W9-BWQ-686

06/2020

PALM BEACH COUNTY
LIBRARY SYSTEM
3650 Summit Boulevard
West Palm Beach, FL 33406-4198

The Shaman of Karres

To purchase any of these titles in e-book form,
please go to www.baen.com.

The Shaman of Karres

Eric Flint
Dave Freer

BAEN

THE SHAMAN OF KARRES

This is a work of fiction. All the characters and events portrayed in this book are fictional, and any resemblance to real people or incidents is purely coincidental.

A Baen Books Original

Baen Publishing Enterprises
P.O. Box 1403
Riverdale, NY 10471
www.baen.com

ISBN: 978-1-9821-2456-4

Cover art by Kurt Miller

First printing, May 2020

Distributed by Simon & Schuster
1230 Avenue of the Americas
New York, NY 10020

Library of Congress Cataloging-in-Publication Data

Names: Flint, Eric, author. | Freer, Dave, author.
Title: The shaman of Karres / Eric Flint and Dave Freer.
Description: Riverdale, NY : Baen, [2020] | Series: Witches of Karres
Identifiers: LCCN 2020000558 | ISBN 9781982124564 (hardcover)
Subjects: GSAFD: Science fiction. | Fantasy fiction.
Classification: LCC PS3556.L548 S53 2020 | DDC 813/.54—dc23
LC record available at https://lccn.loc.gov/2020000558

Pages by Joy Freeman (www.pagesbyjoy.com)
Printed in the United States of America
10 9 8 7 6 5 4 3 2 1

To the world's ambulance and paramedic volunteers.
True shamans.

PRELUDE

The Leewit was unsettled. She usually dealt with that by going up as high as possible and breaking things with supersonic whistles.

Tempting though it was, this time she knew that it wouldn't help. That was enough to make her even more annoyed, which didn't help either.

She really didn't like changes. Not merely changing scenes— she'd seen enough of those on the *Venture 7333*. That was normal. That was fine. It was changes in people that were upsetting. Especially when that person was her.

Being responsible, as they all called it, was deeply annoying.

And the trouble was that there was no getting away from it once you started. She could run... But she already knew that it wouldn't work.

Captain Pausert was watching the Leewit very carefully, out of the corner of his eye. She was stumping around the Winten-berry vines, just off to the side of Threbus and Toll's cottage on the planet of Karres, as he sat on the verandah with Threbus, drinking green Lepti liquor and talking.

He'd learned quite a lot about the wisdom of keeping a sur-reptitious eye on the littlest witch of Karres in the last few years. For some of that time she'd been in his care... In a manner of speaking... As much as anyone ever really had any Karres child in their care. From time to time, ever since he'd rescued Maleen, Goth, and the blond scrap, the Leewit, from slavery on Porlumma, he'd suspected that he was as much in their care as they were in his. Well, Maleen was happily married to Neldo now. But the *Venture* had still been home to Goth and the Leewit for a series of long missions for Karres.

They'd been on Karres itself for a while now. It was always hard to tell quite how long, in the magical timelessness of that place. There'd been a fair amount of learning to be done and a fair amount of debriefing too. And some welcome rest and recuperation to be enjoyed. Time spent getting to know his adopted people. Time spent probably annoying them with the klatha energies that seemed to cluster around him. But that was fair enough, since they'd made his life more than just difficult from time to time.

It was also time spent getting to know more of the witches than just Goth and her family. Time to adjust to the fact that the girl of his childhood dreams, Vala, was actually Goth, via some travel in time. After their adventures in dealing with the Melchin-mother-plant and the Megair Cannibals, Pausert felt he needed a break, and to learn far more about how to use the klatha skills he had. Of course, that wasn't likely to happen. The witches of Karres preferred you to learn on your feet, and as fast as possible. That wasn't because they were cruel, but because it worked, and there was a dire need for that which worked.

Karres and her people were, in the vastness of galactic soci-ety, such a tiny group. Yes, a tiny group with powerful friends in Imperial circles, as the Empress Hailie gradually consolidated her power, bringing in new courtiers and nobles as the Nanite-damaged court was quietly replaced. The Empire had no shortage of nobility who had not been in the court, had not been infected, but it all took time and care. Yet, for now great dangers had been averted.

But Karres seemed to attract trouble. For some reason, quite a bit of it had focused itself on Captain Pausert. Karres, its way of thinking, its people, and its entire existence were always under some degree of threat. If you were one of them, you dealt with it. And right now it seemed that there was another thing they needed him to deal with.

He'd been told this morning that Threbus wanted to have a chat about the *Venture*'s next mission. The Karres prognosticators had apparently been busy.

Something was plainly up...again.

What, he didn't know. But he did know the danger signs with the Leewit.

So he asked Threbus where he was going, this time.

"Well, to Na'kalauf. Partly," explained his Great Uncle Threbus, "to help the Leewit to finish her work with healing Ta'zara."

"But of course it is never as simple as that," said Pausert, prompting.

"Of course not. There is a little war we'd like you to deal with. But Ta'zara is important." Threbus didn't say whether that was to the war, or to the Leewit or to Karres. It could be any or all three, and, Pausert knew by now they'd tell him as little as possible. Prognostication worked better that way.

Ta'zara, the heavily swirl-tattooed warrior-bodyguard from the watery world of Na'kalauf, was, Captain Pausert knew, also watching the Leewit. He was almost invisible standing in the dappled shade, his bulky solid mass as still as any statue. The Megair Cannibals had kept him alive, because he and his group were the toughest foe they'd ever encountered in hand-to-hand combat. He'd been the last survivor...and psychologically broken, until the Leewit had somehow reached into his mind and begun healing him.

That had given her a devoted bodyguard, and led, ultimately, to getting rid of the Megair Cannibals. But Ta'zara had expected to die in that effort. In a moment of insight, Pausert saw that Ta'zara had not just expected to die. Ta'zara had *wanted* to die then, and to die well, to atone for being alive when his comrades had died. Curing that would take a great deal more work.

Pausert had no idea where you even started with that sort of problem. The Leewit was a klatha shaman, a healer, able to reach inside people—and aliens—and fix things at a cellular level. She'd been able to do something for Ta'zara. She'd given him back his courage, and some of himself. But, obviously, there was more. "I'm glad the war is my share," he said, not untruthfully. It was easier to deal with distant enemies than people you saw every day.

There was a wry understanding in Threbus' face. "The war is fairly small as wars go. Not because both sides don't want to kill every man, woman and child on the other side, but just because they're fairly evenly matched, and neither side has the resources to make the fight much bigger. It's in the state, right now, of no actual hostilities. But both sides are ready to get back to killing each other, at the drop of a hat."

"So why do we need to do anything?" asked Pausert. "I mean...there are small wars all the time. They're nasty, people get killed, but they happen. There are far too few of us. We can't really stop all wars."

"Or should we be doing so, you mean? And you're right. Karres doesn't, normally. Oh, maybe a nudge here and there, toward making things better and more stable, but we deal with existential threats to us, and to humankind, not social engineering. But our prognosticators say that what is little more than some border skirmishes now, is about to get much bigger. There's some sort of development happening that will change the equation. And the winning side...won't stop winning."

"And they're the bad guys?" asked Pausert, glad to have that at least clear.

Threbus pulled a face. "Actually...no. The other side are probably what we'd consider 'the bad guys.' The Karoda slavers are not popular with anyone, not even on their own world. But while the people of Karoda may not like them, they like Iradalia less. And a huge amount of money flows through them. That affects the whole economy of both worlds."

Captain Pausert bit his top lip. Slavery was legal in the Empire. Common on some planets, despised on others. He knew that the Empress Hailie wanted to get rid of it. But it had taken deep root in many societies after the collapse of the first empire, after humans had spread from old Yarthe to the stars. Nikkeldepain, where Captain Pausert had grown up, was one of the antislavery worlds. It was about all you could really say that was good about Nikkeldepain. Slavers weren't popular there. And the Karoda slavers were the least popular. They were actually forbidden to land at all. "So what's the problem with them losing?"

"I don't think there is one, or at least not much of a problem. It's the other side winning that's the problem. Because the prognosticators say they won't stop winning. They will take on more and more foes, and . . . bring them in. And that will lead to a war with the Empire, one it is not going to win. The new order, it seems, would be very bad for Karres and bad for humanity."

The Empire . . . well, it wasn't perfect, far from it. But Pausert had had enough history drummed into him at the Nikkeldepain Academy for the Sons and Daughters of Gentlemen and Officers to know that it was a lot better than what had existed before. Still, it was big, scattered and mostly too busy keeping itself together to expand into the border-worlds.

"So . . . you mean I have to see the Karoda slavers win?" asked Pausert, distastefully.

Threbus shook his head. "That, it seems, might be worse. But they do think you, and the Leewit, could solve it. Maybe."

Pausert knew from experience that he wasn't going to get a lot more information out of his great-uncle. But he had noticed one very unwelcome detail in what he had been told. There'd been no mention of Goth. The captain could barely imagine the *Venture* spacefaring without her. So as soon as he could, he took his leave from Great Uncle Threbus—and, if Goth had her way, his future father-in-law—and went in search of Goth.

He found her sitting on her favorite rock, looking out toward the forests where she liked to go hunting Black Bollems. It only took one look to let him know he was right.

"They're saying I have to let you go off without me," she said gruffly.

Pausert had been around Goth for quite a while now, with her growing up, mostly on board the *Venture 7333*. He'd gotten quite good at reading her, despite the fact that she didn't let much show. Goth was angry, upset. Quite possibly dangerous, but that went with being a klatha operative, and with being from Karres. The trick, he'd learned eventually, was not to say anything, because whatever you did say was going to be wrong. Not saying anything could be dangerous too, but less so.

She had gotten up with that lithe ease that was so much a part of her, even more so now that her body was clearly that of a young woman rather than a girl—a change that Pausert found unsettling, to say the least. He was simultaneously skittish, anxious, confused, uncertain—the list went on and on, and buried somewhere within all the other terms was . . . excitement, maybe? Elation?

He wasn't ready to deal with that. Yet. For the Karres witches, the marriageable age was sixteen, which Goth had recently surpassed. But the captain came from a stiffer culture and hadn't shed all of his attitudes. Yet.

Goth didn't say much. Just swallowed and hugged him, quickly. "I'm going to get my bow and go kill a bollem."

"Want company?" he asked.

She shook her head. "Later."

Pausert had to be content with that. Actually, he wouldn't have minded killing something himself. Maybe the team of prognosticators who had foreseen all this. Instead he took himself back to the *Venture 7333*. Old Vezzarn was there. "I wondered when you were going to get here, Captain. They've been bringing the cargo aboard for the last couple of hours. I'm not too happy with the stowage."

"Cargo?" Captain Pausert wondered, grumpily, why no one ever told him anything.

Irritable, he avoided the hold and the cargo, and went down into the *Venture*'s crawlway and checked component modules instead. He was, as he often did, following some inner sense, part of his own witchy klatha mastery, which he poorly understood. It made him, generally, a lucky gambler. This time it didn't let him down either. He let his hands guide him to the units, pulled the ones he found them resting on, and examined them in the light of the crookneck atomic lamp, and then dug out the hyperelectronic surge tester, and checked the readings.

Sure enough, there were telltale flat areas in the responses. He went back to get replacements, and found someone had been restocking the storeroom. Every rack was full.

Karres was plainly doing their very best to prepare him for this mission. Somehow, that wasn't comforting.

Goth moved as silently as she could through the deep woods of Karres. Concentrating on the hunt was easier than thinking about other things. There were other ways to bring food to the table, klatha means, artificial means, but Karres had learned: Sometimes the best ways forward were back. And right now, Goth wanted to go back. Back to Nikkeldepain. Back to being Vala, back to Captain Pausert as a teenager, younger than herself. Well. She didn't really want him younger than herself. Time travel was problematic. She quite understood, now, why age shifts were also problematic.

But that didn't make sending the captain off on another dangerous adventure any easier. Not without her. And her biggest worry was not telling him where she'd be going, because he'd believe he had to come along. She knew him well enough to know he'd feel it was his responsibility. To feel that he'd be neglectful if he didn't.

But that would apparently lead to disaster.

She was sick of precogs. Sick enough to want to prove them wrong...

...but experienced enough to know they couldn't choose what they foresaw. They'd worked out good, systematic means of testing how probable an outcome was. This was apparently rock solid.

That didn't mean she had to like it.

CHAPTER 1

When the shriek of space-alarms is welcome, things are pretty rotten, Captain Pausert reflected.

He'd been near to dozing in the control chair on the *Venture 7333*. That was a good thing considering how little sleep he'd had the last few days, and a bad thing when he was in command of a starship.

He blinked to clear his vision. The screens showed that it was a fairly normal problem on the fringes of the Empire's space, a larger ship following directly down their course. There was only one good reason for that—to try and get in a disabling shot on the *Venture*'s tubes before they had a chance to flee or return fire or try evasive action. It was the hardest to detect too, with the tubes' trail disturbing most sensors. The *Venture* had an advantage over most ships in that she had the latest and best that the Daal of Uldune's shipyards had been able fit into the ship. Otherwise, ten-to-one he would have been taken by surprise.

It wasn't too healthy an approach for the following ship. There were some short-lived radioactives in the trail, but then pirates didn't take a long-term approach to life.

The irony of the situation was that he'd have happily given

the pirates his cargo. There were ten thousand pairs of hyper-electronic manacles in the hold. They were not Pausert's choice of cargo, but an order destined for Karoda. He needed an excuse to go there, but he would have preferred some other excuse!

He toggled the intercom, and woke the Leewit, Vezzarn and Ta'zara. "Got pirates sneaking up astern."

"Good," said the Leewit, her mood plainly not that different from his own. "Let's shoot their front end off, shoot their rear end off, and ram them in the middle!" she snarled, quoting her favorite phrase from the captain's lexicon.

"We could run," said old Vezzarn, warily.

That was true. Not only was the *Venture* more lethal than she looked, but she was somewhat overpowered. She'd originally been built as a pirate chaser, intended to look the part of a small commercial freighter. She'd been sold off, and ended up as just that—a small freighter with high fuel bills and not really enough cargo space for inner-planet work. But for high-risk, high-cost cargos in possibly dangerous localities, she was just the ship a captain needed. Besides, with the Leewit and him aboard they had an ace up their sleeves: the Sheewash Drive, harnessing their klatha powers to outpace any spacecraft.

The downside about the Sheewash Drive was that everyone else wanted it. There was no point in using it if it wasn't an emergency. There were enough rumors about a superdrive and the witches of Karres as it was.

"Run is always better," said Ta'zara, having silently come into the control room. Ta'zara, who was a human battlewagon in unarmed conflict, could move like a ghost when he wished to. "You fight when you have to, in the place you choose, with the weapons you choose."

That made sense, although the captain was all for fighting right now. He looked at the screens and did a quick calculation. "There's an asteroid cluster up ahead. Dirty space, full of debris. Something recently collided with something else and the shattered pieces are still a trap for any starship. Not a great place for us to run at full speed. And three planetoids off to the starboard. Suppose we shift course slightly as if we're avoiding the debris, dive in on the plan-etoid, and catch a slingshot off its gravity well. Then we'll come at them from the flank. The asteroids will give them little space to run."

"And if we blow one or two of those into space fragments,

ahead of their course, they'll have rocks to dodge instead chasing or shooting at us," said Vezzarn.

"As well as chasing us, probably," said the captain. "Right, you'll all need to get to your gravity acceleration couches and strap in. I'll unlock the nova-gun turrets, and then set a course to brush past that closest worldlet at full thrust. As soon as we get out of the gravity well, you get to the guns."

Fun fun piped the little vatchlet, like the sound of sunlight, like seeing a scent, a thing that Captain was aware of, but ordinary senses were not. Klatha-sensitives could "rell" vatch. To others, they weren't there at all, let alone hearable.

The piece of nothingness whirled about in a delighted dance, around the Leewit. The two of them were rather similar, but the Leewit was at least growing up a little more. Pausert almost groaned. He hoped they'd lost Little-bit, the silver-eyed baby vatch, after their last adventure. She'd disappeared for a while, as vatches often did. They regarded humans and their doings as a kind of entertainment, only worth paying attention to when things could go terribly wrong—often as a direct result of the vatch interference. Klatha use attracted them, like moths to a candle. Pausert shook his head. He was a vatch-handler, able to force some of them to do his will, but Little-bit was of the kind that couldn't be handled. His klatha hooks merely tickled her.

"We don't need trouble," he said sternly, knowing it was a waste of time.

But I do! said the vatch, her tinkling little voice inside his head. **Make explosions, big dream thing. I like explosions!**

Whatever he did, Captain Pausert knew that playing the little vatch's game was not a good idea. Neither was directly thwarting the immensely powerful little creature. He had to chart some kind of middle course. That was never going to be easy, but he had years of practice, dealing with the Leewit. She was resisting growing up as hard as any lastborn child ever does, and would have lapses into the hooliganism of her younger years with regularity. But he'd noticed...never when it really mattered. He wondered if that applied to the vatchlet.

He asked it, as he strapped in to the command chair. "Do you ever grow up?"

Almost to his surprise, he got a serious answer, if an incomprehensible one. **We go to the *place*. Some never do.**

"Do you want to?" asked Pausert, fishing for a handle on the strange, nonmaterial creatures.

There was a longer silence. Then the voice in his head said: **Sometimes, big dream thing. Sometimes I don't. Maybe not fun fun.**

"Dying's not fun fun for us either. And that could just happen, no matter how good we are at klatha," said Pausert, missing Goth badly. Wishing he had her at his side. Wishing he'd just had a chance to tell her... because every space battle actually could just be one's last, even for a wizard of Karres.

The battle, if you could call it that, was a short-run thing. The *Venture* had a good turn of speed to her, and she'd been built as a pirate chaser, long years ago on Nikkeldepain. It was almost as if the old ship loved her work, Pausert reflected. The pirates had plainly been unaware that they'd been spotted in their attempt to sneak up undetected. Their first shot, as the *Venture* came racing in from their flank, had been wildly astray. The *Venture*'s return fire from her erratic nova guns had not been. Old Vezzarn had had a misfire, causing some damage to the gun and turret, but the Leewit, whose fire from the nova guns had always been uncannily accurate, was on target. Her purple searing blast had struck the other ship with its full devastating force, destroying what must have been a missile pod. He heard her shriek of glee through the intercom. "Got him! Got him good!"

The explosion that set off was enough to break the other ship in half. One moment it was a pirate, the next two hulks and debris flying off into space in separate directions. Very soon after a small lifecraft detached from what had been the front half of the ship and fled, as Captain Pausert swung the *Venture* away from the target. There'd be metal fragments moving unpredictably and at speed, as they ricocheted off each other.

Vezzarn came down to report on the damage to his gun turret, as the Leewit came bouncing off the walls down the corridor. "Did you see that shot, Captain? I guessed exactly right. We blew his aft right off!"

"So you did," said Pausert, with all the pride of the man who'd taught her to shoot. "Well, if you take the helm for a bit, I need to go and inspect Vezzarn's pod. Lucky you didn't get hurt, old fellow," he said to the old spacer, who was looking a bit shaken.

What happens to the other ones? asked the little vatch-voice in their heads.

The Leewit and the captain paused...and Vezzarn, who was terrified of "witchy stuff," fled, saying something about needing a hot drink.

"What other ones?" asked the Leewit. "So you're back, are you? Huh. Just leaving me like that."

Pausert looked anxiously at his instruments, but except for the fleeing lifecraft, they showed nothing.

The other dream things. In that piece of the ship.

"Pirates left their friends, did they?" said the Leewit. "Just like you left me."

But you are not tied to a pole. They make almost as much air-vibration as you, but there are lots of them.

Captain Pausert had had enough experience of the Leewit's "air-vibration" to work it out. There were prisoners on the pirate ship, screaming. "Which half of the ship?" he asked, pointing at the screens. "That one? Or that one?" As he said that, the front section spun off with another small explosion.

The first one, said the vatch-voice in his head.

That was the larger aft section, still mostly intact. The ship had plainly been an old obsolete Empire C-class merchanter. The cargo holds were just above the tubes—rather like the *Venture's* own structure. Pausert had heard that some of the merchanters had been modified, using some of that space for extra engine capacity. It made them less commercially viable—and they'd already been outclassed, but a lot faster. Ideal for little, except piracy. And that hold, or what was left of it, could well be full of prisoners. "I'll start matching trajectory," said the captain. "Ta'zara. You need to suit up and the Leewit can get old Vezzarn down here, so I can suit up too."

"I should go with you!" protested the Leewit, her lips beginning to purse.

Fortunately, the captain had thought that through in advance. "If there is anyone alive there we'll likely need to carry them. We have one shuttle-bag; we could cram two people in with a suit pony-tank. And if we need...special help on either ship, best there is one klatha operative on each. Besides, if something goes wrong, I want someone who can do astrogation here, in charge. And that's you. Between you and Vezzarn you can fly the ship. If I took Vezzarn, you and Ta'zara can't. If I took you, they certainly can't Sheewash. Besides, it's the captain's decision. Get on with it. I need you here."

She sighed. "Right, Captain."

"And we'll all need blasters from the arms cabinet. Get them and check charges. There might be prisoners there. There might also be trouble." The Leewit didn't answer. Just nodded and ran off, and left the captain to the difficult task of getting the *Venture* into close proximity of the slowly tumbling hulk of the stern end of the wrecked pirate. Captain Pausert could only be grateful that her rocket tubes had also stopped firing with the Leewit's lucky shot or it might have been worse.

The Leewit came back with Vezzarn, and handed the captain a blaster. Captain Pausert noticed the old spacer had strapped one on himself, even if he wasn't going across to the other ship. "Risky business, Captain," he said looking at the screens. "A bit above my pay grade, this sort of piloting."

"Just let me suit up and I'll finish the closing maneuvers. All you'll have to do is hold her there and deal with any problems."

"It's the problems you and the little Wisdom seem to find that worry me," said Vezzarn with a crooked smile, settling into the command chair. "You always get me into jams, Captain, but you always get me out of them, too. I don't forget that."

Pausert suited up and checked his equipment, then checked Ta'zara's and let him run a seal check on his, before taking the *Venture* in on the nerve-jangling final lock-on, with the electro-magnetic grapples. He and Ta'zara exited through the airlock, and then, one at a time, roped together, made the jump across to the pirate hulk with their reaction pistols. That was easy enough.

The question now was how to get in. The hold doors didn't have airlocks. If there was anyone alive in there, opening the doors would kill them. The only possible way was through the torn metal of the massive explosion. That was too dangerous to hurry through—suit fabric was super-tough but it still could be damaged. Besides, it was a mess, a tangle of twisted I-beams and hull metal, and all sorts of drifting debris in the stark dark shadow and silver glare of new-sheared metal. Their headlights on, Pausert let his instincts lead him into the explosion hole. He found a passage which led to a door crusted with ice crystals from air bleeding though the seals. The ice did a fair job of jamming it up, and not all the pulling and thrusting could open it. The door opened toward them, but despite the fact that the air pressure inside was also pushing, it wouldn't budge.

"If I was there I could whistle and shatter it, Captain," said the Leewit, on the radio, with a cross edge in her voice.

"And probably break your helmet, if not your ears," replied Pausert. "Let's get a lever, and have another try, Ta'zara. I don't want to use the blaster."

They found a section of beam, and, with Ta'zara's considerable strength added to Pausert's, they cracked the ice. What was left of the air within wasn't enough to have much effect, puffing out. They went in and closed the door again. It was a scary thing to do, considering how hard it had been to open. But if they were to open any other safety doors, every bit of pressure counted. They kept up the radio chatter to the Leewit so she at least knew they were alive and roughly where they were. The captain wasn't sure what she could do about it, though, if something went wrong.

The first thing Pausert noticed was that the crystal emergency lights on the floor still glowed. Touching the wall, there was a vague vibrating hum of machinery. Some of the ship's system was still alive—and there was mist forming around an air duct. Most of it was iced over, but plainly something was still leaking in. The two of them advanced cautiously, blasters ready. If they met anyone here, common sense might be for a pirate to surrender, but sometimes common sense was scarce in a disaster. Besides, if a pirate had been stalking the corridors of a dead ship in their place, he'd be looking for loot, and would try to kill them.

The next door was easier, and the third definitely had air pressure—and a dead man. The fourth had lights. Weak, flickering, but lights. There was air, but it was thin, probably not enough to breathe. The only remaining door was the door into the tube shaft, engine room—by the door symbols—and into the hold. They cracked that one and went through into the darkness there, the suit lights again providing all the light there was.

See. I told you, said the tinkling little vatch-voice.

They weren't screaming, or not anymore, but indeed there were people, leg-shackled to a long pole. Some of them were definitely alive and gasping for breath. Looking at them, Pausert realized he hadn't thought this through very well. There were a lot of people trapped there! Even if they went back to the *Venture* and fetched the Leewit and Vezzarn's suit and the four spares from the suit locker, that would take at least ten trips or more. Pausert wasn't sure these people would last very much longer—let alone dealing with cutting them loose. Once one end of the pole was cut, they'd have a lot of panicked and terrified people, not inclined to take things in due turn and with the calmness it would take to get them suited up and ferried out along the corridors, losing more air every time, through the dark and chaos and sharp metal. Even with Ta'zara at his side that could be tough.

He couldn't see how he could do it.

Yet the alternative was to leave them here to die. He couldn't see how he could do that either. It was unlikely the pirate ship had had sufficient suits for all these people.

"What are you going to do, Captain?" asked the Leewit. "They're dying. I can feel it."

She probably could. The Leewit was a shaman, a healer with klatha powers.

The problem was he just could see no way of dealing with this number of captives.

"We could use the Sheewash drive to get the hulk into an atmosphere. Use the *Venture* for braking and steering, and hope the grapples hold," she suggested.

The captain shook his head. "They haven't got the time, even if we can make it work. But I might be able to do it with klatha. Can you and Vezzarn line the *Venture*'s hold door up, as precisely as possible, with this hulk? If I remember right, the merchanter class hold door is the standard Imperial, same as the *Venture*'s."

"What are you going to do, Captain?" repeated the Leewit, an edge of wariness in her young voice.

"Try to make a modification on the klatha cocoon I put you and Goth into. An airtight one," said Pausert. He started working through the klatha patterns in his mind . . . a change there . . .

"Move them across in those clumping cocoons? I guess they won't know what they are," said the Leewit, reluctantly. She had not liked being trapped in one, even if it had saved her life.

"No, they weren't airtight, but I hope I can change that. There are far too many for me to do individual cocoons. But I thought I would make a tunnel between the holds . . ."

"It'll take a lot out of you, Captain."

"I know. You three may have to hold the fort before I can undo it. We'll be locked onto this hulk, and that means you'll have to move these people out of the hold, because this hold plainly is losing pressure slowly."

"Right, Captain. How many people?"

"A lot. Keep them out of the control room." Inside the suit, sound was deadened, but in the headlight he could see wide-eyed, terrified people reaching frantic forcecuffed arms to them. There was no time to waste. Pausert concentrated. He knew every detail of the *Venture*'s hull. She was his ship; he loved her. So envisaging layers of the cocoon from just outside the hold-door frame extending into space was easy enough. Now to work the klatha patterns, to trace them in his mind and to change them slightly to be impervious even to air. Captain Pausert could feel himself sweating inside the suit. Such klatha use took enormous amounts of energy out of the user.

"Near lined up as I can get it, Captain," said Vezzarn's voice across the suit radio. "Can't get a perfect match."

That could be a problem. No match, no hold-door opening.

You make vatch-eggstuff, big dream thing! I didn't know you could do that. I thought everything in the dreamplace was soft.

The vatchlet almost distracted him from the pattern he was building out, layer by exhausting layer. "What?"

That's what everything hard in my place is—not like in the dream place. I can go through anything in the dream place, and anywhere. Eggstuff, I can't. I have to undo. I must go talk to the others. This could affect the new game.

Pausert had the answer. He simply kept extending the klatha-force cocoon...right through the hull. Metal was no barrier. He could see the transparent cocoon stuff coming through the wall...

There was of course still vacuum in the space outside the hull, but also inside the klatha-force tunnel he'd created. And now that hull was not entire—the cocoon of klatha force cut right through it. And the hull section—part hull, part door and severed leaking hydraulic servos—sucked out. Captain Pausert heard Ta'zara yell in shock, but he was too exhausted to care.

"Vezzarn, get the hold door slid open. Ta'zara, see if you can cut that bar with your blaster. I'm just going to sit..." He did, before he fell over, as Ta'zara adjusted his blaster and took careful aim at the bar the prisoners were tethered to. The poor prisoners panicked and tried to retreat. That was probably better than having them close in, anyway, thought Pausert.

Ta'zara burned through the bar—a tough job with a blaster that really wasn't designed for that. The melted end glowed white-hot—he still had to hold off the prisoners with the blaster as the ones just back from the front tried to shove the others forward to escape.

"Atmospheric pressure reading from the *Venture*'s hold zero point seven eight ship normal. Looks like you did it, Captain," said the Leewit. "You all right?"

"Yes. Just dead-beat and starving," he answered.

"Use the glucose syrup tube in your suit, Captain," said Ta'zara.

Pausert could have kicked himself for not thinking of that earlier. But that was the problem with being too tired. Thinking logically was difficult. Sucking on the tube even seemed hard work, but it did revitalize him a bit.

"Is there enough atmosphere for me to crack my helmet and talk to these people?" asked Ta'zara.

"Yes. It's losing a little pressure. Down to point seven seven eight ship normal. Safe enough but it must be leaking. There is no time to waste. I can pump more air in to our hold..."

"Don't," said the captain, tiredly. "Let's get them across, close up and then do it."

Ta'zara had cracked his helmet seal and now Captain Pausert could hear the panic and pandemonium from the prisoners—after all, they didn't know that he and Ta'zara weren't just pirates, or just what was going on. "Shut UP!" Boomed the broad man from Na'kalauf. "We're here to rescue you. Be calm."

That might have reduced the volume by a tiny bit, but it did change the tone. "The end of the bar is still too hot for you to get past. Don't push! You will be safe!" shouted Ta'zara, trying to physically hold them back.

Judging by the noise, that wasn't working too well. Tired or not, Pausert knew he had to intervene. He put a tiny klatha-force cocoon on the glowing end of the bar and it dropped off, heat trapped inside. From a two-finger-wide gap, with a molten, dripping end, it was now the size of a large fist, the one end not even glowing. "Ta'zara. Bend it. Use them."

A glance from the big Na'kalauf man plainly took in the instruction and the new situation, and he bellowed at the frantic prisoners. "Pull! This way."

He led by example. The bar bent and the prisoners were able to thrust their way to freedom. Several of them were down, but Pausert was not sure if they were dead or just injured. They had to be pushed and dragged along, until they could let those beyond them off. In the meanwhile, Ta'zara was shoving them toward the *Venture*'s hold. He came back and helped Pausert to his feet. "Move you across now, Captain. The Leewit charged me with seeing to your safety."

Pausert was too tired to quibble, and anyway, his crossing the slippery transparent klatha-cocoon stuff was an encouragement to the others. Some had panicked and had run. A few were helping others, but most of them were fearfully milling around, instead of moving into the light of the *Venture*'s hold. Moving was a good idea, Pausert felt. The hulk of the pirate ship could break up more, and anyway, they were bleeding the *Venture*'s air into the hulk. He said as much to Ta'zara, who nodded and went back. Pausert could hear him chivvying the prisoners along, getting them to carry some of those who were either unconscious or injured, or possibly dead.

Part of the problem was that there were a lot of people to move into a fairly full cargo hold. After a while, Pausert got up enough strength to help marshal them around a bit.

"Captain," said Vezzarn across the suit radio. "We're drifting in on those asteroids. I'm going to need to apply some thrust soon, Captain."

"Get Ta'zara across from the hulk and close the hold doors," said Pausert urgently.

"I am just back," said Ta'zara. "I could find no more prisoners. I have carried the last three over. I think they are dead."

Even if they were, there must have been seventy people crowded into the hold. "Close the doors," said Pausert, "and try to be gentle with the thrust, since no one is strapped in."

He was relieved to see the hold doors close. That had been his major unspoken stress. With that off his shoulders, all he wanted now was to lie down...and eat. The burst of power Vezzarn gave to the tubes was about as gentle as possible, but there was a limit to how little you could do with rocket tubes. It wasn't a Pausert trademark takeoff, but still enough to knock most of them off their feet—except Ta'zara. He stepped over them to the captain, and picked him up as if he was a ragdoll.

"Taking you through to the Leewit, Captain," he said firmly, and pushed and stepped his way through to the inner door to the hold. That was locked, but Ta'zara called through the radio, and got it unlocked. He put the captain down, and pushed back the four people who tried to follow. The Leewit was there already, getting his helmet undogged, and just about pouring some sickly sweet gunk into his mouth. Well, normally it would have been sickly. Now, it tasted like nectar. "Help me carry him to his cabin," she said. "He's pushed it too far, again."

Pausert didn't try to resist, or walk. The Leewit was right, and she sounded far too worried for him to have argued, even if he felt he had the strength.

"We'll deal, Captain. You just recover," said Ta'zara.

And he was happy to do that, right now.

CHAPTER 2

Touching the captain, when he slumped like that, barely able to drink the energy brew she'd gotten out of the robochef, frightened the Leewit badly. She had allowed herself to do what the Toll pattern in her mind said was an absolute no-go for a klatha healer—reading without preparing barriers within herself, without creating a distance between healer and patient. Her Toll pattern was a klatha learning device, a partial replica of the personality of an adult witch whose basic individuality was similar to that of the witch child using it. She usually followed its advice, but in this case...

He'd pushed too far, and too hard again! Goth would never forgive her if she let him die. But, just before reaching into herself to pour some of her energy into the captain...the Toll pattern in her mind was insistent. *Check first. Assess.* Assess and then treat calmly and sensibly, as if it wasn't someone she cared a lot about. Stupidity and panic would help no one and could kill both of them.

So she did. His vital signs were serious, but there was nothing actually wrong with him besides literally being out of energy at the cellular level. It had been strange at first to have the klatha sense of being able to feel the body from the inside. Overwhelming and more than a little scary. It was why one had to be buffered. But there was improvement, even as she worked, checking him out. She could boost those...

The Toll pattern supplied *mitochondria*. But no. He'd get better without that. And much though she wanted the security of the captain making decisions, letting him recover slowly was better for him. And she could cope. She had to: She was the remaining Karres witch on the ship. He would not survive the Egger Route like that. She could only hope he hadn't burned out his ability to be a klatha witch. That happened too, sometimes.

And there was not a bit of use in climbing anything, or whistling at it, either.

Once the captain was in his cabin, being put into his bunk by Ta'zara, she went back to the flight deck, where Vezzarn was sitting in the captain's chair, warily watching instruments. "Is the captain all right, Your Wisdom?" he asked with the nervous respect of Karres and klatha that Uldune's people had—for good historical reason, the Leewit knew. Vezzarn was always respectful, but this was...different, somehow? And then she realized what it was and scowled fiercely at him for reminding her. She was in charge now. No Goth, no Maleen, no Toll, no Threbus. Just nobody. "Yeah. Leave him alone. Anything you need to do, you do. Don't you dare wake the captain. Call me, not him. So: Are we clear of the asteroids?"

"There is nothing of a size that needs worrying about close, Your Wisdom. Except for that piece of hulk. It's still stuck up against us. We can't really boost with it there. It'd mess with the center of mass, and I'm just a spaceman, not up to the captain's level of piloting. Can you undo that?"

"No. The captain has to. We will worry about it if it becomes a problem."

Then there was the issue of what to do about the rescued people. She met Ta'zara in the companionway, just outside the captain's cabin. "He's asleep...or in a coma," he said. "He didn't even know I took his suit off." Ta'zara had removed his space-suit, but not, the Leewit noticed, the blaster. And he too turned to her for orders...well, in a way he always did, but not about running the ship. "What do you wish to do about the people we rescued, mistress?"

"What do *you* think?" she asked.

He rubbed his jaw. "I cannot watch all of them. There are too many for this ship, I think. They need to be put off on some hospitable world, as soon as possible."

"We can't really head for one until the captain wakes up. Which he will." She said that with all the confidence she could muster.

He nodded. "Then I think leave them in the hold, and we will provide what we can. Food. Water."

"And treatment for the badly injured."

He looked at her with concern. "You must not do to yourself what the captain has done, mistress. I know your power, but I know it is not without its cost."

"Yeah. I know. Come on, let's get to the robochef and see what we can do to feed them."

None of it proved quite as simple as the Leewit had hoped. The robochef didn't have any programs for lots and lots of quick food, all at once. It was designed to cater for ten people at the outside, and not to provide drinks for seventy or more. Vezzarn got her a water refill carboy from the storage locker to start with. Food could wait, she decided. She and Ta'zara went down to the hold. Even from outside one could hear the racket and the banging.

"Great Patham's toenails. They better not be damaging the cargo!" she said furiously. Goth had been the one who had worked on making the *Venture 7333* profitable, but now she wasn't here. The captain relied too much on his luck. The Leewit pulled open the hold door—and had to hastily sidestep to avoid the three men and the small crate they'd been using as a makeshift—and hopeless—ram, falling through.

There was no place to go up, so she whistled at them. It was an odd talent, but one that could be deadly. This wasn't intended to kill, just to hurt the ears, and by the way they clutched those ears, it did work. "What do you clumping dopes think you're doing?" she demanded. "Who said you could bash our cargo and doors around?"

There was a stunned silence and then they all started yelling at once and a bunch tried to come shoving forward. Ta'zara dealt with them by picking up two of the makeshift ram carriers and throwing them back in the crowd. He grabbed the fallen crate and used it as battering ram—not on the open door, but the mass of people. "Back, mistress!"

The Leewit did nothing of the kind. She leaned past him and whistled instead. This time it was a real buster of a whistle. She hoped the cargo would be all right. A lot of the people weren't. Quite a few fell over, and all of them tried to cover their ears, and retreat. She realized that Ta'zara had drawn his blaster. "I shoot the first of you to advance. Back. Now!"

There was no doubting Ta'zara's tone. They backed up.

"What's wrong with you dopes?" said the Leewit crossly. "We've clumping well rescued you. I've just brought you water. We'll bring food soon. But not if you're behaving like drunken bollems. You can starve."

"I'm Councilor Stratel..." began one fellow with a fancy-pants hairstyle that had survived being chained up and even being rescued. His clothes hadn't done as well.

"Bully for you," said the Leewit, taking an instant dislike to him. "Now shut up, you clumping nitwit. If I need to know who you are, I'll ask."

He plainly wasn't used to being treated like that. His mouth opened and shut, but no sound came out. That was an improvement.

"Slavery is a vile abuse..." began one of the men Ta'zara had flung back, one of the ram-holders. He was a tall, skinny serious-looking fellow, who looked like he'd never heard a joke he understood.

"You're not clumping slaves, you idiot. We just rescued you," said the Leewit, but the fellow was in full flow, waving his one arm about.

"It's against the basic rights of man!" he bellowed, his face flushed and eyes wild, as he pushed his way forward, and then... fell over.

The Leewit looked at him, startled. That arm was at an odd angle. "Ta'zara," she said. "Give them the water. And then can you carry this fellow up to the spare stateroom. There is something not right with him."

"You have to let me out of here; I'm Councilor Stratel, and you must recover my possessions!" said the annoying man.

"Shut your cakehole, you clumping idiot!" said the Leewit. "Look, I'll be back with food. Sort out who is worst hurt so can we see what we can do."

"I demand to see the captain!" said Stratel.

So she told him to shut up, using some of her best words, before shutting them in the hold again. That was at least a little fun.

Using her klatha senses she examined the unconscious man.

His shoulder was dislocated. She said as much to Ta'zara. "It could have happened when I threw him back into the hold. I can try and pull that." So he did. The Leewit was still rather wary about her klatha-healer skills. It was tiring and sometimes uncomfortable, getting inside the patterns that were people. But she felt the joint slip into place and the changes that caused. She felt like throwing up. Buffering herself from the pain had been among the first lessons she'd had to learn.

But there was more than just pain going on here. The man was fevered and . . . something else was wrong with him. It took her a little time to track it down. He was suffering from poisoning—that she got quickly enough. His liver was enflamed and the toxic metal that was affecting him was being concentrated there. That she could, and did move. She traced the source, down the blood vessels, and came to something that her healer sense had no control over—a foreign body, resting under his rib cage. She had no idea what it was, but it was going to kill him.

Goth could have teleported the object out of the body, but short of cutting him open and healing him up after, the Leewit could see no way of getting it out. Cutting was indeed an option, she knew. It was one other healers took, when necessary. But she was a little scared of trying it on her own. He wasn't going to die, if she isolated it. The toxin was leaking out of one point, and that she could seal. She used his blood to bring calcium and various other compounds from his system and sealed the hole in the object as if healing a tooth. To be safe she put a block and built a lattice around it and then filled it with an impermeable membrane. He woke up as she was finishing. Blinked. Looked around.

"Lie still," said the Leewit. "I'm not quite finished."

"What happened?" he asked in his deep voice.

"You dislocated your shoulder. And you had a fever." The Leewit decided not to mention the poison. "You should start feeling better soon."

"I . . . I do," he said, sounding puzzled by this.

"Right. Ta'zara can take you back to your clumping idiot friends." She was tired from the klatha use and hungry from it, too. She had to eat, pace herself, and be calm. There wasn't anyone else, right now. "I'm going to get food. I'll bring it down."

He sat up gingerly. "I must admit it is some time since I last ate. Since any of us ate. Our captors gave us ration bars and water."

"You need to drink more. Your kidneys are in a mess. So is your liver." She cracked an enormous yawn. "Now go with Ta'zara. You're all right now, and there are more hurt people."

"Thank you," he said. "The leg chains?"

"I got other problems," said the Leewit crossly, just wanting to get to food. "You can manage to walk in 'em."

She did indeed have other problems, the first being that the rescued had not been very good at organizing. So she and Ta'zara had to do that for them, and find them a slop bucket, and take the worst injured up to the spare staterooms. It took time, effort and worry, and fixing some of them would take all she had. The best she could do was keep them alive for now. Time also fixed things, if she could let them have that time.

She wanted the captain awake and on hand. She wanted Goth. She wanted a good tree to climb or spaceguns to aim, and blow the sterns and bows off pirates.

But right now all she had was pancakes and Wintenberry jelly, and a ship to keep going. She wished she knew how long the captain would sleep for . . . or if he'd pushed his klatha power too far.

Pausert awoke, driven by enormous post-klatha-use hunger. Someone had gotten him out of the spacesuit, at least. He still felt as weak as a newborn carteen. He struggled his way into some clothes and made his way to the control room and the robochef. Vezzarn was still at the controls, and looked up as Pausert dialed up the largest portion of Wintenberry jelly pancakes the machine could provide. "Captain! Glad to see you! We're still dragging that chunk of pirate hulk . . . and there are few other things . . ."

"Can any of them not wait until I get some food in me?" asked Pausert, shoveling a huge forkful into his mouth as soon as he'd finished speaking. Death or disaster, he had to have some food, *now.*

The little old spacer smiled. "At the rate you're eating, I reckon we'll be all right."

By the time the fourth forkful hit his stomach Pausert paused for long enough to ask: "Where are the Leewit and Ta'zara?"

"The little Wisdom is dealing with the injured. Ta'zara is along with her to provide muscle, in case she has trouble."

Pausert nodded and chewed. This was a step forward on the first few mouthfuls. He'd just swallowed those. That was the downside of klatha use. Those who knew nothing about it thought it made things easy—but it was all too easy for the user to do themselves major damage—dismind themselves, or actually burn up. Some things took far more energy and mental toll than others. Goth could do tricks with light with very real effort. Teleportation didn't require much more. But the Sheewash Drive and travel by the Egger Route were hard on her.

Just thinking about Goth made him worry. Made him miss her, too, and wish that she was here. The Leewit was a long way from the blond scrap she'd been when they'd first met on Porlumma, years back. But she wasn't Goth.

"Tell me about the problems while I eat," he said. He was feeling a little better for the food already.

"Well, Captain, we've got seventy-eight extra passengers. Six are in a bad way, and another twenty or so have injuries. But we don't really have the air or the even the supplies for them. And some are very grateful, but a few are pretty difficult," said Vezzarn.

"Difficult?" asked Pausert, temporarily halting a mouthful.

"Yes," explained Vezzarn. "Not all of the injuries happened in getting them free, or before. A couple of them tried to give the little Wisdom trouble. They wanted their stuff...things the pirates stole from them. They're convinced that we looted them from the wreck. And then there was the story that we're keeping them in the hold because we plan to sell them as slaves."

"How long have I been asleep for?" Pausert asked.

The little spacer grinned. "'Bout sixteen hours. The little Wisdom said we wasn't to disturb you, unless she said so, even if it was life and death. She said some words you would have washed her mouth out with soap for, about what you did with the, you know, witchy stuff."

"I presume you tried to drop the hulk?"

"It's not falling away, Captain," said Vezzarn. "And I was too scared just to fire the main tubes. If it stayed on, our center of mass would be upset..."

"And falling away it could also collide with us. You've tried laterals?"

"Didn't make any difference," said Vezzarn.

"I thought I said he was to be left sleeping!" snapped the Leewit from the doorway.

"I woke up all by myself," said Pausert. "My stomach thought my throat had been cut."

"You pushed it too hard, Captain. You got to learn..." said the Leewit sternly, and then ran forward and hugged him.

"I know. I also knew they were going to die."

She sniffed and scowled. "Couple of the clumping idiots it would have been a good thing to leave behind. Not really, but they're a pain."

"Some in pain," said Ta'zara with a smile from behind her. "Good to see you, Captain. Some of our new passengers keep demanding the pleasure of speaking to you."

"I hope you knocked their heads together!" said Pausert, irritably.

Ta'zara looked at the Leewit. She giggled. "Something like that."

"Well, I will talk to all of them, just as soon as I deal with undoing the connection to the pirate hulk. I'd blow it apart with the nova guns if it wasn't quite that close that it might damage us. Undoing will probably be as tiring as doing, so we'd better plan ahead. We need to make for the nearest habitable world and off-load these people. I'm sure you worked that out. Have you got a target and route planned?"

"We're sort of on the edge of Imperial space here. The charts show Cinderby's World to be the closest. Four ship days, more or less. It'll not be good on the air recycler, Captain," said Vezzarn.

Pausert caught the look from the Leewit. Using the Sheewash Drive could cut that...but it took klatha skill and energy. The Leewit could do it briefly on her own, but it had usually been something that two or three Karres witches combined to do. In learning the skill the captain had nearly killed them all, but now he was very good at it. Still, it took it out of the klatha user. But he thought he could manage if it had to be done. He was feeling much better for the food already.

"I wonder what is actually holding the ships together?" he said, chewing his lip.

"It could just be how close the contact is with that bridge you created, Captain, or just the attraction of the two masses," said Vezzarn.

"It's not quite like the cocoon—that was just...there. I saw you building this up, Captain," said the Leewit. "Kinda layers. I knew you must be burning tons of energy, even if you are a hot witch. I was watching from the gun turret."

Pausert didn't have to ask what she'd been doing there. "Yes. It's not quite the same. More like fifty of the same thing." He grimaced. "No wonder I was tired."

"I was thinking, Captain, you don't have to undo the whole thing. Maybe...just the first layer."

He looked thoughtful. "Yes. And then try the laterals. I wouldn't be so exhausted and we could use the Sheewash Drive. Get there a lot faster. It'll take us out of our way, though."

"Be a good thing, Captain," said the Leewit. "A couple of the captives...patients...aren't in the best shape. I've done my best for them, but they've got such general damage to their lungs it's like fixing a leak in a sponge."

"We'll try that, then," decided Pausert.

So they did, with Vezzarn standing by to fire the laterals and muttering about witchy stuff.

It worked. They and the wrecked hulk parted company in a last ghostly puff of departing air.

"I'll set a course for Cinderby's World, and then I'll go and talk to these passengers we've found ourselves with," said the captain. "And any of them that don't like it, can get out and walk!"

It took some care, as this was quite a dirty part of space, now, but eventually the *Venture* was on her way to Cinderby's World. And then Captain Edom of the ship *Farflight* from the Leris star cluster—seeing as the Infamous Captain Pausert was known in Imperial Security circles for being associated with the witches of Karres—went down to see their "passengers."

There was an odd, dangerous mood in the hold...for people who had just been rescued from slavery.

"Captain. What are you keeping me in here for? We're not animals!" demanded one, a gangling fellow with a fashionable hair-crop that ill-matched his torn clothes. They had been very fine clothes once. There was a dangerous edge to the voice, and despite the fact that Pausert had a blaster on his hip, and Ta'zara at his side, and an open door behind him, there were still more than seventy people there. And the noise response—half fear and half anger—was nearly overwhelming.

Pausert tried to shout over it. The Leewit took a more direct approach. She used one of her shrill directional whistles at them. They were crowded into the space between the strapped pallets of crates and boxes, and had nowhere to go. But they were keen to try. Most of them clutched their ears, and backed off. Pausert almost felt sorry for them—he'd been on the receiving end of that whistle.

"I can't listen to all of you at once," he informed them, sternly. "You will take it in turns. And if you interrupt, my niece will whistle at you again. Now, we have just rescued you from certain death on that pirate vessel. You're a huge strain on my small ship. We're making as good a speed as possible to take you to an Imperial world, where we'll set you down. I would say we're less than three ship-days travel to it. We've done our best for you, but if you cause me any more trouble I'll just back out of this door and leave you here until we land. Now, have you got any questions?"

"We're not just going to be sold as slaves, are we?" asked a young woman querulously.

"No. Whatever gave you that idea?" asked the captain.

"Well," said an academic-looking man, whose thin, planar face looked more like he belonged in a seminary, in a curiously deep voice, "We're still prisoners. Still in leg shackles. And you have crates of forcecuffs. And we are trapped here in the hold. When we tried to leave we were met by force. We are still very grateful for being rescued from asphyxiation. We owe you our lives."

Those dratted forcecuffs! "We're a small freighter, my friend," said Captain Pausert. "We carry cargo for our own trading and for anyone who contracts us, to smaller and less traveled ports. The forcecuffs were not for us to use—how would a little freighter ever use that many, even if we were a slaver? We were attacked by your pirate-captors and got lucky with our guns. We're armed, because we trade out here. We have a small crew, and very little cabin space, so, except for the corridors, there is nowhere else for you to be, except here. And, honestly, we rescued you, but we have no idea who you are. You were captives, but could be pirates yourselves, or mercenaries, or preachers for all we know. As for your shackles...well, I'll take two of you out of here at a time, and have one of my spacemen work on freeing you. I don't have keys or codes for them."

"That seems very reasonable, Captain," said the deep-voiced man. "And I really am grateful for the medical help your niece has been administering. But if I may ask, why have your crew refused to let us see you?"

"The captain was in a forced sleep," said the Leewit tersely. "I put him into it. He nearly killed himself rescuing you. If it was up to me, I'd make you ungrateful lot get out and walk."

There was a silence.

Then the deep-voiced man said, "I'd like to be the first to say I owe you an apology, Captain. I knew of the evils of slavery, but I had not understood the fear or the brutality firsthand. Thank you from the bottom of my heart."

Others joined in. Eventually Pausert held his hands up. "Enough, good people, enough. We did what spacemen do. Now, do you have any other questions? I have a ship to run."

"Where are we going?" asked one of the freed slaves.

"Cinderby's World," said Captain Pausert.

There was a moment's silence. "Why there?" asked someone with palpable nervousness.

"It's about all we have sufficient air to reach. You're way over our recycler's capacity," explained Pausert.

"But I paid my passage to Marbelly," said the pretty woman, plaintively. "What am I going to do?"

"Be free and alive," said the man with the deep voice. People laughed, but Pausert realized by the surprise on his face at their reaction that he'd been dead serious.

"Captain, I need to talk to you about my property," said the fellow with the fashionable hairstyle. He wasn't looking in the least grateful. "Also, I can't stay in here!"

"It's clumping well here, or outside," said the Leewit coldly. "Captain, that's the one I told you about, who claimed you were looting his possessions! And then he wanted us to take him out there to collect them."

"Great Patham!" said Pausert. He shook his head. "Firstly, we didn't have any time for looting, and secondly, anything you lost to the pirates, you lost. If you want to go and search what's left of their ship, you can charter a vessel and go looking for it. I'll give you the coordinates. You can come back with another vessel, not mine. Anyway, what you lost to pirates is not my problem. If we had salvaged it, it would make no difference to you. Now.

You and you." He pointed to two of the people in front. "Come along and we'll see if my spaceman can get your manacles off. The next two can go when they come back. We'll work our way through you."

Back in the command chair, getting the wires ready for the Sheewash Drive, Pausert said to the Leewit, "Good thing that fellow with the deep voice was there. He seemed sensible enough to make up for some of the others."

"Farnal. He's from Iradalia. He is sensible now, Captain. He wasn't at first. He had a broken arm and a knock on the head, and was talking pretty wild. You know, Captain, I'm going to have to get some bottles and food coloring and stuff. Maybe a few transdermic syringes..."

"Why?" Pausert had had experience of the Leewit's odd ideas of food jokes, of salt when he'd thought he was having sugar, and mud cakes...but he didn't see what this had to do with the fellow with the broken arm and a knock on the head.

"Props. Like when we were with the circus." She sighed. "That was fun. More fun than being responsible." She almost spat the last word out. "For healing. They need medicines and bandages and stuff, so they don't know what I'm actually doing. And that man...he has something strange inside him. A machine of some kind."

"Like an artificial organ or something? They do heart pace-makers in the inner worlds."

She frowned. "No. It was poisoning him a little bit. And anyway, he comes from Iradalia. He told me. That's right out on the edges somewhere."

"Indeed it is," said Pausert, surprised. "It's Karoda's binary planet's name. The system is divided between them. The war we're supposed to deal with is between Iradalia and Karoda. That's a bit too much of a fluke just to be a chance rescue, I think. Is this another vatch-game?"

"Could be. Little-bit's vanished again. I don't think they feel time quite like we do. Now, are we gonna do the Sheewash?"

He sighed. "I guess. It is harder with just the two of us. I don't understand why Goth just left. I mean, without even saying goodbye or anything."

"Guess I do, Captain," said the Leewit, tersely, sounding just like her older sister. "I reckon she was scared."

"Goth's never been scared of anything in her life," said Pausert stoutly.

The Leewit was silent for a bit. Then she scowled. "Scared she wouldn't manage to let go of you. Getting soppy like Maleen."

"Oh." That Captain Pausert could understand.

It didn't make being on the *Venture* without her any easier, but it did make it a lot better. He found the ship without her an empty place, even if there were more than seventy people on board. But they had to get these other people to air, and that meant the Sheewash Drive.

So they did it, and the inner fire burned in that twisted arrangement of wires directing the klatha energy. It appreciably shortened their journey.

CHAPTER 3

Goth had left Karres before the captain. Without saying proper goodbyes, which she was still kicking herself about, but...

She shook herself vigorously. No use being melancholy and miserable about it, even if she was both of those. She'd been taken in one of Karres' fast two-man ships as far as Parisienne—a world undistinguished for anything much except being inside the Empire, a place of gentle and beautiful warm oceans, and the major producer of sheen fabric. Sheen was harvested from the cocoons of a local sea creature, the squill, which had failed to thrive anywhere else. It was pretty, shimmery, strong and soft. There were plenty of fabrics that filled that brief, but sheen had one other desirable property—it wicked moisture away very effectively. You were never sweaty in sheen. It was very popular on hot worlds. It did have one other, much less popular feature. It didn't last. The cocoons broke down to release the sea-squill young three hundred and seventeen Parisienne days after it had been secreted. The fabric, even spun, did the same. Every year there was a rush to get the new sheen garments to the markets as fast as possible. Customers liked their cloth as quickly as possible, and prices were determined by the time since harvest. As a result, Parisienne saw a great deal more fast ships than most worlds, so it was a good spot to blend into the traffic to her next destination.

Her pilot was none other than Olimy, who they had rescued what seemed like forever ago back on Uldune. He set her down on a small island.

There was literally not another person there—which made it a perfect landing spot for a small spacecraft of extremely advanced design that Karres did not wish to advertise. All the stealthing and cloaking gear in the galaxy couldn't stop an accidental sighting—but darkness and twenty miles of surrounding ocean did.

"Your mother put together some tourist gear for you," he said, handing her a small bag. "There will be several dive boats along during the day. They always land the passengers here to have a little shore time—you just join them when they leave."

"Where is the nearest spaceport?" she asked.

"Pagette. The boats all come from Moonah Town. It's a small port, not one of the big centers, but it's got a hover-rail link to Pagette. It takes about three hours, so the dive trips are cheaper than the nearer places. There are enough people, not too obvious. I've used the route a few times now. It's easy and safe enough, and with the tourists, simple not to be noticed."

"No one told me anyone was looking for me," said Goth. "Anything else I'm not being told, Olimy?"

"We don't know if anyone is looking for you. We do know someone was tracking Captain Pausert's cargo, for some reason, but we dealt with that. We're just not taking chances with you. The prognosticators thought this would be a good place to land you, so here you are," he said cheerfully. "You'd better look at the papers that are in the bag with your money. You'll want to adjust your appearance."

He climbed back into the ship, and Goth was left to watch the small craft rise and vanish in a way that the Empire and many others would love to know more about. And then she was alone on the beach, listening to the lapping waves as the sky began to lighten with the dawn. It was quite cool at this time of day, so Goth looked in the bag, thinking she'd add a few layers.

That, she realized rapidly, wasn't going to happen. The bag had a towel and a skimpy swimsuit, jeweled sandals, and a twisted object that folded out into a broad-brimmed hat, and some fashionable eyeshades—and that was it, besides a sequined purse.

The purse, which she examined in the light of Parisienne's slightly mauve new-risen sun, had a cool quarter of a million Imperial maels in it, an Imperial passport in the name of Leinna Dol Armoth and some sunscreen and hair ties. She sighed. *Hair ties.* Essential survival equipment, when you are cast away on a desert island, with no breakfast. Almost less useful than all the money—which was a lot, even for Karres.

So, hungry and a little irritable, Goth sat down to wait. She could have tried to catch some fish or eat the local shellfish, she supposed, but she had no idea if anything was edible, or tasty, and it wasn't worth experimenting for the short time she expected to be here. She sat in the sun, and then when that had become too hot, moved into the shade. Out on the purplish-blue water she could see other islands and what could be a boat in the distance. She got herself changed, and wrapped herself in the towel—it was still cool enough to make that a good thing. She thought about burying her clothes, but as everything that wasn't beach on the island was cloaked in low green vegetation, out of which various odd-shaped trees grew, she settled for 'porting them into a hole in a tree trunk, a long way up one of the trees.

A startled-looking, long-beaked emerald-and-ruby shimmery bird emerged from the hole seconds later, and flew off squawking indignantly. That made Goth jump—and then laugh. She hadn't laughed since they told her what she was going to have to do, all on her own.

It wasn't as good as breakfast and a drink, but it did make her feel much better. So she found a patch of sun behind some trees, and went to sleep. She awoke much later, hot, to the sound of voices and laughter. It was apparent that the tourists had arrived on the island. She went out to join them. There were several boats at anchor along the jetty that jutted out into the bay in front of the island. Her clothing was a close match for what most of the people playing in the shallow water or sitting or lying on the sand were wearing. Goth sat down among them and applied sunscreen, and looked about for something to eat... which she failed to see.

So when a man in a bright orange hat and vest started ringing a bell and shouting "*Calpurnia* passengers, *Calpurnia* passengers! Please embark; luncheon is about to be served," Goth didn't hesitate. She joined the throng of people heading toward the biggest vessel. This was ideal, she thought. Bigger means more people, and less chance of noticing one extra. And there would be food.

Food was a distraction that stopped her noticing that she was one of the youngest in the crowd heading onto the vessel for the buffet. By the time she noticed, it was too late. The vessel was already heading out to sea. It was a hover-jet boat, so they moved both quickly and smoothly away from the island. It took Goth very little time to realize that these were sightseers, not people who had come to snorkel or gill-breathe in the clear water. She used a light-shift to alter her appearance subtly, with just a little regret that she would not get to try the diving. Well, perhaps one day, with the captain...that made her sniff and swallow, and pay attention to the tour guide, rather than thinking about it.

The guide had that sort of singsong quality to his voice that goes with having said the same thing too often, to too many people, who weren't really listening.

"...the Mantro barges follow the migrating sea-squill, collecting the cocoons. Of course there are government inspectors on each barge to make sure enough larval squill remain to keep the fishery healthy. There are also quarterly surveys..." he droned on about the squills, their diet, and how dangerous the migrations were, and how secret the Mantro people kept the process of making sheen. Goth listened and ate. It beat thinking too much.

"And now, ladies and gentlemen, if you could insert your nose smell-filters, we're approaching the Mantro barge, the *Queen Abelard*, and you want to have them comfortable before you get there. We will have souvenir packs of fresh sheen for sale...."

Goth noticed that all around her the passengers were digging in their bags and putting on what was plainly a cruise-issued disposable scent-filter unit. And of course, she didn't have one. Well, there was always a light-shift. They weren't toxin filters... and how bad could a smell be? She'd smelled a few revolting things in her time around the worlds of the Empire and its borders. She could see those around her, and could match the shape of the device well.

They came up to the barge, rapidly. On the high bridge above the wide deck Goth could see a tall, dark-skinned figure—in a rebreather mask, with a long spiky headdress.

"Ah...they have just made a catch. That is the captain himself on the bridge seeing to the winches," the guide informed them.

"The hereditary captain always directs the winching of the nets. To his left is the official government observer."

The observer was a squat little man in a gray and orange uniform, also with a rebreather mask. Everyone else visible on the boat was near naked, so it did make him stand out.

The huge otter-dredge was being emptied into a broad metal hopper, and men in thigh boots were wading through the shimmering catch, kicking and sorting squill with shovels onto the conveyors. On the deck, men and women worked shoulder to shoulder at the stainless-steel tables, knives flashing. Goth noticed they weren't wearing expensive rebreathers or even nose filters. They appeared to come from every race in the Empire, some short, some tall, wearing little more than hats and leather aprons.

Slaves? Goth wondered. Yet they all seemed to be happy, smiling and working frantically. It must be very well paid because many of them didn't look in the first flush of youth or beauty...she was still wondering about that when the smell from the barge hit her. She wished she hadn't eaten, and then, she had to be sick.

She wasn't alone. There were two or three others, also escorted by the crew to the stern, and given rebreather masks so that they didn't inhale the vilest smell ever.

That stopped her thinking about anything much until the tourist cruise had moved on. The vomiting and the dry retching left her exhausted, and happy to rest on a recliner while the rest of the tourists went on being shown the wonders of Parisienne.

It was only later in the hover-rail car heading to the city of Pagette, when Goth got to thinking: How did those workers on the barge live and work with the smell? The guide had said something about the scent being a defensive weapon the sea-squill larvae used to protect their cocoons, but Goth had been feeling too wretched to care. So how did the workers manage? There was something about it that niggled at Goth, but she had to deal with buying clothes, luggage and passage off-world for "Leinna" on a sheen clipper, heading for Morteen, a world in the Duchy of Galm on the southwestern border zone.

That was the sector in which Captain Pausert's father, Lieutenant-Commander Kaen, had vanished. The planet his garrison had been on, where his mother, Lina, had gone on her search to find out what had happened to him. That was the last trace Imperial Security had of her, and, likewise, the last trace that Karres had been able to find. She'd gone over the border, into the uncharted and unpoliced star systems and the worlds beyond. Still: Stars were scattered and thin out that way. There had to be some kind of trace. And there were always people who traded across borders, who were often quite good at evading Imperial Security's watch. All she had to do was find them. And that, in turn, was something Karres' people were quite good at doing. They had had lots of experience.

CHAPTER 4

The air on the *Venture 7333* wasn't unbreathable. It was just...
well, smelly, by the time they were able to send out a call to the
port authorities on the subradio. "This is Captain Edom of the
ship *Farflight*, registered in the Leris star cluster," said Pausert,
giving their current *nom de plume.* "Request landing coordinates.
Request permission for the earliest possible landing slot," continued Pausert, tiredly. "We've got seventy-eight space-rescued
people aboard, and we're running low on air."

There was a moment's silence. "You're short on air and are
coming here?" said a surprised voice.

"You are the nearest Imperial world. According to Imperial
Space Regulation three-two-three section B, landing clearance
or relief must be granted to Imperial citizens in distress. We're
happy to trans-ship them, if there's a vessel that could take
them," said Pausert.

"No ... you're cleared for immediate landing," said Port Control. "Here are your co-ordinates."

While they were descending, Captain Pausert did spare a few
moments' thought for the reaction from Port Control, but he
was tired and it was not an easy descent, with buffeting winds

and—as he looked through the ship-scope—plenty of geography to avoid. Cinderby's World certainly boasted some high mountains. *The atmosphere must be pretty thin up there*, thought the captain as they dropped into a narrow deep valley.

When the ship came to a rest, and the captain looked out at the port, he realized that the atmosphere must be pretty thin generally, let alone up in the mountains they'd come to rest between. The port buildings were in a dome, linked to several more domes by covered passages. Looking at his instruments, Pausert saw that besides enormous volcanic mountains, Cinderby's Word had an atmosphere which had one thing going for it—there wasn't a lot of it. Because what there was, was rather toxic.

Two men in respirator suits—lighter than spacesuits, but airtight, nonetheless—dragged an access tube toward the *Venture* with a grav-sled. What brought men to live on such an inhospitable world? It had to have some draw, since there were thousands of other worlds with breathable atmospheres out there. Still, Pausert didn't really care too much. As soon as he had his cargo of involuntary passengers off the *Venture*, they'd be on their way. They didn't need to refuel yet, and without the extra load, the air recycler would gradually improve their air quality.

Like most plans, this one went awry, and did so quite quickly after the rescued would-be slaves had walked off down the access tube and into the dome, carrying their injured and thanking him. "Port Control. Request you remove the access tube, as we'd like to lift as soon as possible," said the captain into the radio.

There was a pause. "Sorry, Captain. Permission to lift off has been officially withheld. The Planetary Police want to talk to you. And you're under the port guns, which are locked onto your ship."

"Great Patham's seventh steaming hell! What for?" Pausert was confident that the papers his ship now had, and the identity he now had, would pass any muster. Besides, at least in theory, Karres operatives seeing to the cleanup of the Imperial Security Service after it had been taken over by the Nanite plague had scrubbed any reference to Captain Pausert of Nikkeldepain, the *Venture 7333*, as well as Captain Aron of Mulm and the ship *Evening Bird*. In backwaters like this, of course, records could still persist, and affect things.

"Charges of piracy and theft have been laid against you," said Port Control. "Officers of the Planetary Police Force are on their way over to your ship."

Pausert snapped the communicator off.

"How long to warm the tubes, Captain?" asked the Leewit, almost as if she'd read his mind.

"Couple of minutes." He flipped the switches. "The nova turrets are now free. You take the forward one and get a bead on the port guns. They want to play rough with us, they can taste some of their own medicine. Vezzarn, have you sorted that aft gun?"

"No, Captain. But they won't know that. And they won't like the idea of their dome getting holed. Not in this atmosphere."

"Well, I'd rather not hole it either. But all of you strap in. It's likely to be a rough launch." He started the tube-warming ignition sequence, and when he'd done that, snapped open the communicator channel again.

Needless to say, Port Control was having fits. Pausert interrupted them. "You deflect your guns and we'll deflect ours. Otherwise we keep them locked onto you, until we lift. When we lift, if you attempt to fire on us, we'll return fire. Your charges make no sense, and we're out of here."

"Captain Edom. The police merely want to talk to you," said Port Control.

Pausert had heard that one before. But he still said, "Well, let them talk. I'll listen."

"They're on their way across to your airlock," he was informed.

"Tell them to leave any weapons outside. I'm not having them trying to get smart and damaging my ship." If need be he could take off with them on board. Their gunners could decide if they wanted to shoot at their own police or not.

So a little later two members of Cinderby's World's finest were permitted to board the *Venture 7333*. Unarmed.

They were enough to ease Captain Pausert's mind a little, neither of them being typical flatfeet. "I apologize for this," said the plump woman who introduced herself as Chief Inspector Salaman. "It's just that Councilor Stratel insisted on pressing charges. He's a big cheese on Cinderby's World."

"Stinky cheese," said the Leewit. "He was the one with the fancy hairstyle, Captain."

"The one who was so convinced we'd looted the wreck of the

ship and had his property!" exclaimed Pausert. "He's an idiot. We barely got them off alive."

"Off the record, sir, I agree with you," said the female police officer. "But he's wealthy and powerful, and got in touch with the president as soon as he got into the spaceport, insisting we act."

"We'd hardly have saved their lives and set them free if we were pirates, Chief Inspector," said Pausert, trying to keep his temper. "We'd have either killed them or sold them as slaves. Or ransomed your big cheese. As for piracy—they knew all about that. They were captives of real pirates who tried to take us too. We got lucky and scored a hit on their munitions store, and broke up their ship. Ask the others: They were all chained up in the hold, so we got them across into our ship. His 'property,' whatever it is, is either still among the ship's wreckage or on the lifecraft that escaped."

"A lifecraft!" A pregnant look passed between the two policemen. "You interest me extremely, Captain Edom!" said the chief inspector, looking for all the world like a grik-dog that had suddenly gotten a scent. "Adding up for you, Senior Detective?"

The other policeman, a mild, very ordinary looking man who would pass, un-noticed, in a group of three, nodded slowly. "Oh yes, indeed. The trick is going to be tying it up, Sal."

Pausert looked inquiringly at them. "What is this all about?"

"A lifecraft made a landing about four hours before your ship," said the chief inspector.

"Well," said Pausert. "There are your pirates. And possibly that idiot Stratel's goods, whatever they are." It did fit. This was the nearest Empire world, and with the time that he'd been passed out, and then gained by using the Sheewash Drive...well, that would be about right.

"Whatever they are!" The senior detective's face cracked into a smile. "Let me guess, Captain Edom. You don't know much about Cinderby's World, do you?"

"Nothing at all," admitted Pausert. "I can't say it looks a great place to settle, so there must be something here that's worth a fair bit of money. It'd be a mining world, I suppose."

"If anything was going to convince me of your innocence, that answer just did," said the policeman. "Actually, we make our money out of flowers...you might say." And they both laughed.

"Perfume?" asked Pausert.

"No, Captain. They just look like flowers, and it's not the flowers themselves, but their droppings. You've got a little bit of it here on your ship. We produce the catalyst for your air recycler. It's a natural organofluorate, something between what a plant and an animal produces, that drops a trail of little green-ish granules as a waste product. The gatherers follow after them and collect them. The flowers roll with the wind, or can actually creep along. Out here their droppings break down in a few days, but away from the atmosphere of Cinderby's World, it is stable. It's worth many times its weight in gold, and that's what Stratel was couriering to a manufacturer. He's one of the major associates in the company that ships the stuff for the gatherers. Stratel, Bormgo, Wenerside and Ratneurt. They used to be competitors, but they got together a few years ago, and have a monopoly on the export." The chief inspector grimaced. "Smuggling is a big issue, because the companies who own the concessions to harvest it, pay the gatherers as little as they can get away with. So, that is principally my job."

"I see. But what has this got to do with me? Or your reaction to the lifecraft?" asked Pausert.

"On board that lifecraft was another powerful and wealthy man. Also a Councilor. Councilor Bormgo," explained the police-woman.

"The lucky escape he had from space-pirates was all over the newscasts this morning," said the other representative of the police, pulling a wry face. "He was transporting a valuable cargo—a packet of catalyst. The fluoroflower granules he had remain the property of the concession holders until sold. So they're very glad."

"Ah. But they're actually Stratel's granules?" asked the captain.

The policeman nodded. "Or rather, the concession holders who had entrusted Stratel. He's in big trouble with them, and was trying to make you the scapegoat."

"And this . . . Bormgo knew exactly when he was traveling and with what—so he could steal one load and sell the other," said the Leewit. The captain knew her too well. That was almost admiration in her voice. The Leewit was something of a rogue at times. Well. At most times.

"Yes, I suspect that would be what they were up to, but prov-ing it might be more difficult," said the chief inspector, running her hand through her hair. "I tell you, Captain Edom, you've brought us a right Imperial mess. And, yes, I can see that you were just doing your best. Not that the prisoners might not have been better off to die in space than be here!"

"To give in to death without a fight is almost always the weakling's choice," said Ta'zara. "Here they have a choice, I think?"

"A choice between being a gatherer, or not breathing. It's hard to get a free man to do this kind of work," said the senior detective grimly. "But unless they're wealthy people with access to funds, they haven't got a lot of choices here. It's a company town, in a manner of speaking. There's us, the Port Control people and Judge Amorant—we've been seconded here by the sector governor of the Duchy of Camberwell—and that's about it. All the rest are tied up in the granule business. They charge for everything, even the air the poor devils breathe."

"Ouch. I still think most of them would choose breathing over not breathing. Anyway, now that we've solved your mystery, can we leave?" asked the captain. "I think you can see that neither the piracy nor the theft charges stand up."

The two policemen looked at each other. The chief inspector grimaced and shook her head. "It's a legal process, Captain Edom. Stratel hasn't gotten a case, but he's brought one against you. It will have to go to court for the judge to dismiss. One thing at least, Judge Amorant is strict and fair. Between you and us and your ship's hull, he and my force were sent here to try and clean the place up a bit. The spaceport staff petitioned the governor to do something about the situation, and Viscount Camberwell, well, he's a reformer."

"Cinderby's World Spaceport is an obvious pirate-raid target," the senior detective said. "It's hardened against spaceguns, and has endless airlocks. You're a danger to a small part of the spaceport, not the settlement itself. You might as well deflect your guns."

"They make us feel a bit more comfortable," said Pausert, shaking his head. "So what happens now, Chief Inspector?"

"I'm supposed to charge you, take you to the cells, search you and your spaceship, and then have you in front of Judge Amorant for a bail hearing," she answered apologetically but firmly.

"I see. Of course, the tubes are warm, the airlocks are closed, and we could just take off right now," said Pausert, equally firm.

"Believe me, Captain. I did think of that. That's why we came aboard, to show our good intentions. Otherwise I could have insisted you come out or be fired on. Look, I've been in policing long enough to realize a pirate is not going to discharge, free and yelling blue murder, a valuable man for ransom, let alone a cargo of people he could sell for slaves. We...well, we thought this was a trick to smuggle pirates into the port. So we mobilized our defense unit. And then they turned out to be rather battered, unarmed people—and a prominent citizen of Cinderby's World, accusing you of piracy and theft. I realized we were dealing with a genuine rescue. Those people could have been unloaded as slaves here for five hundred maels a piece. I know you're not guilty, that you put your ship and selves at risk to help. But the law is the law. And that is what I do. I uphold the law."

"You're not going to put a little girl in jail, are you?" asked the Leewit, doing her best to look like a little girl, sweet and harmless...in a way that would have frightened Pausert into blocking his ears. But then, he knew her. And could guess what she was up to. "I am scared of jails," she said innocently.

"Er." The chief inspector plainly didn't have children.

"I'll tell you what," said Pausert, stepping into the breach the Leewit had created. "You leave your senior detective here with my niece. I'll go along with you. You're not planning on charging her, are you? And your senior detective can search the ship, under her guidance." He turned to the Leewit. "If I'm not home in time for supper, you can whistle up something, uh, from the robobutler, and have something nice to eat. Have an Egger or something." Pausert hoped he didn't have to use the Egger Route back to the *Venture 7333*. He wasn't that confident of doing it on his own.

"That seems reasonable. I think the judge would be fine with that. I mean it's not like she could fly off on her own. Or do anyone any harm," said the chief inspector.

Captain Pausert did manage to keep a straight face as he agreed with her. The Leewit had quite a convincing coughing fit.

If the two planetary police officers were not fooled, they were better at hiding it than either Pausert or the Leewit. "We'd have to take the adult members of the crew," said the chief inspector.

"I cannot leave my mistress unguarded," said Ta'zara, folding his arms with a calm finality.

"Yes, you can," said the Leewit, equally firmly. "I order you to."

He shook his head.

"Me being safe depends on the captain being here to fly the ship, Ta'zara. So don't be a clumping dope. I'll whistle if need help."

"I'd have to lock the nova guns on their target. They're touchy, and old. Anything disturbing the ship might well set them off," said Pausert. "So I am afraid you'd be stuck inside it, senior detective, until we come back. If you tried anything... well, you'd still be here."

"I'm due some time off," said the officer, managing a smile. "Happy to spend some of it here."

Pausert managed not to smile back. But Ta'zara stepped forward. "I am her sworn defender. Her La'gaiff. Do you understand what that means, policeman?"

The policeman nodded. He could scarcely be unaware of the Na'kalauf tattoos on Ta'zara's broad face, or have been a police officer without knowing. "She'll be as safe as if you were watching her. I won't allow anyone else on the ship," he said, nodding, slightly wide-eyed.

"You won't be able to. Because we're not going to give you access codes, and that means you're stuck here," said Pausert, "until we come back. Now, I'm wasting fuel on my tubes and they'll overheat, so if you'll excuse me, I'll go and shut down the warmup cycle, before we go."

So he did that, and a little later, he, Ta'zara, and Vezzarn set out with the chief inspector for the spaceport. They were ushered through customs—and past an obvious barricade set up to allow the soldiers, now packing their gear, to fire from behind. There were two little groundcars with drivers waiting, and Pausert and the chief inspector got into one, and the other two into the other. "I have to ask, because asking awkward questions is my job," said the chief inspector. "How come your niece has a Na'kalauf bodyguard, and one sworn by their highest oath to defend her?"

Fortunately, Pausert had seen this one coming. "It's a debt of honor. Her father is quite an important man." Both of these things were true, they just had nothing to do with each other.

"I wondered. Normally they only sell their services to the La'tienn level."

"I don't even know the difference," admitted Pausert.

"La'tienn is defense, unarmed, and not in breach of the local law, for a defined period of time. The Empire doesn't have a problem with that. La'gaiff...well, there are no limits, and the guardian's clan will intervene or avenge, if harm comes to the one guarded, and the bodyguard is killed."

"And do the Empire's police have a problem with that?" asked Pausert, reading her tone. "She's a little girl, chief inspector. Not a drug lord or a pirate captain."

"It does make me wish to know who her father is—and why she's on your ship. But that is my job. To notice odd things and to find out answers."

Pausert wondered if he hadn't been too clever himself, again. But that was part of being a Karres operative—trying to outthink your foes, and finding out that what you were really good at was outthinking yourself. Keeping his mouth shut seemed a good idea. So instead he looked out of the window and took in the wonders of Cinderby's World's settlement. That didn't take long. There weren't any. It was a typical dometown—with space at a premium and buildings occupying most of it. The buildings were prefabricated ferrocrete slabs, built to the roof. So there wasn't a view, either. "Cheerful place," he said, as they headed through yet another airlock.

That got a snort of laughter from his escort. "It should be. A lot of money comes into it. But the prices are high. Rents are sky high."

The wealth wasn't that obvious at the jail. It didn't have rats, probably because they couldn't afford the rent. It was rather small, and the three of them had to share one cell. There were other cells, but they were full.

"You're pretty popular," said Vezzarn, taking in the full cells in the corridor.

"Yes," said the chief inspector. "It's cheaper to get locked up than to find a bed. The gatherers come in, get paid, get drunk and commit a suitably minor offense in front of one of my police officers and get locked up for the night. You're unpopular because your ship had most of the police force at the port-dome. Hopefully I can arrange a hearing for you soon so I can free up this cell."

She wasn't joking, either. A few minutes later another policeman came down the passage with a ragged scarecrow of a man, wearing many layers of tattered clothes. The policeman looked around the cells, sighed. "Look, can I put him in with you three?

All the other cells are six deep by now. And you won't be here much longer."

Pausert could only hope so. And it did seem a little odd for prisoners to be asked. By the smell of the man, he wished he'd said no. Their new cellmate was in the final garrulous stage of having drunk or drugged himself to the edge of insensibility. *"I've been a bold gatherer for many's a year..."* He sang tunelessly, before noticing them, and beaming aimlessly at them, and then blinking and screwing up his bleary eyes to try and focus them. "You!" He announced, definitively, and pointing a waving finger. "You ain't gatherers. What they put me here wi' you for?" He sounded quite disgusted about it, which, considering how he smelled, was something of an insult.

Pausert had been through enough port bars to know how to handle this, to avoid the fight. First you tried to distract them. "We just got in off a ship today."

That was, by luck, the right thing to say. "Great Patham! You poor devils. Yer gotta get more clothes. Them breather's won't keep yer warm out there. You try shonky Jok's near the east gate. He's a thief, but they all are, and he ain't as bad as some. Who got yer contract? Don' tell me 's that kranslit Ratneurt?"

"No. Stratel," said the captain, fishing for information.

That got a snort of disdain. "He thinks he's a kranslit too. I uster be bonded to him before he sold me bond to Ratneurt."

Pausert was glad that the Leewit wasn't here to translate "kranslit," or to hear it for that matter. She collected bad words with great relish.

The gatherer went on. "Reckon they'll put you on the north pass. That's where he's gotten his stash caves and they allus put the new ones there. You watch out for them porpentiles. There's a lot around them parts."

"What's a porpentile?" asked the captain, and soon wished he hadn't. Part of that was because the gatherer decided to demonstrate how porpentiles killed gatherers, which involved smothering them. Ta'zara had to haul the scrawny fellow off, before his smell killed the captain.

"I was just showin' him," protested the gatherer. "Let go o' me."

Ta'zara showed no sign of doing so—and then suddenly did, because something had poked its head out of the man's collar and bit Ta'zara on the thumb, before vanishing again. It was so fast Pausert barely had time to see the sleek little head and fiery slit eyes. It was the prickle of klatha again, rather like letting his hands find components that might be malfunctioning, and often were. There was something useful here. Something wrong. "Let's listen to him, Ta'zara."

"His talk comes from a grog bottle, Captain. And something bit me," growled Ta'zara, but he put him down.

The gatherer pulled his layers of clothing clear of his throat. "Y'didn't have to be so rough. I was just warning you about the porpentiles at the store caves."

There was that feeling again. But what was it from? Porpentiles? Or the store caves? Pausert couldn't tell, and went back to fishing, leading the man on. But before they got anywhere, a sturdy policeman came and unlocked the door. "Follow me. Judge Amorant will see you now."

The Leewit realized she was looking as cross as a cornered Tozzimi, when they left. The truth of it all was that she'd given the police inspector a break...and the captain a break, but she was actually wanting a break herself. A break from people. Being a healer was hard in ways she'd never thought about. Even buffered, she could feel their pain, and there was nothing that could stop her seeing their fear.

She really wanted a particularly tall Marachini-fruit tree, which she could disappear to the top of, and spit pips at anyone who came too close. Failing that, the *Venture* would have to do. She hadn't anticipated them leaving someone behind. And now she was stuck with the clumping idiot. She considered whistling him to sleep, or at least unconscious, and grumpily decided against it. She tried her best little-girl smile instead. It wouldn't have fooled Goth or the captain, but the policeman was a dope.

Except, he wasn't quite such a dope when it came to searching. The Leewit followed him around, watching every move. She reckoned it made him a bit uncomfortable, which was good. She also learned a whole bunch of neat new possible hiding places that she hadn't even thought of. That was also probably good, even if it meant someone else had thought of them already. She also talked to him, getting him to answer all sorts of questions. He wasn't a bad old dope really, and he answered what he considered quizzy little-girl questions politely. She kept asking. She figured it wore people down. He was probably telling her a lot of stuff he wouldn't have told the captain—or anyone else.

He explained, patiently, how his wand worked. "The granules have a scent. The wand's sensors pick that up at less than two parts per million."

Among the things she asked was why he was so good at searching, and he said something that the Leewit figured was both serious and odd. "There's a lot of money to be made out of smuggling the catalyst granules. The supply has dropped off a great deal, and that's pushed the price up."

"Why has the supply dropped off?"

"I don't know. The duke's advisors think it's that the cartel—Stratel and his business partners—are holding back supply. They have a history of doing it."

She read doubt in his tone of voice. "But you don't think so, do you?"

"Well, we're seeing a drop-off in the volume smuggled. That could just be that the smugglers have figured a better way." By the way he said it, he badly wanted to believe it.

The Leewit wasn't too sure what it all meant. But the granules were the heart of the air recyclers. And that was something everybody needed in space.

It took up so much of her thinking that she couldn't even play poker well, later, when he finished his search. Well enough to clean out the copper's pockets, but not well. She was a bit disgusted with herself about that.

CHAPTER 5

Captain Pausert found himself up before Judge Amorant—very briefly. The judge wasn't much interested in keeping them in prison. Unfortunately the prosecutor was not of the same mind. "I see no reason why bail should not be granted," said the judge, looking at the papers.

"Your Honor, they pose a serious flight risk. They have a spacecraft, and nothing to lose," said the prosecutor.

The judge sighed. "Bail is granted with the conditional limitation that the prisoners not be permitted to pass though the spaceport airlock. Bail is set at ten thousand maels. Settle it with the clerk or be returned to jail. Dismissed."

So they filed out, with Captain Pausert wondering what to do now. They could draw ten thousand maels on the *Venture*'s account with the Daal's Bank. But the Leewit wasn't going to sit patiently and wait. He could, possibly, use the Egger Route, a way of transporting himself outside of space and time, but he didn't think he could deal with doing so without help and also transporting the other two. And he couldn't exactly leave them here. He paid the bail to buy time to think about it.

They were met outside the court by a rather grave-faced chief inspector. "I am sorry about that," said the policewoman awkwardly. "I should have anticipated that the prosecutor would try to stop bail and Judge Amorant would meet them half way. He makes an effort to be seen as fair. The best I can do is to offer to let you use the communicator in my office. Look, the young lady would be entirely free to leave the ship, to come to you. My officer reports he's done a thorough search, found nothing, and he's desperate to escape another poker game. He wants to know who taught her to play cards."

Pausert couldn't help but laugh at the thought of the Leewit fleecing a green policeman. "That would be your fault, Vezzarn," he said to the old spacer. "He taught both of my nieces." In turning to look at the old spacer, Pausert noticed something odd—the scarecrow who had been put in the cell with them was also there. He blinked but said nothing about it. "I'll take you up on your offer of being able to talk to my niece," was all he said.

So the chief inspector took Pausert and Ta'zara up to his office. Vezzarn said, "I'll just as soon wait out here, Captain. Police offices make me nervous."

"They might ask where you learned to play cards," said the captain, waving. He noticed the scarecrow man was still there.

They went in and soon were talking to the Leewit—with a slightly alarmed looking policeman in the background. "Reckon I'll stay put, so long as I know you're all right," she said, firmly, when he'd explained the situation, sounding very like her older sister, and giving Pausert a brief twinge of heart-sore. "But this fellow c'n leave," she gestured at the policeman, "if you want him to. I've gotten all the money he had in his wallet, and I won't take IOUs." She looked at the chief inspector. "You should pay him better."

The captain was getting better at reading the Leewit by now. Good enough at it to figure out that there was something that she wasn't saying in front of the policeman, and that she wanted him out of the *Venture*. So he played along. "All right. I suppose so," he said with a suitable show of reluctance. "You can let him out then."

"Right, Captain. I'll be seeing you, soon. You give me a bollem-call, when you get here. Out," said the Leewit.

"A bollem-call?" asked the chief inspector.

She was quick, Pausert thought. "A hunting call from our

homeworld," he explained, which was true, but didn't explain just how it worked.

"Well, you're free to come and use the communicator until the case, Captain," she said. "I'll be glad to have my assistant back. Now, you'll need to find someplace to stay. I gather you have sufficient funds?"

"I guess I'll need them," said Pausert.

The chief inspector grimaced. "Yes. The Boromir is good and clean—about the best medium priced of the accommodations. Otherwise the Deward is the most expensive, and there are whole rows of flophouses along the Airlock roads. The closer you get to each lock, the more likely you are to get robbed, especially if you're drunk. I can take you anywhere you want to go, except the spaceport."

"We'll find our own way," said Captain Pausert. "We've got time and it's not like we could go anywhere before the trial."

"True," said the chief inspector and let them go on their way.

Outside they found Vezzarn, and the fellow who had been put in their cell. Now Pausert could finally ask him: "What are you doing here?"

The man grinned disarmingly. "They let me out along 'o you. So I just follered along. And it's too late to get back in jail for a sleep now. 'Sides I come down and woke up, and listened to the judge and that there prosecutor. You ain't bonded to no one are you?"

"No," admitted Pausert. "My ship is sitting on the landing ground outside the spaceport..."

"Captain!" They were hailed from across the street by someone with a familiar face—Pausert recognized the man as the lean planar-faced fellow, Farnal, whom they'd rescued. He was standing in a group of the freed pirate slaves.

"Hello," said Pausert, slightly warily.

"Captain," said the man, hands out in appeal, "is there any chance of taking us as passengers to any other world? These poor souls don't have access to funds, and if they stay here, they'll be little more than slaves. I can pay, but...not a great deal."

"Please, Captain?" said one of the women. "There's not much work here a decent woman can do, and this place is so expensive. We'll never get out. I've got a family on Marcott."

Pausert sighed. "Right now I am as stuck as you are, good

folk. I've been charged with piracy and theft by that fellow Stratel who we rescued with you. I can't go back to my ship until the case is heard."

"What?" exclaimed Farnal. "That worm!"

"Pretty good description," agreed Pausert. "The local police seem sure we'll get off, but then, they were sure we could go back to the ship too. If we do get off, well, the ship could manage twenty people. It'd be uncomfortable and crowded, but there has to be another Empire world close by where at least you can breathe the air within a week or two."

Farnal seized his hands. "Captain. You are a good man. I . . . I had no idea what happened here in the Empire. It is more rotten than I believed."

"Where are you from then?" asked the captain, who knew, but was fishing.

"Iradalia. I was on a mission to investigate the slave trade, particularly the traffic through Karoda." He almost spat that word out.

Pausert was glad the other rescuers were all talking at once. Karoda and Iradalia! There was something very odd about that. "How long do we have before the case, Captain?" asked someone in the hubbub.

"Four days," he answered. "I gather we've been pushed up the roll."

"Four days!" The woman who had exclaimed, shivered. There had been a limit to what the crew of the *Venture 7333* could do about the rescued people's clothing—and the slave-takers hadn't cared. It was easy enough on the ship to turn the heating up but here . . . well, evening was coming on and it was already cooler. They might be in an enclosed dome, but plainly the sun did some of the warming of this environment.

"We will make some kind of plan, Salla," said the gaunt man, looking worried nonetheless. He'd plainly taken on responsibility for the group. They had neither the money nor mental fortitude to do it for themselves.

Pausert felt sorry for them, but that was the difference between these, and Karres people. Karres witches, with or without klatha skills, would have made their own plans. "You could get arrested, and spend the night in jail," he suggested. "I gather it's the best and safest place to sleep around here."

"And they give you breakfast," volunteered the scarecrow local. "Just korma porridge, but it don't cost anything and it is food."

Their planar-faced leader looked somewhat taken aback. "I have never broken the law..."

"I think," said Ta'zara with that gravelly firmness that quelled the other voices, "That you should go into that police station there, and ask for Chief Inspector Salaman. Tell her that someone threatened to harm you if you were to talk about the space rescue. Then she will have to protect you as witnesses."

"What?" said the planar-faced man, looking puzzled.

"I c'n threaten you!" offered the scarecrow, generously.

"And I too," said Ta'zara. "You are afraid, because I was a threat on the ship. And now you have seen me on the streets."

"But...but you aren't dangerous. I mean you were just helping to keep order," said one of the people they'd rescued.

"But I *am* dangerous. The most dangerous man you may ever meet," said Ta'zara calmly. "It is to whom I am dangerous that you do not know. But the police will believe you. They want to. And then you can testify at the case."

"Let us do this," said their leader. "I do not like to bend the truth, but I can see that it will serve us all and justice best in the long run."

So the group of rescued passengers headed toward the police station, which gave Pausert and his companions a chance to move away. "You know, Captain, once that prosecutor gets back to that Stratel fellow, they probably will be looking for witnesses against us. And possibly trying to get us back in jail," said Vezzarn nervously. "I know the type. It's how they work, Captain."

"Yes," said Pausert. "They'll certainly try to arrest Ta'zara. For menaces. You just gave them reason, Ta'zara."

"But you are planning to get us back onto the ship, Captain," said Ta'zara, imperturbably. "You and the Leewit."

The captain shook his head. "I just hope the police don't read me as well as you do. I was planning to fly off and leave them to it, but maybe I need to rethink this. In the light of something that came up."

"I know how you call bollems," said Ta'zara, with just a hint of a smile. "How do you plan to do this, Captain?"

The captain looked at the scarecrow-gatherer, who was in a conversation with Vezzarn—a conversation that involved lots of wild gestures. He seemed very busy with it. "I was going to pay him to lead us around, outside, to the ship."

Ta'zara nodded. "He drinks too much, Captain. Also uses some kind of narcotic drug. He may be less than reliable."

"Yes. But he's not young. And it is tough out there, I gather. He's still alive, so he must be quite good at it. And all we have to do is take a walk around the domes. I can get us in to the field with the ship."

Later, in a small eatery that the gatherer recommended as cheap but good, with prices that made Captain Pausert's frugal Nikkeldepain upbringing reel, they put this to the gatherer and discovered they were wrong about walking. The gatherer, whose name it turned out was Nady, laughed.

"So it can't be done?" asked the captain, wondering if, with his klatha skills and Vezzarn's mastery of lockpicking, and Ta'zara being something of a one man army, they could get through the spaceport itself.

"Well now, it's not that it cain't be done. You cain't just walk around. You'd have to go down North Valley, and over Kassarite Pass, 'n down Jagged-Ferd Gorge. And then the port's got a wall around it, to keep the porpentiles out. I could get you that far. But you cain't get through the wall, and it's got detectors along the top."

"You get us there, we'll deal with that," said the captain.

"Oh, I c'n do that. But you're gunna have to kit up. You'll die in them clothes."

"How much?" asked Vezzarn. He'd dealt with enough smuggling operations in the past, Pausert knew. He'd be the best to negotiate a deal.

Nady rubbed the side of his long bony red-tipped nose, thoughtfully. "You really reckon you can do it? Well, then. I reckon I c'n do you a deal. Less we talk about here..." He looked around warily, "the better. Come on. Let's get moving."

So they did, trooping out after him. He seemed in a tearing hurry, suddenly. "We are being followed," said Ta'zara, quietly.

Nady looked back and swore. "It's some of that kranslit Bormgo's goons."

"Let us go down this little side walkway," said Ta'zara, calmly, steering him by an elbow.

"But it's a dead end," protested Nady.

"Perfect. It will not take long," said Ta'zara. "Wait."

Their two followers came around the corner hastily, looking for them. And then, they saw Ta'zara detach himself from the wall he'd been leaning against—between them and the way out. They were big, heavyset men. One man behind them didn't seem to worry them that much. One of the two reached for a pocket... but his hand had never gotten there. The Na'kalauf bodyguard moved so smoothly it was actually deceptive. It didn't look fast, but he somehow chopped down hard on the reaching forearm, and then literally banged their heads together. As they fell, he reached out to squeeze something in their necks. Squeeze and hold, until he dropped them. "We can leave now," he said.

"Great Patham!" exclaimed Nady. "I ain't picking fights with you, broad-feller. Let's go quick before their friends find 'em."

So they followed, into a somewhat more seedy area, the apartment blocks going right up to the dome. He led them into one of these. Up flight after flight of stairs, leaving Vezzarn panting, and even the captain breathing a bit harder. Sitting in a command chair kept your wits fit, not your legs. Eventually they stopped at a very ordinary-looking door. Their guide knocked on it, a complicated pattern of taps. A voice spoke through the speaker grill. "Who is it?"

"Nady Darrish. I've come about the pipes."

There was a pause. And then the wall behind them swung open—not the door. "This way," said Nady. "Quick. She don't keep it open long."

They went in down a passage and up yet another stair, through what was plainly a blast-door from a spacecraft. It swung open as they got there to reveal a neat office, as might have belonged to any minor businessman. That was a bit worrying, Pausert thought. It was plain they were dealing with some kind of criminal, and he'd had concluded after his various experiences that the really powerful ones tried not to look it.

The woman sitting at the desk didn't look at all criminal. Her age was hard to guess, but it was somewhere between thirty and fifty. She was perfectly made-up, neat hair, good clothing but not too revealing. She had the kind of face which said to a smart gambler: *Do not play cards with me.* And behind her stood another Na'kalauf warrior, plainly her bodyguard. Neither the man nor Ta'zara gave any sign of recognizing or even acknowledging the other.

"Ah. The spaceship captain and his associates. Well done, Nady," said the woman.

"And you are?" asked Pausert.

"I am Me'a," she said with just a hint of a wry smile. "Don't cross me, or you will regret it."

"I actually don't want to cross you at all. I just want out of this dome and back to my ship," said the captain.

"And I want to know exactly what is going on," she answered. "So perhaps if you help me, I can try to help you. Although I am not sure even I can get you through the spaceport locks."

"They was talkin' about going around outside," said Nady. "Seemed to think they could get through the wall."

She looked at them. "That would be worth doing, if you could get back into your ship once you were there. We've thought about it."

"Why haven't you done it?" asked the captain. He was sure now that he'd landed upright among the smugglers. That could be tricky, as he really didn't need the police regarding him as a prime suspect after all. She was undoubtedly dangerous, and she had a bodyguard who was also a Na'kalauf warrior.

She shrugged. "Most ships are not allowed to remain long. Daytime landings only. And the perimeter wall has heat and sound sensors in it, so cutters and explosives cannot be used. They used to have infrared scanners on the field, but the system broke down—and they hadn't ever had an incident, so they didn't bother to replace it." She grimaced slightly. "We keep a close eye on what they have. There are easier ways for small volumes. They would not work well on people . . . Captain Pausert."

Pausert wondered if he should try a klatha cocoon on her, or the bodyguard. "How did you know that?" he said as calmly as he could.

"Subradio, a coded narrow-beam. When your ship landed and I obtained a picture of her, details of the crew and vid image of you and Ta'zara. I sent the details through to my employer, Sedmon of the Six Lives. He guessed Karres would become involved, and he warned me to give you my fullest cooperation."

"Oh." That made a kind of sense. Uldune was still heavily involved in smuggling, even if it had—at least for now—withdrawn from piracy. And it seemed this was a very lucrative trade. "You may not believe this, but we really are here by the purest accident."

"You are quite correct," said the woman. "I would not believe you. But you may tell me anyway. Let me have drinks brought. Sit down, make yourselves comfortable." She looked at Nady. "I think you can remain too. You may be needed, and you know the consequences of not keeping your mouth shut."

So the captain and Vezzarn sat down on the comfortable chairs. Nady perched uneasily on the edge of another. Ta'zara remained standing—as did her bodyguard, impassive, aloof... and watching. Pausert noticed her flickering glance at her own guard, and the tiniest shake of his head. A side door opened and a servitor brought Lepti liquor for Pausert, a fruit drink that Pausert had seen the Na'kalauf bodyguard drink before, as well as something that plainly pleased Nady. A platter of various nuts and small salted biscuits was set on the table. Lepti... which was his favorite liquor. They were all too well informed, thought Pausert. But at least it was very unlikely that Sedmon of the Six Lives would move against Karres. The witches disquieted the hexaperson into a degree of good behavior.

A strange lithe little head popped out of Nady's collar. It made a curious growling chirrup.

The woman sighed, pursed her lips and shook her head. "You have one of those too, do you? Get it some Tar-fish, Palank." The servitor nodded and returned in a few minutes with some little cubes of fishy-smelling something. The creature appeared again and almost seemed to flow out of the top of Nady's shirt. He stroked its mauve fur as it moved. At first Pausert assumed it didn't have legs—but something was definitely moving under the fur. It moved as if it were gliding just above the ground, across to the platter, snatched up two pieces of the fish in its beakish maw and returned equally silently to Nady's shirt collar, to disappear again. Nobody else seemed to find that unusual. The servitor took the rest of the cubes away, which was a good thing, because they were more than just a little smelly.

"So," said Me'a. "Tell me what brings you to Cinderby's World."

So Pausert did, minus one or two details about the klatha use. She noticed, he'd bet.

At the end of it all, she nodded slowly. "So: petty vengeance for not treating him like nobility. And taking it out on an available target, even though you weren't the one who did it to him. That's Stratel all over. And insurance fraud. Well, well, well. The

Daal will be pleased about that. We had not successfully rein-
sured those cargos."

"Uldune insures them?" asked the captain, faintly surprised.

She gave a small snort. "Of course. Banking is not the only
form of robbery. And who better? We can often recover the
goods, at a fraction of the cost of replacement. I think we will
shortly be talking with some of Bormgo's employees. I suppose
the crisis has forced his hand into piracy."

"What crisis?" There was that prickle again. Something important had just been said.

"The shortage of catalyst granules. The Imperials think that
the Consortium—Stratel, Bormgo, Wenerside and Ratneurt—are
hoarding to control the price. They have done so in the past. That
is why they've sent some of their top enforcement officials here."

"But there just ain't much out there," said Nady. "They don't
believe it, but it's true. They ain't producing. Used ter be you
could follow a tumbleflower for a week and so long as the porpentiles didn't get you, you had a pouchful. Now it could take
you a month. Every now and again yer get a good one, but it
just ain't like it uster be."

"The records we've been able to steal show the industry has been
in a slow decline for centuries—but it's only been in the last twenty
years that it has really gone down fast, and the price of catalyst
granules up through the roof. The gatherers used to work within
sight of the spaceport. Now they're going more than fifty times
that distance, to the end of the Mount Lofty range and further."

"And there ain't nothing out there. Just a chance to get onto
the tumbleflowers coming in first," said Nady.

"So these tumbleflowers, don't you get them in other places?"

"Oh, yes. Planetary surveys show them as occurring just
about anywhere. They're very scattered, though. They tend to
concentrate here because the mountains make an enormous
wind-funnel. Early records of the spaceport record them piling
in the thousands against the dome. Of course when the wind
drops they walk away."

"I see," said the captain, who really didn't. "Anyway. Can
you help us get back to our ship? I really need to talk to...ah,
someone on board."

"Goth, or someone referred to as 'the Leewit,'" said Me'a,
knowledgeably.

Pausert scowled at her. He really could use Goth here. "Yes. The Leewit."

"Respect will be given," rumbled Ta'zara.

"I wouldn't dream of doing otherwise to one of the Wisdoms," replied Me'a, using the Uldune term for the witches of Karres. "If you think you can get into the ship by going outside the dome, I am very pleased to help. I'll have rebreathers found for you. Nady here will be your guide. I will send one of my men."

"Strictly speaking," said Vezzarn, "we work for the same boss. I used to work on the Jalreen jewel route. So the Daal has someone along, anyway. You see to that Bormgo's goons. They already tried to track us."

"They did?" said Me'a, her chin rising, eyes narrowing.

"Ta'zara dealt with them in one of your side streets," said Vezzarn.

"Twenty-seventh walkway," supplied Nady.

"I shall follow that up." She pushed her chair away from the desk, and, as the bodyguard stepped forward to open the door for her, Pausert realized it was a wheelchair, and she needed it because she had no legs. "I will take myself, Pa'leto," she said. "I know you would like to speak with your kinsman."

The bodyguard nodded. "Yes, my lady. But first I will see you safe, check the office and then return."

She sighed. "Bodyguards. I used to believe I that gave the orders."

A little later he returned with two other men, who wore the signs of the savage outside weather, carrying a crate. "Rebreathers, goggles, nose plugs and cold-weather gear," he said. "The boys will fit you out." Then he bowed to Ta'zara, held out his hands flat palms out. Ta'zara bowed back and pressed his palms against his. "Kinsman," he said. It was always hard to tell with Ta'zara, but his voice sounded thickened, gruff.

They spoke in their own language. Pausert hadn't picked up more than about three words. But he did get the "La'gaiff" part, and the fact that big tears were flowing down both men's faces, as he got kitted out for the harsh outside world. Then Me'a's bodyguard left, and Ta'zara silently let the locals fit him out as well.

Dressed up, Pausert was sweating. And they would still have to go down all those stairs to get to the street to walk to an airlock, he thought. That, however, was where he was wrong.

They actually went up one more flight of stairs and onto the roof, almost flush with the dome...and there was an airlock. It was already night, and, barring a little starlight—there was no moon—outside the dome it was pitch black. The airlock was open and there were large coils of rope inside. Obviously the smugglers didn't bother with hiding their cargo into and out of the domes. Pausert said so. Nady shook his head. "Not all of it. Got to keep the airlock cops busy."

One by one they were lowered down into the reaching darkness, the wind plucking at them. Soon they were out on the surface of Cinderby's World. Pausert no longer thought he was in danger of being too hot. He wished for an extra layer, already. As soon as they were all on the ground, the ropes were hauled up, and they were alone out there in the night. Nady tied a rope between them and they set off, stumbling through the dark, upward, the only sound, their rebreathers. Pausert stopped being cold.

Once they got up to the ridgeline the full blast of the night wind nearly froze him again. But at least they were walking downhill now, and Nady was using a small atomic light to show the stark terrain. Suddenly he stopped dead. "Back up slowly," he said. "There's a porpentile by the trail."

Pausert stared but couldn't see anything. "Where?" he asked as they retreated.

Nady pointed. "Just there. Look. The rock is too smooth. The edge is wrong."

Pausert still couldn't see anything and said so. "Wait until we're a bit higher," said Nady. "I'll show yer. We want to shift him anyway."

They retreated back up the path some more, and then Nady picked up a flat piece of rock, and said, "Watch." He held up the light, and tossed the rock to land on a sheet of slab-rock, much like any other of hundreds of sheets of slab-rock, downslope.... And the sheet moved, undulating in a curious up-and-down movement. It seemed to swim across the scree, then settled down in a new spot and became something that looked like a rock once more. "I bin doing this forty years now, and there are times when I don't see them. But they don't always attack."

"Is it hurt?" asked Vezzarn.

"Nah. Can't hurt 'em. Not even an ordinary blaster does much to them. Makes a hole—but it doesn't stop 'em. Takes a mining laser or heavy mounted blaster. They're nothing more than rock themselves. They just don't like to have rocks on top of them."

"Why are they so camouflaged? What do they hunt?" asked Ta'zara.

"Gatherers," said Nady with a sort of morbid delight. "They'll smother yer if they gets a chance."

"Do they eat people?" asked Vezzarn, plainly horrified.

"Nah. Jus' kill 'em. And yet, sometimes they won't do nothing to yer."

"Just how do you get away?" Pausert was wishing he'd paid more attention to Nady's instructions, back in the cell.

"Keep yer distance. You can outclimb 'em, but yer can't outrun 'em. And if they gets yer, the trick is breaking the seal. An' you gotta keep your rebreather under your arm like this...they etch anything metal. They suck down around you. If you c'n breathe, they ain't gonna suffocate you. They just gets tired and move on."

"Just how long until that happens?" asked Ta'zara.

"'Bout three days with a small 'un. Could be a week or more for one of the big boys. Yer die then anyway, 'cause they ain't light and anyways yer cain't last without drinking."

"So...if someone put rocks on top of them, would they move?" asked the captain.

"Nope. Not if they pounced a gatherer. Best thing is to spot 'em and not get under them. They like the sun-slopes. They're thick there. Yer only find them movin' across the shade."

That seemed very odd to Pausert. Perhaps the creatures ate metals? Why else would they bother with something that wasn't from their world, which they couldn't eat? Still, he was glad they had a guide. They walked on down the track. It led to a very crude airlock that went into the mountainside.

"We'll rest up here. Got to do the gorge in the daytime," said Nady.

So they went in and found themselves in a cave, lit by glow-globes. It was rank with the smell of unwashed gatherers—several of whom were in the various grottoes off the main chamber. "Nady. How yer going? What you got there? New bonders?" asked one, not bothering to get up.

"Job fer Me'a," explained Nady.

No one asked further questions, after that. One thing that Pausert noticed was that there were several of the sleek fluffy creatures around, moving with that graceful gliding gait, which made them almost look like they flowed across the ground. They must be some kind of gatherer pet, he concluded.

The next morning they left and began walking up the pass. The views were magnificent, with the jagged mountains almost seeming to reach into the heavens. Far below they could see the domes, below the cliff wall that prevented this from being a short walk. When they stopped for a breather, Pausert asked, huffing and panting through his rebreather, why they couldn't have walked the other way along the valley to the spaceport.

"There's a cliff there too. Just a little 'un. But it's a closed area. The concession holders have their store caves in that cliff. And the valley down there is fuller of porpentiles than bubbles in beer. They use flyers to get to the caves."

"Store caves?" prompted the captain.

"Yes, Stratel, Bormgo, Wenerside and Ratneurt each have part of the caves." Nady couldn't spit through his rebreather—but sounded like he wanted to. "They hold back when the demand ain't high, to keep the price up. Funny, we don't see any of it."

They'd seen tumbleflowers in the distance—Nady pointed them out—one being tracked by a gatherer, and another just rolling along. "That one ain't shedding," he explained. A little later they had to dive off the path as two of the tumbleflowers came bouncing down the hill. They were basically a ball of flexible spikes that had pink florets sprouting along the shafts—about twice the size of a man. The end of each shaft branched into little springy tips, letting them bounce hither and thither. "Dry un's," said their guide disparagingly. "Big un's don't shed much. Down in the valley you'll see hundreds like this."

Cinderby's World plainly had much shorter days and although it did not take them that long to get to the top of the pass, the sun was already on its way down when they entered the gorge on the far slope. It was a narrow, awkward and steep descent, with no real path.

"It ain't much used. Too steep for tumbleflowers," explained Nady. And then he gave a crow of delight, dropped to his knees, took a tiny pan and brush from his pouch and carefully brushed up little green crystals into a little oiled leather bag, which he tied closed very carefully. "You're me lucky charm!" he said, beaming around the rebreather.

"That's your catalyst?"

"That's her. That's a lucky break. Musta been one of the big ones, fell in here. They shed a bit now and again."

He was so busy looking around for more, that Ta'zara asked him if he was still looking for porpentiles. "Not in here. Too shady. Oh yes!" He spotted some more of the crystals. It took a little longer to get down the next section, with him hunting hopefully, but as they rounded the next bend they saw the tumbleflower, halfway up a small cliff, relatively close to the end of the gorge. "Is it stuck...or broken?" asked Pausert.

"Nah. It's climbing out. See. It has little suckers on the ends of its branches. They do it when they get stuck. It's just not fast. And they don't get busted. Thems as tough as hull metal. You see 'em bounce after falling over a cliff and just go on rolling. By tomorrow it'll be out of here."

They skirted past, and with Nady no longer looking for the green crystals, they got to the end of the gorge quite quickly. From the end of it they could see the wall of the spaceport's landing apron, and the nose of the *Venture 7333*, sticking out above it, gleaming in the setting sun.

"Come dark and I'll see if I can make us a hole," said the captain, looking at his ship. It would be nice to get into her and get on their way, but there were a few things to sort out here first.

"Ain't going to be that easy," said Nady...but it was. The captain slipped over to the wall with Ta'zara, leaving the other two in the gorge mouth, and used his klatha-cocoon skill, projecting it into the wall opposite the *Venture*. Ta'zara pushed on it and a disk of wall popped out. They waited. No alarms sounded, no searchlight beams penetrated the night, and so they called the others and went through. On the other side the captain and Ta'zara put the plug back in, leaving no sign of their entry.

Once they got to the *Venture*, the captain went along to one of her tubes and began tapping out a repetitive rhythm with a rock—the stamping sound used to call the curious black mountain-bollems to come closer and look.

The Leewit dropped a ladder from the hold door—and they climbed up into the welcome shelter of their ship.

CHAPTER 6

Goth embarked on the sheen clipper *Sheridan*. It was racing to get its cargo of fresh sheen to Morteen, the provincial capital of the Empire's southwestern sector. Morteen, when she looked it up, was described as tropical to hypertropical, and conveniently situated to . . . a list of other worlds, some of which Goth had even heard of. On the hubward fringe of human space, it was a space navy base, with valuable minerals, large flying bugs, lots of money and lots of heat.

A great place to sell sheen, in other words, and a good place for Goth to find another ship to take her further toward or across the border. Sheen clippers were fast and quite luxurious. They were also harder to stay unnoticed in than Goth liked, but then, as far as she knew, no one was looking for her anyway. She had a good cover story, the best fake papers Karres could provide, and plenty of money.

All she was missing was the captain, and the Leewit, of course. But the Leewit was getting toward that age where she'd go off adventuring, either with a couple of other Karres witches or maybe even on her own. That would just leave the captain and Goth.

Right now, that seemed like a really good idea. Maybe they could go to Parisienne, stay as far from the barges as possible, and dive. She'd never gotten to try diving, and by the pictures the spear fishing might be as good as hunting bollems with a bow. Not likely, but she'd like to try it with the captain. She was so taken up with this thought as she made her way down the corridor to the officers' mess—where passengers also ate—that she didn't see a woman in excessively high heels coming the other way, and nearly knocking her off her feet, sending the glass in her hand flying.

The woman in the heels didn't seem too upset about it, though, as Goth apologized and steadied her.

"Not to worry, dear," said the woman, smiling. "It happens. I'll just get another drink for Jaccy. He's winning at the moment."

"Let me," said Goth. "I wasn't paying attention. I'm sorry."

So she bought the woman, who introduced herself as Yelissa, a replacement cocktail at the bar, and did her best at the kind of small talk the captain always managed so easily. It wasn't hard to work out there was a little fishing going on. Of course there was no way of telling who was fishing or why. The woman could just be curious, or she could be anything from Imperial Security to a criminal.

"Yes," said Goth. "Parisienne was lovely. I had a wonderful dive at Ankawayhat." The name came from a glossy brochure of a very expensive resort she had collected while in the spaceport.

"How delightful. And now?" asked Yelissa.

"I'm off to Morteen."

"Also delightful. To the Cascades or for some other reason?"

"Just the Cascades," answered Goth, thinking that had to be safe. Pretty waterfalls for the tourist trade or something. She really had to do her research better! But she hadn't planned on spending any real time there. She had seen mention of "the Cascades," but not really paid attention to it. Her focus was more to the spaceports and likely outbound traffic beyond the Empire's borders. That was where the prognosticators said she was going.

"Well, then you must join us later for a little game! These sheen clippers are fast, but rather dull compared to the passenger liners. Still, there are usually a few handsome young men on these trips," she said archly.

Goth had no interest in meeting handsome young men, but

didn't say so. This led on to more questions, about her home and attachments. It was something she should have prepared better, Goth thought, keeping her answers vague. She didn't want to tell this quizzical woman that home was the *Venture 7333*, and that Captain Pausert wasn't attached yet but would be before much longer—to her.

That just made her miss him and the *Venture* more, and so she let herself get talked into joining Yelissa.

A little later Goth figured out that the Cascades was actually the name of a vast and glitzy gambling casino—one of Morteen's few drawcards. It did have waterfalls in the central foyer, which were something of a local attraction because most of Morteen was as flat as a pancake.

Still, that was pretty unimportant. What was a little more difficult was that old Vezzarn's brand of poker was really all the experience she had of games of chance. Well, they were supposed to be chance. She was being expected to know how to play their variety of poker, and believe that it involved chance. The cozy little group of gamblers in one of the staterooms did know how to play well.

Goth knew enough to know that she should have been losing. She wasn't, and that made her very wary. Wary enough not to bet too high. Wary enough to quietly 'port most of the drink she was given into a nearby ornamental display.

Unwary enough to take a small mouthful of the dregs of the second one Yelissa had brought to her. It wasn't long after that reached her stomach that Goth knew that had been a mistake. She swayed and felt herself slump forward onto the table, her head whirling.

"She must have the hardest head in the galaxy," said Jaccy, the man for whom Yelissa had been fetching the drink. "She didn't even notice the first lot. There was enough knockout in the second one to drop a fanderbag. I was beginning to wonder if the stuff wasn't working anymore."

He was plainly unaware that Goth was still awake and listening, even if she was feeling giddy and had closed her eyes. She felt hands pull her bag away from her.

"Great Patham!" exclaimed the gambler, obviously opening the bag. "She's carrying a small fortune!"

Goth, struggling with the drug they'd given her, tried to

decide what to do. The trouble with klatha was that it really took a clear head. They plainly weren't planning to kill her... yet. They could have shot her or tried to hit her over the head if that was their plan. Yelissa's fishing about who was meeting her, and her family... Goth wished she'd said something else.

"Do you think she's a courier?" asked one of the other men, worriedly.

"If she was, she wouldn't bet their money, or be stupid enough to have it here with her. We'd better check her cabin and papers though. Are you sure she's alone, Yelissa?"

"She said so, Jaccy," said the woman, eagerly. She sounded, thought the part of Goth's head that wasn't really with her, like a pet hoping for a pat. "I'm guessing she had had a messy breakup or something, more by what she wasn't saying and how she was answering."

"Could be, I suppose. A trip to get over it," he sounded amused. "Well, she will."

"Oh, yes. She'll be so happy," said Yelissa. She sounded like she really meant it...which was odd.

"It's a little worrying," said one of the others. "That's the first time we've gotten one with that much money. People with money tend to have families and friends who want to know where the money went to, even if not where the missing person went."

"We'll ask questions when she comes to. It's not like she'll be telling anyone, Paneha. She just won't arrive on Morteen."

Well, obviously they were planning on letting the drug wear off. What they planned to happen after that didn't sound so good. But what Goth planned to do to them wasn't going to be either. So she let herself slump and be carried to a bunk in a separate cabin, let them take her cabin key from her pocket, and waited for the drug to wear off.

It did, leaving her with a headache, and a terrible thirst. "Someone is going to regret this," muttered Goth, crossly. She tried to sit, still feeling a little unsteady, to see if there was water in her prison.

It wasn't just being drugged that made her struggle to sit up, it was also the hyperelectronic forcecuffs on her wrists.

"Don't scream. It doesn't help, and they'll just come and beat you," said someone in a weak, defeated voice. Goth turned to look. It was what once would have been a pretty redheaded woman, if she weren't so pale and miserable-looking and tear-streaked, who was leaning down from the bunk above.

"I wasn't going to scream," said Goth. "I wanted a drink. What's going on? What are you doing here?"

In reply, the redhead burst into tears, and hastily muffled her sobbing into her pillow. Goth managed to get up, and found a door that led to a tiny ship bathroom with a basin and a faucet. The water helped clear her head and ease her headache. She went back and the redhead had stopped crying enough to give her some answers, in between sobs.

It seemed that Mindi—the redhead—had fallen into the same trap that Goth had. The sheen clippers were quite a popular way for people to travel fast and alone—and easy pickings for the gang, who kidnapped and sold those who they thought could disappear. It was easy enough: The only law on a spaceship was the captain's law, and the passengers who vanished were chosen for no one knowing quite where they were.

"And that horrible Yelissa keeps telling me I'll be happy soon," said Mindi bitterly. "I thought I was going somewhere better when I got on this terrible ship. Now I'm going to be a slave."

"Have you tried to escape?" asked Goth, examining the door.

"You can't. There's always two of them. And they have nerve-whips and guns."

"Well, there's two of us now," said Goth. But it was true enough that the slight Mindi did not look like she could knock down a guard, not to save her life. Goth had other ideas, but there was no point in telling the woman that. She'd probably start crying again.

Goth could see that it was more than just a question of getting out of the cabin. They could hardly run this rig without at least some of the crew of the ship, if not the captain, being in the know. And in space...well, the captain was the law, the judge, the jury and even the executioner if need be. Goth could take the Egger Route out of here, or could simply vanish with a light-shift. But that wouldn't exactly help Mindi. The kidnap gang could easily kill her to do away with a witness, and dump her out of an airlock. They probably would, if Goth just left her there.

It was just as well that Pausert wasn't here, because he'd have broken out and be knocking heads together already, Goth thought. Goth planned on doing the same, but she wasn't going to miss any heads that should get knocked. They were going to regret kidnapping a Karres witch. Of that she planned to make absolutely certain.

It might be just as well the captain wasn't there, but thinking about what he might do to them made her smile.

The hyperelectronic forcecuffs were a problem. The force field they generated between them was not something she could 'port away. She could 'port the solid part of the mechanism—or bits out of it—away, but that risked either a rapidly contracting or expanding force field. At best that could cut her hands off, at worst expand and kill her. It was why police forces across space used them. They couldn't be cut or broken off. Without the correct unlocking code the prisoner was in for a worse fate, trying to escape them. Of course, there were ways of dealing with even that problem—a lock was still a lock, and experts like Vezzarn could deal with them, easily, especially on the cheaper ones. Captain Pausert's klatha skills with cocoons would work. The Daal of Uldune would have something in his laboratories too.

There was just one problem. They weren't here, and she was. All she had was the ability to teleport, to shift light around and the ability to read from contact the histories of places. Strong emotions left imprints. Thinking of that she turned to touch the wall . . . and wished she hadn't.

She and Mindi were far from the first victims to be kidnapped and held here. Fear and hurt were in these walls—not in her bunk. The reason, when she looked carefully, was possible to see. It was new. There were scars where the old one had been torn out . . . the walls carried hope, despair and a ram. Not everyone who had been in here had been ready to give up.

But, by the fact that it was still ongoing, that she and Mindi were prisoners now, they probably hadn't succeeded in their brave effort.

When two of their captors came to check, feed, and, it seemed, to question her, Goth was ready for action. It was Jaccy, who, it seemed, was the leader of the kidnappers, with one of his henchmen. They had Clipe needlers, and nerve-jangler whips at their belts, or, in Jaccy's case, his hand. He wasted no time in using it either, swinging it at Goth's face. She ducked, only getting a few of the tendrils across her scalp.

It was enough to make her yell. And to 'port the charge unit out of it as he raised it to hit her again. The whip itself had soft, spongy tendrils, intended to cling and transmit. Without the charge unit it was a bit like being hit by a dust cloth. But Goth did her best to yell the walls down. The Leewit would have been proud of her. It made the unpleasant Jaccy smile and tell her to shut up, and if she yelled again, he'd hit her again. "And it won't help you to scream, anyway. The cabin is soundproofed. Now I want some answers. You make them good or I'll hit you again. Where did all the money in your purse come from?"

Goth had had time to think about this. If they had gotten the idea that she had family or friends who might look for her, they might just try to kill her. Most likely they would kill Mindi as well. "I stole it," she said, sullenly. She took the opportunity to 'port the power units out of the Clipe needlers. No sense in making it easy for them, should they decide to kill the two of them anyway.

That was enough to make the thugs pay attention. "What? Where from?" demanded Jaccy.

"Gambling syndicate, back on Merega V. Illegal, so they couldn't set the cops on me. I still wanted to get a long way away. So I took this ship, because she's fast. I reckoned on Morteen I could get some fake documents, and make my way to somewhere out of reach."

Jaccy actually laughed at that. "You're gonna be out of reach, all right, once you get to Karoda." He raised the whip again. "Now, I'm gonna teach you a little lesson..."

"Don't! Please don't!" begged Mindi. "She's...she young."

"Aw shut up," said Jaccy and turned to swing the whip at her.

Goth realized that the redhead probably wouldn't figure out that she should act as if it hurt. She had to work fast. She'd figured out exactly what was needed to make the light switch work, and 'ported part of that out. The little cabin plunged into darkness, as the butt of the second thug's jangler was 'ported into her hand. It still had its charge unit, unlike Jaccy's. The forcecuffs stopped Goth getting the sort of swing in that she'd have liked, but the yells and screams said she'd gotten a good few tendrils on both of them. She kept it up, until she had the door open. Then it was time for a good strike with the whip at Jaccy's throat, jam the switch on her whip, and to assume no-shape.

Jaccy was screaming at his henchman to get it off him. To kill her. Goth took the opportunity to relieve both of them of their Clipe pistols.

"My gun! It's gone! She's got my gun!" yelled the second thug. They both bundled out of the door, slammed it, and bolted it behind them. That was fine from Goth's point of view, because she was already out of the cabin. They couldn't lock it because Goth had the key—which she 'ported into the bathroom. Mindi would be safer in there for now—if Goth could keep them out—or if she had the brains to lock the door. For good measure Goth 'ported a Clipe pistol and its power unit back into the prison cabin too.

The cabin was down a little passage from the stateroom she'd been kidnapped from, presumably some kind of servant's room. Now free of the jangler, Jaccy and his henchman staggered in, unaware that Goth was in there with them. It took a while for Jaccy to stop swearing, and a terribly upset Yelissa to stop fussing and crying over him, and the henchman to stop apologizing. "I'm sorry, boss. I don't how she got my gun."

"Patham's seventh hell! You're an idiot, Mogon!" snarled Jaccy, unaware that his gun was missing too. "Now just what the hell are we going to do? She's got the key and your gun."

Goth was rather interested in finding out herself. So she waited. It seemed that none of them really knew either, and the best answer they could come up with was to call in the rest of their crew.

That was useful too, and revealed that Goth had been completely right—some part of the ship's crew had to be involved. In all, there were six of them. A steward, the ship's purser, and Jaccy, Mogon, Yelissa and the other gamblers. "We'll have to tell the Old Man," said the purser, worriedly. "He's not going to be pleased."

"He's made enough money off us," snapped Jaccy. "First time he's had to lift a finger."

"He was angry when he had to replace that bunk," said the purser, wringing her hands.

"We paid for it. And we got a good haul out of that Leinna's purse. I say we just kill them and move on."

"How? I mean she's got the key, and a gun. If she hasn't locked the door we could rush her, maybe surprise her. But if we have to batter it open, she'll have plenty of time to be ready to shoot us."

"Starve her out," said Mogon. "She's a madwoman."

"She's a tough one. Must be a high-gravity and high-toxin

world she comes from. She took a lot of knockout, and she took on two of us, with forcecuffs on. I don't know how long she can go without food. Can we cut her water off?" Jaccy asked the crewmembers.

"Not easy. That's engineering's area. And you know the chief engineer . . . well, he's not going to just do it," said the purser, looking at the steward. "Not without coming to look at the problem. From inside the cabin."

"If the captain told him to?" asked Jaccy.

"Not if Patham himself told him to," said the steward. "He's a tough old bird, and his engineers listen to him, no one else. It's always just about open war between engineering and the topside crew. He's the best, the sheen trade needs the best, and he knows it."

"We could negotiate. Lure the two of them out, promise to let them go, and then deal with them," said Yelissa. "They'd be so much happier if they cooperated. That poor Mindi has been so sad."

"Oh shut up, woman," said Jaccy. "Mind you, you might have a point. Let the two of them go hungry a day or two. And then we'll negotiate. We can yell through the door; she should hear it. We've got a few days until we reach Tardelote. And when they're good and hungry we can dope the food we send in."

That was enough to give Goth ideas. They must have a stock of that knockout drug and at least she knew who the enemy was, and that the chief engineer was probably someone who would help, and the captain, wasn't. And for now, Mindi was safe enough. Goth hoped she had the sense to use the bathroom light, because the cabin light wasn't ever going to work again.

CHAPTER 7

Goth needed to think it through, to come up with a plan. In the meanwhile, she had the inconvenience of forcecuffs, and of having to stay hidden in no-shape. First things first. She wanted their knockout drops, and preferably all their weapons. It was easy to 'port things she could see, and small, light things were the least effort, but even the klatha use that she'd made so far had left her hungry. She raided their little chill unit—but other than drinks she wasn't touching, the only thing of interest was a jar with a measuring vial in the lid. Goth muttered to herself about the lack of sensible pockets in fashionable clothing. Then she had a bright idea: She knew the size and shape, precisely, of the bag they'd stolen from her. She 'ported it back, slipped the vial in there, and was in time to follow the steward and purser out of the door.

No-shape was a little more tiring than altering her appearance, and it was hard to walk quietly in the corridors, so she dropped back and became, in appearance, the elderly neighbor she'd had while in the apartment on Nikkeldepain. She wanted to keep up with the steward and purser but they moved a little fast for a gaunt old man. So, making sure there was no one around, she became Hulik do Eldel. She'd spent quite a lot of time studying Hulik, back when she was watching that the Imperial agent didn't get too close to Captain Pausert. It was useful. No one would ever ask why Hulik moved fast.

She caught up with the steward and purser, in worried conversation. All she caught of what they said was "captain" and "after dinner."

Well, that suited her. She wanted that dinner. Of course, someone who looked like Hulik do Eldel wasn't going to just be left to do so. A steward approached her just after she sat down and said, "Captain's compliments, ma'am. Would you like to join him at the captain's table?"

Goth's first instinct was to refuse. It was hard enough to do a light-shift to hide the fact that she had forcecuffs on, and had to lift both hands to put food in her mouth. But . . . she might need to know more about the man.

Within a few minutes she'd decided she really didn't need to. She'd modeled what she expected of a ship's captain on Pausert. He was, after all, the captain she'd spend the most time with. This one was a bossy little blowhard, who seemed to think that bullying the stewards and belittling his officers would impress her. She felt like telling him it wasn't working, but settled for a cool Hulik smile and concentrated on the food . . . and 'porting his dessert to Mindi as he lectured one of his lieutenants. She 'ported an emptied bowl in front of him, and enjoyed hers even more. Her demure "but I saw you eat it, Captain" made it even sweeter.

She excused herself, left the mess, and stepped into the bathroom. There, she returned to no-shape, feeling much better about it now that she'd eaten. The ship had nice clear labels about where passengers were allowed, so it was not that hard to work her way up to the captain's cabin. Hopefully she'd beaten him and the steward there.

She sat down on the floor in the passage and waited, passing the time taking out the Clipe pistol and putting the power unit back into it. She was just getting to the point of giving up when the captain came along. He went in, and she followed hard on his heels, just slipping through the door before he closed it. That was a little tricky because no-shape didn't hide whatever sounds she might make. But the captain seemed oblivious. He immediately poured himself a drink, sat down at his desk and activated a terminal. Goth peered over his shoulder. He had called up a list. A passenger list. There she was, on it, along with her travel ID picture—but he wasn't looking at or for her. She saw Mindi on his scan through. The sheen clipper only carried ninety passengers...

And someone with Hulik do Eldel's face would stand out. The grumpy little old man would have been a better choice. There was a knock at the door. "Who is it?" demanded the captain tersely.

It was the purser. "I was about to send for you," said the captain.

"Uh. Yes, sir. We have a problem," said the woman, beads of sweat on her forehead.

"So you know about the woman who had dinner at my table? Who is she? And how did she get on the ship?"

The purser stared at him blankly. "What? No, we've got a problem with the slaves."

"I've told you before. I don't want to know. You deal with them, just no fuss and I get my money." He'd set down his drink while he spoke with the purser. Goth decided that the time had come to try the dope from the kidnappers on this particular dope. She added a dose to his drink. He took a good mouthful of it.

"Yes, but..." said the purser, sticking a finger in her collar.

"But me no buts. I want to know where that woman came from. She must be a stowaway. She'll be a valuable addition to your livestock." He took another mouthful of his drink. He blinked at it. "I don' feel too well..."

Goth quietly locked the door as the purser tried to catch the toppling captain.

Before the purser had a chance to work out what was going on Goth had her arms around her neck, the Clipe pistol pressed against the woman's cheek. "Don't do anything that will give me a reason to shoot you. And I don't need a lot of reasons right now," she said quietly. The Clipe pistol was awkward in her forcecuffed hands, in that position, and probably wouldn't do more than inflict a flesh wound. But she guessed that the purser wasn't the sort to take the risk.

"Who...who are you? What are you doing here?" asked the purser, fear in her voice.

It occurred to Goth that there was no harm in suggesting

that she wasn't alone and finding out a bit more about the whole operation. "I don't have instructions to tell you. Let's put it this way: You kidnapped someone that my organization is very upset about being missing. Now, I need these forcecuffs off. You enter the code, incorrectly, I lose my hands, and you lose your head. Do it right and you get to live." Goth hoped she sounded menacing enough. In her head the teaching pattern started to prepare the patterns of the Egger Route. Would she survive it, in shock, agony, bleeding out and handless?

She knew the answer was probably *no* even if the Egger Route took her through space to Captain Pausert and her little healer sister on the *Venture 7333.*

"Uh..." the purser hesitated.

The thought of the *Venture,* the captain, and her own fear, made Goth growl. "Do it or I'll kill you!"

Her tone was obviously enough to convince the woman. "I don't have the code," she gasped. "Only Jaccy has that. And Yelissa. Please don't kill me!"

"It's tempting. So: Tell me about your operation. Tell me enough and you'll live," said Goth.

So the purser did. People in a hurry took passages on sheen clippers. They were traveling fast and far—and sometimes alone. The kidnappers, who were a gambling syndicate who worked the route, kept it simple, capturing high-value solitary victims as a source of extra cash. The ship would offload sheen at Tardelote, for trans-shipment to smaller markets—and in among the bales would be doped prisoners for Karoda. The steward and the purser were in charge of loading the sheen into its drop capsule. Sheen didn't do well in a vacuum or if it got too cold, so the prisoners would survive.

"I think it's time you took a little drink," said Goth, when she'd done explaining. "Reach out, very slowly, take the glass your captain was drinking from, and finish it."

"But..."

"It's that or I'll shoot you," explained Goth.

She drank.

Once she'd slumped to the floor, Goth did a hasty search of the cabin, and, failing to find anything obvious to tie them up with, settled for cutting the sheets off the captain's bed in strips and tying and gagging them. It was awkward, with her hands cuffed, but she wasn't going to have them wake up and be on the loose. There was a small bathroom and she dragged them in there. It would have been nicer, she thought, to have her hands not cuffed together to do it. It would also be nice if all the villains could be lighter—or came with wheels.

The wheels arrived at the door, in the shape of the steward and a trolley, knocking. Goth didn't trust her ability to speak much like the ship's captain, but the appearance was easy. She thought the captain's appearance, and a curt gruff "go away" would do—but then she saw what—and who—was outside the door.

"In," she snapped.

He pushed his trolley in. "I'm looking for the purser, sir. We've ... we've got a problem."

Huh, thought Goth. *You think you've got problems.* The man was too distracted to notice she was pointing the Clipe pistol at him. "The slaves—the new ones, they're beating on the wall and the pipes with something. The soundproofing is fine for yelling and screaming, but the vibration carries. There have been complaints from the passengers..."

He finally noticed the gun. Gasped. "Don't kill me, sir! It's not my fault!"

"Shut up," said Goth tersely.

"You ... you don't sound right." He started backing away.

Goth realized he might run. She didn't want to have shoot him, especially in the passage. "Look in the bathroom!"

He did as she said, and she was able to close the door—which he realized as he turned in horror from what he saw in there.

She made him take a drink, too. Soon he joined the other two. That was reducing the number of her foes, if nothing else. It didn't really reduce the problem much, though. She was still forcecuffed, and still had the problem of Mindi.

But there was no point in waiting for a solution to come to her, so she helped herself to the steward's jacket and trousers—and discovered a small Blythe pistol in the pocket. So she searched the others, and when she found both a knife and another Clipe pistol, she was glad to have done so.

The trolley proved to be full of various liquors, so she took it down to the stateroom she'd escaped. And even out in the passage, she could hear the steady thumping of something being banged against the wall.

The steward's jacket had a pen in the pocket, so Goth wrote on one of the napkins from the drawer of the trolley. *Stop banging. I'm coming to get you out,* she wrote. She almost signed it *Goth* but remembered in time to write *Leinna.* She 'ported it into the cabin...and was rewarded a few moments later by silence.

Goth tapped on the door, and was answered by Yelissa. "Who is it?"

"The purser sent me down with the drinks from the captain."

Yelissa opened the door slightly, saw the drinks trolley and Goth's light-shifted face, and let her in.

"Patham knows, I could use a drink after that noise!" said Jaccy, helping himself to a glass and a bottle. "But is this the best the captain could think of?"

"It seems to have worked," said Mogon, doing the same, as the next of them took a drink too. Excellent, thought Goth, who had doped all of the bottles on the top rack. That just left Yelissa—and she would do well to undo the forcecuffs.

Jaccy blinked owlishly, and stared at her... "Who're 'ou?" he slurred, screwing up his eyes and trying to focus them.

Yelissa turned to him, her face instantly anxious. "Are you all right, dearest master?"

Dearest master. Goth could barely contain her snort, as she produced the Clipe pistol. She wasn't going to need it for Mogon. He'd slumped down. The other man was clumsily feeling for something—possibly a gun, but he was plainly having trouble controlling his hand. Jaccy slid to the floor, and Yelissa rushed to cradle his head, before it hit the deck.

"Finish your drink," said Goth, to the still-standing man who was fumbling for a weapon. "And don't try any funny stuff."

He didn't—either finish his drink or try any funny stuff—but Jaccy, his head lolling, managed to say, "Get 'er." Yelissa flew up from the floor like an enraged miffel to attack Goth, not in the least worried by the gun.

It was not quite what she'd expected from the fragile blonde. She'd had her attention on the still-standing man—to find herself attacked by a frantically clawing Yelissa.

Only two things saved her—the first being that Yelissa seemed to have no interest—or fear—of the gun, and made no attempt to get at the weapon. And the second was that there simply wasn't much to Yelissa. Goth had hunted bollems on foot with a bow.

She had muscles, even if she had forcecuffs on. Yelissa just had frantic flailing, kicking, scratching and biting.

The swaying man tried to take a hand too, managing to get his weapon out. The shriek of a Clipe needle shattering his Mark 3 Glassite and his trigger finger stopped him. He grabbed his maimed hand and cried out in pain.

His life had been saved by Goth's struggle, but she ended that struggle by thrusting Yelissa away, and then kicking her in the stomach, so that she went down with an explosive *whuff* of breath.

That quieted her down—which was more than she could say about the screaming man with the bleeding hand. Goth grabbed a handful of the napkins. "Push that onto it. And shut up or I'll have to kill you."

Yelissa tried to get up again. Because she was still in forcecuffs, Goth swung the Clipe over to point at her, traversing Jaccy's body. Goth noticed how Yelissa froze as she did that. "Stay down or I'll shoot him," she said.

Yelissa looked terrified, and stayed down and silent. Someone knocked at the door. "Do you need help in there? Shall I call one of the crew?" asked a querulous female voice.

Goth motioned at the two who were still conscious to shut up by the simple method of waving the Clipe at them, before setting it down on the trolley and opening the door slightly and looking around it. "Thank you, but I'm actually one of the stewards, just treating an injury here. We're fixing that banging noise—sorry, I need to keep this closed while the engineers open the sewer line. It's a bit smelly."

She closed the door firmly, picked up the Clipe pistol again, and waited. When she was sure the quizzy passenger had gone, Goth said to Yelissa, "Give him the rest of that drink, and dress his hand. And don't try anything or I'll put Clipe needles in your precious man."

Yelissa did as she was told.

"Now. I need these force cuffs off. Come here. I am going to put my arms around your neck. If you do it wrong your head will get blown off."

Something about the eagerness in the way the woman stood up and the expression on her face made Goth pull her hands back. "Back off. I've changed my mind. I'll put my arms around his neck." She pointed the Clipe pistol at the unconscious Jaccy.

That produced a look of horror and chagrin, and very reluctant but careful cooperation.

Her hands free at last, Goth stood up, enjoying the movement.

"I would have died for him," said Yelissa sullenly.

"I figured. But why?" asked Goth.

"Because it would have killed you and he would be safe," answered Yelissa reverently. "I would have been happy to do that."

"You're a dope, and he's not worth it. But if you want to keep him safe you'll behave yourself," warned Goth.

"You won't take him away from me?" Yelissa pleaded.

"Great Patham, no! You can keep him." Goth saw the expression on Yelissa's face and actually felt a little sorry for her. "As long as you behave yourself. Now I need to tie you up before I can get Mindi free."

Searching around, Goth had no luck finding rope or cord—but she did find the kidnappers' supply of forcecuffs. They were the programmable kind that she could enter her own code into, so Goth cuffed the doped men and Yelissa. Then she went down the short corridor to the room into which they'd locked her and Mindi. She knocked. Then knocked louder. "It's me. Leinna. You're free. Unlock the door."

There was silence. Then a muffled voice said. "I'm going to open the door. I'll shoot if it's not Leinna on her own."

Goth decided on a little light-shift, just in case.

The door opened a crack, with the spiky nozzle of slightly wavering Clipe pistol emerging first. Then the door pushed slightly wider and the redhead looked out of the darkness around it. "Oh! Leinna! I was so afraid for you. Where are they?"

"Unconscious and forcecuffed, except for Yelissa. She's just forcecuffed."

Mindi said something that would even have impressed the Leewit about what she wanted to do to Yelissa.

"Yeah, well. Just hold off a bit so she can undo your forcecuffs," said Goth.

"That—she kept telling me I'd be happy!"

"She's crazy," said Goth. "Come on. Let's get you free. Then you can help me drag them in here and lock them in. I wish the bad guys came in lighter models."

Goth had learned from her previous experience, and did some searching for weapons. That produced quite a collection, and rather a lot of cash. They even had Yelissa help carry them back to the room—and put them in there with several of the drink bottles—all but for her precious Jaccy. "But you can't separate us," she said, her voice edging on hysteria.

"You keep them doped, and we'll look after him, and I'll see you get to go with him," promised Goth.

"But..."

"Otherwise, no." The woman went, tears welling in her eyes.

Goth just had to wonder what she saw in a dope like Jaccy. It wasn't like he treated her well, or even showed he cared about her, but in the meanwhile she had to stop Mindi from having one of the drugged drinks. "They're full of their knockout drops. I'll get something else."

"And some food please. I haven't had anything since you got out."

Goth felt a little guilty and hungry too. "But I sent you the captain's dessert."

"Oh. I thought...I thought somehow they'd gotten that in there. I thought it must be drugged and I used the plate to bang on the pipes."

Goth grinned. That was one mystery solved. "I'll get us some food and drink."

"Please don't leave me here with him." There was real fear, edging on panic, in Mindi's voice.

"I guess we could lock him up. Tie him down, in case he wakes up," offered Goth.

Mindi shook her head violently. "No. I'm still not staying in here."

"Well, fine. We'll gag him, and use another pair of forcecuffs to attach him to the bar and leave him in here."

Goth took Mindi back to her own cabin. She wasn't surprised to find that it had been rifled through, but as she had very little for them to search, it wasn't in too much of a mess. She left Mindi there and went to the galley, where she found a robobutler and ordered three meals. She figured Mindi could eat two and she wasn't wrong.

After they'd eaten they got into a serious discussion about what steps to take next.

"What now?" asked Mindi. She was a good few years older than Goth, but turned to Goth for answers. "Do we turn them over to the captain?"

"Nope. The captain is one of them. He's in on it," said Goth.

"But what can we do, then?" asked Mindi, wringing her hands.

She plainly regarded captains as one step down from Patham. And out here, in deep space, that wasn't far wrong.

"I figured we'd send them off in our place. Seems about fair," said Goth. "And honestly, if we leave them, they'll either starve, or get out and start doing it again. And if they get out, they might come after us."

The last part seemed to act as a powerful argument to Mindi. So then it was just up to Goth to organize the practical details. Fortunately it wasn't that hard, merely a case of ferrying the drugged prisoners into the drop capsule, along with bales of sheen marked *Tardelote, transshipment*. Yelissa was willing enough to be drugged too, as long as they forcecuffed her to Jaccy.

Then it was a quiet trip to Morteen, with no more excitement than someone trying to cheat in a game of cards, and the fact that Mindi would not let her out of sight, and that the crew were covering up the sudden disappearance of their captain, purser, a steward, and some of the longer-term passengers. The crew did break into the stateroom Jaccy and his associates had used, but as Goth and Mindi had removed themselves and all traces of themselves from there, that didn't help them much.

CHAPTER 8

The Leewit nodded knowingly, after listening to what had happened. "See, Captain, people say things to kids that they wouldn't give away to adults. That copper said more than he realized, answering my questions. I kept on the 'Whys,' 'cause I figured it would be a good thing if I made him tired of being asked questions all the time. Grown-ups can be pushed like that. The Imperials are worried, because they think the cartel—this Stratel, Bormgo and whatever—are holding back supply. But the policeman—he was an all right old dope, even if he can't play cards—he doesn't think that's true. He thinks that if Stratel and his friends were cutting the supply to push up the price, the smuggling would step up instead. It hasn't. He thinks there really just isn't the catalyst to be had."

"And he's right. That's what the smuggler boss says," agreed Pausert.

"An' what we gatherers say, but the Consortium thinks we're holding out on 'em. Selling to Me'a," said Nady.

"Why would you be selling to yourself?" the Leewit asked.

"Not himself. Me'a—that's what the smuggler boss calls herself."

"That's neat!" said the Leewit, proving it wasn't just something that had appealed to one young girl, once. "But Captain...what happens if the stuff really is running out?"

Pausert shrugged. "Nothing and everything. Well, nothing immediately. Space travel gets slowly more expensive. They used to travel in space before air recyclers... It's just the slow end of small ships. The catalysts don't wear out. There just won't be any new ones. Ships wreck, are lost, get blown up by pirates."

"That's sort of what I figured," said the Leewit. "So we can't exactly cut and run, Captain. It needs fixing."

That was Karres for you, thought Pausert. It borrowed you a fair bit of trouble, but it was what they were. "No. I was wondering if something had changed. Something that could be reversed. Or if there was a disease or something." That, after all, was what the Leewit's core klatha skill was. She was a healer.

"They've been gathering for thousands of years," said Nady. "This place got found not long after they left old Yarthe, they say. An' might have bin used before that even. I seen some old laser-cut stone walls with doors too small for people, over North Pass way."

"So what's changed?"

He shrugged, rubbed his head. "Nothin'. Gatherers goin' further out, mebbe? There's more porpentiles than there use to be, I'd say."

"Porpentiles?" asked the Leewit.

So they had to explain porpentiles.

"Could they be eating the tumbleflowers?" she asked.

"Nah. They let them roll past. Even roll over them. Seen it meself often. Porpentiles don't do nothing but lie in the sun."

"And smother gatherers," pointed out Pausert.

"Yeah. But not always. I seen a new boy, not an hour into workin' his bond, and he walks right past one. Big 'un. Next day he walks past it again...and it's fine. A week later it's still there...and he's just found his first granules; he's full of himself...and it kills him. But nobody never seen them do anything to a tumbleflower."

"Any chance I could get to see one of these tumbleflowers, Captain," asked the Leewit. "Can you touch them?" she asked Nady.

"Oh, yeah. If they're not movin' you can touch them all over. Gatherers have tried poking 'em, patting 'em, stroking 'em to see if they'd drop their crystals. It don't hurt, but it also don't help," said Nady.

"And there was one in the gorge—not more than twenty minutes away," said Pausert. "I think if we took a rope you could get to it. You could see if it was sick, maybe? Can you work on alien creatures?"

"I reckon," said the Leewit. "I fixed the nursebeast, didn't I?"

They left Vezzarn, so that the Leewit could use his rebreather, slipped out of the *Venture* again and went back to the gorge. The tumbleflower hadn't completed its climb out yet. Looking down the steep cliff, Pausert unhitched the length of rope. "Tie onto the end of the rope, Leewit. Three of us should be able to pull you up, even after all those pancakes."

Ta'zara neatly snagged the end of the rope and looped it around his own waist. "I will go down first."

"You weigh a lot more than the Leewit," grumbled Pausert.

"Yes, but if you put the rope around that spike of rock, I can lower myself. You will not have to take my full weight."

The captain knew by now that it was useless to argue with Ta'zara about the decisions he'd made concerning the Leewit's safety, so they went along with his plan. Then they let the Leewit down to a ledge next to the creature, which had ignored Ta'zara, even when he touched it.

The Leewit had brought a headlight from the *Venture*, and in its light the captain saw her put her small hands onto the long spokes of the tumbleflower, and hold them. The plant creature just went on slowly hauling its way up the cliff. She pulled her hands back. "You can pull us up, Captain."

On the lip of the gorge, Pausert asked, "So was it sick?"

"Nope," said the Leewit, shaking her head. "Just old."

So they retreated to the *Venture* again. Once they were safely back inside, the captain asked her about it. She shrugged. "I can feel what's going on inside. Feel broken bone, feel blood vessels and where they should go. Feel nerves and follow their patterns and read something about what they feel. The tumbleflower is different from what humans—or even the nursebeast—felt like, but I . . . there is no other word for it, I understand how it works, and what's broken. And there is nothing much broken in the tumbleflower. It's just old and tired of rolling. It's not like there's a brain really for it to think."

"I ain't sure wasn't me you was reading," said Nady. "Old and tired o' rolling. An' not much brain to think."

The sleek little head popped out of Nady's collar, eyed them all, and yawned. And then it turned back and stared unblinking and utterly motionless, at the Leewit.

"Clumping demorgop!" exclaimed the Leewit, pointing. "What's that?"

It gave her a peculiar hissy-growl in reply.

"Rochat," said Ta'zara disapprovingly. "Smelly beasts. Take a lot of time and effort and do nothing useful."

"Ain't true. Why, Kiki here she's no trouble an' she keeps me comp'ny. She's real affectionate and friendly." Nady stroked the creature under the chin. It bit him, and disappeared back into his shirt. "Um. When she feels like it," he added.

"So...what are they, actually?" asked the Leewit. "Can I have another look?"

"Nope," said Nady. "She comes out when she feels like it."

"People keep them as pets," said Ta'zara. "They're some kind of alien beast that seems to like hanging around people. They're not very bright and you can't train them. There are some on Na'kalauf—brought back from contracts. But they won't breed there."

"Breed here, but it's too cold for 'em. Most of the miners have one," said Nady.

"Or are had by one," said Ta'zara. "My sister's mother has one. She spends half her share-money on spoiling it."

"The question is, what do we do about the situation here," said Pausert, hastily, seeing Nady open his mouth. "Look, besides us being arrested and having to go to court...we could warm the tubes and blast out of here right now, but there's a long-term situation here, which affects K...all of us. The sooner dealt with the better, and it is something the various parties—the government and the Consortium can't see because they're all part of it. They all believe the others are to blame."

"I think I need to go have another look outside," said the Leewit.

"For what?" asked Pausert.

"I don't know. But maybe I need to look at some more of the tumbleflowers. Besides, I had to sit in here while you all got put in jail and met Me'a."

No one seemed to have a better idea, so Captain Pausert agreed. They had time, and his gambler's itch said it was a good idea. Vezzarn was left to look after the *Venture*, and before dawn they slipped out and back into the wilds of Cinderby's World.

They walked for some hours, and had one encounter with another tumbleflower, which the Leewit was also able to touch—and, again, failed to diagnose anything but age. It was younger than the first one, she said, but still had had many years of rolling.

"We c'n try the other side of Torg Pass," suggested Nady, pointing to a notch in the mountain. "Usually find more there, but more porpentiles too."

So they did. Ta'zara insisted on them walking in formation— Nady ahead, Pausert behind him, and then the Leewit, with Ta'zara just behind her. He didn't explain, but Pausert figured it was probably the best defensive strategy the Na'kalauf bodyguard could come up with—Nady to spot the problems, Pausert to deal with them—and himself to deal with sudden attacks from the back.

They'd just gotten over to the sun side of the pass when it all happened. Nady was perhaps ten paces ahead of the Leewit, and Ta'zara just behind her, when the porpentile undulated out of a narrow gully, between them. Ta'zara reached out and grabbed the Leewit, and put her behind him.

Nady turned, and yelled "No!" through the speaker of his rebreather. The porpentile—which had been turned toward the Leewit and Ta'zara—twisted and leapt. In a sinuous lunge, it spread and covered Nady.

The old gatherer had been fast enough, barely, to get an arm out. All they could see of him was his hand sticking out from under. The fingers moved.

Ta'zara stopped his charge from running forward. "We can't just leave him like that," said the Leewit.

"We can't get it off—or at least that's what he said," explained the captain. "If he can breathe, it'll eventually give up."

"Ain't dead," came a voice from under the porpentile. "C'n breathe."

He might not be dead, but he certainly sounded hurt. "How do we get you out?" asked the Leewit.

"Cain't."

"Will it attack us?" she asked.

"Not while it has got me."

"I could whistle at it, Captain," said the Leewit. "Bust it up inside, good and proper."

"Not through the rebreather speaker," said the captain. "You'd bust that first. And no, you can't take it off. This air is pretty close to poison."

"Oh. Great Patham! I hadn't thought of that," said the Leewit. "So what do we do now, Captain? Can you cocoon him? Or it?"

"I could make holes in it. It might work. I don't want to make holes in him. And it is hard to tell how thick it is, or what it might do."

"Jest leave it alone," said the voice of Nady from underneath it. "I'll wait it out."

"You're hurt," said the Leewit.

"Might have broke something. But you get on. You cain't stay out here. Could take three days or five."

"The big problem, even if we were willing to do that, is knowing where to go," said the captain. There had to be some kind of answer to this. It made no sense. Both the Leewit and Ta'zara had been much closer. Why did it attack Nady? It had looked like it was just going past, and then had done that huge turn.

The Leewit had stepped up to Nady's hand. "Mistress, don't," said Ta'zara, leaping forward. "I cannot allow..."

The Leewit looked at him sternly. "No. It needs doing," she said, and calmly put her hand on the porpentile. Nothing happened. And then she said, "Clumping Great Patham's seventh steaming hell, Cap'n! It's the same animal."

Pausert, who had also started forward, noticed that the porpentile had done nothing in reaction to her touching it. So he asked, "The same as what?"

"The same as the tumbleflower," explained the Leewit. "I mean not the actual same animal, but organized the same inside. I can even feel where the arms were. It's just folded itself flat and those things that looked like flower buds have kind of grown to each other."

"Is it well, but old too?" said the captain with a smile, making a joke of it. "It's bigger than a tumbleflower, even spread out."

"No... it doesn't feel old," she said.

"Hungry for gatherers?" asked Ta'zara.

The Leewit blinked. "It just eats sunlight."

In his head the story of the young gatherer suddenly came back to Pausert. The porpentile wasn't hungry. It had ignored the fellow... until he found some granules of the catalyst. "It has to be the granules. That's what it's after!"

"Well, it cain't have them! They're under me," protested the gatherer.

"I think we need to do a little digging here," said Ta'zara. "If I haul that slab of rock out, we might be able to reach." So he and the captain pulled, and wriggled the piece of rock free, making a narrow gap. He stuck his hand in . . . and pulled it out hastily . . . with the red rochat attached to his thumb. He shook it, and it let go. Then, bounded across to a rock, where it hunched, looking at them with slitted eyes chittering with rage.

"I'll try again, now that pest is out the way," said Ta'zara. So he did, but he could not reach far enough.

It took the captain, who had slightly longer arms, to reach in and cut the gatherer's pouch free and pull it out. He opened it and pulled out the little oiled leather bag.

"Look out, Captain!" yelled the Leewit.

The porpentile was surging toward him. So Pausert threw the bag to Ta'zara. It turned to chase him and, just in time, he threw it to the captain. It was very fast and turned back like an agile fish. Pausert slipped on a rock and flung it—badly. The Leewit scooped it out of the air, and tossed it across to Ta'zara. The porpentile whirled after him. "Captain! What must we do?"

"Open the bag and pour the stuff out!" he yelled.

So Ta'zara did, throwing the crystals out on the ground.

Nady sat up and yelled in outrage. "Thieving claim jumper! That ain't yours!" He struggled to his feet as the porpentile surged over the scattered green granules and settled on them. The raging old man limped up to it, and started pummeling it with his fists. "Yer kranslits! Now I'll have ter wait until it moves . . ."

He backed away, because it was moving. Well . . . not so much moving as simply breaking apart, the fragments blowing away. The Leewit caught one. "That figures," she said, in a tone of satisfaction. She stepped over to Nady, who had sat down and was clutching his ankle. "Look." She held out her cupped hands to him.

"A tumbleflower. I ain't never seen one that size before. But where's me granules?" he asked plaintively.

"I think that *is* your granules. Or what happens when you mix your granules with a porpentile. That's why you're running out. They haven't been breeding properly."

"But I still ain't got my granules. Or my Kiki." The rochat was nowhere to be seen. He sniffed plaintively. "She's gone an' left me. And I lost my granules. I was goin' ter buy her some coalfish."

The rochat suddenly appeared out of the Leewit's shirt, and bounded across to him. "How did that get there?" demanded the Leewit as the rochat oozed its way up to Nady.

"Them always go to where they can stay warm. You better take her with you. I ain't going back with nothing, an' my stash gone and my leg ain't right," he said gloomily.

"What you have to do is get to your feet and lead us back," said Ta'zara.

"I think we need to go back to the dome. Me'a is going to be very, very interested. She needs to know this," said Pausert. "And I think you may become a hero to the gatherers, Nady."

"Being a hero don't buy no drinks. Those crystals was worth a five-night drunk!" complained Nady.

"If I'm right, you'll be bought drinks for the rest of your life-time. You just worked out how to save gatherers from porpentiles."

"Huh. Most of 'em would rather be dead than lose their stash," said Nady, but he tried to stand up. And sat down again, with a gasp of pain. "Ya should o' left me under it. I'm bust."

"And that would have helped you how?" said Ta'zara dryly. "Let me have a look..."

"I'd have died rich," said the old gatherer, grumpily letting Ta'zara push him into lying down. "Now, even if I get back, I'll starve. Kiki will go off with someone else because I can't afford to feed her."

"You can't take riches with you," said Ta'zara. "Leewit, do you need the leg exposed?"

With her klatha senses, the Leewit felt the sharp broken edges of the bone in Nady's leg. Ta'zara had splinted it and numbed the nerve. The Leewit moved everything carefully until the bone edges touched, going into place like that last piece of jigsaw puzzle. She knitted little lattices between the broken edges. Healing should be faster and better with the framework she'd created.

Except that it wouldn't. She realized that it wasn't that Nady had merely had a porpentile fall on him. It was that the bones themselves were brittle, short of calcium. This break was just something inevitable, just happening a little sooner than it would have anyway. Part of her said *you've used enough energy, leave it*. But another part of her knew there was more to healing than just treating the immediate problem.

The Leewit had the teacher-pattern in her mind to guide her, to help understand what she was finding: The problems centered on the gatherer's liver. That problem was affecting a lot of other things—among them the hormones that controlled his calcium levels. Nady was slowly stripping calcium off his bones when he needed it. And was not—as other humans did—replacing it. It all came down to a compound his liver was still breaking down. To the klatha healer one cell was just as big as one organ. She could fix the damaged cells, but there were millions of them—in this size-less dimension, as hard a work as fixing something far bigger. She'd die before she got done.

The teaching-pattern led her. She made his own immune cells know the compound that was destroying his bone—change its shape by joining on to it—and that, it seemed, would send it to his kidneys and out, without doing the damage it had been. Satisfied, she gradually pulled back from the klatha healing trance... but as she did, she grasped from the teaching-pattern what she'd done. What the substance was.

It was Nady's drug habit, a euphoric drug of some kind. It wouldn't poison him now—but it also wouldn't work to make him happy anymore. The teaching-pattern was...almost smug. It had taught the Leewit how to deal with many poisons now. The Leewit herself was not smug. It worried her. She wasn't quite sure how or why, but it did.

"Can he walk?" asked the captain.

The Leewit realized that he had his hand on her shoulder—lending her strength. Like touch-talk klatha, strength-lending seemed to function best with actual contact. He looked tired, but she didn't feel as tired as the last time. Well, maybe she was getting better at it. She wasn't ever going to tell anyone, but this was hard. Or maybe it was the captain's klatha strength she'd leaned on. She'd asked for his help before, but not this time. It was a weird thing, suddenly understanding what Goth thought was so wonderful about the captain. She'd said when the Leewit asked, but it hadn't made sense back then: *You never have to ask him twice.*

"Nope. But it doesn't hurt, does it Nady?"

The old gatherer blinked. "No. It feels fine..." He would have tried to stand up and undo her work, but for Ta'zara thinking faster than either she or the captain did, and pushing him down.

"We'll carry him. It's a pity we have nothing for a stretcher, but he's a skinny drink of water," said the captain. "We can't be that far from that cave, and at least he can tell us where to go."

"And keep an eye for more porpentiles," said the Leewit.

"I shall watch for those too," said Ta'zara. "I will carry him first, Captain. Lift him onto my back. He can tell us where to go."

So the captain did, ignoring Nady's protests. At least the porpentiles were unlikely to trouble them.

Pausert was glad to let Ta'zara take the first shift of carrying, as they headed on down the pass, so he could suck at the glucose tube in the rebreather. That gave him time to recover, and time to think. The answer to the shortage of catalyst was that the porpentiles weren't splitting into baby tumbleflowers, that was plain. But how should that news be handled? "Nady. The porpentiles—do you get them elsewhere? I mean elsewhere on the planet."

"Wouln' know," said the gatherer. "I never been past Mount Lofty."

"You said the surveyors found tumbleflowers elsewhere," said the Leewit.

"Yeah, but then yer can see one of those easy enough. Them survey blokes wouldn't see a porpentile unless it jumped on 'em."

That could well be true. "So they could just live here in these mountains?"

"Could do, I suppose," said the gatherer. "No one cares really."

Soon they swapped over, and the captain had to concentrate on his feet on the rocky trail rather than the problems of Cinderby's World. They took two more turns each, before the airlock to the cave came in sight.

Once inside, it seemed that the decision on how the news should be handled was made by the only member of the party who wasn't dead beat from carrying extra—either a pack or the injured gatherer—and that, of course, was Nady. He had plenty of energy and breath for it. He was certainly eager to use both—and he was quite a storyteller, with a tale of something that held his audience in mortal fear. He had all the other gatherers around him—and after a few moments the Leewit said to Ta'zara, "Go stop him jumping up."

So Ta'zara did, pressing a hand onto his shoulder every time the gatherer tried. Nady still had his audience in the palm of his hand. Captain Pausert smiled to himself, enjoying just sitting and resting, listening to a tale that was already a lot more dramatic than it had been, growing and growing. He had been quite right about one thing. Nady would probably never pay for another drink in a bar on Cinderby's World.

As an option, keeping it all a secret was off the table.

CHAPTER 9

Goth had one small clue, and a world to search. She knew that Captain Pausert's mother had booked her ticket to Morteen, while the captain was in space as a cadet officer of the Nikkeldepain Space Navy. She'd sent him a message from there, saying she'd settled nicely into her new job at the Morteen Xenobiological Research Institute, wishing him the best and congratulating him on his engagement to Illiya—the daughter of Councilor Onswud. Pausert had said, somewhere during their travels, that he didn't think his mother had approved, and that was why she'd accepted the new post.

Goth had read that message. Subradio transmissions were expensive enough, over range, to make actually sending written messages worthwhile. Touching it...she could read a great deal with her klatha power of what wasn't said.

There was sadness there, which was natural for a mother moving far from her only son. But there was also elation, and... deceit. A part of the information that Karres witches had obtained after the precognitives had predicted the need for this mission, was to track Pausert's mother's banking details. She'd actually left Nikkeldepain a relatively well-off woman—both with her income from Great Uncle Threbus' research institute, and the final proceeds from the sale of his estate. Half of that had gone to Captain Pausert and his failed miffel-fur farm. But the other half had gone to her account.

On Morteen, after a relatively brief period, it had all been withdrawn and the account closed.

And that was the last trace of her. The limited search that Karres operatives had carried out indicated that she was no longer on Morteen. Nor had she left for any Empire world, or at least not under her own name or identity.

But then Morteen was a border world, and there was some traffic out beyond the Empire's limits and sway. Empty worlds, alien worlds, worlds with little colonies of human émigrés, rebels, criminals, refugees, pirates. Dangerous country and large empty starspaces.

And worlds, many of them, blasted clean of life or fragmented into space debris.

It was while patrolling this frontier that Pausert's father had vanished. He'd been a sturdy ten-year-old then, and nearly sixteen standard years had gone by since. It had been seven years since his mother's last bank withdrawal.

That was a cold trail to try to follow.

Goth started with that disadvantage, but she also had to sort out the life of her fellow would-have-been slave. Mindi was free and, with the money taken from their captors, at least able to afford to look after herself. But she was also terrified to let Goth out of her sight. That was understandable, but a nuisance.

And if, as seemed very likely, Goth's search took her far beyond the Empire's borders in amongst the dead worlds and savage places of the beyond, that was no place for anyone who was not a klatha operative.

With a sudden shock, Goth realized that she'd just learned one of those essential life lessons she would never quite have gotten with the captain at her side. The universe was not full of Karres operatives—or even people like them. Yet people like Mindi were just as human. Goth knew that from spending the last two weeks close to her, trusted because they'd been through something terrible together. A friend who knew nothing about Karres or klatha. Goth now knew all the details of Mindi's childhood, family, all about her loves and lover. It had been quite an education! Mindi could find determination and courage for herself—but she liked to have someone else to lean on, to look after her.

The gambling-slaving syndicate's loot had seen to it that Goth now had more money than she'd been given by Karres—plenty to give Mindi a good start. The woman was reluctant to take the money and go off on her own, or even to take a space liner back home without Goth as an escort.

Goth liked Mindi. She was capable enough, and capable of being brave. But she would always turn to someone else to make decisions, to give her courage. To lean on. Huh. Goth liked to lean on the captain, sometimes. He was a leanable-on sort of person, but it wasn't quite the same with him, was it? It was more like lean together. Well, there was nothing for it. Mindi needed a minder, and, judging by what she'd said, she desperately missed the man she'd been engaged to marry, despite the argument that had had her book onto the sheen clipper, as the first ship off-world.

That called for a subradio conversation, regardless of the expense. After several weeks, Goth knew his name, where he worked, and a lot more besides. So: Once they had deposited their baggage, Goth took the unsuspecting Mindi into the subradio office and asked to book a call, handing over the details on a note. She paid the large requisite fee, and they sat in one of the booths.

"I could have stayed in the hotel, and locked myself in, I suppose," said Mindi. "Who are you calling?"

Just then a worried male voice came over the speakers.

Mindi's shriek probably deafened the poor man. It took a while—an expensive while—to reassure him that she was no longer kidnapped. It took a little more time to organize him a passage on a sheen clipper, but Goth knew, at least, that she would be able to leave her rescued companion in someone else's hands quite soon.

It seemed to settle Mindi too. She was still nervous, but would stay alone in the hotel room while Goth started her hunt for just where Pausert's mother had gotten to. Goth soon discovered one of the big problems with a world where the main attraction was gambling: Large bank withdrawals were common. Pausert's mother's place of work and former apartment yielded no more clues... except an unusual spice. The place had of course been re-rented, but it was fortunately empty again. Goth pretended to be a possible tenant, trailing her fingers across the walls, reading the history that strong emotions had left for her klatha sense.

The problem, as always, was separating out the relevant from everything else that happened. Old structures were worse than new ones.

Goth realized the renting agent was giving her an odd look. "I'm sorry. I was...elsewhere. Something just reminded me of a friend." She described Pausert's mother.

The agent scowled. "I thought we'd gotten rid of the smell."

"What smell?"

"Paratha spice. We had a terrible job getting rid of it after that woman left. I can't rent this to you if you also use it. And I'll have to increase the deposit."

"Thank you, but I don't think it will suit me," said Goth, and went off to investigate paratha spice. As it turned out, it was very illegal but was not, strictly speaking, a narcotic. According to the databank she consulted, paratha was a plant-based flavor enhancer. That sounded harmless enough—except paratha apparently made everything taste like paratha. Your taste buds thought that it was the most wonderful flavor ever, even if your nose did not agree. No food without it tasted worth eating. And the cheapest boiled wallroot tasted as good as the finest and most expensive delicacy—as long as you had paratha. It didn't appear to do those who consumed it any harm, and they could eat food without it. The food just lacked any real taste to them. The spice came from somewhere out beyond the borders of the Empire; Morteen seemed to be its main point of entry.

So that was the dropped odd-shaped bottle and the joy she read off the stone top of the counter. From there and back to the xeno-botanical institute: where a night-time visit to their files revealed that Doctor Lina had been asked to investigate the chemistry of the illegal paratha spice. Had in fact been granted some funding to purchase some—money she'd returned, just before resigning.

Now, Goth merely had to track down just who was smuggling the stuff in for her next lead. That should be easy...

Only it wasn't. Her visits, light-shifted and in no-shape, to various portside bars could have bought her any other drug she might have wanted, but not paratha. Paratha she eventually found through Mindi.

Mindi, having gone through relief and happiness that her dear Woton was coming to fetch her, was now doing alternating spells of worry that he might be kidnapped, or that he might still be very angry, impatience, and a desire to welcome him with the finest treats. The last part Goth encouraged, because at least something could be done about that. It seemed his favorite food was a complicated kind of cake, the ingredients of which could only be obtained from an expensive specialist. And while Mindi asked about limbnut flour, Goth put her hand on the counter, and her klatha senses read elation and despair—and a small odd-shaped bottle woven into it.

She grabbed Mindi. "We have to go. Now!" And she hustled the startled young woman out.

"What was wrong?" asked Mindi, once they were on the slidewalk and well away.

"Just a feeling," said Goth. "After the last time on the sheen clipper, I like to listen to those feelings."

Mindi nodded earnestly, and they went in search of another delicatessen.

It was late that afternoon when Goth came back to the shop, slipping into no-shape and watching and waiting. She expected to find that the shopkeeper was selling it.

But he wasn't. He was buying. She had to wait until the shop closed to see that. He sent his employees home, locked the doors, turned off the lights that weren't in the window display and walked through to a back room. Goth followed, just to make sure he'd left, and to see if he turned on any alarms before she searched the place, using her klatha skill to get the past from its walls. But he wasn't leaving. He went into what had plainly been intended as a storeroom—and still had a few boxes in it, as well as a simple cot, closet and a chair. Two of the boxes had been pushed together to make a table, on which reposed a loaf of ordinary bread on a cutting board, and a set of very precise scales. The owner cut a slice of the bread, unlocked a small cupboard set into the wall, and took out the odd-shaped bottle. Then, he carefully weighed out some of the pungent spice, sprinkled it on his bread, and started to eat it in tiny, appreciative bites, savoring each mouthful.

Goth stepped back into the shadows and out of no-shape. She took out her Clipe pistol and stepped into view. "Got a few questions to ask you," she said in her best Hulik-the-professional IS agent voice. "Stay calm and answer them, and no one gets hurt."

The man sighed. "Do you have to spoil my one pleasure, my one decent meal of the day? Can't it wait until I'm finished?" And he took a large bite of his bread.

Goth had expected pretty much anything else as a response. She actually didn't quite know what to do. So she 'ported his little spice bottle into her hand. When he stopped his careful chewing and realized it was gone, and that she was holding it... That got his attention.

"Please. I...I've paid for that one," he said. "And I haven't got any more money. I'm selling off all the stock I've got. I should have enough to settle up."

"You can have it back if I get the answers I'm looking for," said Goth. "I want to know where this stuff is coming from."

He looked at her and sighed. "You're either from some kind of antidrug-enforcement agency, or someone planning to muscle in on the trade. So I can't really tell you. It would stop my supply, and then I'd starve to death. It's a horrible way to die, especially for a lover of fine food. So just kill me. If you let me finish first, that would be kind."

"I'm not competition, and I'm not part of any antidrug agency, and you can finish your meal and have your bottle back. I just need to track the source down. I want—"

"Don't do it, girl," he interrupted. "I thought if I got the quantities small enough it would just be a flavor enhancer. But you can't. I tried. Patham, I tried."

"I don't want to eat the stuff," said Goth, rolling her eyes. "I just need to find the planet it comes from."

"I suppose that would be the most effective way of destroying it. Anyway, I can't tell you. It comes from somewhere out past the frontier. I just buy it. And if you destroyed the crop, I couldn't."

"I've no interest in destroying it. I've no interest in it at all, I'm just looking for someone who is on that world. A missing person," said Goth, irritably. "Just tell me who you buy it from."

"Drymocks. Purveyors of furs, luxury goods, fine liquors and spices. Now can I have my paratha back? Please?"

Goth took a long careful look at the spice bottle, memorizing the details...and noticed that the bottle had been sealed with some kind of hard wax, and that in it, there was a neat little imprint—small letters pressed into the wax, broken by the bottle being opened. Other than that, it was a plain if oddly shaped bottle. The spice itself was a dusty red.

The man was getting anxious, had gotten up—and still had his breadknife in hand. She could have dealt with that, but there was nothing to gain by not giving it back to him. So she held it out. He snatched it and clutched it to himself. And now he seemed more inclined to talk. "You won't try it, will you?" he said, anxiously. "It's not worth it. I thought . . . I thought it was manageable. It's not. Not even in the smallest quantities. Now all my food—even Vegtam caviar—just tastes like ashes."

"I'm not planning to, no. As I said, I'm actually looking for a missing person . . . or persons."

"They wanted me to sell it in my shop . . ." He started to cry. "Thirty years I've spent building up the business, the best and finest flavors. All lost to me now. I can't taste them anymore."

Goth left him to his regrets. A little more research found the wholesaler, Drymocks. And standing in no-shape she saw a last layer of little bottles on a pallet in their secure store—and overheard that the SS Bolivar was due soon. They hoped that the supply would last . . .

She had a ship's name, and, while she was there, she took a bottle of the paratha to examine. She understood, when she looked at it, why Pausert's mother had dropped the bottle. Because imprinted into the wax in tiny letters was Pausert's father's name: LT. COMDR. KAEN ISN.

Goth just had to wait for the ship to land at the port. It was, she established, a regular visitor to Morteen. It had a shipping agent, and they had a schedule—at least its official one. It wasn't a fast ship, plying a regular route between several worlds on the borders of Imperial space, finishing its route on Iradalia, before taking a long run back to Morteen. Goth's heart skipped a beat seeing that. Iradalia . . . She knew the captain had been heading toward the long-simmering war between Iradalia and Karoda. Be rather neat if she ended up there . . .

In the meantime, she had her own pair of lovebirds to settle. That proved less difficult than she had feared. Woton, when he arrived, was a solid young man. He was initially rather suspicious of Goth having had a role in Mindi's disappearance and kidnapping—but once the hugging and kissing had eased off and Mindi had tearfully told him her tale, that changed. Then he was just embarrassingly grateful. He was now curious, however, about how Goth had managed it all.

He had, she decided, some of the common sense Mindi lacked. So she gave him a story he could believe. "Let's just say Imperial Security has a number of agencies, and they recruit people from higher-gravity worlds and give us special training and equipment. I can't really say any more. My superiors wouldn't be pleased at me saying that much, or... well, I should have left Mindi. That was not part of my task, and I don't want it trickling back to them. That could have bad consequences for all of us."

It was amazing how people's imagination filled in the gaps. Goth was sure she couldn't have made up all those details if she'd tried for a month. It made leaving quite easy—which was helped by the fact that Woton was a skilled hyperelectronic engineer, a trade much in demand at the Cascades.

Goth was very glad to be on her own again. She celebrated by visiting the Cascades and, after wandering around a little in no-shape, being quite glad the Leewit wasn't here. Her little sister liked to play cards, and had never really accepted that it was probably her klatha skill that made her win. Even when Goth had pointed it out, the Leewit didn't consider it cheating. She took a serious objection to ordinary cheating, though. Goth did too, but Goth didn't break things with her ultrasonic whistles. She just relieved the cheats of their own money. She even gave some back to the victims.

Still, there were quite a lot of Imperial maels in her purse by the time the *SS Bolivar* got into port, and offloaded its cargo. That was just as well, because the agent wasn't keen on selling her a passage. "It's a freighter, miss. They don't take passengers."

"You have before," she said.

He looked at her in surprise. "How did you know?"

Goth did not say, *Because the desperation, and hope, of that passenger left a trace, a memory imprinted in this greasy ferrostone countertop.* Instead she said, "I got a message from her."

The man actually looked relieved—and his response was not quite what Goth had expected. She'd meant a message before Pausert's mother Lina had left Morteen. He didn't read it that way. "Oh, good. She got there and back, then. I was worried. But she insisted."

That was a fair thing to worry about, really. From the start of this mission it had been obvious to Goth and to the Karres witches that the odds against Pausert's father being anything other than dead had to be high. The imprint of his name proved that hadn't been true.

She'd also given him quite a lot of money, Goth read. But he didn't mention that.

"I am prepared to pay you handsomely for the passage," said Goth.

The man sighed. "Look, young woman, it's dangerous. You know . . . at least I think you do, that they don't go where the schedule says they do. No one from here really wants to go to Iradalia. It's just that they are a world that doesn't share their landing records with the Imperial landings record register. And they're far enough away to justify the time."

Goth hadn't known, but she did now. Not that it made any difference—except . . . given the ship's speed, and the time that it would take to get to Iradalia, she could narrow down the possible destinations outside the Imperial border. That information, she could—and would—send back to Karres. Just in case.

"I'm prepared to pay for a passage. Regardless."

"I'll ask the captain," said the agent. "He may not agree. They ship out tomorrow."

"Give him a call," she said, pointing at the communicator.

The agent shook his head. "I'll talk to him when he comes in. Come back in about an hour."

Goth nodded, walked out, and quietly slipped herself into no-shape. But she was getting tired now from her too frequent use of no-shape, and shifted a bit too slowly. The agent had followed her to the door and locked it. So she had to 'port the key from his pocket, and let herself in—by which stage he was already in his office and on the communicator, talking to someone.

". . . says she got a message from her." Goth could only hear one side of the conversation, but the other person had obviously replied.

"I thought so. It's odd. We should be careful," answered the agent.

The person he'd called replied again, and the agent supplied, "She's coming back in an hour."

Even standing too close for comfort, Goth couldn't hear the

reply, just the burr of a gravelly voice. The agent answered, "To Iradalia? All right. But—" He was plainly interrupted at this point. He sighed and shook his head. "Look. You deal with it. Off-planet. And you'd better send someone. I want no part of this."

He put the communicator back down, went to open his door, and failed to find his key in his pocket. Goth took advantage of that time to go through his desk drawers and steal his blaster from them—and, when he came back, she let herself out. When he came to the door again, feeling in his pockets, and looking around his grubby floor, she 'ported the key back on his desk. Then she went out quietly and walked over to the port buildings where she sent an expensive subradio message, before returning to the agent's office. She was just in time to see two spacemen enter. She followed them in, again in no-shape. She was getting even more tired, but she thought she could maintain no-shape for a while yet.

"It has to be a trap of some sort, Merko. There's no way she got back to Imperial space. She must have meant she sent a message before she left."

"The question is just who is behind this search. Can we afford to just make her disappear?" asked the agent, worriedly.

The smaller spaceman shrugged. "Can we afford not to?"

"Look," said the agent. "She's just a very young woman. If there was any real muscle behind her, they'd have sent them. Odds are she's some kind of relative. It must be a wealthy family, to spend that kind of money. But it's been a good few years."

"Then make the deal, but get her on board now. Make sure there's no record that she did," said the larger of the two spacemen.

"I don't like it. This is not what I agreed to . . ." the agent protested weakly.

"You'll do what we want, Tobi. Or else."

The agent glowered sullenly back at them.

Goth took the opportunity to slip out, and then come back to the doors, rattle them, and knock loudly.

The three within looked at each other and at her, as Goth walked in. "I've thought about it," she said, ignoring the two spacers and just addressing the agent. "I need a few more hours to consult with . . . well, other people. I'm not too comfortable with what you told me."

The agent looked at the other two again and said gruffly, "It's go now, or not at all. This is the captain and first mate. They just came to tell me their departure has been set forward. And it'll cost you twenty thousand maels."

That was a huge amount just for a passage, but Goth paid it over without a blink.

"You must be quite wealthy," said one of the spacemen.

"It's money my Aunt Lina left me," said Goth. As soon as the money was put away, she calmly 'ported it right back into her purse.

"Well, we'll take you across to the ship then," said the other. "Not long until takeoff."

"Oh. I was hoping to send a message..." said Goth.

"Give it to me, I'll see it is sent," said the agent.

Goth shook her head. "It'll wait."

"I can have your luggage fetched for you."

"That would be useful," Goth said, smiling innocently. She gave him her hotel name and room number. "But I had better go with these gentlemen now."

So she went along with them, to the *Bolivar*. It was much larger than the *Venture*, and plainly armed. Pausert would have had a fit if the *Venture 7333* ever looked that dirty. The *Bolivar*'s captain and first mate didn't seem to care or notice. The little cubbyhole they told her was to be her cabin had to be emptied of junk first. "I'll get someone to clean it out. We weren't expecting a passenger," said the *Bolivar*'s captain. "Have you been on a working ship before, miss?"

"Oh, yes," said Goth sweetly. "I was on one, once." She left out the many ensuing times. It was a dull ache thinking of the *Venture*.

"Well, the heads are down there, the mess is up the stair. Stay out of my command deck," he said, tersely.

"I am sure I'll be fine, Captain," said Goth, not promising anything. "And I may as well clear this stuff out of the cabin. That'll save some of your hardworking crew some effort."

He nodded. "Just put it in the passage."

Goth did manage to close the door on the clutter, before stalking after them in no-shape, in time to hear the mate say, "... space her?"

"It's that or sell her to Karoda," said the captain, grimly, "but you can still sometimes get answers out of the slaves they condition. This is too sweet a business to take a chance on."

Talk drifted away from her onto loading, and Goth slipped

back to her little cabin. She was now very tired from her too
frequent use of no-shape—quite hungry, too—but was set on
clearing the place out by just tossing everything. Then it occurred
to her that she had time...and this might well be where they'd
put Pausert's mother for the trip. And, on touching each item,
and reading the story behind it—another tiring, hungry-making
process—she found that to be true. Some of it didn't even take
klatha skills: An old space-navy ship-bag at the back of a pile of
boxes of spare parts had women's clothing in it, and her name.
Now, if she could just avoid being tossed into space or sold into
slavery, she could find out just what had happened to Pausert's
mother. At least, where this link of the chain led.

She could only hope that it was a short chain.

And she really wished she had something to eat.

CHAPTER 10

Me'a grimaced. "This is a most appalling mess you present me with, Captain. My inclination is to have nothing to do with it. But I have been in coded subradio contact with the Daal of Uldune. Sedmon of the Six Lives has instructed me to give the Wisdoms of Karres any support they need. And that, in particular, applied to three of you. You, Captain Pausert. A particularly dangerous witch called Goth. And the Leewit."

The Leewit glowered at her. "You bet."

Me'a allowed herself the faintest hint of a smile. "Sedmon knows my weaknesses. I was specifically told not to gamble with you. Any of you. And part of that gamble would be the knowledge that there is a third, powerful, dangerous Karres witch unaccounted for. I have—listed among the powers she is reputed to possess—the ability to be invisible, and probably undetectable. So I need to ask: Where is this Goth? I think it would be wise, from my point of view, to include her in my calculations."

Both the captain and the Leewit scowled at her, but, before they could say anything Ta'zara said calmly, "Not to be told. This is your weak flank, lady. You must know you have it, and live and behave accordingly."

Me'a sighed. "Strategically sound. But tactically, we need to penetrate two layers of guards. I want all the assets I can get. Besides, I hate the idea of an exposed flank."

Ta'zara shrugged. "Live with it, lady."

Me'a shook her head. "I prefer..."

A communicator on the desk buzzed. "Planetary police just entered the building."

"How many?" asked the other Na'kalauf bodyguard.

"Just one. Chief Inspector Salaman."

"On her own?" asked the bodyguard.

"Yes," replied the voice over the communicator.

Me'a pursed her lips, shook her head again. "It must be a trap. We'll be clear in less than three minutes."

The communicator voice interrupted. "She says to tell you she's on her own and needs to talk to you and the people from the ship."

"It seems they pay more attention to comings and goings out of the airlocks than we realized," said Me'a, sourly. "Well. We'll be out of here with her then. If she's providing a distraction, they won't get it. If she really needs to talk—we can talk elsewhere."

So they were all bundled into an elevator—which certainly beat climbing all those stairs, even going down. That led into a tunnel with a small groundcar in it, which took them through the dark...somewhere.

"They'll bring the policewoman along presently. If need be it can be collapsed. Expensive, but hard for any copper to follow," said Me'a.

"I think," said Ta'zara, "that my mistress should also be hidden. We do not need to tell the policewoman we have a way back to the ship."

"There is a screen she could sit behind," said the other bodyguard.

The chief inspector arrived a few minutes later. Blindfolded. "We took a tracker bug off her coat. She seems clean otherwise," said one of the escorts.

"That would be my assistant. He's upset about this," said the chief inspector. "Now, am I going to be allowed to see?"

"I think not," said Me'a.

"I think I can manage to speak without seeing. I assume the enterprising Captain Aron is here."

Me'a held a finger to her lips and then replied. "That is for us to know. Now what do you want?"

"Something completely illegal of course. A temporary alliance, or at least a consultation. One of my informants among the gatherers brought me word of . . . an unusual story, involving Captain Aron. About granules being devoured by a porpentile—and that creature breaking up into little tumbleflowers."

"I see," said Me'a, not helping.

"I don't," said Chief Inspector Salaman, with a slight smile. "So your identity is still shrouded in mystery."

"Who was your informant?" asked Me'a.

"A gatherer by the name of Malketh. And he's safely off-world already. You frighten them quite badly. But that wasn't what I came to talk about. The Consortium are bound to get to hear of it as well. They still have the largest supply of granules, and the most to gain by keeping them rare."

"So do we," said Me'a.

"To some extent that is true," admitted the chief inspector. "But the Consortium have large stocks, and can hold out long after the tumbleflowers become too rare to support gatherers. And no gatherers means no smuggling. On the other hand, the Consortium's expenses are very high because they've made a vast profit for many years, and expenses have a way of catching up and resisting any attempt to reduce them."

"Our expenses are very high too," said Me'a.

"Only because we put a lot of barriers in your way," replied Chief Inspector Salaman. "Because there is a lot of money to be made off the tariff, which exists to make money from a very lucrative business."

"And your point is?" asked Me'a, dryly. "Governments do not reduce spending, either. You will still want the money."

"True," admitted the chief inspector. "But in this situation, Camberwell's Spacecraft Yards are a much bigger business, and much easier to tax. And they're dying under the huge cost of air recyclers. You could still run a lucrative business, as long as your margins are good. You're more adaptable than the Consortium."

"Flattery, Inspector, gains little advantage with me," said Me'a. "But I will consider what you have to say. I suspect you propose breaking open the Consortium's store caves, and getting the porpentiles into them."

"Yes." The chief inspector sighed. "It has been hard countering you, because you anticipate what I might do."

Me'a steepled her fingers, and permitted herself a wry smile, before saying, "I preferred having your predecessors here, Chief Inspector. They reacted. You also anticipate my moves. Reacting to them is so much easier to deal with."

"Well, there's a good reason for breaking the Consortium. If the price of granules falls, there will be not much revenue to be raised by taxing it. I will be reassigned back home to Camberwell," said the chief inspector.

"At last you give me a good reason," said Me'a, dryly. "Now, what do you propose?"

"The court case against Captain Aron has become very contentious. The Consortium have arranged a major demonstration to demand the execution of the pirate. I have, as a result, had to pull our guard from the security area around the caves, to keep public order," said the chief inspector smoothly. "Of course their own security and perimeter are still there."

"So this is not quite the open-and-shut case you told us it would be," said Pausert.

"Why, Captain Aron, how surprising to have you here," said the chief inspector, mockingly. "It will indeed be a little more interesting than we thought, thanks to your sending me a large group of people to feed in my jail. It's not the way to earn yourself popularity with the local gatherers hoping for somewhere to sleep."

"Er..." said Captain Pausert.

"But, however, they have provided some valuable testimony," said the chief inspector. "Including some detailed identikits of some of the pirates who captured the liner that Councilor Stratel was on. I have files and pictures of a rather large number of the people here on Cinderby's World. As I knew where to start with Bormgo's goons, we have some remarkable matches. People who were on the lifecraft. People that these rescued slaves would never have seen in their lives."

"That's good, isn't it?" said the captain, warily. Every time he had had a brush with the law on various planets—from the trouble he'd gotten into rescuing the witches of Karres on Porlumma in the first place, to Gerota Town on Pidoon, he had come off the worse, or at least financially poorer.

"It should be. Of course it all depends on what other bits

of testimony Councilor Stratel can find. Anyway, under the circumstances, with the possibility of rioting, I have been able to prevail on Judge Amorant to relax the bail conditions for the young lady's bodyguard, as they cannot fly the spaceship. Now, I had better get back. My assistant is likely to start doing foolish things if I don't return soon. I will see you in court, Captain."

She stood up. "And I am sorry I couldn't put a face to the legend."

"You are fortunate that you could not," said Me'a. "Take her back."

After the policewoman had gone, Me'a said irritably, "It would be worth doing this, no matter what Sedmon of the Six Lives said, just to get rid of her. This raid will have to happen when the police are watching the court case."

"Might be when they're expecting it," said Pausert.

"No," said Ta'zara. "Not a strategy they would expect. You're talking about letting the porpentiles into the caves. They expect robbery, not that."

"Actually," said Me'a, "I thought robbery sounded more attractive."

"Then I guess you'd have the Empire, the Daal of Uldune, and us—the witches of Karres—after you," said the Leewit, walking out from behind the screen, stroking a small rochat, which was hanging over her shoulders like a purple fluffy collar.

"Where did you get that from?" asked the captain. "You'd better give it back," he said.

"It's a baby and needs looking after," announced the Leewit. "It was lost back in the tunnels and followed us out."

"They do live down there," said Me'a. "Live and breed."

"I'm sure someone else would love to have it and would look after it," said the captain, knowing he'd lost, but still trying. "There's really no place for it on a spaceship."

"They seem to do perfectly well on spaceships," said Me'a. "And they cope with the foulest of conditions. They cheerfully breathe the air outside the domes and they can eat almost anything. They are common on my homeworld, even if they don't breed there. I had one as a pet, when I was young."

She seemed to be taking a rather nasty pleasure in both Pausert and Ta'zara's reaction to the Leewit's new pet. But it was her turn next. "Why haven't you got any legs?" the Leewit asked.

Me'a straightened up in her chair and said, her eyes narrow and hard, "Shut up, little girl. Or else..."

In reply the Leewit whistled at her. A two-pitched shrill and directional whistle, which hurt Pausert's ear drums and shattered several pieces of glass, and made Me'a clutch her ears and wince in pain. The captain—and Ta'zara, stepping in front of the Leewit—prepared for consequences. A cocoon would protect her, the captain thought, preparing the klatha pattern. But it might be best applied to the Na'kalauf bodyguard...

The Leewit stepped out from behind the bulk of Ta'zara. "It's important," she said. She didn't sound like a small girl at all, but far more like her mother Toll. Pausert was willing to bet she was channeling the teaching pattern in her head. "And don't make me whistle again. The next time I will break your ear drums and leave you deaf, if you're lucky."

It was plain that Me'a was used to being in control and was not ready for this kind of situation. So the captain did his best to put a bit of caution into her calculations. "She's a Karres witch, Me'a. And she's a healer. Don't do anything hasty."

Me'a turned her steely look on him. "It's not a question I tolerate. You are in my control. I have three hundred..."

The sound was abruptly cut off, because Pausert had put her into a klatha cocoon.

The Na'kalauf bodyguard reached for her and his hand struck the cocoon. He was ready to fight—as were the two other of her men in the room. "What have you done?" he demanded.

"Something only I can undo," said the captain. "And probably saved her hearing. Now I think it is time we all calmed down. The Leewit asked her a simple question."

"And I still need to know," said the Leewit. "I've been able to feel it...like a sore tooth ever since we got close to her. And she can't hear you now. She can breathe, but that is about it. If anything happens to the captain she'll die like that. Not even a Mark 20 Blaster has any effect."

"It is my task to keep her safe," said the bodyguard.

"She's safer than in a vault in the Daal's Bank," said the Leewit. "Clumping unhappy about it, but safe."

"I'll let her out, if you keep her from doing anything stupid," said the captain. "But if she puts a foot...uh, hand wrong, back in she will go. She'll be safe all right, until I let her out."

"She does not like to have her . . . condition spoken of. But I will do my best. I bind myself to that," said the bodyguard. He stepped up and pulled a wire free of its connectors. "That will stop her calling the others, until I have spoken to her."

"And you too," growled Ta'zara, at her other two men. They nodded, wide-eyed.

So Pausert reversed the pattern. Like the Leewit when the captain had done it the first time to save her life, Me'a had not taken kindly to being imprisoned in the klatha cocoon. She started with swearing—well enough to get the Leewit to laugh. That didn't seem to help. She stopped and ground her teeth. "Right. This farce stops now. Pa'leto, Mazan, Teem, take them down."

Nobody moved. "They're a threat, Pa'leto. Take them. Or I will."

"No, mistress. To get you free I gave my oath that I would stop you doing anything stupid."

"And that would be suicidal," growled Ta'zara, "let alone stupid. Think about it, instead of yelling."

That silenced her. She sat and glowered at them for a few moments. Then she said, "I understand why the Daal of Uldune warned that you were to be treated with great care. What did you do to me?"

"For us to know," said the Leewit.

"But you don't want to have it happen again," said the captain.

"You could get a funny hat like the Daal," said the Leewit. "He thinks it protects him."

"And does it?" asked Me'a, her voice slightly more normal.

The Leewit just looked at her, and grinned.

Me'a took a deep breath. "I have learned something of a lesson. But I am sorry, my . . . condition, is off-limits. It is something I must live with." The steeliness was back in her voice again.

"She's a Karres healer, Me'a," said Pausert.

"It is untreatable. A degenerative condition, not that uncommon on my homeworld."

Pausert started to get some idea quite what made the smuggler boss tick. Looking closely, the lines around her eyes were probably from dealing with pain. She was younger than he'd thought at first. She had to be ruthless and driven to get that far, that fast, in a large, powerful organization, especially in a wheelchair. Pity was something she actively fought off. In a flash of insight, Pausert knew that hope was too.

"It's not only for you," said the Leewit. "There'll be others. I need to know in advance." She stepped forward and took Me'a's hand.

"Don't touch me...oh. What did you do?" demanded Me'a, in a tone between suspicion and awe.

"Stopped you feeling the pain. It's still there, I just blocked it for now," said the Leewit. There was that adult tone to her voice that Pausert knew meant she was getting help again from the teaching pattern the young of Karres had imprinted in their minds. It allowed them a lot more freedom, and more help when they needed it.

"I don't allow myself drugs." That same steely control came through in Me'a's reply.

"No drugs. I just stopped the nerve from producing the chemicals to send news of the pain to your brain. It's not going to last. Now shut up. I need to concentrate." Her hands glowed slightly with klatha force.

Pausert walked over, put his hands on her shoulder, and then moved to the other shoulder because the rochat squirmed away under his hand. He willed himself to lend her his strength. They stood like that for quite a long time. Me'a eventually decided to put an end to it. "I need my hand back."

"Shut up," said the Leewit, and then added a few more words in another language that made Me'a open her eyes wide in amazement. "Nearly done." Then the Leewit pulled her hands away and said, "Now I need food. Lots. Pancakes with Wintenberry jelly."

"What?" asked Me'a, taken aback by the change in direction.

"She's used a lot of energy. She needs food. Now," explained Ta'zara, with a suggestive crack of his knuckles.

Me'a looked at him, looked at her bodyguard. "See to it," she said to one of her men. "Now. Just what have you done to me? When will the pain come back? And how did you know our native language? Such bad words too!" Her tone was...odd. Almost plaintive.

The Leewit yawned and flopped into a chair. "I only like the bad words. You had an autoimmune disease. I've stopped your body reacting to it. You'll get some odd aches, and funny sensations as the nerves get used to it. It was starting to affect your hands too."

"Do you think I didn't know?" snapped Me'a, sounding more like herself. "What have you done...?"

"Lemme eat, and I'll explain," said the Leewit, tiredly. She looked very small and frail, and the captain put his hand back on her shoulder, supporting her, until the food arrived. Then she ate with ravenous speed, and startling volume. The small rochat stuck its head out, and snatched a bite—but it had to be quick about it.

The passing time had obviously given Me'a time to think, and to calm down. "Shall I have more food brought, Your Wisdom?" she asked politely.

"Reckon I'm about done," said the Leewit. "But the captain could probably use some."

Me'a nodded. "It shall happen as fast as possible, Your Wisdom."

The Leewit wiped her face on her sleeve, and her hands on her trousers. "You're not hurting anymore, are you?" she asked of Me'a.

"No. It is something I have lived with for a long time. Is it... really going to last?" There was a desperate appeal in her voice.

The Leewit nodded. "Yep."

"I want to believe you, but..." Me'a's voice faded off.

"You'll see," said the Leewit. "I don't care if you believe me or not. I gotta sleep." And she leaned herself into Pausert and snuggled down into the chair.

The captain had helped himself to two of the new plate of pancakes. "Rest," he said, calmly, looking at the smuggler boss. "We're going to have to get her back onto the ship, and Vezzarn off it before the trial."

"That can and will be arranged," said Me'a.

And so it was. It seemed like Me'a had given them a degree of cooperation before—but now all her power and assets were at their disposal. It appeared this was not the only tunnel under the dome city, and the ropes had been a mere minor route for the less trusted. They had a route to outside—several, in fact. One of them came out a few hundred yards from the spaceport perimeter. Another had targeted the store caves of the Consortium. "We're not there yet," admitted Me'a. "But you did disturb a plan that is only weeks from completion. It won't matter, now."

CHAPTER 11

Sitting back in the *Venture*, all together again, just the four of them, was a pleasant respite, even if the trial was still coming. Late that night, long after the Leewit had gone to bed, Pausert was sitting in the command chair, thinking. It was a comfortable and familiar spot, and, Pausert had to admit to himself, one he kept hoping Goth would suddenly appear next to. But instead it was the Leewit, in her nightclothes, who did. "Can't sleep," she said tersely.

That was the Leewit's way of saying she was upset about something. So Pausert got two hot drinks and sat down to listen. They talked of all sorts of things, of places they'd been, and people they knew. Pausert just let the conversation take its own course. He'd learned from Goth and the Leewit: They'd tell him sooner or later. If you asked directly, they wouldn't answer. The conversation soon drifted to talking about Me'a and the plans to get into the store chambers. The captain observed: "It's like we're dealing with a different person."

There was a long silence from the Leewit. And then she said, "We are. The disease—well, the effects of it—changed the way her brain worked. It...she was pretty horrible under it. It made her...what's the word...obsessive. That's gone. It's kind of not her anymore."

Pausert had learned to read some of the Leewit's tones and mannerisms. She wasn't finished. So he waited.

Eventually she said, "It was killing her. But in a way I've also killed her. I could do the same to Ta'zara, cure him. Take away his ability to remember what happened on the Illtraming World with the Megair Cannibals. But...I don't think I can do that. I feel bad because I don't, because...the other Na'kalauf guard said Ta'zara's name means 'the laughing man.' I knew that, because I can translate his language, but I've never heard him laugh."

Sometimes, Pausert realized, you had to get a grip on the fact that the Leewit was still very young, and having to deal with matters that adults struggled with. "Then don't," he said calmly. "We're Karres people. We do what needs doing. Sometimes that means doing nothing, or finding another way to skin a miffel."

"Huh," said the Leewit. It was a thoughtful *huh*, but the captain was still wary. The Leewit's fuse had gotten longer as she grew, but it hadn't made her less explosive. And he felt they were heading for an explosion somewhere down the track. But she uncurled herself from the seat, stood up and gave him a hug and headed back to her cabin, leaving Pausert to wonder what was coming. It wasn't that long in getting there—Ta'zara slipped into the command room. The broad man could be remarkably silent for someone so large. "She is asleep," he said. "I just stayed long enough to make sure."

"You were listening?" asked Pausert.

"I am her La'gaiff. Her bodyguard. I need to watch over her. But she plainly wished to be alone with you, Captain," explained Ta'zara. "You are quite right. It is...needful that I remember my brothers, my clansmen. Our people require it. Please do not let her take it away from me."

And then he too left.

The courthouse was packed. If it had to get any fuller it would have needed a second layer of people. "They must be expecting to hang us," said the captain, darkly.

"It's free entertainment," said Inspector Detective Salaman. "Nothing much else is free here."

"Not even us," said Pausert, wryly.

The case began with all the usual formalities, and soon the captain was learning how wicked a fellow he was. He felt quite proud of his antics as a star-marauding pirate. How he'd disabled the helpless passenger liner with vicious green blasts of his ship's guns, before his men had captured the passengers and consigned them in manacles to the hold as slaves.

The prosecution had two of the rescued prisoners and Councilor Stratel as witnesses, telling a curiously identical story, down to all the fine details. The captain held off cross-examination until Stratel had been called. "So you saw this happen with your own eyes did you, Councilor?"

The man looked disdainfully at him. "Yes, as I said, we were in the main observation deck of the *Moria* when your ship attacked us."

"And you saw me leading the pirate boarding party?"

"Yes, I recognize you clearly."

"You saw the atomic blasts of our fire?"

"Yes. It hit our ship's control room, murdering innocent spacemen!" said Stratel, wiping away an imaginary tear.

"Ah. You saw that, did you?"

"Yes, a terrible, unprovoked attack on an unarmed peaceful passenger liner."

"Very interesting," said Pausert. "I looked up the *Moria* in the Imperial Ship Registry. Firstly, she was armed. Secondly, she was built on a class G Starchaser framework, on Camberwell. The observation deck is one hundred eighty degrees from the control room. You can't see one from the other."

"Well, I didn't actually see the shot hit," admitted Stratel. "But it was obvious where it was going to hit."

"So you lied under oath," said Pausert pleasantly. "You do know that our ship has been examined by the planetary police. They have seen all our armament and can attest that we have rather old nova guns. They're out of fashion because they're rather hard to aim and are unreliable. But they're what we've got. I don't know what you saw out there, sir, but it wasn't our ship. Now the common atomic blast-cannons do produce a green ionized blast, but nova-gun fire looks purple."

"I misremember the color. It's not relevant," said Stratel, crossly.

"All of you misremembered the color. All of you remember the same place on the ship being struck."

"Well, that was what you vile pirates hit," said Stratel.

"Liar, liar, your pants are on fire!" said the Leewit loudly, and had to be hushed. So did the laughing crowd.

After that, they adjourned before the captain, the crew of the *Venture*, and their witnesses were to address the court. A message came to the captain and his crew: "Me'a says that you're to drag it out a bit. The rock is harder than they thought. They don't want to use explosives but may have to."

"The court recesses for lunch," said Pausert. "Tell Me'a that if she can get me out there, I can deal with it. She can arrange it with the chief inspector."

It wasn't that hard to drag things on—the process was slow—with each of the *Venture*'s crew making their statements. The prosecutor tried to trip the captain up and failed. But he thought he would have it easy when the Leewit stepped up to the stand—and had to be provided with a stool to stand on so she could be seen. You could hear that by his tone as he said, condescendingly, "Now, little girl, of course you don't understand..."

"Why did that man"—the Leewit pointed at Stratel—"give you all that money? Mr. Judge, is he supposed to be giving that man money?"

And while everyone else was staring at the prosecutor, the captain, who knew the Leewit too well, saw her purse her lips, but this directional whistle was not one human ears were meant to hear. The Leewit had come a long way from just breaking eardrums and shattering fragile things with her whistles. She'd been working on new types and effects. Sound could do strange things to the human mind...and in this case the human sweat glands and tear ducts...it could even frighten one quite badly.

The judge eventually managed to get the crowd to quiet down, giving the prosecutor time to compose himself. That didn't help him very much, though, as the Leewit managed to ask him far more pointed questions than he asked her, trading shamelessly on being a little girl who didn't understand anything, when she was told that she was there to answer questions, not ask them. Her questions always seemed to reduce him to a stuttering panic. He gave up very quickly. His questioning of Vezzarn, after that, was hasty and not very effective. By the time he got to Ta'zara, he'd gotten his wind again. And he might as well not have had it. Questioning Ta'zara and hoping to trap him was a waste of effort. The bodyguard had very precise recall, and wasn't afraid of anything, let alone some windbag.

Then things took a turn for the worse for the prosecutor... and for Stratel. That wasn't surprising seeing as the Daal's Bank on Uldune were the insurers. The insurance assessor had actually taken a fast ship to look for the wreck of the *Moria*—and to the coordinates Pausert had supplied for the hulk of the pirate ship.

"We wished to recover the cargo if possible," he said, primly. "The vessel *Moria* on which Councilor Stratel traveled was disabled by having her stern tubes shot out. The damage was consistent with an atomic Mark 17 ship atomic cannon. This was the type of weaponry found on the wreck of the pirate vessel, which was struck amidships, causing the munitions pod for class ADE ship-to-ship missiles to self-destruct. The damage to surrounding areas was consistent with a single nova-gun discharge. An extensive search of both vessels failed to find the goods we had insured. However, we were able to find the serial number on the pirate vessel, and to track it back to the original manufacturers. We obtained the identifying serial numbers of the lifeboat, which was missing."

"Objection, Your Honor," protested the prosecutor. "This is irrelevant."

"It does not seem so to me," said Judge Amorant. "Please continue."

"The lifeboat was tracked to the port records of Cinderby's World. A business associate of the insured was listed as on board. We are thus declining payment on the basis of probable fraud. That is all, Your Honor."

If he'd dropped a bomb on the court it might have had less effect. Eventually the judge had to order the court cleared, and a recess until after lunch. The prisoners were led out...and into a waiting transport. They were underground on a little carrier within minutes, being kitted up for outside—just in case.

"We've still got some distance to go. The rock has been hardened," admitted the lead driller.

"Can you get us onto the surface?" asked Pausert.

"Already got an exit. But there is a guard on patrol up there. Me'a said we weren't to kill anyone." He sounded puzzled by that.

"I will deal," said Ta'zara, calmly. "Can we get close to them?"

"Yeah, I'll show yer. But they're armed, and they got orders to shoot to kill. And there are lots of porpentiles out there. Y' got to be careful."

Ta'zara nodded. "I will deal." He was careful—because he was officially in prison and unarmed. But it seemed like a man of Na'kalauf was never really unarmed. He selected two pieces of rock and waited for the patrol to come past the little gully they were hiding in. Pausert was ready to act, cocooning...but he never got the chance. The rock was a distraction and the two hired guards were not expecting trouble. Nor did they see it coming, or were likely to remember it. They were tied up and left in the gully, while Pausert and Ta'zara donned the guards' jackets and walked out onto the exposed rock above the store caves. There were other patrols in the distance, and in front of the cave doors, according to Me'a's information, the main cavern which joined all the individual Consortium members' caves came very close to the surface here.

Pausert cocooned a tube of rock with klatha force. He hoped that would be enough to break through, that he and Ta'zara could push it in.

He wasn't prepared for Ta'zara to jerk him off his feet and haul him backward as from the rocky ground came a whistling shriek and a wild dust storm, full of sand and small rocks. As an attempt at "quiet" it was a complete failure.

He and Ta'zara retreated from the rock-and-sand gale as the normal human-space air and pressure escaped. It was a challenge—because they had to dodge a steady stream of porpentiles eagerly undulating toward the dust plume. Then, obviously, the entire tube of rock fell in and the atmosphere from the caves gushed out, some freezing into a white mist. A mist full of surging porpentiles.

"I think we'd better get out of here," said Pausert through the breather mike. "Me'a is not going to be pleased."

"Neither are the Consortium—those porpentiles are going into the store caves. They must be able to smell the granules or something. It's going to be a big cave system full of little tumbleflowers by the time they open it."

"They'll start climbing out too, I should think. Remember, they have those sucker-feet."

They went back to the others, who wanted to know what had happened. Pausert explained as they made their way back through the tunnel to the little tracked carrier, and back to their nice comfortable, safe holding cell—where the chief inspector was waiting to hear it all again and to tell them they had very little time before court resumed. Pausert was expecting Me'a to be rather unhappy about the way the break-in had occurred. He was sure the smuggler had planned to share the loot from inside the store caves with the porpentiles. But she hadn't planned for an *all for the porpentiles, none for her sharing*, of that the captain was sure. She'd changed, but not that much.

The chief inspector, however, was rubbing her hands in glee. "Best of all possible outcomes," she said. "I've been getting reports in already. They haven't quite worked out what happened. They think part of the roof collapsed. The entrance has an airlock door—and they sent their people in to secure the granules. Only when they opened the inner door, the airlock flooded with dust-bunny size tumbleflowers. They had to open the outer door to not be packed solid with them, and now they're rolling out of the entrance—and the hole—like smoke. It couldn't be a worse outcome for the Consortium . . . or for that smuggler-woman. The Consortium just went broke. And the insurers won't pay Stratel, and I've got enough to arrest Bormgo. Now it's time you got back in court. I've been feeding and housing a lot of witnesses to cancel out the two Stratel bribed to repeat his lie."

The stories of some of the other rescued slaves were not quite all the same, unlike the coached accusers had been. But they were believable and at times tearful. They would have given great entertainment to the court, if the gatherers and quite a lot of other people hadn't been brought some whispered news and started leaving at almost a run.

"What is going on?" Judge Amorant asked eventually.

"I believe there's been some kind of natural disaster at the granule store caves, Your Honor. I've had to deploy some of my people to keep order," explained the chief inspector.

"Hmm. Well, let us continue," said the judge. So they did. But the prosecutor had given up even trying to cross-examine anyone.

At the end of the witnesses' testimony he stood up and said, "Your Honor. I would like to move this case be dismissed."

"You should have done so a while ago," said the judge, dryly. "In fact, it should never have been entered onto my rolls."

The judge proceeded to be rather flattering about their rescue, Pausert thought. As he hadn't ever had anything but trouble in his encounters with the officers of a court before, this was a welcome change.

The Leewit gave the prosecutor one last whistle, and one for Stratel as well. It honestly didn't look as if it made any difference to him. He was looking sick and green.

"So," said the captain to the chief inspector once they were out of the court. "If you're done with us, we'd like to get back to the spaceport. I'd rather not have to have another meeting with Me'a."

The chief inspector smiled. "I hope she is very angry with you, Captain. I still want to know why you were consorting with her, and why you have a very expensive bodyguard for your niece, and just how you got the caves open, as I know they had some serious armoring. But I think I owe you enough to forego getting those answers. I believe I have a few riots to deal with—the Consortium owe quite a lot of people money—and some arrests to go and effect. I neglected to tell you that Bormgo was charged with piracy this morning. We're searching for him. Stratel is likely to face a few charges himself. But I think being bankrupted on a planet where he has made himself hated may be worse than anything I could do to him."

However, any daydreams that the captain had of avoiding meeting Me'a again before they got away on the *Venture* were doomed to fail. She was sitting in the *Venture*'s control room, waiting for them. "I do have some employees who are rather skilled at working out airlock opening codes," she said, calmly. "But that proved unnecessary. Your ship was refitted in the shipyards on Uldune. As a precaution, the Daal's instruction is that an override code be fitted."

"I see," said the captain. He was coldly angry. "Do tell your master that I wonder how Hulik will find being married to Sedmon of the Five Lives. This is the second time the Daal of Uldune's little tricks have given Karres trouble. I know the hexaperson is a man of power, but this has to be stopped."

Me'a grimaced. "I suspect the Daal would be just as angry and certainly a lot more dangerous to me if he knew that I had obtained and used that code. Judging by what he said about avoiding any conflict with you, and giving you my full cooperation,

I suspect he did not know that you were one of the witches of Karres, when this was done. But I mean you no harm, and will leave if you order me to."

She sounded quite apologetic. Pausert wasn't that easily fooled. Neither was the Leewit, by her tone. "What do you want, Me'a?" she demanded.

"Passage home, for me and my bodyguards, as soon as possible."

"We're full," said Pausert.

"Your hold, however, is not. I took the liberty of having loaded not one, but four portable suites, each with four bunks. They will provide considerably more comfort than you were able to offer your passengers. And I have a second air recycler."

"Just where is your home, Me'a?" asked the Leewit.

The smuggler boss sketched a slight smile. "I would have thought it was obvious, or that Ta'zara might have told you. Na'kalauf, of course."

Pausert got his gambler's klatha instinct about that statement. "Very well. Are the Imperials going to be chasing after you?"

"Your trial and the events with the store caves provided a unique opportunity for them to be too preoccupied to notice. They don't know we are on board either. So I suggest we depart as soon as possible," she said coolly.

The Leewit's rochat stuck its angular head out of her shirt and hissed dismissively at her, and disappeared again.

They were able to clear the port quite soon after that. The passengers were all strapped in, and the captain made one of his trademark takeoffs, which might possibly have given Me'a second thoughts about traveling on the *Venture*.

CHAPTER 12

Sitting in the cleared cabin, Goth thought about her situation. They had brought her bag from the hotel, hastily and badly packed. She could wait until they decided to take steps to make her a slave or toss her off the ship into space. She could do her best to see that went badly wrong for them. Or...

Or she could take steps before they even tried. The best and simplest step, now that she'd established that this was definitely the ship she needed to be on, was not to be there when they came hunting for her. So she stepped into no-shape, and took herself into the gangway—just in time, as the mate came along and locked her cabin door. But she was no longer inside it.

Goth set off to explore the ship. It was plain to her that it was a space-traveling garbage dump. The crew obviously had no love for it. There were quite a lot of cabins they could have put her in, it turned out, even a long-unoccupied stateroom of dusty splendor, and very little clutter. It even had its own robobutler—in need of restocking, but that she could do, and did, from their stores. The luxurious room would do for a base, and had, in addition to the standard lock, a plain old-fashioned sturdy bolt. Even in a time of hyperelectronic locks, that was hard to beat.

The ship had a lower crew number than it was built to carry—seven that she'd been able to count. Goth decided they were as dodgy a lot as she'd ever encountered. She checked out the ship's guns and its missile pods, and found them to be in good order. They plainly expected trouble. She checked out the hold, expecting to find trading goods of some kind, even if it was as useless as a tinklewood fishing rod. But most of it seemed given over to food, drink, building materials and agricultural tools—and weapons. Military grade blasters in one crate, and two crates of power units for various caliber blasters. Any customs inspector might have had a few questions about those, but it was plain this ship had few troubles in that respect.

Goth spent a happy hour reorganizing the consignment labels. The blasters became canned soup, and the power units became toilet paper. The toilet paper became nails... and so on. There'd be no way of telling what was in the crates without opening the lot. And if they needed power units in a hurry, they were in for a nasty shock.

No-shape wasn't as tiring as some kinds of klatha. But Goth was still glad to return to the abandoned stateroom and use the robobutler, which was an excellent, top-of-the-range product. She laid down to sleep on the dusty bed, which made her sneeze a bit, but it was still more comfortable than the cubbyhole they'd put her in would have been.

She awoke to the sounds of takeoff, and hastily got herself strapped in. Not long afterward, she heard the sound of doors being crashed open down the passage. Some yelling. It seemed like they'd discovered she wasn't locked up in the cabin they'd put her in. How the Leewit would have enjoyed that!

Then she heard someone trying the door of the stateroom. It was bolted. "She must be in here!" said a female voice.

"But... but it's the boss's cabin!" said another, shocked voice.

"Where else could she be?"

"Lots of places," said the other voice, plainly uneasy.

"But this door is locked."

"Forz might have locked it. Or the skipper."

"Yeah? Well you go and check. I'll stay here."

Goth could have kicked herself for not thinking this through. As quietly as possible she slid the bolt open, unlocked the door and turned the lights out. She just had time to do that when the sound of several people outside alerted her to their return.

"It's a reinforced door," said a voice she recognized as the mate. "If she's locked herself in, we'll have to wait until we get to Lumajo to get a cutting torch."

Someone then tried the door. "Great Patham, Felap! What an idiot you are. It's open." The door swung open.

"Ought we to go in, Forz? It's the boss's cabin," said the same nervous voice.

"If you don't tell him, I won't," said Forz.

"Yeah. But he might find out..." The whiney voice sounded like that might be a really bad idea.

"Skaz, shut up. Get in and search."

Someone flipped the light on. Goth was safe in no-shape. Then she realized that she should have stayed lying on the bed, because the dust betrayed her. And by the drawn weapons they were planning on tossing her out of that airlock, dead. "Someone's been here! Jines, you and Felap search the bathroom."

They did while the others peered in cupboards and corners and under the bed. Which was quite fun, except for the dust. Goth felt that sneeze building, and building. You can't stop a sneeze.

She hastily 'ported a glass into the bathroom and dropped it. And muffled her sneeze as best as possible. Luckily, the breaking glass had had enough effect to make the sneeze irrelevant. "You broke one of the boss's glasses!" yelled one of the searchers, with the meaty sound of a blow.

"Ow! I didn't! Jines, you must have done it. You always blame me! Stop hitting me. I've cut myself." Whiny Felap fled the bathroom, clutching a bleeding hand. "Forz. It wasn't me. Stop her."

"Don't you drip blood on the carpet! Get out, you fool. Come on, all of you out. She's not here. I'll lock it up as soon as you're out. I'll bring you back to clean up the glass later, Felap."

Goth got out too. That was a little tricky because you could still be bumped into, in no-shape. And you could have someone stand on your foot in their spaceboots, and not be able to yell. Goth did shove the woman really hard, so she fell and nearly shot the mate, Forz.

It was all Goth could do, watching the fight, to not betray herself by laughing. She had to bite her sleeve, and retreat a bit, in case they heard her snorting, trying to breathe, not sneeze again, and stop laughing. They'd been all for killing her and dumping her out of an airlock, and had had something to do with the disappearance of Pausert's mother, at least. They were in for a rough trip, she decided. Besides, they ought to keep their ship cleaner.

Goth soon had a fairly firm understanding of the crew and the workings of the *Bolivar*. Getting to know them didn't help Goth like them one bit more. They had two theories on what had happened to her. One was that she'd fled the ship before takeoff, which was possible. Their watch was not very good; they even admitted that themselves. That worried them a lot. They really didn't want anyone disturbing their very profitable business. The second idea was that she was still on board, hiding. And, as Forz held by that theory, they searched. And searched. Goth could have followed them around. But it was easier to sit in Forz's cabin and wait. It was boring, so she whiled away her time making holes in his socks, cutting the stitching on the back of his trousers so they would rip suddenly and soon. It wasn't a very grown-up thing to do, Goth admitted. But who wanted to be grown-up all the time? She'd had to be, and pretend to look that way, for too much time on this trip. She just wanted to go back to the *Venture* and back to being herself. And back to the captain. That couldn't happen, yet. So instead she unpicked stitches.

When they were done searching, Goth collected her bag from the junk they'd just piled back into the little cabin they'd tried to lock her into... And then had second thoughts. She took her clothes out of that bag, put them into Pausert's mother's ship-bag and filled hers with some of the stuff lying around. Then she went back to the cabin belonging to "the boss," whoever he was.

As Forz had made Felap clean it generally, as well as just clean up the glass, the stateroom was now less dusty and more pleasant. Goth soon found that "the boss" had a comms link to the bridge and the mess, with a one-way vision set. She could watch and listen to them, without leaving the comfortable cabin. It was locked, now. But, as Goth had the key-bar, that wasn't a problem for her.

One of the first things she learned, sitting and listening to them, was just how they passed across the frontier. It was a huge area of space, and a clever—or lucky—skipper could avoid coming in detection range of Imperial Space Navy ships. There were patrols, and their routes were randomized and secret. The sector was renowned for several invading raider fleets having attacked worlds of the Duchy of Galm, as well as considerable smuggling, and was thus heavily patrolled.

Apparently that secret could be bought, and had been. The *Bolivar* dropped into orbit around a dead sun and waited among the frozen worldlets for a patrol to pass—a patrol they knew was coming, and where it was going to. There was no need to dodge the watchmen, when all they had to do was corrupt someone who knew what the patrol routes and times would be. Thus the *Bolivar* passed across that poorly defined bit of space that divided the Empire from the star-swirl toward the galactic center, into an area of dead worlds, blasted ruins, and poorly mapped stars.

The ship was doubtless heading for one of them. It was, judging by the crew's wary behavior and the readiness of the ship's guns and missile pods, plainly somewhere they thought was dangerous. That might be wise, but Goth decided to help them hurry up. Power to the air recycler was controlled by a simple cutoff switch, to allow it to be removed or worked on. It was up in the power conduit access near the engine room. Goth could have built one, but she settled for simply switching the circuit to the indicator light that showed it had power. Normally it glowed when it had power. Now, it glowed when it didn't.

That of course did not apply to the ship's own air-monitoring system, which started flashing warnings. "Captain, we're getting air-quality warnings," said the nervous crewman on watch, waking the sleeping captain with a call to his cabin on comms. Goth couldn't hear his reply, but it was enough to have him calling various other crewmen from their beds, including a rumpled Forz and Felap. The two of them and the ship's second engineer started checking. They soon found that the air recycler was without power.

"Oh. Well. That's simple then. We'll just give it an alternate power source," said Felap. He sounded quite relieved.

That got him slapped on the ear from the second engineer. "You're as dumb as a dung-grubber, Felap. Do you know how much power that takes to run?"

"Uh. No."

"Well, I do. We'll have to open the conduit hatch," said the engineer, hastening in that direction.

So they did, as Goth watched from no-shape. "Well, that's got power," said the engineer, looking at the happily glowing telltale light. "We'll have to open the conduit. There must be a break somewhere." He was grumpy and worried at the same time, as well he might be. It was a horrible, awkward job, as Goth knew from helping Captain Pausert, but the ship couldn't run long without recycled air.

As soon as they got started on that, Goth flipped her switch. It would take a little while before the air quality was back to normal, and the air-quality warning stopped. None of the three working on undoing the bolts and moving the panels and testing the current induction went to check the recycler again.

Goth 'ported the power wrench when Forz put it down, and changed its direction setting and torque so it tightened instead of loosened. So the next bolt he put it on tightened and snapped with a scream of metal—and a scream of rage from the engineer. "You idiot! Now we'll have to drill that one out and we don't have time on our side!"

He hit Forz, and Forz hit him with the power wrench. And Goth got knocked into the wall by the captain coming down the gangway at a run—and hitting both of them. And kicking Felap for good measure. Goth took her bruises away and left them to it.

She was listening on comms when Forz—with a swelling black eye—reported to the captain on the bridge. "I don't know what we did. We opened the conduit up, and by the time we got to the recycler room, it was working again."

"I was about to call you. The air-quality warning light has been flicking out. So it's getting back to normal."

"There must be a short or a break somewhere that we fixed accidentally. It's worrying, Captain," said Forz, sounding scared enough for Goth to almost feel sorry for him.

But not sorry enough not to wait until he was fast asleep, when she disconnected the monitoring system input. All the ship repair she'd learned from Captain Pausert and Vezzarn was proving useful. As she knew it would, that had the control panel flashing dire warnings and sounding an alarm, because as far as it was concerned the ship was becoming an airless vacuum.

The crew all went running for the airlocks, for the spacesuits. The ship's automatic doors hissed closed, sealing Goth off on the bridge. The yelling and panic were pretty noisy even by the Leewit's standards, Goth thought. The Leewit would have been impressed by the swearing, too, when Forz couldn't remember the access code to open the bulkhead doors. The captain had to put in the override from the bridge, and Goth learned that code too.

The engineer, seeing the recycler power light off, had promptly flipped the switch, cutting power to the recycler. Goth plugged the air-quality monitor back in—which, seeing as the recycler had only been off for moments, promptly stopped the alarm. Skaz and Jines in the meanwhile, in total panic, had climbed into the airlock, ready to abandon ship...out into the airless vacuum of space. Fortunately for them, they couldn't remember the outer airlock code and had demanded it over the intercom—and were getting a bawling out by the captain instead.

The bulkhead door opened and Goth walked down to where the engineer, his second, and Felap—who was more hindrance than help, as usual—were frantically opening the conduit covers again, as the air recycler wasn't running because it had no power. Goth let them get all of it opened up, before flipping the switch again.

The engineer was slightly more thorough than his junior officer, and came back to check the switch. He swore and promptly flipped it off again, and ran to check the recycler. Goth had to work pretty quickly to get the original switch in place before he came back. It took him several frantic runs to get Felap to stay and flip the switch and have him satisfied that it was working properly.

But neither he nor the crew were a happy bunch of spacers. Being out here with a faulty air recycler was more terrifying than having to fight raiders or pirates or inimical aliens. "We can't slow down and probe, Captain. We've got to get to a safe world with breathable air and then I can take the whole thing apart," said the engineer. "And that's Lumajo. I never thought I'd be glad to breathe its stinking air and even see those little furry apes again...but it will be air."

Goth had decided to fish for information too. As well as hiding herself in no-shape, she could also bend light into other images—and project them onto the air. She could make them good enough to fool most people, but for this use...a little wavy faintness and transparency were more useful. She used Lina's image...in gangways when a crew member was alone, and near the tail end of the alter-watch. She hoped it would spook them into talking.

It spooked them, all right. But not into telling her anything she didn't know. "We didn't do anything to her!" was the most she got out of that. But their nerves soon had them believing in phantoms, phantoms beyond her deliberate creation. "We should turn back," moaned Skaz, her voice shaking in conversation with the crew in the mess. "It's not safe. And there's creepy stuff going on. I heard footsteps behind me last watch, but there was no one there."

There was a murmur of uneasy assent, rapidly quashed by the captain and the mate. "We're more than two thirds of the way to Lumajo," said Forz.

"And there's an Imperial Space Navy exercise between us and Morteen," said the captain. "We'll push on as fast as possible."

That suited Goth. So she held off from harassing them with any more recycler issues, and settled for just making their lives miserable by sabotaging the robobutler in the mess so it would only produce Sargothian seaweed stew and sickly sweet drinks. She had a perfectly working robobutler in the comfortable cabin— but it was a measure of how much they all feared whoever this absent "Boss" was, that they were too much afraid of him to suggest using it.

The *Bolivar* raced on toward its destination, its crew complaining this was the worst trip they'd ever had. That also suited Goth. They'd been all set to give her the worst trip of her life—and the last. She spent the rest of the trip removing power units from as many weapons as possible. There was a box marked floor-cleaning liquid in the store, and that seemed a good safe place to store them.

They were all plainly relieved to swing into orbit around a planet—Goth could see it on the vid on the comms link. Not as clearly as she'd like, but enough to see that it bore what looked like the scars of interstellar war. Parts were dense green, other areas stark and white with black streaks. Even from this great height, she could see octagonal structures down there. They must be huge. Like any world, Goth knew that it was a big, varied and complex place, but it plainly wore the marks of having been densely settled.

The *Bolivar* wasted no time on contacting planetary authorities or requesting landing permission. She just began to drop in on the planet they called Lumajo, targeting a site somewhere between a huge octagon and a far smaller one, which as they approached revealed itself as a cleared area of jungle.

Goth had very little idea what she was coming to. Other than mentions of stink, the hairy little apes, and the fact that the place was a source of a banned substance, she hadn't gleaned much from the conversation of the crew. Mostly they talked about what they'd do back on Morteen, if they talked about planets at all. She had no idea how she'd even start to find Lina, how many people there were here, or quite what her plan was. But she'd eaten well and slept as much as possible. That would have to do for preparation.

The landing jarred her to the back teeth. Captain Pausert was good at putting a ship down as lightly as a feather, no matter what you thought of his takeoffs. The *Bolivar's* captain wasn't—but they were down in one piece. Now to get out and get searching...

The crew had been in a hurry to get off the ship. That was understandable, but did leave Goth with the main airlock closed, and the ramp up. She had all the codes to the airlocks and could open it and put the ramp down, easily enough, but that would be rather obvious to any watcher. By the noise, they were offloading cargo.

Invisible in no-shape, she went down to the cargo hold, where the sulfurous air of outside hit her, along with the smell of the hairy little... men. Well, they were sort of humanoid anyway. They looked less like humans than the Nartheby Sprites. They were offloading, and jabbering away in a singsong foreign tongue—which might actually have been a kind of singing. The words weren't universal galactic, anyway. One phrase seemed to recur: "blong khagoh."

They were watched by a couple of rough-looking spacers with blast-rifles and jangler-whips. Goth walked quietly down the ramp and onto Lumajo, where the gravel of the spaceship's landing area shivered with heat, beneath a distant white sun. The sky was an odd dirty yellow color, and the air didn't smell much better away from the chanting little locals. Exploring the rest of the place would involve getting over some high double fences that looked electrified. There were guard towers, too. It looked more like a military camp or a prison than anything else.

Goth figured it was likely that, if either were still alive, Pausert's mother and even his father would most likely be inside the wire. She waited a while at the gate, and then walked back to the ship for a bit of shade. The sun might be a small point in the sky but it was hot and vicious. She could feel it burning her.

The hairy locals were loading the boxes and crates onto a large wooden trolley, with rough wheels made from cross sections of tree trunk. Sitting in the shade of the ship, Goth had time to study them. They were as hairy as a lelundel, and had little tails. They were shorter than the Leewit, but a little broader. How they saw anything was a mystery, because their faces too were hidden in their hair.

Once the trolley was piled high with boxes and crates, coils of wire, steel beams of various shapes and sizes, the spacemen chased the little humanoids—on average half their size—to leashes on the drawbar. With the little humanoids chanting rhythmically again, they hauled the load toward the gate. Goth walked along in the shade, wishing she had the hat and sunglasses from Parisienne. They were still with her luggage on the ship.

They dragged the trolley through the gate and to the compound beyond, which boasted a palace-like building and primitive-looking factories and warehouses beyond that, and, behind yet another layer of wire, scruffy-looking huts. The trolley-loads of goods were being taken to one of the warehouses, where they were offloaded and packed away. There were several shiny new ground trucks in the building that certainly could have done the job, Goth noted, before they locked the place up again.

The little humanoids were marched to the huts behind the next wire barrier. There was no obvious sense in following them so Goth took her sunburn along behind the guards, heading for the big house. She'd met some rough types over the years, traveling around in the *Venture* and with the circus. These men, listening to their talk, made Lesithanian fishermen look polite and nice. They smelled about as bad too, even in the sulfurous air. They were plainly in a hurry to get indoors, and about that, at least Goth could agree. The palace-like building was air-conditioned, which was welcome.

It took Goth a while to get her bearings inside, raid the kitchen, and find a quiet spot to eat. It was going to take her time to explore, and she'd have no choice but to use up some energy staying in no-shape. So far she'd found that some of the place was given over to dormitory-like rooms as well as a communal hall, where the crew of the *Bolivar* were doing some catching up on meals that didn't look very appetizing. Goth was tempted to help their ill-luck along, but instead concentrated on eavesdropping for clues. It wasn't particularly productive. Most of what they were talking about she'd heard before back on the ship. And all the others could talk about was "the Gaks."

It seemed the Gaks were the little humanoids. They'd apparently burned out several fields a few days back. They were arguing about the best response. Goth went on her way, exploring. Warily, she tried touching walls and objects to "read" them. It was a dangerous thing to do because if she got drawn in, she could well fall into a trance—which would stop her being light-shifted into no-shape.

Mostly, though, it turned out to be quite safe. There were few strong emotions and deep thoughts to leave traces. Every old place had them, but this building was quite new, and not, as it were, full of the past. She went on searching, and eventually came to the prisoners at the back. They were locked into a separate section, which Goth got access to by following someone carrying buckets of food . . . food that reeked of paratha. It didn't look appetizing, but Goth realized it didn't have to.

This section of the building consisted of a series of small metal rooms, with barred doors and a caged walkway, which she found led to the factory plant. Here the walls told a different story. Here she really had to be careful. But the despair and anger were not just in the walls. They were in the people still trapped in the little hot rooms. The air-conditioning was not for prisoners.

Neither Pausert's mother nor his father were among the handful of prisoners. That was worrying. Goth followed the person delivering plates of paratha-laced slops, which they slid into a grid on the bottom of each door.

No one said much. They just eagerly took their plates. This was one prison where the prisoners thought the food was great, at least. The food deliverer left them to it, and walked out. Goth wasn't quite quick enough to follow her, but she could always get out some other way. There were several empty cells, so Goth took herself into the farthest one, to have a rest from no-shape and read the walls.

It was a grim experience, and a grim story. The last prisoner had been a guard who had stolen something from the boss. That told her about the people she was dealing with, but not the reason she'd come here.

The next cell, however, was the jackpot. Goth learned a great deal about Lieutenant-Commander Kaen, Pausert's father. He'd been quite badly injured and in a lot of pain when they had brought him here. But he had recovered and there was something of an imprint of his memory of the place, machinery he had worked on, and the little humanoids.

The oddest thing was there was no memory of fences. This was a man she'd never met, who had left the traces of his determination, anger and pain for her to read—but he reminded her a lot of Pausert, which made her quite snuffly. There were no other empty cells. A couple of the other prisoners were talking in a despondent fashion about the problems they had with one of the machines.

Goth figured she'd regained enough energy and slipped back into no-shape; then, went down the caged walkway to the factory. The harsh sun was down, but there was some light from a pair of moonlets on the horizon. Goth could see it was a simple bottling plant with what, on examination, proved to be a big drying room for huge leaves, and a crushing plant for the same. The whole place reeked of paratha. The building was not particularly secure, and it was easy enough to get out of. In this it was unlike the main building, which did not look easy to get into. That was solidly built and had a guard house on the doors, and pillboxes on the corners.

Goth decided to go back to the *Bolivar* and collect her bag. There was a cargo-hold door that should be accessible. After the terrible heat of the day, it was already cool and Goth could bet it would be freezing by dawn. The first of the moons was below the horizon, and the second was touching it. It'd be pitch dark soon. There was wire in the way, but she could deal with that. Teleporting a piece out of it worked. She'd walk across in no-shape, get a good meal from the robobutler, a shower and maybe sleep there. And she could bring the sunshades and hat with her, as well as some clothes for cool nights.

The idea had seemed good, but nearly got her killed. She made her hole, making sure she was well clear of the electrified wires, and started walking fast, as she wanted enough light to at least find the cargo door.

And then suddenly there was far too much light. Searchlights sprang to life on the watchtowers, an alarm shrieked. Goth froze for a moment, crimping her eyes against the glare. She was in no-shape and quite safe, but some instinct made her run, anyway, which was just as well as blaster bolts seared the place she'd been standing. She took off at a zigzag run, back toward the fence, with them firing at her from the watchtowers, just as if they could see her.

She realized that they could. They must have some kind of infrared detector. The Toll teaching pattern said she could no-shape infrared too. It wasn't easy to learn while you were running, but she did it. And kept running for a bit for good measure.

The shooting stopped. But that was definitely a bit of an ionization burn on her shoulder. Did she need the Egger Route...?

Not quite yet, she decided. She was too close now. But the wound hurt and she was fairly mad about it—partly at herself for being caught like that. Well, if they wanted to shoot at infrared images she'd give them some to shoot at. She could split light images—and infrared was still light. There were four targets for them, moving ones, ones that they could shoot at to their hearts' content. She pushed the split light images toward the watchtowers. Sore or not, she had to suppress a giggle at them shooting at the bases of each other's towers. Someone was going to fall, hard, when those came down.

Unfortunately, someone must have realized that could happen. They stopped shooting—and plainly were calling for reinforcements. The occupants of the palatial building came—armed, scared—and opened the gate. Goth decided that going to the ship would just have to wait. She went back out of the spaceship compound, where someone had just found her cut wire.

Goth knew that sooner or later they'd figure out she had to have come from the building compound. And then they'd search that, in earnest. Wincing a little at the pain from the burn on her shoulder, Goth decided it would be sensible enough to make them assume she'd come from outside—and hopefully left that way. So she took a piece out of the outer wire... which caused sirens and alarms, not exactly what she'd had in mind. Obviously the outside perimeter had some sort of detector, to make sure it wasn't broken.

What was out there that they were so scared of? These people were not exactly soft inner-planet dwellers, terrified of the wild. Listening to them, it was all about the Gaks. "There's bound to be a charge soon!" said someone, warily looking at the dark jungle beyond the cleared area around the fence.

Those funny little hairy humanoids? Goth couldn't see it. And her shoulder was sore. So she went back to the palatial building in search of some burn ointment and a dressing. That proved harder than she thought it would be. Even in no-shape, you had to dodge being bumped into and also go through doors before they closed. Someone running nearly sent her flying, and really hurt her sore shoulder. And then they slammed a door in her face.

She recognized the next two coming out—the whiny useless Felap and the *Bolivar*'s mate, Forz. "Why can't we get the Gaks to do it? Or some of the boss's guards? Those crates are heavy."

"Because when the Gaks come they want to be able to shoot anything that looks like one, not worry about if these are tame ones or not, you idiot. And we'll take a ground truck. If there's a big rush they'll need extra blaster charges. Now get a move on."

"I still don't see why I have to do it. Ow. You didn't have to hit me," complained Felap.

"I don't have to but I'm going to," said Forz. "Come on."

Goth followed the complaining Felap around to the factory, scrambled onto the back of the ground-truck before it rose on its repulsors, and enjoyed a ride out to the *Bolivar*. She was feeling a little faint by now. Inside the ship she could take a rest and have a good look at her injury. Part way across it occurred to her that their supply of blaster power units was now in a crate labeled TOILET PAPER and if the Gaks did attack they'd have to throw nails at them. Even feeling sore, that made her smile.

Once inside the *Bolivar*, the two went looking. "Manifest says it should be packed here," said Forz.

"Well, it's not," said Felap, looking at the space-crate label. "Says toilet paper."

"Patham's seven steaming hells! Those idiots offloading must have shuffled things about. Look for it."

They both did and soon found the suitably labeled crates. Felap whined about how heavy they were.

"You'd moan more if we didn't have them," said Forz, lifting the other. "They say the last time the Gaks massed an attack there must have been ten thousand of them."

"Why don't we just stay on board, then? Just in case."

"You're a little worm, Felap. Anyway, Pnaden said that we're to get the ship offloaded and ready tomorrow. They'll be bringing the cargo. He wants a quick turnaround."

That really didn't suit Goth. She could cope with the Egger Route and one person...but there was a chance of it being two. For that she'd want a spaceship. So once they'd gone, she'd have to wait for their return. Or take steps to see that they couldn't leave.

First, though, was food and a cleanup of the nasty burn on her shoulder. Then...well, she had the ship's codes. Part of her wondered if she should just seal the ship, take off, and put it down somewhere else. That was something she could probably manage. Pausert handled takeoffs and landings with the *Venture*, but both she and the Leewit had been taught how to do it. He'd even taught them how you ought to do it, instead of his way. But that wasn't quite the same as actually doing the job.

Once she'd eaten, and had a wash, she was yawningly tired. But there was no telling when they might discover that they'd taken two crates of nails, not blaster power units. So she set about making sure that they didn't find them. Engineering had a store for lubricants and cleaning material so she put the boxes in there. That involved quite a lot of the heavy lifting and carrying that Felap had moaned about, and hurt her shoulder. Then to make sure that they didn't leave, she removed two electronic units from the tube warmup mechanism. They might be able to find them, or replace them—she really wasn't sure how well equipped their spares were. But, from her experience with the *Venture*'s disaster on the world the Megair Cannibals had claimed for their own, she knew that they weren't going to have a spare multiplier link from the main sequencer. So she took that out too. By this time she was exhausted. She just had to rest, to sleep, somehow, somewhere.

But some instinct said that using the boss's cabin was probably not a great idea. So she moved her bag out, and took herself to the tip-of-a-broom-cupboard they had given her for a cabin. She cleared enough flat space to lie down on, curled up, and slept.

CHAPTER 13

Goth awoke to the sound of people moving around in the ship. She should have thought to bring breakfast along with her, she realized. Best to find out what they were doing, she decided.

What they were doing was offloading the cargo, in double quick time, and preparing the ship for takeoff. That preparation included cleaning up the boss's suite, so Goth was glad not to be there.

Actually, it seemed the ship would be a good place not to be soon, so she took the parts, the hat and dark glasses, and a spare jacket and left on one of the ground trucks—which, today, they were using as well as the trolley pulled by the chattering little humanoids. The stores were being packed into a warehouse, but Goth decided that the spaceship spare parts should be put somewhere where they were less likely to be accidentally found. So she went into the factory, which was running full tilt, crushing paratha and packing it into tiny bottles that ran down a conveyor to get sealed. The sealer was against the wall, and had some space behind it. Goth slipped the units into the dusty cavity behind and below—and nearly got herself caught, by touching that machine's casing and losing her no-shape.

It drew her in. It was full of memories. This was where the injured prisoner Lieutenant-Commander Kaen had been put to work. He'd fixed that machine...and sent his name out with every single bottle sold. There was also the image of a little hairy humanoid somehow tied to his hopes and fears.

"Who are you?" one of the prisoners from the cells asked. Goth was no longer in no-shape, and just standing there.

"New prisoner," she said. "I was sent to work here. But they didn't tell me exactly where I had to go. Everything seems to be a bit of a mess this morning."

Inwardly Goth was cursing. She didn't want them searching where she'd been seen—or describing her too closely. She used a light-shift to alter her appearance. But habit caught up on her: She'd been using the ghostly image of Pausert's mother to try and frighten the crew of the *Bolivar*, so that was the face she chose. And then seeing the startled look on the face of the other prisoner, hastily modified it.

The woman looked at Goth again, blinked, and rubbed her eyes. "For a moment I thought you were that Lina woman. The one who ran off and got herself killed by the Gaks. Did they tell you where you were supposed to be working?"

"No. They just chased me out of the cell they put me in," said Goth sullenly. "I want out of here."

"Huh. Fat chance," said the other prisoner. "Where are you going to go? Leave here and the Gaks will kill you. And even if you got away from them, what are you going to eat out there?"

He shook his head. "Wait here. I need to shut down my crusher. I was told to get Pilsk to help load plants at the nursery. But you'll do. Pilsk is a borgum."

Goth had a few seconds to scoop some debris over the parts behind the cover, before the other prisoner came along and led her out, toward the warehouse, where a bored spacer was sitting on a small armored ground vehicle. "You took your time, Vanessa. Who's this? It's not Pilsk."

"She's a new prisoner, Heffner. What's your name, woman?" asked Vanessa.

"Orthia," Goth supplied. She'd had time to think of that and prepare.

"Didn't know there were any new ones. Come with the ship, did you?"

Goth nodded.

"Well, come on, there's work to be done," said Heffner. "We're to put a thousand seedling trays on the ship."

"The boss is taking them off-world?" asked Vanessa.

"Yeah, but not you, Vanessa," said the spacer, sardonically. "You should have known better. You're lucky to be alive. And you, Orthia? What did you do?"

"It was just borrowing," protested Goth sullenly. "I didn't really steal it, no matter what Forz says."

The other two laughed, obviously not believing her. "You drive, Vanessa," said the spacer. He climbed into the gun turret, and Goth sat herself down in the second seat. Vanessa started the ground truck and they went into the compound that held the scruffy huts of the humanoids, and then out of a far gate, toward patchworks of fields, all growing the big-leafed paratha. On the one edge of the fields was a long, low building. By the time they got there, Goth had decided that the spacer and Vanessa—despite being a prisoner herself—were both on a par with the crew of the *Bolivar*, if not worse. It was time to ask some direct questions, and get some direct answers.

The spacer was armed. Vanessa obviously wasn't. Still, his hip-blaster's power unit was easily portable, but he might have something else. And Goth had learned a great deal from that sore shoulder. She gave them a false light image to use for a target. The image also had her Clipe needler in hand. "Just stop right there," said Goth.

The spacer took one look and dived sideways, clawing out his blaster. His look of horror when it didn't fire was a pure pleasure. He hastily pulled at the power unit . . . which wasn't there. He started to reach for a pocket, and Goth let a Clipe needle blow dirt all over his face. "Lie very still," she said. "Otherwise you're going to lie still forever. I want some answers. If I get them, you get to live. If I don't I'll find someone else to tell me."

"Give me the gun, Orthia. You can't get away. There's only one ship. And the boss doesn't care about hostages."

He was brave, Goth had to give him that. He was also misinformed, at least about the getting-away part. "Even if he doesn't care, you do. At least you care about staying alive," Goth said. "Vanessa. Tie him up. There's rope in the ground-truck."

"One of the patrols will come around, Orthia. Look," she

pointed at an armored groundcar across the fields in the distance. "Give up. Me and Heffner will say nothing. We promise."

The only fit answer to that was: "Get the rope, Vanessa."

Vanessa's tying was deliberately loose, but once she'd finished tying Heffner, Goth checked the ropes, Clipe needler against his spine. As she expected, they were too loose. She then made Vanessa tighten them up properly, after which she searched Heffner and removed a spare power unit from a pocket and a rather nice knife. "Now load him in to the ground-truck, Vanessa. Do your best to help her, Heffner. Otherwise I'll just tie a rope to your feet and drag you behind like a bollem."

"Are you crazy? You'll never get to the ship," complained Vanessa, nonetheless trying to pick up an uncooperative Heffner, who just looked sullen.

"I'm not going to try. Go on, Heffner. Stand up before I shoot you in the leg so you have a reason for behaving like you're crippled. I need some answers out of you."

He cooperated, but Vanessa went on trying to talk. "I'll help you but you must let us go."

"I've come to look for Lieutenant-Commander Kaen and Lina. We've tracked both of them this far. You get to go free when I find them."

"You'll never get off this world alive," grated Heffner. "Anyway—the scout-pilot and the woman are dead."

"Then I'll have their killers."

He snorted. "Good luck. The Gaks killed them. And that's nothing to what we'll do to you. You can't get away."

"Actually, it's you who can't get away. Your ship won't fly again. I did that last night. That was the alarm you heard. You're all stuck here."

They both looked at her in horror. "But . . . but we'll all die," said Vanessa.

"We'll make you fix the ship. And you are just as stuck!"

"I may fix your ship. But I am going to want answers first. Sit down, I am going to tie you to the seats." Goth could see the patrol vehicle heading around. But before the other armored vehicle got to them, Goth had the ground-truck started and headed slowly back toward the base . . . and then, once the patrol had gone past, turned around again. The "slowly" part had been more a case of learning to drive the vehicle, but it really was quite simple. Light-shift on a moving vehicle was quite hard, so Goth waited until she was near the edge of the fields before doing so. The jungle of tall, feathery looking trees was not that far off.

Her passengers didn't know that light was bending around them. "Where are you going?" demanded Vanessa, her voice high and panicky.

"Away. I want to ask you some questions in peace. Then I might bring you back," answered Goth.

"The Gaks will kill all of us, you mad fool!" she yelled.

The prisoners were unaware of the invisibility of the vehicle. Goth picked on a thinner-looking patch of brush, and gunned the ground-truck forward. "The sooner you answer all my questions, the sooner I let you go. If I get the information I need, that is."

"We'll tell you anything you want to know. Just don't go into the jungle," begged Vanessa.

Goth ignored her and kept going. She'd given up on the light-shift while they drove. It was hard going at first, but the problem now was finding a path through the vast feathery trees. It was quite dim under the canopy. Both prisoners were begging her to go back and struggling to free themselves. She stopped. If these little humanoids were dangerous... right now all they would see was a tangle of shadows. "So what happened to Lieutenant-Commander Kaen and Lina? Tell me."

"They did pretty much what you did, you crazy woman. Ran off into the jungle," said the spacer.

Piece by piece, Goth got the story. The lieutenant-commander had been shot down in an ambush arranged by the boss's contacts in the Imperial Space Navy. He'd made a crash landing on Lumajo.

"The Gaks brought him to us on a stretcher," said Vanessa. "He was hurt pretty bad. No one expected him to live, but the boss thought he'd question him, so we put him in one of the cells. He got better while the boss was off-world. We made him work in the plant. He was a good engineer, and he fixed things. But one day we found he'd cut a hole in his cell and slipped away during the night. The ship wasn't here—it had just left. Look, I gave him extra food. Heff wasn't even here yet."

"Hang on," said Goth. "You say the Gaks brought him to you on a stretcher. I thought you said they'd killed him?"

"That was then. They got crazy later," said Heffner.

"They treated us like gods back then," said Vanessa.

Digging through their answers, Goth began to form a picture. This had been a pirate and smuggler base, before the little humanoids had brought them gifts of paratha. Paratha had just started becoming big business, when Lieutenant-Commander Kaen had been shot down. A then-young Vanessa had been one of a smuggler crew, before she'd gotten herself imprisoned and effectively enslaved. Something had gone wrong between the smugglers and the locals, and except for the little tribe living in the compound, it was now open war. Things had been hostile before Kaen had fled, and by the time Pausert's mother came a few years later the only way to get the paratha—for which they now had a valuable, captive market—was to grow it. They'd had to fort up and the Gaks attacked them on sight. And it had only gotten worse since, with the base nearly being overrun twice.

"That's what the nursery is for, see," said the garrulous Vanessa. "The boss is trying to get a plantation working somewhere else. This is getting too hard. Only the last lot of plants died."

It seemed that the answer to whatever had happened to Kaen and Lina would have to come out of the Gaks. Humanoids she couldn't even talk to! If only the Leewit were here. If only the captain were here . . . no. He would have been doing his best to destroy the entire smuggler base by now. "All right. I've heard enough. I'm cutting you free—well, I'll leave your hands tied. Your base is back there."

"What?" they both exclaimed.

"I'm letting you go. That's what I said I'd do."

They both looked at her. "But . . . we're in the jungle. Outside the perimeter," said Vanessa.

"I'm going further into it. So you're better off here. And I'm not taking you with me," said Goth.

Both of them were silenced. Then Vanessa asked, "Could you give us a lift? Please?"

Despite the situation, Goth burst out laughing. Oddly, that frightened both of them into scrambling out, and running frantically, diving and weaving behind trees.

It was something of a window into their minds, she realized, starting the ground-truck up again. They'd assumed she was laughing for the reasons they'd laugh—which plainly were pretty awful. And there she'd been about to take them a bit closer to the perimeter. Vanessa had said "please," and that even worked on the Leewit.

Goth pushed her way between the huge trees as best as possible—which meant reversing out a few times, something she was not very practiced at. Inevitably on the fifth time, she got the ground-truck stuck. Well, she'd have to walk. The dappled shade was tricky for no-shape, and right now the forest seemed silent and empty. She'd vanish when she needed to, she decided.

Walking was easier to do than drive, but she had no real idea what direction she was going, or how to find what she was looking for. The only form of life she'd seen was a slim, lithe streak of red fur, on a creature with an oddly beak-like mouth. But she'd find them. She'd done enough tracking and hunting on Karres.

Unfortunately, they found her first, and, as Goth didn't see them, she had no chance to hide.

All she knew about it was a sudden agonizing pain in the back of her neck. She grabbed at the spot trying to turn to see what had hit her.

It was a feathered dart, about as long as her hand. As the world blurred and she fell, she saw one of the humanoids peering around the huge bole of a tree, a long pipe in his mouth.

That was the last she remembered, until the world swam into focus again. Looking at her was someone she recognized. Someone, if somewhat older, she remembered clearly from Nikkeldepain.

Lina did not look pleased to see her. In fact she looked very grim. Her first words were not pleasant either. "Young woman, you're dying. Now: You can make that quick and painless, or slow and painful."

Goth tried to sit—and found that she was tied up. Her mouth tasted dreadful, and she felt absolutely wretched. She swallowed. "Lina? I came to find you."

"So they still know my name. You're young to be involved in their vile business. Now, I need to know certain details..."

"Don't you recognize me? I'm Goth...Vala."

Pausert's mother looked at her. And looked again. And then shook her head, and rubbed her eyes as if to clear them. "You can't be! I mean you do look like her...but she'd be ten years older than you look."

Goth managed to laugh weakly. "Nikkeldepain. The Threbus Institute. The makemake stings."

The woman shook her head incredulously. "But...what are

you doing here? I mean...you were such a nice girl. Pausert was heartbroken when you left."

Goth thought that was good to hear, even if she felt like she wanted to throw up. "I'm going to marry him as soon as I'm old enough. Which I already am now."

"But...my dear, what are you doing here? With Pnaden's thugs..."

"Looking for you, obviously. I came the same way you did," explained Goth.

Goth was not prepared for her future mother-in-law to burst into tears. "Dear Patham. I've killed you."

Goth had had enough of being tied up, so 'ported a bit of the cord away and sat up. The world swayed quite a lot, with the effort. "I'm still alive," she said, crossly.

Pausert's mother swallowed, and she struggled to get control of her voice. "For now, yes. But it's a slow poison, irreversible. It'll kill you in the next three days. I'm so sorry, Vala." A slow tear ran down her face. "My poor girl. My poor son. And I can't even tell him. There is nothing we can do. I'll have them take you to the octagon."

"I'm not planning on doing nothing," said Goth. "I don't suppose you've gotten any blankets or thick jackets? You need to wrap me up."

"It's the effect of the poison on the darts. It's really very warm."

"I'm not cold, Lina. I need them for padding. I'm going to have to leave you. And I don't think I can take you with me."

"You can't leave. The only ship..."

"Well," said Goth "They can't leave either. I took a few parts out of their ship. I have my own method of traveling. It's hard. I would try and take you, but I feel so rotten that I don't think I can. Stay safe. I'll be back."

"But Vala," protested Pausert's mother. "I'm sorry, but you'll lapse into unconsciousness in about three hours. You can't fly a ship. We're too far from an Empire hospital, even if they could do something, for you to get there. Each time you wake after that will be shorter. The best I can do is to take you to the octagon..."

"The best you can do is get me some blankets or coats. Now. Trust me."

The woman looked doubtful. "I..."

Goth was feeling really wretched again. "Look. Everything you heard about your Uncle Threbus is true. He's my father, and I can do even stranger things. Now please, get me some padding, quickly. Or I will go without it, and that can get me hurt."

"Threbus!" She exclaimed, shaking her head, disbelievingly. But she got up and left the little leaf-thatched room, and soon returned with two of the little hominids helping her to carry a large bundle of soft bright-colored fluffy fabric, the color of the creature she'd seen in the forest. "Is this any good?" asked Pausert's mother.

"Wonderful." Goth struggled to her feet. "Can you and the little aliens wrap me in it? I'll give Pausert your love. I'll try and come back soon. I have the coordinates."

"But...you're dying. And they're not aliens. They're the Gyak. But we'll wrap you up if it will make you happier. I wish..." She shook her head and stopped. Then said something in the hominid language. They started rolling her up in the fluffy fabric.

"Then I'm going to die after I get back to the captain," said Goth. She was feeling awful, but the Toll pattern in her mind would help with the Egger Route. And...well, if she was dying, there were ways of shutting down her body and mind, a defense Karres witches used as a last resort. Rescue would have to come to her then, but it would slow everything in her body down. Right down, to the point where she'd seem dead. She'd be as close to being in stasis as could be, without a stasis chamber.

It might still not be enough, she knew, as she slipped into the betweenness that was the Egger Route, and swam toward the *Venture*. Karres people did not die easily, but they did die.

CHAPTER 14

The *Venture* had made an uneventful if crowded journey to Marbelly, and discharged their grateful passengers. They set out again on the long leg to Na'kalauf.

On the evening watch of the third day, the captain and Leewit both became aware of the distant drumming vibration of the Egger Route. The captain wasn't sure if people who were not Karres witches even felt it. But both of them hastily grabbed things to cushion the incoming person.

The captain desperately hoped it would be Goth. Nothing, he realized, could make him happier.

But when it was, and he saw her face, the happiness was erased by fear. She looked as if she were dead. She lay there, flaccid, eyes open but glazed as they tore the fabric around her away. The captain felt frantically for a heartbeat, but just felt the faint vibration of the Egger Route. The Leewit, however, was already busy at what she did best. With great effort, Pausert pulled his hand from Goth and put it on the Leewit's shoulder, willing himself to lend her his klatha strength. To the last drop, if need be. He deliberately didn't say or do anything to distract her, until she stood up.

"Is she dead?" he asked, full of despair and rage at himself for letting her go without him.

"Huh? No," said the Leewit. "Just let's take her to a bunk. This is going to take a while."

Pausert felt his knees almost buckle. He thought if he was going to fall over with relief, it might as well be next to Goth. He knelt down next to her. She was no less pale and her eyes were still open and unseeing. "But I couldn't feel her heart."

"It's beating. Just fast and shallowly. Pick her up, Captain, or do I need Ta'zara to help you?"

Pausert picked her up as if she were a fragile piece of precious ten-thousand-year-old porcelain. She'd grown a lot from the scrap just entering her teens, which she had been when she came aboard the *Venture* the first time, although she was still slender. But right now he could have carried her if she were made of lead.

"What is wrong?" he asked as he carried her to her cabin. No one, not even as crowded as they were, had been allowed in there.

"Poison. It's pretty nasty," said the Leewit.

"Can you heal her?" he asked desperately.

"I hope so," growled the Leewit. "But the sooner I get working the better."

Pausert got Goth onto her bunk at a run. "What can I do?" he asked, full of a terrible helplessness. Right then he'd have given up all his klatha skills, his ship—anything, just to make her well.

"Going to need to cut this cocoon off her. Scissors. And we need to get fluids into her. Tell Ta'zara I need him—I'll tell him what to prepare. And then you'll have to lend me your strength again."

Pausert rushed out to find Ta'zara and scissors. He nearly knocked over Vezzarn. "Take over the helm," he said briskly. "Where's Ta'zara?"

"In the mess..." The spaceman never got a chance to finish, before the captain ran off. Ta'zara was in the mess, with Me'a and both of her Na'kalauf bodyguards. "The Leewit wants you. Goth's cabin!" he said, and turned and ran back, beating Ta'zara by seconds.

They cut the beautiful fabric away from Goth, not caring how magnificent it was. Ta'zara was sent running to the robobutler, and the captain stood and lent his strength. He was rewarded by a blink and the faintest movement of Goth's mouth, as the Leewit worked her klatha skill.

And then she stopped. To Captain Pausert, Goth looked no better. Yes, he could see a faint rise and fall of her chest and her staring eyes had drooped closed. But she was still ghost-pale and very still. "What's wrong?" he demanded. "Why did you stop?"

The Leewit sighed, and said, "Because I've clumping well done what I can for now." She sounded much older than her years. That wasn't the Toll pattern talking, just a really tired Leewit. Pausert was feeling exhausted himself, just letting her draw on his strength.

"But..."

"I can't just fix it," said the Leewit. "There are millions of cells involved."

"But...is she...?" He knew he was pleading for reassurance, scared she could not give it.

"I've destroyed the poison. Stabilized her as best as I can. Got her liver producing...what is the word? Enzymes. I've done as much as I can. Now...it's just time. And hoping it's enough."

Pausert squeezed her small shoulder. "You've done more than you should. I can feel it, little one. Eat. Rest. I'll sit with her."

"I want her well as badly as you do, Captain." There was a catch in the Leewit's voice.

"I know. Eat and rest now."

"You need to eat and rest too. I leaned on you a lot there. Drew from you."

Pausert shook his head. "You send someone with food. I'll call you if there is any change."

The Leewit shook her head. "Going to have to get some more fluid into her. In through the veins, if need be. I've never done that before. Got to learn."

"I have, mistress," said Ta'zara. "We are trained in battlefield medicine. I have brought the drinks you ordered. Also the ship's medical kit. It has intravenous drip kits." He looked at Goth. "Finding a vein will be hard."

The Leewit nodded slowly, thoughtfully. "I need to drink some high-energy fluid myself. Then I will direct you." That was the Toll pattern speaking, through the Leewit. "I can feel the needle from the inside of her. I'll drink the drink you brought me for Goth."

A few minutes later the Leewit sat with her hand on Goth's arm—with a temporary tourniquet made with some of the fabric, and gave Ta'zara instructions. Pausert noticed she had gritted teeth through a lot of it. But they got a drop of dark red blood out of the needle and were able to take off the tourniquet and to hook up the drip bag.

"Phew. That was the clumping horriblest," said the Leewit, rubbing her own arm. "I had to open up and feel that needle. Now I am going to get a big stack of pancakes and Wintenberry jelly. I'll send some up for you, Captain. I hope we don't need the Sheewash Drive, because I don't think I could push a noodle, never mind the *Venture*."

"I hate to ask, Leewit. But . . . should I try the Egger Route to Karres with Goth?"

The Leewit shook her head. "Kill her for sure. That's why she's in such bad shape. Mind you, it was going to kill her anyway. The ionization burn was pretty minor, even if it says someone tried to shoot her. But that was not all by a long way. She had to take the Egger Route. That was a nasty poison that she got into her. Came in through that little wound on her neck. That's going to scar badly. It has killed quite a lot of the tissue."

"Someone is going to be very sorry for this," said Pausert, between gritted teeth.

"If they did this to Goth, they probably already are," said the Leewit. "Or you and me can take it in turns. Being a healer is teaching me some really nasty whistles. Bust them up inside."

That was an aspect of the Leewit's klatha healing skills that the captain had never thought about. Anyone who could stop you dying could probably make you wish you were dead.

Pausert sat in the cabin with Goth through the entire night-watch. His only comfort was that she was warm, had a pulse and was breathing. Ta'zara brought food. The Leewit came and put her hands on Goth—and curled up on the chair and catnapped. The little rochat slipped out of her collar and glided onto the bed, before Pausert could stop it. It sniffed curiously at Goth—well, not so much at her as at the remains of the fabric she'd been wrapped in. It ignored Pausert trying to quietly chase it away, and snuggled in next to Goth. Pausert couldn't see what harm it was doing, so he left it be. The Leewit didn't sleep for long, but woke and checked Goth again. She looked unusually grim and worried.

"What is going on?" he asked. "Is it getting worse?"

"Not really. It's . . . she's not really winning . . . or really losing. The fluids have helped. She seems to have a secondary infection of some sort too."

"Can you deal with it?"

The Leewit shook her head. "I was going to, and I can. But that'd be cleared through her liver. That's got enough to cope with right now. And it is giving her a fever, which means the poison isn't working as well as it could. I should have thought of that."

"Your rochat has taken a liking to her," said Pausert, pointing to the creature's nose, just visible next to Goth.

"Little pest," said the Leewit. "Runs off and leaves me for somewhere warmer. They're like that, Captain. She's feverish, so she's hotter'n me."

"So what do we do now?" asked Pausert, feeling terribly helpless.

"More IV fluids, more watching and waiting. If she loses any more ground I'm going to have to dismind her and put her in deep-tran. You remember. Like Olimy when he had the encounter with Moander."

Too well did Pausert remember. The Karres agent had survived, but it had needed all the skills of a team of Karres healers to see that it happened—and Pausert knew that it had been touch and go.

Waiting and watching was hard. But by the time the second IV drip was nearly done, Pausert had some relief at least, seeing Goth move. She was trying to burrow deeper under the covers. He felt her forehead and it was hot—so he woke the Leewit. "Sorry," he said, as she yawned. "But she's feeling really feverish to me. It is temperature-controlled in here, and she's acting really cold."

"Cold," said Goth, in a tiny weak voice, so quiet it could barely be heard.

"We'll get you something warm," said Pausert. "Just lie still."

"Captain?" she said, blinking. "Can't see properly."

Pausert squeezed her hot little hand. "It's me. You're safe back on the *Venture*."

"Don't leave me."

"I'm not going anywhere," he said, keeping his voice calm, somehow.

He was rewarded by a faint squeeze from her hand. She was shivering. "Right," said the Leewit. "Time to do some more."

"Leewit?"

"Yeah. It's me, big sister. Now shut up and let me work. My turn to say that to you now." The Leewit's voice cracked slightly, but her hands were steady.

The next few days would forever feature in Pausert's memory as a long, grim, terrifying blur. Fortunately, they were in an area of space that made little demand on his ship-handling. But it was three days later that the Leewit, having been called by the captain because Goth was sweating buckets, put her hands on Goth and started to cry, tears streaming down her face. Pausert went through a moment of utter horror...and then realized the littlest witch of Karres was smiling. "We've clumping done it, Captain. She's turned the corner."

The relief left him weak at the knees. "Why is she sweating like that?"

"Fever breaking. We can change her sheets soon, and make her comfortable. She's going to sleep for a fair while." She looked at him. "And so are you."

"I want to be here if she wakes. I've slept often enough in the command chair."

The Leewit looked hard at him. "You'll go to bed now, or I'll have Ta'zara drag and tie you there. She'll sleep now for at least twelve hours. I've seen to that."

The captain yawned. "Wake me in ten, then. I have some ship and astrogation chores I had better see to."

"Wake yourself," said the Leewit, with a shadow of her usual impish grin. She yawned too. "I'm going to get Ta'zara to give me a hand with the sheets and go and crash onto my bunk. And sleep until I wake up."

The Leewit had been rigid about being woken every two hours to check, and had only slept because the Toll teaching pattern let her know it was essential. That was enough to send the captain to his own bunk, only stopping to pass the order to wake him on to Vezzarn.

He woke before being called, and went via Goth's cabin to the bridge. She was sleeping peacefully, with none of the tossing and turning discomfort he'd seen for the last few days. Her forehead was cool to a careful touch, and, though she was still ghost pale, there was just a hint of color about her cheeks. He went down to the bridge whistling—only to stop suddenly, because the command chair was occupied by Me'a.

"Is there something I should know about you taking control of my ship?" he asked.

"Other than the fact I have a spaceman's ticket, and Vezzarn also needs to sleep, no," said Me'a. "I assume by the whistling, that there is some improvement in your new arrival?"

"Yes." The captain realized that Me'a would likely have known that Goth wasn't actually on board when they left Cinderby's World. "But that is Karres business, Me'a."

"I feel that if Sedmon of the Six Lives doesn't know that the Karres witches don't actually need spaceships to travel, he doesn't need to know. Although it doesn't seem to leave the user in a good state."

Pausert opened his mouth to explain, realized she was fishing, and smiled. "I'll need to do some astrogation checks. You can stay there. Seeing as you're available and qualified I may as well use you."

He checked their course, checked the fuel levels, and ran a few checks on the telltales in the engines. The *Venture* was running as smoothly as if new, rather than having been built generations ago. He patted the old pirate chaser's console affectionately.

"She's a good ship," said Me'a. "A lot faster than she looks, and well cared for."

They were words that were music to the captain's ears. "Flattery, Me'a. What do you want?"

She laughed. "You've been taught well, Captain. To satisfy my curiosity, of course. But I don't think I will get the answers I want."

"Not likely. I haven't got them," said Pausert, standing up. "If you need me, I'll be in Goth's cabin. Page me."

She nodded. "That does at least answer one of my questions, Captain. I had wondered, given the briefing I was sent from Uldune."

Pausert decided to go while he was at least leaving her wondering about some things.

Goth was still asleep when he'd gotten to her cabin and she stayed that way until after the Leewit arrived. "Huh. Goth, you lazybones," said the Leewit, wiping the last of her breakfast off her chin. That was enough of a change in way she'd treated her older sister from the last few days, enough of a return to normal to help the captain relax a bit. The Leewit put her hand inside the covers and onto Goth's neck.

Goth tried to burrow away from it. "Get your cold, sticky

hand from off me," she said, sounding at least something like her usual self.

In reply, the Leewit simply pulled the covers off her head. For a moment Goth looked daggers at her, and then caught sight of Pausert, and started smiling and reaching out a hand. The captain knelt down next to her, took it and gave it a squeeze, his voice too choked up to say anything.

"The two of you look like stunned breadfish," said the Leewit in disgust. "And I'll have my rochat back, you pet thief." She stuck her hand under the cover and emerged with the lithe creature, which she popped into her shirt.

The captain finally managed to find his tongue. "I've missed you," he said. "So much." It wasn't his best speech, but Goth seemed to like it a lot, because she struggled up enough to try and hug him.

"I didn't know if I'd see you again, Captain," she said in his ear.

"You're safe now, little one."

"Not sure if I am. I got poisoned."

"You sure did," said the Leewit. "Me and the captain are going to have a little meeting with whoever did that."

Goth shook her head. "I don't think they meant to."

"Going to teach them to be more careful then," said the Leewit. "You worried me stiff. And it's your job looking after the captain, not mine. I'm not doing any more of this 'responsible' stuff. Now lie down. You're getting better, but you're as weak as a newborn bollem. An' I don't want my work undone."

Pausert gently put her down. "She kept you alive, Goth. I think for now you better listen to her," he said, his heart full of happiness. "Even if she doesn't wash behind her ears unless we tell her to."

"Do so!" said the Leewit, and blew him a raspberry.

Goth managed a laugh. "I guess it's not just a great dream. No one could dream anything quite like you, Leewit. You're right. I do feel pretty weak and battered."

The Leewit had taken hold of her shoulder again. The captain knew by now she was using touch to "read" her patient. After a moment, she withdrew the hand. "And you're staying in bed for the next while. We'll need to feed you up, but kind of slowly. You frightened me, doing that sort of silly stuff. You shouldn't let her off on her own, Captain."

"I'm not planning to again, if I can help it," said Pausert. "Now could you get her something to eat? I'm not sure what will be best."

"Come to the mess and I'll tell you what to order from the robobutler," said the Leewit.

"I'd like to stay with her."

"You'll clumping well come and carry it back, and make sure she eats, but not too much. I got stuff to do," the Leewit informed him.

And in medical matters, she outranked him, Pausert knew. So he went.

Which was the right thing to do because she wanted to talk to him. "She's made big steps, Captain," said the Leewit, tucking her arm in his, all the rudeness she'd displayed in Goth's cabin vanishing. It had probably been an act, Pausert realized. "But you're to keep her in that bed if you have to tie her to it. She'll lose ground real easy at this stage. Lots of rest, small meals often, not too rich."

The Leewit made a face. "I'd hate that, and I expect she will too. Goth's not good at sitting still. You're going to have your work cut out for you. She won't listen to me."

That was true of the Leewit, too. But as the captain found, not entirely true about Goth's attitude. She didn't give him the trouble he expected, and she was inclined to do what the Leewit told her to. "Not normally, see. Just, well, healing is her klatha strength," admitted Goth.

Goth did sleep a great deal, and it was actually quite hard to get her to eat much. But as the days passed on the trip to Na'kalauf, her appetite seemed to improve. So did the amount of time she spent awake. It took a while for the captain to hear her story—which was probably a good thing, since it gave him a chance to get mad and then at least partly get over it.

"Well, I know where our next destination is," he'd said, gritting his teeth.

"I don't think so, Captain," said Goth, seriously. "I think I need to recover. And I don't think, after all these years, that a little extra time is going to make any difference. She's well established and safe. I told her we'd be back, and Pnaden and his thugs aren't going to be leaving, unless they find the pieces I took out of their ship."

She was very firm about that. When Goth was very firm, it was really not worth fighting, Pausert knew. She seemed to have a reason she wasn't telling him, though.

CHAPTER 15

Goth knew too well just what they were tiptoeing around. She'd come close to dying and she had pushed her klatha use too far and too hard. She had met people whose klatha use had burned out. People who had been hot witches once.

She wondered if it wouldn't have been easier just to do what others who tried to do too much had done: burn up.

But the captain... he'd just been so pleased to see her.

So she tried to 'port a glass. All that happened was that it rocked and fell over. That brought the Leewit, who grumpily told her she needed to take it easy.

She tried, but it wasn't easy. Sleeping was the best escape, so she did a lot of it. She was also fighting another demon. She'd gone off on her own mission and she could see why the prognosticators thought she would be better for that. Captain Pausert would have gotten furious and tried to take on the whole lot, head on. But... in a way, she'd failed. This was the first big failure in her life, and she wasn't dealing with it well.

It was with all of this sitting on her, that the *Venture* closed on its next destination, Na'kalauf.

✧ ✧ ✧

Na'kalauf was a water world, a blue jewel hung in space in a setting of moons. From far out they could detect no trace of land, but as they swung into a braking orbit they could see that the blue below was not all uniform. Zooming in on the screens, Pausert could see the color came from traceries of white—bands and patterns of them across the face of the blue jewel below them. He was aware that Me'a, her bodyguards and Ta'zara were looking over his shoulder. "So where are we going? Where's the spaceport?" Goth was up, and sitting in the second's chair, enjoying it. This was the first time the Leewit had allowed it, and it was a beautiful sight.

"So what are all the white lines?" asked the Leewit, peering at the screen.

Ta'zara answered her. "The reefs. The sea breaks onto the reefs. Our Nuii lie inside the reef." His voice was strained—a little higher-pitched than usual.

No one had answered his question about where the spaceport was. So the captain zoomed the view on the screens a little closer. Now one could see the breaking reefs with the deeper blue of the ocean outside and paler turquoise areas within—surrounding endless small islands. "So just where are we going? Where is the main spaceport?" he asked again.

"No one wants to answer in case we start a war," said Me'a, with a wry smile. "We are from different clans. Related ones at least, so it could be worse. There are no spaceports, Captain. Any Nuii that tried to build one would have everyone else go to war with them."

"Why? I mean, Na'kalauf bodyguards travel. They go off-world. So how do they do it?" asked the captain.

"How and why in the same question. 'Why' is because our clans have a long, long history of war and raiding. It is what we are and why Na'kalauf guards are what they are. 'How' is easy. There are lots of beaches to land on. As much of it as you could want for a space fleet, if you choose the tide right. Fortunately we are close to the right tide."

"And if we aren't?" asked Pausert, warily. The *Venture* might be old, but she was his ship.

"Well, your ship is going to end up with her tail in the water, but only on the full flood tide—when all the moons align, on the war tide. But if you choose your time, it is all dry."

"Um, when is that?" The moons varied in size and distance, and didn't look particularly aligned.

"The Tide of the Dead comes around once a year. Our year, that is," said Ta'zara.

Pausert was aware of that prickle of klatha that went with his gambles. He exchanged a quick glance with the Leewit. Both Goth and the Leewit always had that curious lithe tension in their posture, like a hunting miffel. But long experience had taught the captain to spot when that was heightened. Right now the Leewit looked like all that tension was about to explode into action. That was usually pretty messy.

"What's the 'Tide of the Dead'?" the Leewit asked. When she was being like this, all the little-girl speech patterns and mannerisms disappeared. The captain wondered if she put them on, in between, or if this was more of the effect of the teaching pattern in her head. The girls both carried their mother—and some others—with them always. A teaching pattern would have helped him, Pausert had often thought. But they seemed to think it would be better if he learned everything the hard way.

Me'a answered. "The opposite of the flood tide, of course. If all the water is drawn to one side of Na'kalauf, the reefs on the other side have it drawn away."

"I wasn't asking you, Me'a. I was asking Ta'zara," said the Leewit, now definitely sounding very like her mother Toll.

There was a long silence. Then Ta'zara sighed and answered. "It is the time when all of the reefs around the Nuii are exposed. It is uncrossable. No war canoe can get through. The channels are dry, the reef corals are a wide barrier of knives no living warrior could pass through. It is when the battle warning-call sounds, calling the clans from the fields or from the lagoon or reef, home to protect the Nuii—but there can be no possible raid coming to defend from, then. It is the time when the clans call the dead back from the sea. Only their spirits can cross the reef then. The living call them, sing their deeds so they be remembered, so they can stand with their comrades again. Without that they are lost, forgotten. Their war brothers sing their deeds so they can return and guard their kin." He shook his head and turned away, walking rapidly down the corridor to the cabins.

There was a long silence. Finally, Me'a broke it. "His whole clan group was killed. He will have to sing them all home by himself. Their kin will be waiting. That...is unusual, these days. The Imperials frown on the Na'kalauf going to war, and while bodyguards have to come home over the reef at the tide—it is rare. He will have to sing them all home by himself."

"That has to be pretty hard," said Pausert, awkwardly.

One of Me'a's two bodyguards broke that silence. "It is the task of the living to honor their clan dead, to tell of how they conducted themselves, as warriors of the Aiwi, the clan. Then the warriors or the children of the warriors all sing of their deeds, so the dead and the living can hear. He can sing them home, but not of his own deeds, for them. The clan will have to send some of its elders to find any that witnessed, so they can sing of it. The old men travel under the truce flag, and go to ask. It has been done before."

The man paused. And then he continued, reluctantly. "But you have said they have all fled. Fled beyond reaching."

"Yeah. I guess so," said the captain, thinking about it. It wasn't strictly fled as *gotten rid of, back to their own universe*, but that would do. Ta'zara had expected to die in that effort. It was the price he had been willing, almost eager, to pay. He had not expected the witches of Karres to 'port him to safety at the last moment, as the Megair Cannibal fleet slipped through the rift into their own dimension.

He had not expected to have to face this.

"A word, Captain, in your shell-like ear. In private, perhaps," said Me'a.

"There are no secrets between me and my crew, Me'a."

She shrugged. "Very well. From what I have gathered you know nothing of how Na'kalauf's society works. We are a poor world, and our only thing of great value to sell is the services of our warriors. A warrior has an oath of loyalty to their 'warlord.' In the case of the La'tienn oath—which is what almost all off-worlders get, it is simply that of personal loyalty and defense for a fixed period. The loyalty while they serve their contract time is total, and the fighting skills they bring, great. That isn't cheap. Part of the payment goes to their families, and part to the clan—who must care for the family, if the warrior is killed, or for the warrior and their family, if the warrior is injured."

She looked at the Leewit. "There are higher oaths. They are granted, rarely, outside the clan—because they commit the clan too. And they are lifelong. It has been a century or more since that happened with an off-worlder. Ta'zara was part of a new defense squad—a thing of huge cost, to a very wealthy smuggler of illicit substances. A rival to the smuggling network of Sedmon of the Six lives—so he had reason to need them. Their new employer was killed by shrapnel from a missile fired by the Megair Cannibals.

"Ta'zara's squad had no one to die in the defense of, so, strictly speaking, the clan is no longer responsible for providing for those families. Warriors, and bodyguards, die before their 'warlord,' preserving his or her life. Normally, when their charge falls despite their best, the La'tienn walk away. These could not. They lost their lives, and their families and clan lost their income. Not only does Ta'zara have no word of how they died, because he did not see them die, but the families and the clan have lost their breadwinners. It's not a huge clan, but an old and proud one. This is a blow in every way, not just to him but to those families and that clan."

"Um," said the Leewit into the silence after Me'a had finished. "Are you saying I should be paying Ta'zara?"

Me'a's two bodyguards looked surprised. That must be pretty shocking, thought the captain, as the one thing about Na'kalauf bodyguards was that their faces never gave much away.

He tried to decide what to say. But before he could say anything, the Leewit continued. "'Cause it's clumping not like he just works for me. What I've got is his, if he needs it. I clumping well told him so. He always says he doesn't need anything."

"You have it right," said Me'a, approvingly. "It would be an insult to offer money to a La'gaiff retainer. But it is traditional to provide for his needs and give him gifts that he can distribute to his kin. And it is also traditional for the kin and clan of the 'warlord' to thank, in a similar fashion, the warrior for any exceptional services."

"Ah," said the captain, "And when and how is this done?"

"Either at the time of the service, or a time of the warlord's choosing, or for great and signal services, in front of the clan, at the Tide of the Dead. Oh, and because Na'kalauf is a very traditional culture, such gifts are usually made in gold coin. Na'kalauf doesn't hold with banks or credits."

Captain Pausert pulled a face. "There goes another plan."

Me'a looked at Captain Pausert with just the slightest hint of a smile about her face. She never showed much on that poker face, so that was a lot. "I am, as it happens, transporting quite a lot of gold, as I was returning there. Some I have an immediate need for. But having operated in the wider world I would sell some and take payment in a bank draft of Imperial maels. As long as it was transaction with a bank I could trust."

"Like the Daal's bank on Uldune?" said Pausert.

"Why, that is my own banker," said Me'a. "I think I could trust them."

The Leewit, Goth and Captain all looked suspiciously at her. It was the Leewit who spoke first, though. "You trying to pull some kind of stunt, Me'a?"

"Actually, no. For a start I think that would be foolish. I was given very explicit instructions—and a warning about what could happen otherwise—about giving you as much assistance as possible, by the Daal of Uldune. In person, by subradio. That doesn't happen...except it did. My job as much as anything was always to be a step ahead of the Imperial authorities, to anticipate their moves. Anticipation is what I am good at. I guessed you would not know the traditions of Na'kalauf. I worked out that the gold might be useful. Besides, I wasn't going to leave it on Cinderby's World."

The Leewit looked at Pausert. "Captain?"

He nodded. "Consider it done, little one. The *Venture* owes some of her wealth to your pack of cards."

"And," said Goth, "Karres kind of owes him too. So do the Illtraming, although collecting might involve going back there. But from Karres' point of view I have about half a million maels in my purse. If you'll take cash that is, Me'a."

"Half a million!" exclaimed the captain.

Goth shrugged. "It started at a quarter, but a few people tried stupid stuff on me."

"I would accept cash," said Me'a. "Without trying any stupid stuff. There is also the matter of my own debt to the Leewit. I have been thinking about that. I am still free of pain. I am..."

"You and me are going to have a talk about that," said the Leewit. "Soon."

Me'a's normal poker face showed dismay. "You mean...it's not cured?"

"You are," said the Leewit. "But it's kind of more about what you said about this ailment being common on Na'kalauf."

She grimaced. "It's not common. It happens, though. As far as we know—knew—it was untreatable."

"It's treatable. Doesn't even need me. But I have access to memories of healers going back all the way to old Yarthe. They'd never seen it elsewhere."

"The cure would be of huge value to our people. Killing the child, and then parents killing themselves afterward, is the only way out right now. I was very late onset. It was expected I would kill myself."

"Yeah. It's kind of about that late onset," said the Leewit, reaching into her shirt and pulling out her pet rochat. "You had one of these as a pet, didn't you?" The animal squirmed free and jumped across to Goth.

"Yes. It died when I was young. I remember the fur making me sneeze, but I was very fond of it," said Me'a. "You mean the disease comes from them?"

"Nope. It's not strictly a disease. Complicated stuff, to do with your genes. In a way having one of these, making you sneeze... stops the body attacking its nervous system. Kind of like having little fights with your sister," she looked at Goth, stroking the rochat. "Stops you having big fights with someone else. When your rochat died, the disease had nothing to stop it."

Me'a sat there, her lips pursed. Then she made a little *ksck* noise and the rochat—which had been investigating Goth's ear, leapt off her shoulder and bounded over to Me'a. Me'a sat there in her chair, stroking it. There were tears quietly trickling down her face. Eventually she said, "I loved my little Sklar very much. When she died, I said I would never let myself get that close to another animal."

She took a deep breath. "To think I just left Cinderby's World because the business opportunities declined. I may have to go back. But I have sufficient contacts... they breed there, particularly in the tunnels. Strange that they should have such an effect."

"Yeah," said the Leewit with a very odd smile, the kind of smile that always made Pausert wary. "Very, very strange."

"In the meantime," he said, "we have a world down there, and I still need to know where I am setting you down."

"The ever-practical Captain Pausert," said Me'a. "I'll give you the coordinates later—we're on the wrong side of Na'kalauf at the moment. If you set me down, my guards can take a trade boat to their own Nuii. Then you can take Ta'zara to his Nuii. It's relatively close—two days' paddling. It's a little faster by rocket ship. Come, Pa'leto. I think it is time we packed our things. We will be home soon."

The guards said something to each other in their own language, and looked at her. She gave them a wry smile. "My men would like to respectfully buy passage to Ta'zara's Nuii after they finish their contract, bringing me home. They claim that it will be easier sailing. It's not that they wish to be there, to hear Ta'zara sing his brothers home, so they can say they were there. Not at all." She shook her head. "So, Captain. Can we save you fuel? I am so kind. I will take a trading vessel home, and retain my men as guards until then."

"And we'll buy some of your gold off you, so you have less to guard. Just as kind," said Goth. "You've been getting into bad company without me around, Captain," she said, looking at Me'a.

Me'a laughed. "I was going to say 'you have no idea,' but given that Sedmon of the Six Lives wears a special cap to prevent the powers of the witches of Karres, I will merely say, 'Yes, Your Wisdom, he has.' And leave it at that." She turned her eyes to her guards. "Can we go? I have things to prepare."

As soon as the captain heard her cabin door shut, he turned to the Leewit who was feeding salty seaweed crisps to the rochat that had returned to her from Me'a's lap. It was not sure it liked them. "Just what did you mean by 'very, very, strange'? I noticed. I've learned to notice. There was salt in the sugar last time."

The Leewit stuck out her tongue. "I haven't done anything for ages. All this being responsible. But it is strange. The rochat... it gave Goth a disease too. The temperature she had. It might even have fixed her... possibly. If she hadn't just clumping well come down the Egger Route. But it helped. And I found it gave Me'a a kind of treatment too. That was also working, except she wouldn't normally let them near her. And Nady... that drug he was using should've killed him. Only he got a bug from his rochat. It's something that needs a rochat to host it—but it helps the people that catch it from the rochat."

"Pretty good bug. Good for all that ails you."

"Yeah. Except for one thing. It's not the same bug every time.

Somehow the rochat is making some kind of variation, depending on what's wrong. I'm not saying it does everything, but I tested it once I figured it out. It might make you sick, but it's helping your body deal with things that'd kill you otherwise. Diseases just don't work like that. There is something very strange about these little animals."

"Very, very strange indeed."

"Yeah. And that's not all that is strange. When I look inside Tippi . . . she's more like the tumbleflowers than people. I mean, like really alien."

"Yes?"

"Really alien doesn't have bugs that can live easily in humans. It just . . ." she rolled her eyes. "I haven't even got the words for all this yet! It doesn't work like that. Just like the Melchin plant could sort of live in humans, but not breed."

"It does sound like it could still be useful to the people with Me'a's condition."

"Pretty much fix it if they're young when they get the rochats, and keep them. A good deal for the rochats. But that's not all that's odd. I asked Nady. He said rochats had always been around on Cinderby's World. So I did some looking up of stuff. I kind've leaned on that detective inspector to let me look into the history vault. And yeah, in the reports, real early records record three animals. The tumbleflowers, the porpentiles and the rochats."

"Maybe that's where they come from. You said they were like the tumbleflowers on the inside, at the cellular level."

"Yeah. Quite like. But . . . here's the thing, Captain. What did they eat? I mean this little girl is really a greedy-guts, but they all eat. And Cinderby's World has got nothing else."

That was true enough. Cinderby's World was effectively a pretty good place for tumbleflowers or porpentiles and not much else. "Must have come with one of the early spacers, I suppose."

"Could be. But you know what else is weird? That cloth Goth was wrapped in—that's rochat hair. I've been trying to find out where else they could come from. And it looks like Cinderby's World or the Iradalia system."

The captain's klatha gambler's prickle was raising the hair on his neck. There had to be a tie between all of these worlds. But before he could think much more about it, one of Me'a's bodyguards brought a set of coordinates for their landing. He also brought something that probably wasn't much use elsewhere that spaceships landed—a set of tide tables.

Calculating off those the *Venture* had about ten hours to reach her landing spot, and a further six hours before the first small returning tidal water would come into the lagoon around Ta'zara's home village. With six moons, tides on Na'kalauf were complicated... and huge. The water would drop by nearly the full length of the *Venture*, standing on her tail fins. They really didn't want to get the tide chart wrong.

The captain set the *Venture* down as lightly as a feather on the vast expanse of white sand around the feathery green trees of the little island. There was still water in the lagoon, but it clung to the edges of the reef, and there was plenty of near-flat beach to land on. There were two other ships there, too, and another set down a few minutes later. But what really struck the captain as he brought the *Venture* gently to rest was the line of people on the shoreline. Watching.

"They wait to see who has come home," said Ta'zara, heavily.

"Uh. Do they know?" asked the captain. "I mean about the Megair Cannibals."

"I sent word. They know."

CHAPTER 16

The Leewit had spent a fair part of the ten hours successfully convincing her bodyguard that she was asleep, and instead sitting and talking to Me'a, learning a lot more about Na'kalauf, the clans, the honor code, the oaths, and just how everything worked on Ta'zara's homeworld.

She'd clarified a small misunderstanding right at the start. Me'a had suggested she needed a translator, and the Leewit had been able to explain this was not the case, with a fine display of bad words that had Me'a's two bodyguards struggling to keep straight faces.

"Do you know what you just said to me?" asked Me'a.

"Yes," said the Leewit, smiling in a way that would have made the captain careful—but Me'a was not yet quite so experienced. "And I can say some more, if you like." And did.

Me'a sat very still in her chair. And then started to smile. "Do you know how long it is since anyone last called me rude names, at least to my face?" she said in the language of Na'kalauf.

The Leewit sat down and answered in the same language. "A long time, I guess. They didn't want to upset you, because you were crippled, and then, later, because they were too scared to."

"I preferred the latter," said Me'a, the smile vanishing.

"Yeah. I figured. But you don't get either from me."

"I am still adjusting to that. I am . . . not used to it."

"Yeah. You're kind of used to being the cleverest, most dangerous and frightening person around," said the Leewit. "But I didn't come to talk about you. I need know about the Tide of the Dead, and what I gotta do for Ta'zara. Because it needs doing right."

"I would be glad to help." She looked at the two guards. "In fact, I think we would be honored to help. If you two can stop laughing."

That actually made them worse. But they both bowed, and when the first of the two managed to control himself, said that they too would be honored. So the Leewit acquired a lot of background about how the clans of the sea peoples worked, and just what she had to do.

The Leewit went along with Ta'zara to greet his clan elders in the Nuii, to be introduced as the one to whom he had sworn his highest oath, committing himself—and them, if he failed—to defend her. She greeted them—as only the Leewit with her klatha gift of languages could—as if she came from Na'kalauf. That was something of a surprise, plainly, a welcome one, but . . . The clan had known of the deaths of the squad, but it had been made fresh and raw by Ta'zara's returning alone. So after the politenesses had been done, she stood up, and turned to Ta'zara.

"Warrior. I give you leave to remain and speak with your kin. I am honored to have met your clan."

One of the old women got up. "You will honor us by joining us at the feast of the living and the dead?"

The Leewit had had this explained to her. "Yes," she said. "My warrior has no comrades to recount his deed and battles. As his Ta'taimi, even though I am not of the sea people, I claim the right to do so."

There was a collective "ah!" at that, and two of the other elders got up and escorted her back to the *Venture*.

"That went very well," said Me'a.

"How did you know?" asked the Leewit.

"Your escort. If it had gone badly you would not have had one; if it had been so-so, one young man or woman. Good, one elder. Very well, another. You got three: the war counsel, and the old war chief and his brother. Anyway, you said the right things. I am more practiced at reading their faces than you are."

"How do you know?" asked the Leewit. "You were back here. I could have called them tree-bollems with unhappy rumbly tummies for all you know."

"Spy ray," Me'a said cheerfully.

"Huh. You've got a fat cheek. So: Can we see what's going on with Ta'zara and the clan?"

Me'a raised an eyebrow, but flipped out a screen from the arm of the wheelchair.

In the twilight the same three elders came to fetch the Leewit, along with Ta'zara. The captain thought he looked tired and strained, but that was not really surprising. The rest of them had to remain back on the beach away from where piles of dry branches were being piled for the feast fires. "When they have recounted the deeds of their living and the dead, someone will be sent to call us to the feast," explained Me'a. She sniffed loftily. "The food won't be as good as that of my Nuii, of course."

Darkness fell on the atoll. Na'kalauf's sun sank into the sea, and the last redness of it faded behind the dark bulk of the island. The white sand was dim in the starlight. By strict instruction there was not as much as an atomic lamp burning in the ships. The only sound was the distant surf breaking on the outer reef.

And then, somewhere, a lonely trumpetlike sound started. It was enough, the captain found, to start the hair on the back of his neck standing up. The horn call got faster and louder.

"The war call. They call the spirits of dead warriors back across the reef," explained one of Me'a's bodyguards, quietly.

Then there was silence again. And then a single drum beating. Then a second, and then more, and more, and more, as the fires on the dry sands of the lagoon were kindled. "Each family beats the drum for their own dead, answering the call. When a Nuii has no one to answer . . . then its dead are forgotten. Lost. Now, they are home. Now the warriors will sing, and the honor feast will be prepared. Ta'zara must sing for his lost brothers. He will give what tokens he has of them to the lagoon, so they may watch over it. It is hard because he has little from their last battles, and he did not see them fall."

"Well, at least he doesn't have to tell them about them getting eaten," said Goth.

Me'a laughed. "That wouldn't worry them. The sea people used to eat their enemies too, you see. These days it doesn't happen much. But it was only cowardly enemies who were not fit to eat. In case you caught the taint from the meat," explained Me'a.

"No wonder he dealt with the Megair Cannibals so well," said Goth darkly.

"Hush. Your little sister has just stood up and claimed the right to speak for the living."

In the circle of firelight the Leewit felt very alone, standing up in front of all these people she didn't know. She wasn't used to making pretty speeches. Giving them a nice collection of insults in bad language was more what she was used to. Then she realized that Ta'zara had gotten to his feet too, and was standing there, still her bodyguard for life, still the man who had reached through his own breaking to try to defend her. This was as needed as fixing broken bones or bleeding wounds, which was what she did. She was a healer. She could do that well. She could do this well. She had to.

So without embellishment she told some of the adventures in dealing with the Megair Cannibals. She told of his fight with the Melchin's mind-controlled thugs and how he fought, although he was injured and wounded and saved her and her sister. She described in great detail his fight and conquest of Gwarrr the great eater, the Megair Cannibal chief, and his taking control and leadership of the Megair fleet, where he expected to die.

She turned to Ta'zara: "It is said that a brave man knows no fear of the great shark. But a truly brave man is the man who has been savaged by the shark and barely lived, and goes back to the water to face it again. Ta'zara, you faced the shark not once but again and again. For yourself, for your brothers-in-arms, and for me. It is a great honor for my family to have me served by such a warrior. Now: It is customary for the Ta'taimi to reward a warrior for his service." She whistled, and Me'a's two bodyguards came dogtrotting across the sand carrying a small but plainly heavy box, and set it down at her feet.

The Leewit opened it, revealing layers of gold coins. She looked at Ta'zara. Looked at the elders. She realized she'd learned quite a lot in the circus—and not just about fanderbags and circus tricks and the plays Richard Cravan and Dame Ethy produced, but about playing the crowds. She waited for approving grunts to fade to silence. Then, regal as any empress, she said, "Not enough. Not nearly enough. Fetch more."

The two men trotted off, and returned with another box. She repeated the performance. Three more times, she did it. Then she bent down and took a double handful of the coins and put them into his hands. "From my own hands to yours, the gift is given. Use it as you see fit." She could see, both by Ta'zara's astounded face and the approving faces of the clan, that Me'a had instructed her very well on this. She could see the relief in Ta'zara's face. He could not bring his squad home, but he would be able to see his dead squad brothers' families and the clan provided for. She hadn't realized how that must have weighed on him.

He bowed very low, stood up and said, "Thank you, mistress. It is an honor to serve. Not only did you give me my freedom from captivity, you gave me healing, and you allowed me to avenge my clan's dead. That was gift enough. But for this, for my clan brothers and their families, I thank you."

"It is my gift. And it is still not enough. But it is what is in my ability to give," she said formally.

Several of the elders of the clan got up and came over to them. "What's going on?" asked the Leewit, quietly.

"They come to escort you to sit with them," said Ta'zara with the broadest smile she'd ever seen on his face. "It is a great honor. I must sing my brothers home now."

"Ah. Well, you can tell them that Goth can get the stones of the arena to tell the whole story. So there are witnesses," she said.

"That too is a great gift, mistress."

Pausert didn't understand what the Leewit had been saying, or the singing that followed. He got the pride and sadness, but the words themselves meant nothing to him. After the first "shush" from the intent Me'a, who was watching both the distant spectacle and had it on screen of her spy ray, which had her two guards' eyes also glued to it, he left the words to mean whatever they meant. Judging by the three that did understand, it was pretty gripping.

But, watching the Leewit, standing there, he felt a kind of

sadness as well as satisfaction. The little blond waif he used to have to tell to wash behind her ears was growing up. Oh, she'd be back to being the Leewit as soon as she got back on the ship. But soon she wouldn't need him or Goth. She'd probably go adventuring on her own. And then he'd have her to worry about too. A teaching pattern was all very well, and yes, it let the children of Karres grow up and get an education in ways the Nikkeldepain Academy for the Sons and Daughters of Gentlemen and Officers hadn't. But he was still very protective about the youngest of the witches. He was pretty protective of the middle one too, of course. Goth had been happy to be back on the *Venture*, seemingly very happy to see him. He could tell that something was troubling her, but he knew by now she'd only tell him what it was when she was ready to.

After the feasting—and it was a great feast, no matter what Me'a said—they'd all returned to the *Venture*. There'd be two more days of small tides before the huge tide that would make the landing beach vanish, and they'd agreed to spend that time sitting on their tubes and letting Ta'zara have some time with his extended family. There was no telling when the *Venture* might be back this way again.

Ta'zara's face always gave little away, but when they returned to the ship in the small hours of the morning he just looked more at ease. He—not the captain—had carried the fast-asleep full-bellied Leewit back to the ship and up to her cabin.

Once they had put her in her bunk and covered her up and closed the door on her, Ta'zara put his hand on Pausert's shoulder. "My thanks, Captain. That was a great gift, and given with a great kindness and understanding."

"It's more or less the Leewit's share. Besides, you did a lot for us," said Pausert. "She did well tonight, didn't she?"

Ta'zara beamed. "She did very well. Indeed, I think what she said about the shark will become part of the Aiwi's legend. My clan thought I had placed them under an obligation and now they want to adopt her into the clan. She spoke very well." He laughed. "And then she ate very well, which is also important to us. And I too have some peace. Tomorrow, when she wakes, I will take her to meet and talk with my family. My sister, her children, some of my friends from the clan. The elders will want to be visited too. You will not mind waiting on us?"

"We haven't exactly got a deadline for Karoda, and the next leg is beyond the borders," said Pausert with a smile. "Goth says that after all these years there's not really a reason to drop everything and run. I don't know that I agree. I have some unpleasant plans for whoever that dart came from. But Goth doesn't agree with me on that, either."

"Fortunately, bodyguards merely have to defend," said Ta'zara.

Goth was actually having a terrible time. Firstly, she just still felt as weak as a newborn. To someone who had spent her whole life full of energy, it was horrible. All she wanted to do was sleep and cry and she did not approve of either. And secondly... Well, secondly was sort of her own fault. She had said it, and didn't know how to unsay it. When she failed to 'port the water glass, she realized she'd pushed her klatha ability too far. She'd gotten home, but home wasn't Karres anymore. It was the *Venture*, with the captain. It had been a stupid thing to say; but she'd been trying to find a way to tell him. She hadn't even been able to tell the Leewit. The Leewit could fix her body, but she couldn't do anything for Goth's klatha ability. And she'd had that, ever since she could remember. It had gotten stronger with age, and then her ability to read objects had developed—and now she couldn't even 'port a glass. So she'd said, sort of fishing, sort of looking for reassurance, and sort of looking for a way to tell him, "Could you ever marry someone who wasn't a witch of Karres?"

And the captain had told her, in no uncertain terms, that the answer was no. That he was as good as promised not only to a witch of Karres, but to a specific witch. After all, who else could cope with his own erratic klatha powers and help him with the Sheewash Drive in their ship?

Which, under almost any other circumstances, would have been music to Goth's ears.

Later the same day, the Leewit went bouncing off with Ta'zara. It hadn't occurred to the captain that the littlest witch of Karres could have been worried, but watching her doing cartwheels—and falling over on the beach—he realized she had been carrying the weight of dealing with Ta'zara's problems. Now, she plainly felt them lifted from her shoulders, to judge by the shrieks of laughter from the beach, echoing up through the open gangway. Ta'zara was grinning broadly too—and then showed her how cartwheels should be done.

The captain came to realize he wasn't alone, watching them. Goth was still asleep, but Me'a had silently wheeled herself into the bridge. She too was watching the Leewit. "The stuff of legends, Captain. My men will be taking their leave shortly. I have paid them off and they are free to return to their homes. They are eager to do so too, with stories to tell, as well as their pay. They will find trading vessels with the tide." She paused. "Do you mind if I delay my own departure? I wish to speak to the Leewit. I would also be interested in hiring the *Venture* to transport a cargo of young rochats from Cinderby's World—or from Iradalia or Karoda. They also exist there. I have arranged this with certain of my associates of my own clan."

"I'll talk to Goth, when she wakes up. She does the cargoes and the bookings..." The captain looked at the ex–smuggler boss. Well, she knew that they weren't exactly just a tramp merchant ship carrying high-value cargoes on less-traveled routes. "Unless we get other instructions."

"Understood. I know very little of the Wisdoms and their business. Sedmon told me I would be very wise to keep it that way."

Pausert had to laugh. "You're not alone. Half the time they don't even tell me what I'm supposed to be doing. I'm not all that sure they know, or at least not too far in advance."

"But they have placed you at some considerable risk at times, Captain, or so I have gathered from things you and your crew have let slip. They plainly think you can cope."

"Karres' way is to learn or to die, Me'a. If you can't cope you don't belong. They do back us up, but they leave us to it, a lot of the time. We've got...skills, each of us."

"And you operate as a team?" she asked.

"Yes. Well, the younger witches tend to travel in groups. And, um, select or take along a guardian. They don't raise their children the way most Empire worlds do. Many of the older witches do operate alone." Having said that, the captain looked at her suspiciously. "You're fishing again, Me'a."

Me'a nodded. "It is my skill. Or at least one of them. I have been told that I do it well. However, Captain, you need have no fear. I wish the Wisdoms no ill. In fact, I have been considering my own future in the light of the debt I owe. We of Na'kalauf always pay our debts." She made a face. "It's why the sea people have so many feuds. You have given me much to think about, Captain. My men will want to come and pay their respects before they leave, but I will go back to my cabin for now."

The Leewit knew, no matter what anyone else might think, that what she had done to help Ta'zara was just a step. One of many needed. But she couldn't explain that to people. Clumping idiots. She didn't even really understand it too well herself. But her teaching pattern did. And that step had been hard and was behind her now. She was going to have a good time today . . .

In Ta'zara's Nuii, the Leewit found that whatever else she and Ta'zara thought they were doing today, having an easy fun day stopped with the cartwheels on the beach. They knew now that she was a healer. And it seemed all of them thought they were sick, even the ones who definitely weren't. Being a healer meant you wanted to help, but how much help could she give without burning herself out? Fortunately, Ta'zara figured that one out. With the help of some of the elders, he reduced that to just a lot instead of a flood.

But there were people here who needed healing. And some who needed more healing than others, and more time and strength than she had to give.

It was incredibly hard. But the worst came toward the end of the day, when a young couple brought their crying baby to her. In their eyes she could see desperation and fear. On touching the child, she stilled its pain . . . and she understood why it was sore. The baby had the start of the same disease as Me'a.

The Leewit was already exhausted. Fixing that . . .

Tippi stuck her nose out of the Leewit's collar, and it struck the Leewit like a bolt of lightning . . . She pulled Tippi out and held her next to the baby's face. The little girl sneezed, and Tippi wriggled over and sniffed it. She sneezed again. "Phew. All right!" said the Leewit, putting her fingers onto the baby's neck. Down in the cells she could feel the reaction. She held up Tippi. "She needs one of these in the house. Now and always. Look, I think you both suspected she might have Iberra. Living with a few sneezes . . . will stop it developing. She can have a normal growing up and life."

"But nothing cures Iberra," said the father, his face grim. The mother cradled her baby and started to weep, which started the little one up again.

"Do I need to whistle at you to stop that?" said the Leewit crossly. She'd whistled at a few people already that day. Word got around. "It doesn't cure it. It *stops* it."

"Like a shield," said Ta'zara. "I have seen it. It is true."

"Really?" There was desperate hope in the mother's voice.

"I swear it by the spirit of our forefather Ke'taka," said Ta'zara.

"It'll make her sneeze a little at first. But it...it gives the disease a small enemy to fight, so it doesn't attack her. She is little enough that the damage that it has already done will recover and heal."

The father looked at Tippi, at his wife, at the baby and then back at the Leewit. "Great lady," he said. "How long do we have? I cannot get one of these animals soon. They are expensive and rare."

Ta'zara, for the first time since the Leewit had met him, started to laugh. Eventually he managed to get the words out. "There is a price on everything, Je'tara. You will have to stay with my sister. I will arrange, and she will tell me she was right about the smelly little things. And she will tell you how to raise your child, and a great deal more she knows nothing about, but your little girl will be fine. It is high price, cousin, but that is what it will cost you." And then he started laughing again. Maybe it really was that funny, thought the Leewit. But maybe he just had a lot of laughing to catch up on.

It was infectious. The young warrior began to laugh too, holding tightly to his wife. Finally, they got control of themselves. He bowed to Ta'zara. "It is a high price. But my little one is worth it." And then there was doubt. "You are sure it will work?"

"Absolutely certain," said the Leewit. "And Me'a's planning on shipping rochats in. I'll tell her you need one."

"Me'a?" asked the young warrior.

"She calls herself that," explained Ta'zara. "Li'jani of the Katipi Nuii. The daughter of the war chief there, the one who developed Iberra later in life. You see—she grew up with one of these pests. And then it died." He gestured at the Leewit. "My Ta'taimi found out and stopped the disease. It is too late for her legs, but it stopped the pain."

The warrior nodded, belief and acceptance finally getting home to him. Then he drew himself up. "I have very little to gift you with, great lady. But I would offer my service."

The Leewit was starting to get used to the way the sea people thought. She'd not really known what to do with the gifts the people had brought. They were generous, if sometimes not really what one wanted on a spaceship—like the smelly ropes of dried fish that Tippi had found very attractive. The Leewit had been about to say *no, thank you* to the first gift when Ta'zara had caught her eye, and shook his head almost imperceptibly. When they left he'd explained: "It would be an insult. And it is a way of showing that they value what you do, and that they respect you. Something which is given for nothing has no value and is abused."

But now she was faced with someone who plainly didn't have much and was giving her what he had and was willing to give up life with his wife and baby for it. And it was something she didn't want or need. Yet... Ta'zara had explained: that to be offered something and refuse was an insult. The difference between the bodyguarding work most of the Na'kalauf people did and what Ta'zara did was simple: It came in the difference between offering and asking. You could ask a warrior, and he would agree and a contract would be drawn up. That was simple business. But if someone offered... it was different, entirely.

So she took his hands. "You are mine, now, to command."

He bowed his head. "Yes, Ta'taimi."

The Leewit couldn't help but notice that his wife had started to cry again, softly. "And mine to take care of. The respect of the clan comes from how well I do that, correct, Ta'zara?"

Ta'zara nodded. "Your standing with the clan depends on that, yes."

"So I can show off by how well I do it?"

Ta'zara managed to keep his laughter to a slight shaking of the shoulders. "I don't think we would quite put it like that, but yes, mistress."

"Good!" said the Leewit cheerfully. "Then to look after you, Je'tara, I must see to the health and welfare of your child, who is sick. Until she is of an age to look after herself, you will stay to care for her. Then you can come and spell Ta'zara. Or if I send for you."

"But great lady, I am willing..."

"I know you are. But I have responsibilities. To you. And Ta'zara. His sister worries him."

Ta'zara couldn't stop himself laughing at this point. His sister worried him all right. She had a very big mouth, the Leewit had decided. But the young warrior's wife's tears were at least also divided by laughter.

Later, as they walked back to the *Venture*, she asked Ta'zara if she'd done right.

"I am your warrior, not your war counsel," he said. "It is not my place to advise, just to defend and fight for you, at your order."

"Well, I'm telling you to tell me. It's a kind of fight, and a kind of defense," said the Leewit.

"Then I think you did very well indeed. You will have to call him for work, but he has just returned from his last contract. It is customary for men to take some time between contracts, and the Nuii needs some men here. The loss of my clan brothers is felt. Even by my sister... one of those was her younger son."

"Oh!" That did sort of explain things.

"She will find relief in Je'tara's little one. Of course she will constantly tell them what to do. But she has a good heart under it all. It is a gift to me, Ta'taimi. And yes, a good way to show off your status. My clan, who are the best, will now claim they are even better."

The next day wasn't a whole lot easier.

There were queues. And most of them didn't look sick.

"You are now quite famous, and they think you will become more so. Each of them wants to be able to say that they or their child was seen by you," explained her new warrior, Je'tara. "That is partly my wife's fault. She has spent much of the night boasting to everyone about her man's new Ta'taimi. She is determined that if you need to show off, she will help as much as she can."

"Umph. I think I'll whistle at all of them. Those that don't run are really sick," said the Leewit crossly. "I thought I could go fishing or something. Goth and the captain are going fishing. It's not fair."

"I can tell them to go away."

"No," said the Leewit, regretfully. "Tell them I'm going to be especially rude to the ones who are faking."

Unfortunately, as she later discovered, the Na'kalaufer still considered that a treat, and a story to tell.

✧   ✧   ✧

It was a long and tiring day for the Leewit. The tides dictated that they'd be leaving by the next afternoon. And when she got back to the ship, she'd barely had time to sit down and drink caram juice and wonder when Goth and the captain would get back from fishing, when Me'a came in.

"I thought you were going to catch a boat home. We're going to have to charge you rent," said the Leewit grumpily.

"I was," said Me'a, "but I have thought about it for a long time, and waited to ask you something. You have never been anything but rude to me since you met me. Others you are sometimes polite to. But me, never. Why?"

The Leewit looked at Me'a in her wheelchair. "Because I felt you needed it."

Me'a nodded slowly. "It took me some time to work out what you were doing, but I am in your debt. I was about your age when the disease struck me. I think that was the last time anyone treated me as you have. It is a great gift, Your Wisdom. I have thought at great length about what I needed to do to adequately reward you for what you have done for me, and for others who would have suffered my disease."

"I didn't ask for any reward," said the Leewit. "I have lots of dried fish."

"No," said Me'a with a slight smile. "You did not. Instead you gave me more healing. You called me a silly cow. I did not understand immediately. But I think I do now. You showed me neither pity nor fear. Not showing pity... that I understood. It took me a little while longer to work out how powerful you were, that you need not show fear because you could kill if you wished to. If you can reach into people to heal, you can reach into them to kill."

"I didn't mean it that way. I just did what I always do."

"I know. It is as much part of you as breathing. You showed yourself to be someone whom it would be an honor to serve, to be my Ta'taimi, if you will accept my service. It is fitting that you should be rewarded with what I have. I am Me'a, and I pledge myself to your service. You may not see that you need me yet, but you will. Ta'zara is a great warrior. I am a great organizer. A tactician, of some repute, it is said."

"Can you play poker?" asked the Leewit.

Me'a nodded. "Not very well. It's been a long time. I am sure you will explain the rules to me."

The Leewit looked darkly at her. "Huh. With an answer like that I'm gonna have to stick to playing for points, not money. That takes the fun out of it."

"Chicken stakes," said Me'a, cheerfully. "Never more than a tenth of a mael."

"Why do feel I'm being suckered?" said the Leewit.

"Because you are. It adds up remarkably quickly, and is much easier to lead someone into debt with just little bets. It will, of course, be my privilege to instruct my Ta'taimi into certain skills."

"And," rumbled Ta'zara, "to recall that as her hearthman what you win is the property of the Ta'taimi."

The Leewit turned to him. "So...what do you think?"

Ta'zara smiled. He seemed to find that so much easier now. "She is a very bad woman. She cheats at cards, and she is good at that. Her bond-guards told me so. But my work is not to think for you or decide for you. I am your warrior, not your war counsel."

"If I were your war counsel, which I am not," said Me'a, "I would point out that the captain and your sister plainly intend to marry. And in the fashion of marrying people, they may well settle down for some years and have children. It is my thought that the Leewit does not plan to settle down just yet."

"No," said the Leewit gruffly. "You got something there. Goth's going just like Maleen. All soppy. I still want to go back to the circus."

"I could assist. Arrange. Do some of the tasks the captain does, while Ta'zara provides the rest, and I have some skills that could get us out of trouble," said Me'a, persuasively. "You are, of course, the Ta'taimi. You decide and you order. But as far as many of the worlds of the Empire are concerned—they will treat you as a child. I can act as your proxy. Fool them that I give the orders."

"I think I am going to talk to the captain about it," announced the Leewit, and went off to do so. She found him and Goth in the control room, having just gotten in from their fishing expedition. Holding hands. It did make a sharp point out of what Me'a had said. Both he and Goth looked...very happy. Like they were sort of part of each other.

Abruptly, the Leewit realized that they were, or would be soon. Goth was of marriageable age now. She and the captain had always had a tight bond, but the nature of it was changing. The

Leewit swallowed hard. She didn't like changes, as a rule—and this one was going to be especially hard on her.

"Come to talk to you two," she announced. Goth didn't take her hand away from the captain's, she noticed. That had changed too.

"We're listening," said the captain.

"Yeah. Well, you two are going to get married, aren't you?" asked the Leewit.

"I told the captain about that long ago," said Goth. "When we get back to Karres. If this trip takes too long, I'll be on the shelf," she said with a laugh.

The Leewit didn't find it funny. "Yeah. Well, I figured. So I better do some planning. 'Cause I'm not going back to Karres yet."

The captain looked startled. "But..." he paused, looked at Goth, inquiringly.

Goth shrugged. "She was too little to go off on her own when we went to Porlumma. But she wanted to come. And the prognosticators told Toll and Threbus you'd be along. I guess they have plans now too. Usually younger ones get paired or grouped. We're kind of free agents...sort of."

"I'm busy making plans all by myself," said the Leewit. "Well, with Me'a. And Ta'zara."

Goth grinned. "You know, I was just saying to the captain that I'd bet that Me'a had made some kind of plan to come along."

"So...you think it's a good idea?"

"I think she would be hard to stop," said the captain. "Or at least hard to stop her following us. And it'll be easier to watch her from close by than when she is following us in her own ship."

"She's got her own ship?" asked the Leewit.

"It set down yesterday." Goth pointed to a ship visible on the viewer. "She came up to the bridge and asked us if she might contact her. Maybe she doesn't want us to know she's gotten her own communicator. Maybe she was just being clever, figuring out not telling us would make us mad when we found out. I reckon she is pretty smart. She's the kind who likes to think a few steps ahead all the time."

"Which is fine until the steps don't go the direction you thought they would," said the captain.

"We *could* stop her," said the Leewit. "I mean she's rich and sneaky, but we've got klatha."

"Yep. But do you want to?" asked Goth. "She's even got a ship for you to use."

The Leewit turned away hurriedly, because she hadn't wanted to think about that. When the captain married Goth...the *Venture 7333* was his ship, not hers.

The captain seemed to know what she was thinking. "This is your ship too. There'll always be space on her for you." He paused. "Unless you put another stink bomb in the air recycler."

That made her laugh. "Going to clumping well have to think of something worse now!" And she went off to find Me'a and Ta'zara.

"I think that they think it's a good idea. Why didn't you tell me you have your own ship?" she asked Me'a.

"Because it is never good to show all your cards. That is something the Wisdoms of Karres know, don't they?" She rolled her chair forward and held out both hands, palms up. "Will you accept my service?"

The Leewit looked at her. "So what am I supposed to say? If you were being my advisor." She spoke Na'kalauf, because of her klatha skill, and she knew the word didn't quite mean *advisor*. More like *war counselor*.

"Put your hands on mine and say, 'Yes, I accept you. You are mine,'" said Me'a.

"Is that all?" asked the Leewit.

"Yes. It doesn't really matter quite what is said. That is where the Na'kalauf's people differ from the Empire. Binding is easy. The more serious it is the easier it is because there are fewer conditions. For La'gaiff, there are no conditions at all. It is the unbinding that is hard. So you do not bind yourself lightly. I have considered this and reached my decision." There was a calm certainty in Me'a's voice.

"And what is my side of this?" asked the Leewit. "I haven't got much gold. And I have to leave some with young Je'tara."

"Such gifts are the traditional reward for great service," said Me'a. "Which I would still have to do. And I have a lot, and as my property is now yours to use, it will not be a problem. You can make it my task to see to it."

"All right then," said the Leewit. "Do it."

CHAPTER 17

The trip to Iradalia-Karoda was relatively uneventful other than the normal happenings of interstellar travel. There were a few encounters with possibly hostile ships, but no need for the Sheewash Drive. Navigationally it was quite a clean piece of space. They did what was normal on such legs—the *Venture* got cleaned, checked over, and the Leewit played cards with anyone she could. Even Me'a.

"I should command you to stop beating me," she said sourly.

"Of course. If that is your command," said Me'a.

"No. That'd be no fun then," the Leewit grumbled. "My turn to deal."

The captain spent some of the trip learning more wrestling skills from Ta'zara. It was a useful way of working out his limits, and working up a sweat.

Goth spent her time—very much in private—trying to 'port things. And to her horror, failing. There didn't seem to be a teaching pattern to tell her what to do. And she just couldn't bring herself to talk about it, yet. Not with anyone.

The Iradalia-Karoda system was rather beautiful, if you looked at it from space. One reddish and one bluish world spun in close orbits around each other. The binary planet had several rings around it, obviously the remains of moons that had met each other a bit too closely. "Wonder how long before the whole thing falls apart," said the captain, looking at the place on the forward viewscreens.

"If you live on Iradalia—that's the bigger, redder one—you believe it is only the divine grace of Irad that stops it happening tomorrow. If you live on Karoda you know they're getting a tiny bit further apart," said Me'a.

"You've been here before?" asked Goth.

"Early in my career. Iradalia produces some lovely gemstones, the export of which is very highly taxed. And of course there is a rich profit in avoiding their import and transit taxes and customs."

"And Karoda?" asked Goth.

Me'a raised her eyebrows at her. "Bespoke slaves. Willing slaves, who like being slaves. I don't know what they do to them, but that left nothing for us to make money on. Karoda had nothing of inter-est to smugglers, and is not an easy or safe base. We make most of our profits by not giving monies to governments and selling goods which the government laws don't allow. Karoda doesn't have taxes, or even much in the way of laws. It's a pretty wild place, as the Iradalians find out every time they've tried to invade it."

"Oh. I gathered there was some sort of war going on," said the captain, fishing.

"There has been for centuries. It's quite funny in some ways. It's a bit one-sided, really. Karoda's people can't be bothered to do more than womp their troops every time the church of Irad sends them in. Iradalians tend to make pretty bad fighters. Very few of them know which end of a blaster shoots, and even wrestling is considered evil in the sight of Irad. A hundred Na'kalauf warriors could walk all over Iradalia in a month. If Karoda was organized, or could be bothered, they'd go over and flatten the place."

"Why do the Iradalians keep trying then?"

Me'a shrugged. "It's supposedly about the slaves. But Iradalia makes a lot of their state's money out of taxing those same slaves."

"What?"

"They control the rings. Any ship getting in or out of Karoda needs to pay transit visas, and their goods pay a transit tax," she explained. "So: Karoda makes a lot of money out of Karoda slaves, but Iradalia's main source of income is ships going in and out.

They even charge tax on the slaves. They claim that is intended to make the immoral business too expensive."

"I thought you said Karoda could lick them in a fight," said the Leewit.

"Yes, but they'd have to want to. And get organized enough to do it." She grimaced. "The Karodese don't organize well. Or take orders well."

"You say they charge transit visa fees... I think I just figured out that we got burned on that cargo," said Goth with a scowl. "We got paid to transport it. Now we'll have to pay their taxes."

"Sneaky."

"But I thought Karres organized that cargo," said the captain. Goth had taken over looking after the *Venture*'s money, which he had found a relief. She was good at it, and seemed to like doing it, as much as the Leewit liked playing cards.

"Yeah. It's still booked through us, though. I reckon we'll get it back," said Goth, sounding cross. "But someone set out to cheat us."

"Karres is not in the business of destroying every cheat," said the captain.

"Huh. We gotta clumping start somewhere," answered the Leewit. "It might as well be with them."

"Maybe later. We've got our primary job to deal with, remember," said the captain.

"If I might ask," inserted Me'a, "what is this primary job?"

By now they all knew that Me'a knew a fair amount about Karres—as much as Sedmon of the Six Lives did. But after talking it over with Ta'zara privately, they were pretty sure her oath to the Leewit was a near unbreakable one, so the captain didn't try to avoid the subject. "We're here to stop the war between them."

Me'a shook her head. "Captain, you may as well try to stop the tide. The war has gone on for centuries. It'd only end if one side won. And that can't happen short of sterilizing one or other planet. Karoda wouldn't give up while there is one living person left, and they're a culture that lives by their guns and fights all the time—except when the Iradalians attack, when they all go after them. Iradalia believes they have a religious duty to conquer Karoda, but they... well let's just say you can't train soldiers when you have none, and most of your instructors don't know which end of a blaster shoots, and mostly end up running away. You're not even allowed to have a weapon on Iradalia. They'd have to hire mercenaries, and they won't do that because they believe it is the duty of true believers in Irad to destroy the evils of Karoda."

"All the evils . . . or just slavery?" asked Goth.

"All of it. Slavery gets talked about most, but really the whole way of life on Karoda is something the Church of Iradalia can't handle."

"And the church gets to decide?" asked Goth.

"Iradalia is a theocracy," explained Me'a. "The high priests decide everything."

"It sounds pretty terrible."

"For some understandings of terrible," said Me'a. "They're very kind. No one starves. Everyone gets rations. Everyone does what they're ordered to."

Something about the way she said it plainly made the Leewit suspicious. "And if they don't?"

"Well, the priests' secret police would kill you. It's not a society for disagreeing," said Me'a.

"I understand why Karres doesn't want them winning. They didn't want Karoda winning either. The prognosticators say both would be bad," said Pausert.

"There's no pleasing some people," said Me'a. "Seriously, for Karoda to win, Karoda would have to change, become organized, and then yes, they'd be dangerous." She looked at Ta'zara. "When it comes to combat with arms, at range, they are better fighters than the warriors of Na'kalauf. They do that all their lives, and have for centuries."

"They sound really friendly," said Goth in a sarcastic tone.

Me'a smiled. "They are. Provided they feel like it. Everyone is armed, and everyone is ready to use those arms. They're mostly very polite, very honest and very friendly. It's when they stop being that that it that turns ugly fast." She looked at the Leewit. "Best not to call them names first, Ta'taimi."

"Huh," said the Leewit. But it was a thoughtful *huh*.

They were soon in hailing frequency. It was demanded what ship they were, and their destination. Captain Pausert gave their current identity, and their destination as Karoda.

The voice over the communicator informed them they would need to dock at the customs asteroid, and gave them the coordinates. "All cargo for Karoda need to be inspected by customs priests of the Theocracy of Iradalia, and you need to pay the appropriate transit taxes. Attempting to evade these will result in your ship being destroyed."

The captain snapped the communicator off, having seen the Leewit drawing breath. "You can't whistle at them. And you can't use dirty words on them either," he said, sternly. "I'm still the captain here."

"And you'll probably get a chance once we're being inspected, little sister," said Goth. "Iradalia sounds like it might make Nikkeldepain look like a fun place."

"It's rather dull," admitted Me'a. "Except of course when they decide you're going against the will of Irad, like by selling your gemstones instead of giving them to the temple to sell. Or if they catch you selling forbidden goods. Don't be fooled by the customs inspectors offering to buy things in a whisper."

"Anything else we should know about?"

"Sometimes they'll pick on a ship just to make an example of it, but other than that, no."

The Leewit thought the docking facilities on the asteroid outside of the rings were relatively busy, if rather primitive for something that had so much traffic. So were the customs officers. All of them stank of something that made her want to sneeze. Still, it was all going fairly smoothly, until the customs officers went into the Leewit's cabin. That was probably never a great place to insist on searching anyway. It got worse when the white-garbed customs officer said dismissively, "Out of my way. I have work to do, little girl."

"It's my cabin. I'm going to make sure you don't steal my stuff," said the Leewit, folding her arms and pursing her lips slightly, ready.

The Iradalian customs officer looked affronted at that. "You cannot stop me pursuing my duty. Aha! Officer Shimdram!"

The other customs man came in too. So did Goth, behind him, from her cabin which he'd just finished inspecting. "Look!" said the first customs official. "Blasphemy!"

He was pointing at her latest picture. The Leewit liked painting. It wasn't her fault that paint sometimes liked her too. She was getting better at it. In this case she thought she'd actually done a pretty good job of painting the planets and the sun. It was pretty with the rings.

"What is this?" demanded the customs officer in a tone of horror.

"It's a picture, you stupid kranslit," the Leewit informed him.

"It is not permitted to make images of Irad! We shall have to confiscate it," said the customs officer.

"What picture?" said the Leewit, giving Goth a meaningful look. Goth would do no-light and make it vanish. Or play other light tricks and make there be one in every corner...

Only she didn't do either. She just smiled at the Leewit, which wasn't the sort of help the Leewit expected from Goth. She always helped out. Always! The Leewit didn't think she even thought about it. Neither of them did...until Goth didn't.

"That blasphemous image!" said the shocked customs officer. "It will have to be removed and purified, and you will be charged."

At this point things got very noisy. The Leewit didn't see that she could whistle without affecting Goth, but she could yell at them. That brought everyone else—the captain, Me'a, and Ta'zara, old Vezzarn, and at least ten more customs officials.

The Leewit, on a bit more thought, could see that maybe being arrested before they even got to Karoda was not really what the prognosticators of Karres would have seen as a great way to deal with the situation. Or perhaps it was... She had great confidence in the captain's and Goth's skill at breaking out of jails and escaping traps. Even escaping planets. But then, maybe it was time she started thinking about how she'd do it without them.

"All right," she said. "You can have the picture."

That didn't, at this stage, seem like it was enough. And it seemed that neither Goth nor the captain wanted to take it further. Ta'zara had quietly broken the collarbone of the man who had tried to put his hand on the Leewit's wrist—and Me'a had somehow positioned herself in her wheelchair in front of the Leewit. "Is it not written that no man shall lay his hand on the daughter of another, without consent?" she asked, pointedly.

The result was them being herded out of the *Venture* to the office of the chief customs official. He looked, the Leewit thought, like he had had indigestion—for about twenty years. "I think we'll make an example of you," he said, looking at the *Venture's* current papers and manifest. "An example..."

He stopped suddenly. Looked again at the manifest. "Oh. Er. It's really a small infraction, Officer Shimdram. Stop making such a fuss and let them go." He gave the captain an insincere smile. "A misunderstanding. There will be a small fine, twenty maels, added to your visa and transit tariffs. That will be . . . ah . . . three hundred and fifty maels. If you pay the clerk on your way out you can depart immediately."

"But . . ." protested the customs officer. "They attacked Officer—"

"Not another word, Shimdram," said the chief sternly, casting another look at the manifest. "You're in trouble. Remain here. You . . . Officer Walbert. See these good people back to their ship via the cashier. You do have the funds to pay, Captain? Otherwise, if your cargo is cash on delivery as they sometimes are, it could be settled on your return."

"I think we'll just pay it," said Pausert. "Thank you very much." And they followed the suddenly nervous customs official out.

Within a few minutes they were back on the *Venture*, cleared for departure inward to Karoda. "Captain," said Me'a. "With all respect I think you should take off and head out-system just as fast as your ship can go. Something is very wrong."

"I got that idea too, Me'a. But sticking our necks out is what we do. What did you spot that was wrong?"

Me'a grimaced. "Iradalia breeds petty officials. They never turn suddenly reasonable. The rate that he charged is less than one tenth of the normal. And," she tapped the arm of her wheelchair, "I locked a spy ray onto the chief official. He put a shield down, pretty quick—he had one sitting on his desk—but not before I got one word. Maladek."

"What's that mean?" asked Goth.

"It's the name for their secret police. Their spies, their secret service. Someone has to keep everyone in line. They're a nasty lot. The ordinary people are terrified of them."

"And it had something to do with our cargo. That was our manifest he looked at," said Pausert. "You're right, we're running into trouble. If you like, you can disembark before we leave. You'd get another passage, fast enough."

"That would run contrary to my oath. Besides, Vezzarn informs me that whatever mess the Wisdoms get you into, they get you out of. But I do think we should have a look at that cargo for Karoda"

"It's a load of hyperelectronic forcecuffs."

"All of it? I mean, have you checked the crates?"

"It sure looked like they were all the same," said the Leewit. "I was with that customs snoop on Cinderby's World when he looked. He had a scanner and a bunch of hyperelectronic tools himself. He was comparing weights and densities of the crates. All of that consignment were exactly the same."

"Senior Inspector Dru," said Me'a. "He was one of the sharpest they had, at picking up contraband of any kind. Whatever is there will probably be legal, at least in the Empire. And nothing is off-limits on Karoda."

"Let's open one of the boxes, and have a look. We'll claim 'opened by customs for inspection,'" said the captain. "And have a good look at the works of the thing. After all, we have got an expert on locking mechanisms with us, eh, Vezzarn?" He lifted an eyebrow at the old spacer.

"I'll do my best, Captain," said Vezzarn.

The crate they picked had nothing in it but the hyperelectronic forcecuffs it claimed to have. Vezzarn took a couple to his work desk and was soon peering at the first through his jeweler's magnifier and probing it with his electronic tools. Then he picked up the second. "Hmm," he said, pushing it aside after a few minutes. "It's a standard, fairly cheap forcecuff, each one with an individual resettable access code, Captain. But they've been modified."

"What have they done to them?"

"Well, they've put in a short-range receiver, which will accept a code to override the locking code, so they can be opened and closed remotely. It's the same code pattern, and the same frequency on both."

"So...they can set prisoners free. That could be interesting," said the captain. "Sort of thing Iradalia might arrange, I suppose."

"Your problem, Captain," said Me'a in an odd voice, "is that you are too nice to see into the heads of really nasty people."

"Why? I mean what else..."

"It's a bomb, Captain. A really clever bomb. Looking at the number of crates and the number of forcecuffs, a really powerful one."

"Uh. How..."

"What happens to forcecuffs if you give them the wrong code? Their field expands and goes critical. That would cut a prisoner's hands off. Several thousand—all doing it at once, their hyperelectronic fields intersecting...you'd see it from space. And that is what they want."

"They want to destroy the slavers badly enough to blow up their base and kill some poor slaves who happen to be cuffed with them. Ouch," said the captain. "That's nasty."

"I don't think that is what they want, no," said Me'a, grimly. "They want to know a locality, and attack just that instead of having to try and fight their way across all of Karoda to find it. They fail at that, but if they put a massive force right on a base that had just suffered a huge explosion, they would succeed. The high priests of the temple of Iradalia know that there is, hidden somewhere in the mountains, some device that the Karoda slavers use to indoctrinate people into serving and serving joyfully. It's a lifetime compulsion, and the Karoda slave will find reasons to serve joyfully, whoever they are bound to. They'll even die to make whoever they are bound to happy. You think the high priests of Irad want to destroy it? No. They want to own it, to have it, to use it. They could then make people follow their religion, and do anything they ordered. The first people they'd line up for treatment would be their enemies from Karoda. They'd have some of the deadliest fighters in the galaxy as their loving slaves. And any captives would end up the same way."

Suddenly, the reason why Iradalia winning this war could be far worse than Karoda's slave trade was very clear.

"We could disable their bombs, Captain," said Goth. "Or warn the slavers. I don't like them much after my brush with 'em, but I can see the alternative could be worse."

"Five thousand forcecuffs might be a bit much for Vezzarn, my dear. We'll just have to tell them their cargo is pretty useless."

"Well, Captain, actually," said the old spacer, "I can change the code easily enough. They're all set with the same code. I can access the controllers on the right frequency and give the disarming code. Then, when I have access to their controller, I can reset it."

"That wouldn't help much, if what they plan is sending the wrong code," said the Leewit, seeing the problem immediately.

"There is one other possibility," said Me'a thoughtfully. "If you can gain access to all their controllers, Vezzarn, you should be able to reset not just the codes but the transmission frequency they have to be sent on."

Vezzarn looked thoughtful. "I could do that. It's fairly simple coding. Child's play really. They bought cheap and nasty."

"Good," said the Leewit. "I want to stay and watch and learn it. It could be useful."

"Then I had better too," said Me'a.

A little later, the Leewit finally got a chance to talk to Goth alone, when she took the now modified sets of forcecuffs back to the crate in the hold, and found Goth doing tallies of the goods there. They carried some trading goods on their own account—gambles that the captain felt might pay off, and, given his luck, often did. Goth liked working out the business side, and had done most of the ship's accounts for a few years now. Her way of relaxing herself—if she couldn't take her bow and go hunting—was to count the stock. The Leewit couldn't see why, but Goth liked it and there she was.

"What's going on with you, Goth?" said the Leewit. "You knew I wanted you to do a light-shift on my picture. But you didn't do it."

Goth sighed. "Yeah, well..."

The Leewit poked her in the ribs. "Come on. Tell."

Goth shook her head. "If there is one thing I have learned going off on my own on Karres business, it's that you have to find out what you're breaking up before you just start doing stuff. The captain would never have found out about the forcecuffs and what those smelly Iradalians were planning, if we'd gotten into a fight then and there. And you're getting to the age where you won't have the captain or any other hot witch to turn to, often times. You'll have to get out of the messes on your own, or with Ta'zara and Me'a doing their best. And while their best is pretty good, they can't do klatha. So don't get into messes you can stay out of, just for the sake of getting your own way," she said, severely. "I need you to start learning that."

The Leewit scowled. "You could have clumping well told me, instead of dropping me."

"That's the Karres way," said Goth, turning and walking out.

Goth knew she was going to have to face up to telling them sometime, and soon. She just wasn't quite ready yet. Just as she wasn't ready to try 'porting anything again, yet.

She didn't *feel* any different, here in the comforting cocoon of the *Venture*. She just knew that she was.

CHAPTER 18

Once the *Venture* was safely inside the space debris that made up the very decorative but dangerous rings, and was able to move into orbit around Karoda, it was a case of finding the spaceport their cargo was consigned to. There was certainly no shortage of them, all eagerly broadcasting their wares and rates to the passing ship.

They would certainly be happy to have the business—or so they said. There were five surrounding a particularly jagged piece of geography. "The ring," said Me'a. "The Karoda slaver base is somewhere in those mountains. They use all of them for landings. The mountains are full of caves, and most of the tracks go underground. Slaves are big money, more than most of the rest of Karoda's industries and exports put together. They do have a lot of other businesses, everything from wine to rare minerals, but nothing that makes that sort of margin."

"So: Karoda's people support them?" asked the captain.

"Not really. The Karodese just believe in minding your own business. They don't like anyone—least of all Iradalia—telling them what they can or can't do. As I said, we looked into it as a base, at one time. The 'tax' that Iradalia would put on our ships transiting made it not worth it. Besides it is quite a dangerous place."

"Dangerous in that they'll shoot you?" asked Goth.

"Let us just keep it at 'dangerous.' They may shoot you if they don't like you, or they feel you're a threat. There are a number of vicious predatory animals and, as the smaller of the worlds in a binary pair, it has earthquakes and volcanos. And forests with plants that will kill the unwary, across much of it. If you want controlled and safe, go to Iradalia. Oh, and it has a season of torrential rain, and that's the dry season. It's quite pleasant when it is not raining."

"Sounds like a nice place, except for the rain," said Goth. "I better get out my bow." She wasn't joking either, Pausert knew. "I would have thought they would have shot all the dangerous beasts."

Me'a gave a crack of laughter. "They do. But they breed more. They like having them out there. And it doesn't rain all the time like on Vaudevillia. It just rains hard most afternoons, and then clears up. That's in the tropics, but that's also where most people live."

The spaceport, when they landed, proved to be in the middle of a busy little settlement, which ended abruptly in jungle just beyond the last building. Various tracks led off under the trees. The tree leaves had a peculiar reflective shimmer to them, making the Leewit screw up her eyes. "I reckon I could do a lot of eye-fixing here," she said.

"They're odd-looking trees," agreed Goth. "A bit like those on Lumajo, just even shinier."

"They accumulate metals—aluminum and some others—in a microscopic layer in their leaves and reflect back a lot of the radiation they aren't using. It is cooler under the trees. It also makes the heat signature of things under the trees very hard to trace. Cutting down trees is something most people on Karoda will shoot you for."

"I'll avoid it," promised Goth.

"Huh," said the Leewit. "They shoot at us, and they'll be sorry."

The captain laughed. "Well, Me'a. See what you are taking on. Right, we'd better get to off-loading that cargo. I think we'll just keep Vezzarn on board, on the forward turret. Any problems and you can let the port have it with the nova guns."

"We need to go armed ourselves, Captain," said Me'a. "It's the way it is done here."

So the arms locker was opened, and blasters strapped on. "What are their customs officers like, Me'a?" asked the Leewit.

"They don't have any."

And indeed, this was the case. Just a port operator in a broad hat who wandered over and asked for the landing fee. He wore a pair of Mark 5 blasters, one on either hip, and a belt of spare charges. That seemed his only badge of office, but the captain took his cue from Me'a, and accepted him as what he claimed to be, and showed him the waybill.

"Soman Consortium. That's their warehouse over there," he said, pointing. "You want to hire a cargo float? Save you a lot of carrying."

"How much?" asked Goth suspiciously.

"Twenty maels."

That was very reasonable, and certainly beat carrying crates in the heat, so they accepted. The port operator took the money and said, "The Soman Consortium are in town. I can let them know they've gotten a cargo."

"That will be kind," said the captain.

"That will be five maels, actually," said the port operator, with a grin. "You up for outgoing cargo? I could try and line some up."

"For a fee," said Goth, smiling in spite of herself.

"Naturally," he said. "It's business. It might take a day or two. There was a ship yesterday, one of the regulars, but she only hauls Soman cargo. People carrier. So it'll be Likan leaf and Maturian liquor most likely. For Morteen. Give me a few hours after the rain. You'll go into Labrun Town, I assume? You've got to try the wild galpin steaks at Ma Leerin's place. I'll get someone to let you know when I've got something."

"For a fee, naturally."

"Blaster charges aren't cheap," said the port operator, cheerfully.

"I could like this place," said Goth to the captain.

The captain nodded. "It does seem friendly enough."

That impression changed while they were unloading the cargo into the Soman warehouse. The warehouse was little more than a roof on steel posts—open, as were the others around the spaceport. The only visible difference was that this one was bigger. The fact that thieves probably would be shot seemed to have reduced the need for locks or fences. While they were there, a group of about twenty heavily armed men drove up in three flatbed floaters. "This the cargo for Soman?" asked one, leaning out of the cab.

"That's what it says on the consignment note," said the captain.

"Right. You want us to sign for receipt?"

"They told us we had to get that to get paid," said Me'a. "Not that we'd care, otherwise."

That seemed the right answer to give. Men got out of or off the flatbeds to start loading, and the driver signed the consignment note. Then someone got out of the third flatbed cab, looked at the captain, and shouted, "You! What in Patham's name are you doing here?"

Captain Pausert looked at the stocky, rotund man. He'd swear he'd never seen him in his life before. "Delivering a cargo," he said, calmly.

"That's not likely!" snapped the man. All around them heavily armed men stopped what they'd been doing . . . and reached for their weapons.

"That's Bormgo. From the Consortium on Cinderby's World," said Me'a, quietly. "I knew he came from here, but I never made the connection."

"Who are they, Borm?" asked the tall man who had signed the receipt.

"He's the one who shot up Herc's ship. And then busted things open on Cinderby's World. He was working with the Imperial cops."

They were facing a semicircle of twenty blaster rifles and other weaponry. "Coppers. Coming to Karoda," said the tall man, shaking his head. "And they're using kids and cripples for cover."

"We're not Imperial police," protested Pausert. "They arrested us on Cinderby's World."

"Yeah? They seem to have let you go. They don't usually do that," said the tall man with a sneer.

"We weren't guilty. The judge let us go."

"They were in it up to their necks," said Bormgo. "Very thick with that Chief Inspector Salaman."

"No, we weren't!" protested Goth.

"I think I might whistle at them," said the Leewit, crossly. "Seeing as no one else seems keen to do anything."

"It will wait," said the captain, sternly, before turning to say,

"I'm sure we can explain. Our ship was just in the right place at the wrong time."

"Oh, really," said Bormgo. "Well, I guess we'll find out who is right and what is going on. You'll tell us happily, after a little . . . treatment. Take them along, boys."

So that was how they found themselves being loaded up onto the flatbeds along with the cargo of forcecuffs in their crates. Well, almost all the cargo was in the crates. The slavers took some out to forcecuff them.

The floaters edged their way along under the trees down a winding trail that took the *Venture*'s crew up toward the mountains. The Leewit, sitting next to Pausert, waited until their captors were talking and laughing among themselves to ask him what his plans were.

"We're getting to their base; we might get to find out what's going on, and deal with it."

"I like 'shoot their front end off, shoot their rear end off, and ram them in the middle,' more than all this stuff."

"Patience. That's the 'deal with it' part."

"Huh," said the Leewit. "I've gotten some new special whistles I want to try."

"I'm pretty sure you'll get a chance."

"Or make a chance," said Me'a, quietly. "There is fair amount of rumor about how the Wisdoms of Karres operate, but it is something of a surprise to me. It's not the way I would have done things, but at this stage I am following Ta'zara's advice: to watch and learn. Give the word when you need me to do anything."

One of their captors climbed back from the armored cab, to where they'd been put into a barred section on the second to last floater. He stopped in front of Ta'zara. "You're one of those Na'kalauf fighters, supposed to be so tough, aren't you?"

"I am from Na'kalauf, yes," said Ta'zara calmly.

"That'll put your price way up," said the slaver. "An absolutely loyal bodyguard for life has gotten to be valuable."

"I already am a life-sworn bodyguard," said Ta'zara, with calm finality.

"I guess that's about to change . . . agh . . ." The last part of that was as the man cartwheeled over the edge of the flatbed.

The floater behind them stopped and plainly radioed theirs, because the entire caravan stopped. It was noticeable that the first thing their captors did was to deploy a watchful force—looking for attack from the forest. And it was plain the last thing that their captors thought could have happened was that the man, with a broken head and a broken leg, might have had his leg broken before he fell, not after. He wasn't in any state to tell them, and so, after some rudimentary first aid, they loaded him up again and the floaters moved on, now with two watchful guards on the back with weapons at the ready, looking into the trees.

"I could cure him," said the Leewit, quietly.

"That would be awkward," said Me'a. "You see, at the moment, they think someone or thing out of the forest must have knocked him off. Not Ta'zara breaking his knee."

"You will not allow them to steal my loyalty, mistress?" asked Ta'zara. "It cannot be permitted."

"Besides the mess it would cause. Half of Na'kalauf knows he is the Leewit's life-guardian. Breach of that oath...well, any man or woman of Na'kalauf would kill Ta'zara," said Me'a. "If they ever found out that these Karoda slavers even tried to change that, it would probably mean war."

"I would kill myself first," said Ta'zara.

"No, you won't," said the Leewit crossly. One of the downsides she had found to being a healer was that she was aware of the pain of others—at least if they were badly hurt and close. She could block it...almost entirely. "We're going to shoot their bows off, blow their stern off and ram them in the middle, just as soon as the captain gives the word...hey. We're going into a cave."

They were. A whole labyrinth of them, by what they could see in the headlights. It was rather clear why Iradalia's soldiers had never worked out where the slaver's base was. The floaters left no trail through the caves. Eventually they came out of the oppressive darkness and back under the forest canopy again. But the Leewit had no idea in which direction lay the spaceport where the *Venture 7333* stood. Then they drove through more forest, and back into a cave. It was a shorter journey this time, only broken by some blaster fire at a shrieking flying creature that swooped down out of the darkness to attack the guards. In the woods beyond that they saw a pack of long-fanged creatures watching them from the shadows. "They're as big as a bollem," commented Goth, who had been mostly silent on the trip.

"Yes. I think the return journey is going to be interesting," said the captain. "But I dare say we'll manage. We've got a few skills they don't have, don't we?"

"Um," said Goth.

The caravan of vehicles had arrived at an overhanging cliff into which a door was set. Not just a door, but a hull-metal door, triple-layered, big enough for the floaters to drive through, under guard turrets fitted with spaceguns. Even if the Iradalians got here with an army, it wouldn't be easy to get in.

In front of them loomed another door, equally impressive, equally well armed. Anyone breaking in this far would be in a fire zone. A solitary guard came out and went to the driver of the lead floater and spoke briefly to them.

"Ah. Password. Melon. Answer, Cantaloupe," said Me'a.

"How do you know?" asked the Leewit.

"The spy ray in my wheelchair. And a bone-induction ear-piece. I've been listening in on them for most of the trip. I have not learned much of value. Bormgo is convinced you are more than you seem. The rest think he's either wrong or stupid, but he is quite high up in the Consortium. So ... when do we take action, Captain? I took the liberty of sending positional data to Vezzarn on a narrow-beam transmitter. We can communicate with the ship."

"Just let us get inside," said Pausert, grimly. "I think I've had about enough of patience."

But they were ill-prepared for the fact that the slaving operation was an old one, and had long since developed a method of dealing with potential trouble from slaves. The floaters' driving cabs had sealed windows, and the cavern had knockout gas.

CHAPTER 19

The captain awoke somewhat blearily to find he was in a prison cage—a cave with floor-to ceiling bars—and his ship coveralls had been replaced by a bright orange one-piece garment. He was sharing the cell with about twenty other prisoners—although, if they crowded them in, there was space for five times that. Ta'zara was also waking. His first question was: "Where is the Leewit?"

"I don't know," said the captain, grimly. "But we're going looking for the others." He held out his forcecuffed wrists to Ta'zara. "Tap in the opening code. I want to be able to slug a few of these fellows."

Of course these were the cuffs that they'd brought along, and that Vezzarn had worked on, so Ta'zara could and did. No sooner had he done so than one of the others in the cell—a bent, elderly wizened man in an identical orange one-piece who had been industriously sweeping the cell a few yards from them—started yelling. Ta'zara might still have been forcecuffed, and groggy from the drugging, but the fellow never got to draw a second breath to yell again. Hastily, watching the others in the cell, the captain freed Ta'zara from his forcecuffs.

"Can you do the rest of us too?" asked one of the other

prisoners quietly. "Someone may check on what the yell was about. Probably another trusty." He pointed at the unconscious sweeper. "He's already a Karoda slave. Happy cleaning the cells and keeping watch on the prisoners. I guess he was too old for the Mantro barges. And he was telling us we'd all soon be happy too," he grimaced. "I'd rather go down fighting."

He wasn't the only one holding out his forcecuffed manacles. In fact, all of the other prisoners were.

"I wish we could," said the captain. "We only have the codes to these new ones. But we'll break you out of the cell, anyway. We're going."

He used his klatha ability to cocoon off the lock—which as it was no longer attached, they pushed out. That left them in a cave passage, lit by glow-globes. They met another trusty coming around the corner—this one did not even get to scream. The only problem was there was a choice of passages beyond, and no clue to which lead where.

The Leewit, Goth and Me'a also awoke in a barred-off cave. Me'a still had her wheelchair—but they'd been stripped and given a new pocketless garment. The Leewit was the first to wake. The first thing she noticed was that Tippi the rochat was not in the shirt of her new garment. In fact, wasn't anywhere. That was enough to make her angry and worried, leaving aside being drugged and caged. They could use the Egger Route to escape, but what had happened to Tippi?

She felt rotten so she tried using her healer skills on herself. Her teaching pattern said she'd been doing that already, which is why she was awake first. A little time would still be needed to clear the anesthetic gas through her liver, but it was happening. She set to work on her sister, and then Me'a. Knowing what was needed made it easier, and by the time they were awake her own feeling of sickness had largely gone. All she was, was hungry, angry and worried about her rochat. "Time we got out of here," she said. "The captain can catch up with us. I need to find Tippi."

"Dears, you mustn't try to escape," said one of the other women in the cell, a dumpy older woman, barely looking up from her work of polishing the bars with a rag. She beamed at them quickly before going back to concentrating on her work. "You'll soon be happy."

"I'm going to whistle at you," said the Leewit, "And you're not going to be happy." She pursed her lips.

Goth put a hand in front of the Leewit's mouth. "Wait. That's important. I've heard it before. I need to ask why we're going to be so happy?"

"You will be taken to the Ghandagar. I know you are afraid, but really it will be so much better afterwards. You will have service to be happy in. Believe me it is the best thing that could happen to you. I was never happy before. I was rich and powerful, but not happy."

"Jaccy's woman, Yelissa," said Goth. "I never realized she was a Karoda slave. Like this woman obviously is."

"It's not slavery, child. I love to serve and I am happy. I never was that before."

The Leewit looked at the woman with her cleaning rag. "This is what they do to their slaves?"

"I'd say so," said Goth. "Nasty."

"It isn't," said the woman, calmly. "And you will find this is true too."

The Leewit walked over to her. "Hold my hand, will you?"

The woman took it . . . and moments later slumped to the floor. The Leewit had to stop her head from hitting the ground.

"Good thinking," said Me'a. "She would have tried to stop us. But how did you do that?"

"Shut up," said the Leewit, fiercely. "I need to concentrate. I need to work out what has been done."

And she did. The good part was that she understood it, with a little help from the teaching pattern. The bad part was that it would be hard to undo. It wasn't a very complicated neural change. That wasn't the problem. The problem was—at least as far as the slave was concerned—that she really did feel just about exactly as people did when they were really happy . . . only a lot more. The Leewit knew, even without her teaching pattern, that any human would struggle to step away from that.

It shared some characteristics, neural pathways, hormone and endorphin production stimulation of what humans called "love," the teaching pattern explained. The brain of the slave had been changed, physically forming new pathways to ensure this.

The Leewit, not used to not knowing how to deal with something, found herself not knowing what to do this time—except for making certain it didn't happen to her or the captain or Goth. Or Ta'zara or Me'a or Vezzarn. Or, actually, anyone else. "Right," she said letting go of the woman's hand, leaving her unconscious on the floor. "It's time we got out of here. Goth, can you 'port us some keys? Or a piece out of the lock? Hide us in no-shape so we can go looking."

Goth took a deep breath. "I can't."

The Leewit looked at her crossly, her mood not helped by what she was trying to process. "Don't be a dope, Goth. Stop waiting for the captain to do everything."

"Don't you be a dope, little sister," said Goth. "I mean I *can't*. I can't 'port anymore. I think I can still read things because this place is giving me the grue. I don't want to touch anything. But my other klatha skills seem to be gone. I burned out. I used too much getting back down the Egger Route."

The Leewit stared at her and blinked. And then shook her head. "That..."

"Hush. There is someone coming down the passage," said Me'a.

It was several of their heavily armed captors. The Leewit was quite pleased to see them right now. She got to whistle, finally. To use some of her directional whistles was just more pleasant than dealing with thinking about all this stuff. The first whistle was a thin, high-pitched whistle, a refinement on the whistle she had used on Moander. The delicate components of those heavy blasters' charge units became shards of fragmenting glass. There was quite a lot of heat generated in the process, to judge by their yells and desperate attempts to get rid of bandoliers of charge units. You could see that in the sudden flare of the burning units, as the passage lights also exploded.

But the Leewit was in no mood to stop there. Sound, she'd found, was a lot more powerful than people realized. It could stun, induce anything from terror to confusion and make various muscles—including the ones controlling sphincters—suddenly relax.

When she'd finished, Goth said, "Great. Now we're still trapped, but in pitch darkness. And they stink."

A light glowed into life, on Me'a's wheelchair. "Fortunately they don't seem to have examined my chair too closely. I can cut the bars and get us out of here. If you want to go, that is? I think being somewhere else might be a wise move."

"Sounds like a good idea to me," said Goth.

"Yes," agreed the Leewit. "I need to look for Tippi. And bust their enslavement machine."

"Very well," said Me'a. "I have some thermite putty. If you apply some around the bars for me we should be able to depart this cave, hopefully without bringing the roof down. You will have to close your eyes and cover your ears, of course."

"Get these forcecuffs off first," said Goth, practically. "But then, yes, let's blow this place."

So they did. The thermite putty ringed around the bars weakened them enough to make pushing them out easy, and they were able leave the darkness, the stunned captors and smoke, and head down the passage. "Your Wisdom," said Me'a, as she struggled to steer past the bodies. "Not that I want to complain, but this is quite hard to negotiate in a wheelchair."

"Then why don't you use your floater-boosters? I've seen you do so for stairs often enough."

"They use a fair amount of power. I'm not sure when I will be able to recharge. And, after your whistle some of my utilities are reporting damage, even if I wasn't on the front end of it. I've gotten my diagnostics repairing what can be dealt with. This chair is normally as powerful as a small tank. Now it's more like a small armored car."

"Oh. I didn't think..." admitted the Leewit.

"I still have more than enough functionality and a few weapons," said Me'a.

"Just stun them next time," said Goth, tersely. "Now let's find the captain and Ta'zara."

"I reckon they'll find us," said the Leewit. "I want to find Tippi. If they've hurt her..."

"The gas is unlikely to have affected her," said Me'a, soothingly. "Remember rochats can survive outside on Cinderby's World without any form of rebreather. And they're very hard to catch—or even to hurt."

"They still better not have hurt her," said the Leewit, darkly. "Or I'll do a lot worse than I'm planning to do to them anyway. And that isn't going to be pretty."

"Let's settle for stunning the next one, so we can get some answers," said Goth. "And I'd like a working weapon, if possible. Right now I feel sort of helpless, and I don't like it."

"Well, you're—" started the Leewit.

"Ware!" said Goth, as another one of their former captors stepped out of a doorway built into the cave warren. Before the Leewit could even whistle, the man jerked violently and fell over, shuddering.

Two thin wires trailed back from the dart in him to Me'a's chair. "Electrical paralysis. You wanted one alive for questioning. I suggest we hurry, though. I hope he's cooperative."

"He will be," said the Leewit grimly. She went over and whistled gently in the bulky fellow's ear, while Goth helped herself to his holstered military grade blaster, and a belt of charges. The Leewit knew exactly what that whistle, from so close, would do.

The problem thereafter wasn't getting the man's cooperation, it was getting the man to stop stammering. Fortunately, it turned out that he was one of the guards who had overseen the stripping and redressing of the gassed new prisoners. And yes, they had seen Tippi the rochat. She'd bitten an unwary hand and fled the scene. Someone had tried to shoot her.

At this point the Leewit slapped him. "You get up and go and find them. Tell them—and all your other friends—that if Tippi is hurt or killed I'll see to it that they die slowly over a month, in pain. And just so you can tell them what the pain will be like... this is how it will feel." The Leewit tweaked his nerves and he shrieked and then lolled into unconsciousness. "And not just for seconds either," she said, grimly. "Come on, let's go." She got up.

"While I understand you're worried about Tippi," said Me'a, "do you think we should just be charging around looking for her?"

"Yes, of course!" said the Leewit.

"I mean, we need a plan, a method, or sooner or later they will be luckier than we are. And they'll be expecting us after this. They'll shoot first and ask questions later."

"So what do you suggest?" asked Goth.

"It appears that the captain also has very special abilities. I would suggest finding him first and combining his skills with yours. We're outnumbered and, little as I like to admit it, outgunned. It's that or gain some high-value hostage."

Both of those proved quite difficult, however. It was obvious that word had gotten around that some of the prisoners were on the loose, and the Soman Consortium was out in force to try to kill them. The Soman Consortium also had some idea where they were going—which was not an advantage that Goth, Me'a or the Leewit had. They went into the next cave...and into an ambush—with several slightly too hasty blaster bolts having betrayed the ambushers hiding behind a stack of boxes.

There was a sharp and sudden click and two transparent crystallite screens appeared in front of the wheelchair, as well as the hum of hyperelectronics. At this point Me'a used her wheelchair's armory. A shriek of rocketry and the boxes and most of those behind them disappeared into an explosive cloud. Advancing into the dust and smashed debris, the Leewit finished the contact with a stunning whistle that the echoes in the cave multiplied.

As they moved forward, Goth picked up a handheld communicator from the chaos. Its lights still blinked. A voice from it said, "Macsell, Macsell, respond. What's happening in D5? Do you need backup? Ramio and his squad are coming down from the upper sector."

"They're obviously coordinating. Let's listen in," she said. So they did as they moved on. The chatter over the communicator told them two things—firstly, their enemies knew roughly where they were and were sending more fighters. And secondly, they weren't the only problem the Soman clan had. There'd been a slave breakout. At least twenty slaves were scattered in several groups though the caves. They were apparently armed, or at least some of them were. "That'll be the captain and Ta'zara," said Goth, plainly pleased.

"That is good. But it doesn't help us," said Me'a. "I suggest you both stay behind me. The crystallite should be proof against any mechanical attack, and the hyperelectronic shield will diffuse the effect of blaster bolts."

"I have another idea," said the Leewit. "Can that chair shut out sound?"

"It has a spy screen that should do that."

"Right," she said, reaching for the communicator. "Can you get Goth into it? I'm going to give them a few whistles."

"A few seconds and I'll do my best to shield my own equipment!" said Me'a.

"Better," said the Leewit. "I'm planning to bust theirs up a bit, and put the frighteners on them. And to use some new words I've learned, seeing as the captain isn't here."

✧   ✧   ✧

Captain Pausert and Ta'zara were finding the resistance stiff, despite the fact that they'd removed quite a lot of heavy weaponry from the first of the Soman Consortium's men to come into contact with Ta'zara. The Soman men might be good with weapons, but at hand-to-hand combat, they were not so good. The captain could shield them, but it took energy—and then, to respond, he had to take down the cocoon. At first the other prisoners had just followed them, but, as soon as they found a few more weapons in what was plainly the slavers' rest room, the captain put a stop to that. He handed out weapons on a first-come-first-serve basis. Even in forcecuffs they could still shoot.

"All of you have a choice of slavery for life, or fighting and maybe dying," he said. "Split up into small groups. They've got the heavy weapons and numbers to deal with us in one group. But that advantage goes away if they're fighting small battles everywhere. You'll win some and lose some. If we stay together we will probably all die together."

They were in a maze of caves, where the Soman Consortium knew where they were, and the desperate escapees did not. It was a tough fight. The captain was forced to cocoon two of them when they stepped around a corner to face a barricade, and a Mark 20 tripod-mounted blaster cannon, pouring fire on them. He wasn't sure how they could get out of this one. The cocoon stopped the blaster effects, but if he stopped using it for long enough to fire back, it would be all over for them. He would have to wait for them to run out of charge—and by the size of the power pack they had, that might take a while.

And then, abruptly, he saw the gunner and his four companions let go of their weapons, clutch their ears—and then run away. He opened the cocoon. "The Leewit is on the loose," he said, with a broad grin. He saw relief all over Ta'zara's broad, normally near expressionless face. "That is good. She is my duty to guard. Let us go to them."

"We may not see them. Goth will have them hidden in no-shape."

"They will see and hear us. It is time for the war chant of my clan. The Leewit and the woman who calls herself 'Me'a' will know then that it is us."

The war chant echoing through the Soman caves might also have made their enemies run, thought Pausert. But there was no sign of Goth, the Leewit, or Me'a. Just dropped weapons and the still-smoldering remains of a hand communicator.

"That's how she did it," said the captain, pointing. "I suppose we'll just have to go on looking."

The Leewit's actions had not destroyed the Soman Consortium, but it had left them unable to communicate, badly rattled and looking to fort up in large groups, rather than searching for the escapees.

Not surprisingly, the next people who shot at Pausert and Ta'zara were some of the escapees. Fortunately they were rotten shots and no one got killed by the new armory they had picked up, and equally fortunately the other escapees had a captive. He wasn't the ideal guide—until Ta'zara gave him the benefit of a one-on-one war chant. Then he was much more cooperative.

The problem was, even with a guide, they had no idea exactly where the others were, or where they were heading. It was just a case of hoping they were lucky. So the captain decided that it was time to rely on his klatha-sourced luck. Which way felt best? He paused. Saw how he felt about the choices. "We'll go that way," he said, pointing to a small cave mouth.

The prisoner looked openly dismayed. "You can't!" he blurted. "It doesn't lead out; it leads to the Ghandagar. We...we can't go there without breathing equipment. I...you would end up as a slave."

The feeling was much stronger now. "Then you better hope we catch up with Goth and the Leewit before that."

But raw fear made the man frantic, and gave him hysterical strength. He broke and ran.

Ta'zara cursed. "You should have let me hold him, Captain."

"I thought having your hands free to fight was more valuable. Come on. They might find out where we're going from him, but we still need to get up there in time."

So they headed for the Soman Consortium's slave-maker, "the Ghandagar," whatever that was.

They were at least able to travel largely unhindered now, Goth thought. Of course, they still had no idea where they were going, but it was better than being shot at. The long passage they were in now sloped upward, and at least had fewer branches. They'd only passed one in the last while. Me'a had been quite keen on going down it, but the Leewit wanted to go on. Goth came down on the onward side. She found the caverns of the Soman clan incredibly depressing. All she wanted to do was get out of them. With everybody else, of course...but at least this cave sloped upward.

And eventually led into tree-filtered daylight.

Not a great deal of it, though. There was just one tree. They were in a small rock bowl surrounded by towering cliffs. The bowl itself, barring the one tree, was full of a strange and spiky rock formation.

As they came out of the cave mouth, a heavy door slid down behind them. Me'a turned hastily to look, as did Goth. It was also plainly hull metal. "Oh, oh," said Goth.

The Leewit just said "Tippi!" in delight and rushed forward to pick up the rochat from between the rows of curved and spiky stone going into the structure above. And then Goth became aware of a smell she remembered all too well...the smell of the squill cocoons off the Mantro barge on Parisienne. She was going to throw up... She leaned forward, grabbing one of the stone pillars.

And immediately became aware of three things. The first was that the essence of putrescence, squill-cocoon scent...was making her feel good. The second was even more horrific. Her klatha ability to read the imprinted history of strong emotions in objects had not gone away. And what she was touching was a thing with many such enormously strong emotions...mostly happy ones. The final fact she became aware of was that what she was touching might be mostly silicates, but was alive.

She pulled away, and yelled out, "Leewit! It's alive. It's the slave-maker! We have to get out of here!"

The Leewit shook herself, and whistled. That had no noticeable effect.

Me'a fired another rocket to explode in the structure. It knocked a few of the spikes off but had no other effect, except to make the feeling that Goth really loved the stink of squill cocoon even more intense.

The Leewit turned to Me'a. "Don't. That hurt it." And she leaned in and grabbed the spiky stone that was the Ghandagar, the slave-maker, her hands glowing with klatha force.

It took seconds before Goth suddenly was aware again of just how revolting sea-squill cocoon scent was, and how that smell made her anything but happy. "Goth," said the Leewit, "there's a little vial of some horrible stuff jammed in between the filaments in there. Get rid of it, please. I'm doing some repairs."

Goth went looking. She had to follow her nose, even though she'd rather not have. She soon found the vial in a nest of long green-gray dangling strips of rock, next to a small storehouse. Even getting that close made her gag. She tried holding her breath. No good. She'd have had to take a breath and be running in from a lot farther away. In desperation, without thinking about it, she tried 'porting it elsewhere.

And to her surprise she felt that familiar surge of klatha power as the vial vanished.

The shock and relief were almost enough to make her fall over. She sat down, hastily, before she fell—and found herself touching the rocky filaments again. Reading the past. It was... not easy. Besides the emotional turmoil of terror, sadness, and then the strange "happiness" there were some very alien images there as well.

Some of them were oddly familiar. She got the full sensory emersion, with the reading of the past. Details that meant nothing to her and a smell she'd smelled before—*paratha*! The spice that ruined the taste of everything in comparison. Strange aliens combing the stone filaments... With difficulty, she pulled herself away, and went back to find Me'a and the Leewit.

She put her hands on the Leewit's shoulders, lending strength. "My klatha! It's back."

The Leewit didn't even look up. "I know, stupid. It never went anywhere. It can't partly go. It doesn't work like that. And I treated you, remember. I would have known. You just tried too soon and too hard. Now shut up. This is complicated. They hurt the poor thing. And then Me'a shot it. And it is half-starved. Short of minerals."

"What does it eat?" asked Goth warily, wondering if they were diet items for this... alien her little sister was healing.

"Leaves. Leaves from different kinds of trees... but it can't collect them," said the Leewit with a faint air of puzzlement.

"They used to bring it leaves. And brush its filaments. It likes that. Long before it was left here alone and hungry and lonely. Long before the humans came and found it," said Goth. "It doesn't like them. They don't look after it. It wants to go home. Back to the ones who look after a poor Arerrerr."

"Arerrerr?"

"What it thinks of itself as. A sort of noise it makes. It's not very bright. It has thought these things very often and been very sorry for itself. Oh. And it remembers rochats. Along with the aliens that used to look after it."

"What's going on?" asked Me'a, warily. "I dropped some bugs in the tunnel up here. I'm picking up some sounds. They're coming this way."

"The Leewit is healing the thing. The Arerrerr."

"But...that's the thing that made willing slaves for the Karoda slavers. Is the Leewit enslaved?"

"Don't be silly," said the Leewit. "Anyway, that was the Soman, using it. They blocked its own scent gland, and they put the smells they wanted fixed into the neural pattern there. It thought it was making them love it, making them happy loving it, looking after it, feeding it, caring for it. That's what it does. It is a kind of pet. It just works better on the human nervous system than the one it was made for."

CHAPTER 20

"The thing is," said Me'a to Goth, "we are basically trapped in here. I mean, yes, we have the Leewit curing this creature. In a way that's the most valuable hostage we could have, but we're rather stuck here with it. And if the Soman Consortium got it to do what they wanted once before, they can again. It's not something we can carry away in our pockets."

Goth shook her head. "Even if we have to destroy it, I'm not leaving it to either the Somans or the Iradalians. Or anyone else for that matter. At least now I have my klatha skills to add to the Leewit's. I can hide us so they simply can't see us. I can 'port things. But I want to go back through that door to find the captain. And Ta'zara."

She felt faintly bad about the afterthought, but she really, really wanted to see Pausert. Her klatha was back...if it had ever gone away. She wanted to tell him, so badly. If they could be together now, as compared to when she thought she'd lost it and couldn't bring herself to tell him.

"It's possible—but not that likely—that I can blow that door down. But there must be some way of opening it. I assume there's a mechanism this side too, in case they got stuck out here. The

Soman crowd must come up here, I suppose, if only to feed the creature."

"Yes, but it is probably hidden. There's a little hut back there. It's worth checking, I suppose. Then I can try the door for what imprinted memories it might have." Goth wrinkled her face in distaste. "It's not likely to be a pleasant experience. I'll see what I can find first."

The hut proved to be a cold store for vials—labeled and carefully ordered. It didn't take long to figure that those were the odd pheromones the Somans had been using to make... what did the Leewit call it? The Arerrerr. There was a lot labeled sea-squill exudate. So exactly how the Mantro barges got their willing workers was now more than plain. Goth put a handful of the vials in her pocket. They'd 'port easily and might make a good weapon if they were just thrown hard.

She was looking for any possible switches or controls when she heard the Leewit calling, so she ran back. The Leewit was sitting down, resting against one of the Arerrerr pillars, or rather, legs. She looked, Goth thought, tired and young. She was also trying to talk around some sort of compressed seed bar she was cramming into her face. The rochat was fastidiously eating a few crumbs with the look of doing her a huge favor.

"Energy bar," said Me'a. "Do you need one, Goth? I have a few stored in the chair."

"Let her eat them," said Goth. "I haven't done much. What are you calling for? Are you winning?"

"For now," said the Leewit in a spray of crumbs. At least it might have been what she said.

"Swallow and tell me what you called for."

So the Leewit did. A drink, provided by Me'a, and she was at least audible. "Goth, there's some of those seaweed flakes on my table on the *Venture*, ones that I was feeding to Tippi. You know, the ones in that funny-shaped bottle. I know it's far, but the Arerrerr needs them. Or rather, it needs selenium. Its body chemistry is kinda like Tippi's. That's why the rochats thrive and breed on Cinderby's World, but don't on Na'kalauf. And the poor Arerrerr has been short of it for a long time. There's some selenium here, but not enough and it's been here a long time. The lack is slowly killing it, and I need some for repairs."

"I'll try. It's long range." Goth knew exactly what the object looked like, exactly where it was in the *Venture*, even if she had no idea where the *Venture 7333* was.

But as it turned out, 'porting it was almost ridiculously effortless. Either the *Venture* was much closer than they realized, or she had suddenly grown in teleporting ability. She did know that progress with klatha use was usually like that. It wasn't linear progress, but sudden steps. Sometimes people just never climbed up that next step. Maybe she had. After the stress of the last while, it was a nice thought.

The rochat was headbutting her hand and giving her its odd growl in its attempt to get the bottle—so she nearly dropped it, passing it to the Leewit. The Leewit looked sternly at Tippi. "One flake. It needs it more than you."

By Tippi's behavior, the rochat didn't care how badly the Arerrerr wanted it. She wanted it herself. But the Leewit ignored her complaints and went and reached up and into a stalactite-fringed opening above them—and pulled her hand out quickly. "Huh. Nearly ate my hand too," she said. "I guess it was really hungry. I still am. You couldn't 'port me some pancakes with Wintenberry jelly, could you, Goth?"

"Nope. Not unless you left a bunch ready made outside the robobutler, you greedy little bollem. Eat some more of Me'a's energy bar."

"Hush," said Me'a. "I'm picking up something from the bugs I seeded behind us." Then she beamed widely. "Ta'zara. He's giving a war chant. I feel sorry for any Soman people that run into him."

"We have the door between us and them," said the Leewit.

"The captain will sort that out," said Goth, confidently.

And indeed, he did. Minutes later a piece fell out of the door, cocooned and cut off from the rest of the metal, and the captain and Ta'zara pushed it open.

Pausert was prepared for an enthusiastic greeting, but not quite the rapturous one he got. Goth seemed to be literally bouncing off the cliff wall in quite her old lithe, lively way. And she kept stopping and kissing him again. The Leewit had hugged him and Ta'zara, but was now all business. "Right, Captain. We need to take Arerrerr out of here. They'll just abuse her. And they haven't been feeding her properly."

"Arerrerr?" asked the captain, warily.

The Leewit patted what he had taken for a natural rock formation, limestone perhaps. "This is Arerrerr. The Soman Consortium
have been using her to condition the slaves."

"What?"

So they had to explain. It was a confusing explanation, but
Pausert had had years of making sense of the Leewit, and Goth,
and both together. He looked at the vast creature. At the small
cave opening they had just come out of. "Um, can it move?"

"Quite slowly. But she won't fit in that hole. Not anymore.
She was put in here when she was little."

"For safekeeping," added Goth. "She was going to be fetched.
Only... they never came back."

"Who never came back?" asked the captain, still trying to
get this all sorted in his head.

"Captain! We've gotten something big coming up the passage,"
interrupted Me'a. "The bugs are picking up some serious power
fans. It must be some kind of tank!"

"I can hide us in no-shape," said Goth.

"I'd rather blow their front end off, shoot their rear end off,
and ram them in the middle!" said the Leewit. "Have you still
got some of your exploding rockets, Me'a?"

"Three. But they have limited facility against armor. On the
other hand, we have what's probably the most valuable hostage
in the place. I don't think they'll come in shooting."

They didn't come in shooting. They came in stinking.

Me'a had wheeled to the opening and focused a scope from the
arm of her wheelchair down the passage. "If I can get in range I can
get a spy ray on them... oh, it *is* a tank. A Mark 7 Sirius. They're
pretty well shielded against everything. And they have a range of
target detection equipment that is second to none. We're in trouble."

Ta'zara, looking over her shoulder at the screen display of the
tank which barely fitted down the tunnel, said, "We can drop the
tunnel on them. But then we'd be stuck here too." He sniffed.
"What is that smell!"

Goth smelled it too, and laughed. "Sea-squill-cocoon exudate. They think we're enslaved to it, will love it. It's the job the
Arerrerr was set up to do when we came up here."

"Uh," said the captain, swallowing. "That's some perfume! I
hope it didn't work? I'd hate to put that on after shaving."

"The Leewit stopped it," said Goth.

"Thank Patham! But even hiding in no-shape is going to be hard. I feel I might have to throw up."

"I have gas-filter nose plugs," said Me'a.

"Good," said Goth. "Put them in quick, because I doubt if they have any. They're in an airtight tank. Let's see how they like their own medicine."

And when she 'ported an open sea-squill-cocoon exudate vial into the tank . . . it proved that they really couldn't live with their own medicine. Less than twenty seconds later, the hatch on the top flew open and several gasping, gagging and vomiting Soman soldiers scrabbled out. Of course, seeing as they had a vial of the stuff outside, it wasn't a lot better in the passage. Still, they were in no state to resist Ta'zara. They would have been in no state to resist a newborn.

"Well," said Me'a. "I think we have transportation."

"The Arerrerr won't fit," said the Leewit. "We need to take her to the *Venture*. We need to get her away from here."

"I get the feeling that we're going to have to bring the *Venture* to her," said the captain, looking at the strange misshapen rocklike creature. "I could probably set the ship down on the plateau above us, and then we could use our tractor beam to load her into the hold. It would depend on her weight, but that is the best I can think of, at the moment. Which means we need to get back to the *Venture*."

"I suppose so," said the Leewit reluctantly. "Okay. I'm going to put her into a healing trance. At least she won't know we've left her. And they won't be able to abuse her. I've fixed her, gotten rid of the plug they put in, but they would probably do it again."

"Why hasn't the Arerrerr just made us all love her?" asked Goth, suddenly wary about her little sister's "fixes."

The Leewit grinned. "She thinks she has. I've put in a little nerve shunt for now. It's temporary, but we're safe enough. Just give me a minute or two."

So they did. The Mark 7 Sirius was brought forward and turned around, and a few minutes later, with all of them aboard, they set off back down into the Soman caves. Fortunately, Me'a was as adept at driving the tank as she was driving the wheelchair which was now strapped onto the back. They used one of the rear guns to bring down the rock at the entrance to the tunnel, blocking it, and went looking for trouble.

They didn't have to go that far to find it, but the "trouble" had expected the tank to be on their side. And they didn't expect a vial of sea-squill exudate to get 'ported high up into the cave above them and to smash in their midst. It was, Goth reflected, a small payback for all those who had been sent to work on the Mantro barges.

"I have accessed the tank's data and mapping system," said Me'a. "It's got the entire Soman cave system in it. Including holding cells, their living quarters, armories, ammunition stores and storage caves. The passages which are accessible to the tank are marked. So where are we going? Straight out by the shortest route?"

"I think we may as well clean up this rat's nest properly. And certainly free any other slaves we find," said the captain. "We should head for the main living areas. That's where most of them will be, I suspect."

The presence of the tank did simplify things. Obviously, news had gotten around, it seemed with extra panic added. The tank had very little opportunity to use its guns. The slave holding pens were next on the list. The captain and Ta'zara had freed some, and those had already freed others. Of course they also ran away from the Mark 7. But they were easy to avoid shooting at, thanks to the one-piece overalls.

Then they went about systematically destroying the Soman Consortium's armories, assets and stores. It was only when they came to a cavern that was full of boxes they recognized—the cargo of hyperelectronic forcecuffs—that the captain held the Leewit back from her gleeful experimentation with the tank's varied weapons systems.

"I've got an idea for those," he said. "From what I can work out we're pretty near the surface, close to the doors. As far away from the conditioning creature—the Arerrerr—as possible really. We'll use them later."

"Those doors are something of a problem," said Me'a. "Looking at the maps on the screen, we won't be able to access the fortification and the spaceguns with the tank. And we can't get out without going past them. Two layers of them. With spaceguns. That is something that outguns us, and will destroy our armor."

"We'll have to take them out first, before we and the other prisoners try and bust out of here."

"I guess. But we ought to finish off the slave pens first. There's another close to here. It's where they put the slaves after they had been conditioned, preparatory to shipping them out."

"That could be awkward. I've never felt anything quite as intense as what the Arerrerr did to us, and we just got the start of the treatment. The effects are reversible, but I don't think the victims are going to thank me."

Security for the treated slaves was plainly less of a priority. Where they'd had to blast through steel bars for the untreated prisoners, these were kept behind a locked door that the tank simply drove through. Unlike the untreated ones, these at least were no longer in forcecuffs, but did wear the orange overalls. There weren't many in the dormitories right now.

They came rushing out of their quarters—about fifteen of them—and ran straight at the tank. "Are they trying to attack us barehanded?" asked Goth, incredulously.

"They're not coming to attack. They're coming to love," answered Me'a, dryly. "Look at their faces."

"They're in love with a tank?" said the captain.

"They're in love with what we smell of. We never took off that bit of sea-squill exudate that the Somans had on the outside. The tank's air filtration and purifier has cleaned out most of the smell from in here, but I would guess it is dumping that waste straight into the outside air. So the tank smells even more of it. So do we, probably. You'll find this lot are the slaves who weren't desirable for individual buyers, so were gotten rid of by selling them to the Mantro barges on Parisienne."

"Oh. Well, that'll stop them wanting to do anything but help us. Hey! Look. We know that one! It's that long thin drink of water you rescued, Captain. The tall guy who was a captive in the pirate vessel we blew apart. The fellow we gave passage off Cinderby's World to. Farnal. The one who organized the other prisoners."

"Well, at least he looks happy now. He was a pretty miserable sort," said the captain. "Mind you, he tried to do his best for the rest of the captives. I mean he paid their passage, looked after them."

"At least they won't want to give us trouble," said Ta'zara.

"Except by being too clingy," said the captain. "But what do we do with them?"

"Well," said Goth. "First off, I think we get rid of the sea-squill stink on the outside of the tank. This lot don't look like they can think straight with it that close." So she 'ported it elsewhere. "And then I think we go and talk to them."

"Yeah," said the Leewit. "See what can be done, I suppose. I'll go. It's healing they need."

So they got out. That is to say, the Leewit, Me'a, and Ta'zara got out. Ta'zara first, then giving Me'a her chair off the back—which had fans to get her down. Goth and the captain stayed in the tank, on guard.

It was rapidly apparent that Ta'zara's martial arts skills were not going to be needed. The slaves were still in a state of happy euphoria—and they associated the tank and the people in it with that. They were only too eager to cooperate. They were perfectly willing to let the Leewit draw Farnal aside. He smiled at her, recognizing her.

"What are you doin' here?" she demanded. "You managed to get captured twice! Did you think we'd always come to your rescue?"

"No, young lady. To be captured was always my mission, my service to the Church of Irad. We had studied the routes preyed on by the slavers and pirates selling to Karoda very carefully. I was among those sent out to be captured, so I could be the hand of Irad in destroying the beast. I was here to destroy the creature which turns men into slaves," he said with a sadness underlying his happy smile. "I was always intended to be captured. I wanted to be."

"But...you helped the others escape Cinderby's World," said the Leewit. "You helped them get home when we freed them."

He nodded. "They were free, but in trouble. They needed guidance, and support. That too is a good deed in the service of Irad."

"And just how did you plan to destroy this beast?" asked Ta'zara. "Because it is plain that you failed."

"I cannot tell you, sir, in case others succeed. It is probable will be others taken. There were quite a number of us sent out."

"He's got a bomb in his belly," said the Leewit to Ta'zara. "It makes sense, now. The captain was wrong. They don't want to capture the thing that conditions the slaves. They wanted to kill the Arerrerr."

The older man gaped at her. "How did you know...?"

The Leewit shrugged. "It was making you sick. I examined you, remember. I treated you, made you get better."

He sighed. "Our technicians were worried about that. They had to interface Irad's will with our nervous system. It was a risk, but one I believed was worthwhile. After all, it was a small sacrifice to be made. And yes, the ruling faction of the high priests of Irad do favor capturing the beast. Our group hold that it is evil incarnate, and it must be destroyed." He frowned, just slightly. "The levels of corruption there . . . you would not understand, but we found that several of the high priests are active in the financing of vessels engaged in piracy, and shipping conditioned slaves inward to the Empire. That was how we knew where the true vessels of Irad's will—those of us carrying the bombs—had to be placed in order to be captured. To destroy the evil thing which makes Karoda slaves."

"Well, it's not going to be destroyed," said the Leewit. "But we're not going to have it making more slaves either. In case you hadn't figured it out, we're busting up this place, cleaning up the slavers. It's over. But the Arerrerr is not going to be killed or go to Irad. It's not evil. It's just an animal. The Soman were evil, and your high priests would have been eviler. So we're dealing, see. It's all over."

"I am glad. It is too late for me, but it always was something I was willing to die to end." He smiled wryly. "The oddest thing is, I know it to be false, but the rapture . . . It is in itself a love I have never felt, even in my service to Irad. I understood how it was abused, how it made slaves, but not the way the slaves felt. The misuse was evil, but the love and joy it brings is of itself not."

"Yeah. But it's not real," said the Leewit.

"It is to us. It is odd to find myself a slave, an evil I have fought all my life. And yet . . ." He sighed again. "I understand what was done to us. But I am sure all of us will make our way to Parisienne and try to find a place on one of the barges so we can serve. I know what we love and where it comes from. We were told. It is worthy."

The Leewit rolled her eyes. "You're really messed up."

"Maybe. But I feel more whole than I ever have," he said calmly.

The Leewit shook her head. "Wait. I gotta talk to Me'a and the others."

✧   ✧   ✧

Sitting in the tank, keeping a wary eye back the way they'd come, Goth finally had some time to be alone with Captain Pausert. To tell him how afraid she'd been that she'd lost klatha skills, and how glad she was having them back. "So you and me can still be together, Captain."

He squeezed her hand. "I never saw it as any different, Goth. And I wish you'd told me. I could have told you that you were wrong. You 'ported that power wrench for me, when you were helping me with those calibration checks."

"I did? I don't remember," said Goth, wrinkling her forehead. She remembered doing the checks with the captain. It was a slow, tedious and awkward job that he always saw to himself. He was exceptionally good at it. Klatha luck, perhaps.

"Sure you did. I don't think you even thought about it. It's so natural to you, and you were busy with the micrometer readings, when I asked."

"Oh. But...but that was weeks ago!" said Goth, flushing. All this time...

"Yes. But it doesn't matter. All that matters is you're back to being yourself. Anyway, it's not like I'm that good...by Karres standards," said the captain. "Not that useful. I mean the cocooning is useful, but I think it's in some ways like making vatch hooks."

"You're a hot witch, Captain! You can handle the Sheewash Drive," said Goth, automatically supportive.

"Like just about every other witch," said Pausert.

"You're way stronger than most. Stronger than Maleen, and our family are known to be some of the best. And you can do the Egger Route. And you're probably the best vatch-handler ever."

"And as a result we have little to do with vatches these days," said Pausert. "Except Little-bit and her like and they come and go, and there's not a lot I can do about them."

"Just keeping the big ones away is pretty useful. Super useful actually. They used to use us as playthings. Now they leave us alone. That's huge."

"I suppose it is useful. It just didn't feel that way. To be honest with you, I keep feeling as if the vatches are still around, just on the edge of my perception. They can be as sneaky as humans, if you ask me." He glanced around, as if expecting one to appear. "Anyway, Goth, klatha is something we use but klatha using isn't what makes *you*. Goth is who she is. And she's also Vala, the girl of my dreams when I was a boy growing up on Nikkeldepain—when I knew absolutely nothing about klatha or you using it. I just thought you were wonderful. That was enough for me, then, and I haven't actually changed that much."

"I know," said Goth, gruffly. "You're pretty solid, Captain."

At this point the Leewit peered in the manhole on the turret. She looked disapprovingly at them. "Huh. I need some advice about what to do with silly people in love with real stinkers. I reckon you would be the right people to ask."

"What have we done to be stinkers this time?" asked the captain, cheerfully.

"She," said the Leewit, pulling a face at her older sister, "should have talked to me."

"That's different," said Goth equally cheerfully. "I'm usually a stinker for talking to you."

The Leewit sniffed. "Crumping kranslits to both of you. Now what am I going to do with these people? It's not right to let them go and be slaves on the Mantro barges. But it is what they want to do. What they will be happy doing. I know it's just the Arerrerr's work, not real. But what it has done to them is real to them. I don't know what to do now."

She stroked Tippi's sleek head, which had popped itself out of her shirt, looking to be petted. The rochat did seem to do that when people were distressed, and the Leewit plainly was distressed. "I can fix them, I could even make them forget, but... it's a bit like Ta'zara and the Megair Cannibals. They don't want to forget. Even the guy with the bomb in his belly. The one we rescued, and transported to Marbelly. Farnal. They'd rather be dead than be without what it's done to them. Most of them would probably kill themselves in despair—having had it and then having had it taken away. My teaching pattern... says people often do that when they lose what they love. The best I could do is make them forget what happened. And in this case that is hard. It's a primitive part of the brain. We respond to smells at levels far below the thinking part of the brain. And this got hooked into all their emotional feedbacks and pleasure centers without any throttling down. They could forget the incident, but they will always know that they lost something. Something they found really precious. They don't want to forget it."

"Bit different from wanting to forget," said Goth. "From what

I can work out, the Arerrerr was a pet. It needed looking after, and looking after it made the aliens feel good. Maybe even happy. A bit like Tippi. The Arerrerr doesn't need much, just some leaves and some petting. In some ways it doesn't give much, rather like Tippi. I don't think it loved its aliens. Oh, it misses them, because they did a good job and it was comfortable, well petted and looked after and happy. But I am pretty sure they loved it. The image of them telling it they were coming back for it . . . it was heartrending. And loving it and looking after it made them happy. Just like looking after Tippi makes you happy."

"Yeah. I reckon you're right. They all look like you two dopes. But I still don't see what I can do about it. If they realize I'm going to take that away . . . it's going to take more'n Ta'zara to hold them still."

The captain looked thoughtful. "Is it possible to turn this change in their minds away from loving sea-squill smell? I mean, now that it is set."

"You said it was pretty simple," said Goth to the Leewit.

"It is. I think it will reinforce the more exposure they get. But at this stage, it's just one neuron path. It's associated with smell. Very basic neural function."

Goth smiled to herself. You could hear the teaching pattern helping the Leewit. She skipped from her usual language, clinging to the fact that she was the youngest and liked being the youngest. "The guy with the bomb. Can you claim he needs treatment to take it out?"

The Leewit scowled. "Not too keen on surgery, Goth. I'm still sort of scared of it."

"Teleport surgery? I know they do it on Karres. Mother told me. We did a small bit with the nursebeast on Nartheby."

The Leewit brightened. "Oh. Yeah. Hang on." She stood, plainly referencing her teaching pattern. "Yep. We can try anyway. It won't hurt him. You and I work together . . . touch talk. I could direct you and you 'port it out of him?"

"If I know how big it is and can get a mental handle on it. If I get the wrong bit, it could do some damage, but it wouldn't be cutting him open. And while you're in there . . . you shift that neural pathway."

"Yeah. Um. Maybe. But to what?"

"Each other?" suggested the captain. "They'll need someone

not to take advantage of them. At the moment they desperately want to please... Mantro barges and the stinking work on them. Make it any one person and that person could take terrible advantage of them. If they're looking out for the best they can do for each other, well, that would stop that."

"I like that," said the Leewit, thoughtfully. "Even though they'd be like you dopes, but still. Come on, Goth, Captain, we're going to need your strength. Me'a can guard us with the tank."

"So what do you need to do the change? They used scent vials for the Arerrerr," said Goth.

"Hadn't thought of that. I'll need a scent sample from each and all of them. That could be hard."

"Separately?"

"No, all together will probably do. The reaction will trigger off any of the molecules, even in low concentrations."

"No-shape, and if you give me something to collect the samples on, I could do it," said Goth.

"There's a first aid kit here, with some absorbent swabs," said the captain, producing them.

"Perfect," said the Leewit. "And I will make them sweat a bit for you. I got a new whistle for that!"

So Goth went out, unseen, and simply took dabs off the skin of the suddenly sweaty and slightly nervous happy people.

When she came back, they did a changeover, with Me'a taking control of the tank, and the others going to the wary group.

It was obvious that the Leewit's whistle hadn't made them easier to deal with. "You all got your nose filters in?" asked Goth of her companions.

The others nodded. "Okay. I'm going to crack a vial of sea-squill smell."

"Make it real quick," said the Leewit. "They don't need to smell a lot of it, and neither do we."

So she did. It worked. "Look, we need to do a follow-up medical procedure on you," the Leewit explained to Farnal. "You've got that bomb in you, which will eventually blow up."

He nodded earnestly. "That could hurt others. Innocents."

"Well, I couldn't do this earlier, because my sister wasn't with me. But I reckon we can help."

"But how? It was a major surgical procedure to put it in," said Farnal.

"You leave that to us," said the Leewit. "We're using new techniques. Trust us. We rescued you, saved all those other slaves, treated your injuries, and then got you off Cinderby's World."

"This is all true. You have displayed your goodness, and I think you have been a hand of Irad. I will trust you," said Farnal.

They took him into one of the dormitory rooms, and got him to lie down.

The Leewit put her hands on his shoulders. "The transdermic injection may sting briefly," she said—and touching him obviously induced some kind of nerve-based anesthesia.

"You've been watching those medical shows," said Goth to her sister.

"Yeah," said the Leewit. "Need to fake something besides klatha being used. Goth, hold onto my shoulders and I'll try and lead you in. The teaching pattern says I can do this. I hope it works. Captain . . . if you lend us strength."

Goth found it nearly as disturbing as reading history from objects was. She found herself seeing the layers of tissue and blood vessels that her sister moved her power through and along, with the man's heartbeat loud in her ears. The Leewit transported her down between the ropes of intestines and their rhythmic move-ment and little gurgles, to a spheroid with a couple of spiky protrusions, one of which had plainly connected to the spine, and the other to a major artery. Suddenly the vision zoomed in, and she could see those connections were closed off with some hard white substance. And then they zoomed out and did it again. She could hear the Leewit's voice somewhere in the distance, yet within her. "That's it. Can you take it out? Not breaking the blockers I put in."

'Porting always took careful visualization, but she had that now. So she took it out.

She was not really prepared for being in the middle of an earthquake.

When the shake and tumble had stopped and she found that she was still somehow seeing the world from inside the gut cavity through the Leewit's klatha senses, she asked, "Did it go off?"

"No, you dope. Just the bomb suddenly wasn't there in his abdomen," said the Leewit's distant-near voice. "Everything rushed in to fill the space. I nearly lost control for a bit. I got a few minor bleeders to fix. All right. You can go out now."

"Not sure I know how to."

"Just let go of me. You're squeezing a hole in my shoulder."

So Goth did. The bomb from Farnal's belly lay on the floor rocking slightly . . . inside one of the captain's transparent force cocoons.

"I didn't know if and when it might go off," he said. "Best to be safe I thought."

"Swab," said the Leewit.

So Goth gave it to her.

A few moments later she pulled her hands away, and smiled at the two of them. "That was easier than I thought."

"I feel like I went through an earthquake," said Goth.

"Well, next time we shouldn't actually be in there when you do it. And my shoulder is sore. But the job is done. He'll wake up in few minutes. He'll be a little sore, but no longer in love with anything that smells of sea-squill."

"That's a win for him. So what about that bomb? Will it go off?"

The Leewit shrugged. "My teaching pattern doesn't cover bombs, and the captain hasn't given me any to 'speriment with. And I did *so* ask him to." She stuck her tongue out at the captain.

"Yeah. Well, it is sitting in a cocoon over there. What do we do with it?" asked Goth.

"You 'ported it here? You dope," said the Leewit. "Don't you think somewhere else would have been smart?"

"Easy, you two," said Captain Pausert, grinning at them. "Here. I brought two of the ration bars from the tank. You'll probably need them and they might make you better tempered. I don't know that much about bombs, but it's safe in the cocoon. Vezzarn's the right man to ask, but Ta'zara or Me'a might know more."

They both took the ration bars, and ate. "Tastes as bad as Me'a's energy bars, but not as hard on the teeth," said the Leewit at the end of it.

"Better than nothing, but not nothing better," agreed Goth. "How hard was changing the Arerrerr's work?"

"Piece of cake. Quick too. Easier than chewing that ration bar. I could do the others without them even knowing, now I've done one."

"So let me hide you in no-shape and we'll go and do it. It'll be easier than getting them to trust us first."

"It is sort of without consent," said the Leewit.

"Uh-huh. If any complain you can undo it, and make them want to work on the Mantro barges to smell sea-squill all their lives. We don't want to spend too much time on this. The Soman crowd probably still outnumber us. They're just in a mess right now."

"I guess," said the Leewit.

So they went out.

The captain looked at Ta'zara, still standing at the doorway, and sighed. "I suppose I should be used to them."

Ta'zara smiled. "As the man said of storm wind: 'There is no stopping it, so you may as well go with it. Who knows where you may end up?' It is good that my mistress considers what she does, though. She is growing, Captain."

"Yes. Both of them are. I'm the one who feels like he is shrinking. What do we do with this fellow? What do we do with this bomb?"

"Leave both, I would say," said Ta'zara, calmly, looking out of the doorway at the group of people. "I think I can work out where they are."

"Why? Is Goth's no-shape less than perfect? She would want to know."

Ta'zara shook his head. "Come and look. The ones they've treated are quite obvious."

They were. The faces and postures showed it. They glowed with happiness, with pleasure at being with those their modified nervous systems told them they adored.

"I don't want it done to me, but I can see how it works," said Pausert quietly. "And how they made such good slaves. I'm glad we've put a stop to it."

"It is a particularly evil thing to take advantage of," agreed Ta'zara. "Still. I believe they were very expensive, and therefore treated quite well. Ordinary slaves are often not treated well because they are quite cheap."

"I don't care. It had to stop," said Pausert. "And we need to make sure it doesn't start up again."

"On this we are in complete agreement, Captain. The Arerrerr's power can be terribly misused. Besides slaves... Soldiers could be made into utter fanatics. I am not sure quite how the Leewit plans to do it, though."

Ta'zara seemed convinced she had a plan. Privately, though, Pausert wondered how such a creature's abilities could ever be kept safe from abuse.

While he was still pondering this, Goth and the Leewit returned. "Done. I think. They kept milling around," said the Leewit, tiredly.

"I kept track," said Goth. "Being able to know where things are in space goes with 'porting them. People are no different. How's the patient?"

"Breathing fine," said the captain. "But I'm not much on medical matters, as you know. He's been stirring a bit."

"He's waking up," said the Leewit. "He's about due."

And indeed, Farnal sat up a few minutes later, and blinked at them. "Did you succeed? You seem so young for a surgeon."

"Look on the floor," said the Leewit.

He did . . . and then flung himself hastily on top of the bomb. "Get out! Get out quickly!"

"It's shielded," said the captain. "A hyperelectronic bomb-disposal shield." It was simpler than trying to explain what that actually was. And, for Karres and its operatives it was far safer to keep its mechanisms secret.

The man got up, rubbing his plainly bruised stomach. "Good, dear ones. I was so afraid you would be killed." There were tears in his eyes. "I thought you would just deactivate the switch. It is not possible to remove it from the body without activating the timer. It only has a brief time before exploding. I think you should still leave. I could not bear it if you were to be hurt."

Goth looked at the Leewit. And the Leewit looked back at Goth. "We both held the swab."

It took Pausert a few moments to work it out. "Well. At least we know they won't attack us. I suppose we can leave this bomb here. Unless you have another use for it, that is?"

"Thinking," said Goth. "Come on, Farnal. There are lots of people out there who will be happy to see you. And you them."

They went out of the dormitory room and left him to join the others, returning to the tank. Me'a had been busy in there. "I've used the spatial maps and the data to position a remote probe in the passage leading to the gateguns. I used that for a direct line-of-sight spy-ray penetration. They're preparing a coun-terattack. I'm listening in on their planning. I've even managed to penetrate their systems. I'm trying to use that to circumvent their comms shield. I am stealing all their data while I am in there... Here. Let me put the sound and visual up on screen. Ta'zara, we need to plan."

Her fingers danced across the hyperelectronic keypad. Onto the tank's central display screen came the image of the people of the Soman Consortium—or what was left of it, in the fortification behind the gateguns.

There were still quite a lot of heavily armed men. There were even a couple Goth recognized. Bormgo... and the obnoxious Jaccy from the sheen clipper *Sheridan*. He must, somehow, have gotten them to not to condition him as a slave. Yelissa was there too, clinging onto him. Well, Goth understood that now. It was still a surprise to see them there.

"That's the nasty piece of work who drugged me on the ship! The one who wanted to send me here to be turned into a Karoda slave," said Goth.

Pausert cracked his knuckles. "Which one?" he demanded.

"Can you keep it down?" asked Me'a. "I'm trying to listen. It always pays to know what your enemies are thinking and doing."

"It might pay better to 'port them a little bomb," said the captain, tersely. "It was, come to think of it, really intended for them. I think delivering it might stop them thinking or doing. Can you do that, Goth?"

"No problem. I can see where it is going. But will it go off? What about the cocoon?"

"I can take that off anywhere. I made it. I know it. I don't have to see it or touch it. We can take it off here and we can set the trigger."

"Better we go to it. Leave Me'a to watch and listen in."

When they went out, they found the conditioned slaves in a tight huddle on the far side of the room. They went into the cave room where the cocooned bomb lay.

"Now we need to work out how to activate it," said the captain bending forward to pick it up. "I'll just..."

The cocooned bomb suddenly glowed searingly. "Oh," said the Leewit. "Maybe it really didn't like being taken out of his belly."

"I guess that's the end of that idea, Captain," said Goth.

Pausert looked at the glowing sphere. It was bright enough to make him narrow his eyes to slits, but that was the only effect it had. "Not really. If you can 'port it like that, I can undo it anywhere. And that version of the cocooning doesn't even allow gas molecules to pass. Just visible light."

"Easily done then," said Goth. She took his hand. "On the count of three I'll 'port."

Pausert found it the oddest thing. He'd never really gotten quite how teleportation worked with klatha, before... And now he was doing it. Well, experiencing it as if he was doing it. He wondered if he could... but first to reverse the pattern that made the cocoon. He only had to start it for the energy field to stop resonating and collapse.

Goth looked up at him, her mouth slightly open. "So that's how it works!" she said. Plainly she'd had the same experience. She squeezed his hand hard. "You're a hot witch, Captain."

"And so are you."

"Come on," said the Leewit. "Let's go find out what happened. I think I felt the explosion. And that bit of rock fell down."

Out in the main chamber quite a few more pieces of rock had fallen down. The group of former slaves had retreated to a far corner. The Leewit, Goth, the captain and Ta'zara scrambled into the tank. Me'a shook her head at them. "Just when I was piggybacking on their system to get a tight beam communication to Vezzarn. The shielding is tight on this place. They're calling their associates home to help, and I thought we might as well do the same—and you go and collapse the roof on them."

"Their safe cave caved in?" asked the captain.

"That was what the spy ray showed," answered Me'a. "We've got our former slaves approaching the tank. I have been thinking about what you did to them, Leewit. I don't think sweat samples from everyone worked quite the way you planned." She smiled wryly. "We did do some investigation into just how the Karoda slavers conditioned their slaves. We didn't find out a lot, but the scent material was refined—I think to take out all the elements which don't just belong to a specific individual. That lot... probably love all of human kind. The sweaty ones, the most."

"Oh," said the Leewit. "Yes. I suppose so."

"It could be worse," said the captain. "And I assume the specific bits will keep them fond of each other. Let's see what they want."

"Probably to make us sweat," said Goth. But this was not the case. They wanted reassurance and direction—and to know what was going on. And to tell the *Venture*'s crew they knew their minds had been messed with. "Could it be done to others who have so been conditioned?" asked Farnal. "It is morally wrong to tamper with the minds of men, but compared to loving the smell of sea-squill, and wishing to be in that smell..."

The Leewit wrinkled her brow. "Prob'ly not," she admitted. "It's a self-reinforcing pattern. This was the best we could do for you to escape it. It was possible because you had so little time and chance to smell sea-squill stink. You still won't find that as revolting as most. But people who have been conditioned and getting feedback for a while? Nope."

"They are to be pitied," said Farnal. "We will have to see what can be done for them. No one understands this condition better. Now, you said you had been busy freeing other slaves, and that there was a little more to do before it was done. How can we help?" He smiled. "We have talked together. We will do whatever we can for you, even to death. As long as we can do it together." The group surrounding him nodded almost in unison. They seemed to have made him into their speaker, but it was plain they agreed.

"What you can do for us is to stay alive and get out of here," said the captain. "Their command and control center—the roof collapsed with the explosion. But they have sent out a call for all their people. There's going to be extra trouble, and probably some more explosions before we're done. We don't want to be worrying about you. We're going to try and deal with the front gates now. I'd stay back for a while. Arm yourselves if possible." He saw the doubt on their faces. "You may need to defend each other. Karoda is a tough place, even outside the Soman base."

"That is true," said Farnal. "I was one of the survivors of the '03 war. We must arm ourselves, brothers and sisters."

"You do that. Also tell any other slaves you see that they have to head downhill. The caves are confusing but the exit is the lowest point," said Me'a.

"We will spread that news."

"Right. We're going to break out," said the captain. "I believe there is quite a loud siren on this tank. When you hear that, it's time to head for the exit."

"Actually, there is even a public address system," said Me'a.

"Even better. Listen for it. We'll give instructions as best we can."

They closed the hatch and headed through the tunnels that the Somans had converted the cave system into, toward the inner gates. "Of course, I am not even sure that the tank can blow them open, or where their controls are," admitted Me'a. "And, just as we're not sure how well hardened those hull-metal doors are, we don't know how the blowing of their command and control center affected the spacegun chambers or their power and manning. I mean all the lights in this cave-tunnel complex of theirs have stayed on. The power supply must be robust."

"Just get us to the gate, Me'a. We'll deal," said Goth.

That brought a chuckle from Me'a. "I begin to appreciate, fully, the warnings that Sedmon of the Six Lives gave about the need to give the Wisdoms of Karres my full cooperation. I didn't quite get it back then. Not the full implication."

"Ha," said Ta'zara, cheerfully. "You have seen nothing yet. When you have been where I have been..."

The inner gate being reached, they could see it for the first time, as they had been unconscious when they came in. It had big and fairly simple mechanical hinges. "Could blast those," said Me'a.

"We can, just now. But that looks like a personal access door," said the captain. "The Leewit can just give a little whistle to get rid of any lurkers, and Goth and I will go in no-shape to check it out."

"Can I try out the public address system?" asked the Leewit. "What sort of whistle do you want, Captain? A frightener? A stunner? Or why not both?"

"Both sound good, in that order, if you let us put on earmuffs first!" The tank had earmuff-mouthpiece combinations for its operators, and these could be set to mute. Those outside the tank were not so lucky.

Goth had to admit that she was having the time of her life. Having thought that she'd never be able to use klatha again and she and the captain could never do Karres' work together, let alone the sheer power of actually using their klatha powers together as they had with 'porting Farnal's bomb...it felt like opening a whole lot of presents on her birthday. "The no-shape I have us in is basically everything. No radiation is getting out, and the light is bent around us."

"Is it an effort?" asked Pausert.

"Y'know, it's odd. It's much less effort, now. I had to do a fair bit of it on the sheen clipper. This...is harder, but feels easier. It's as if I have come back stronger after nearly dying. Klatha progression is sort of stepwise, not linear."

"Well, don't you go nearly dying again. I'm quite content with you as strong as you are," said the captain, giving her hand a squeeze. "Now...this door. Shall I just cocoon the lock out of it?"

Goth shook her head. "It's got a security pad. Probably needs an entry code."

"Well," said the captain. "I could try my gambler's luck on it. That seems klatha driven."

"But it doesn't feel right," said Goth. "I can hear it in your voice, Captain. So why don't we make ourselves a little door in their hull metal?"

"Now that does feel right," said Pausert. "Pick a spot. I'll cocoon it. That worked remarkably well on the spaceport wall."

"Save your cocooning for their spaceguns, Captain. It takes much more energy. I'll just 'port a nice doorframe shape line... to over there. Minimum effort."

The chunk of hull metal was still remarkably heavy. It dropped slightly to the ferrocrete floor, but that was only a fingernail width or two, with a laser-cut line around it. Otherwise it stayed in place.

"I'll just have to give it a shove, I suppose," said the captain. He did and it moved very slightly. So they both did. "Might have to get Ta'zara, or the tan..."

It gave way suddenly and they both fell inward on top of it. For a moment Goth's no-shape cover was disrupted.

The fire systems of the Soman defenses were not disrupted.

CHAPTER 21

The killing zone in between the Soman gates was a searing blaze of heavy blaster fire. Nothing could have lived through it.

"I guess they really aren't pleased to see us," said the captain, from inside the cocoon. The cocoon of klatha force had proved impervious to blaster fire before. It hadn't had to do so this time because they weren't in the killing zone anymore.

"I didn't know I could 'port people!" said Goth.

"It's a big step up, isn't it? Your father can, though."

"Yeah. But I mean Threbus...he's one of the hottest witches on Karres."

"I guess I know what that means," said Pausert with a smile. "So, how do we deal with the situation?"

"The same way, I guess. If I took us out of there, I can put us back. But in your cocoon. Can you still work your cocooning on the spaceguns? I'll start dealing with the blaster cannons."

"Sounds like a plan to me," said the captain. "I'm not entirely sure what happens when a spacegun hits a cocoon. They must be pre-ranged or they'd blow the other walls apart. They won't do their ferrocrete any good."

"We're not planning on leaving this place in much shape for

any future tenants," said Goth. "And I for one trust your cocoons, Captain. Let's go."

The Leewit would have been envious if she had seen the results. It turned out that putting a cocoon onto the point where the space-gun nozzle protruded through the hull-metal wall, and including some of the wall, meant the entire force of that weapon had to go somewhere. And that somewhere wasn't out. Half the wall blew out and Goth and the captain were bounced by flying chunks of metal and pieces of rock. And most of the force had blown back through the gun emplacements. That explosion continued to run in a chain of other detonations and blooms of fire and smoke.

When at last it was silent the cocoon lay against the far wall with a pile of debris around it. The front doors had also blown open. A couple of surviving Soman gunners were staggering toward the forest margin. One entire side of their defensive entry was shattered into several pieces, some with still-molten sections, others looking like they'd been one of the Leewit's artworks that she'd gotten angry with and crumpled. The other side had had several holes ripped into it also, from the pieces of debris.

"Next time," said Goth, trying to rub an elbow in the tight quarters of their cocoon, "I think we should 'port away, as well. We got lucky."

"And bruised," said the captain. "I think I may have a black eye. It was a bit like going over a waterfall in a barrel, wasn't it?"

"Yeah. But I think they went over it without the barrel. Hello...what's happening there?"

The one inner door was slowly pushing forward, sticking on the debris, with the broad nozzle of the Sirius tank's main gun leading the way. Another shove and the tank pushed into what had been the Soman antechamber.

"We've got company," said Goth. "I suppose we had better get up and say hello."

"See if they draw fire first," said the captain. "Then we can deal with it, without getting caught in the crossfire."

Which was sensible, but there was no blaster or any other fire. So the captain undid their cocoon, and they stood up.

Goth took a deep breath to call out, promptly felt very woozy and had to sit down again.

The next thing she knew she was waking up in the tank.

"What happened? Is the captain all right?"

"I'm fine," said Pausert from just behind her. "There was just a bit of their knockout gas."

"You gave me quite a fright," said the Leewit. "Don't do that again!"

"I'm not planning to. But things happen even to hot witches," said Goth. "Got anything to drink? My mouth tastes like a bollem pen."

"Here," said Me'a, passing a water-suck tube. "The tank's supply."

Goth sucked on it gratefully.

The Leewit had not quite gotten over the relief of seeing the captain and her sister stand up in the middle of the zone of destruction they had caused—and the horror of seeing them immediately fall over. It had only been Me'a's quick intervention that had stopped her flinging the hatch open to run to their rescue. That would have ended up with all of them gassed, and easy victims for any foe.

The tank did have an airlock exit. And Ta'zara, raised on Na'kalauf, was an excellent diver, quite capable of holding his breath and carrying them both in. Me'a had an external analyzer going by then. "Gas. Ambrox. Short-term anesthetic. They'll be fine in a few minutes, Your Wisdom. The concentration is quite low. With the doors open it should be gone in a few minutes."

The Leewit, hand on her sister's neck, was busy assessing that for herself. But it was correct, and the captain had already begun to sit up, slightly confused and, briefly, ready to cocoon—or whatever his befuddled mind with its klatha-harnessing power might do—to protect and attack whatever it was, before the Leewit managed to stop him. That was probably just as well, the teaching pattern in her mind told her. Klatha manipulation really needed good mental focus.

"I see what you mean," said Me'a to Ta'zara, in the tongue of Na'kalauf, looking at the devastation. "And that was just two of them. I wondered a little what they had done to Sedmon of the Six Lives, to intimidate him like that. Uldune usually sets about eliminating possible dangers."

"Strategy, Ta'taimi. When your enemy can eat you for breakfast in one bite, and then ask when the food is coming, make sure you are not his enemy. It is fortunate that the Wisdoms have no need or desire for what they could take easily."

"And she is a great healer, on top of it all. My oath is given. I had little idea of what I was giving it to, though."

"She would free you if you asked."

"Are you crazy, Ta'zara?" said Me'a with a smile. "We're going to wreak havoc, man of the Ke'taka clan. We will be legends. They will tell of our lives, and our passing over the reef, for a thousand years."

He smiled broadly. "Of that I am certain. And as her Ta'taimi, you ought to remember that she has the gift of understanding any language she chooses."

"There's a lot to remember with this job," said Me'a, with an answering smile.

"It's mainly keeping the Wisdoms fed and keeping up with them. We do get to fight, sometimes," said Ta'zara.

"But there is also some need of stopping them from plunging in immediately," said Me'a.

"Oh, that too. But it is not always practical or possible."

"So," said the captain. "Next steps? I have ideas, but I want your thoughts."

"The gas is mostly dissipated," said Me'a. "We could put out a call for any prisoners wishing to flee to do so. The floater bay is close by. There are vehicles to be taken. I suggest we, and they, remove from here as soon as possible. This was merely their central processing base for slaves. The Soman Consortium has holdings across most of the habitable area of the planet. A lot of their forces are coming. I've been monitoring their channels. They've been trying to contact the command and control center. They believe the entrance fortification capable of withstanding a long siege. But, obviously, they know that the Somans' chief asset, the slave conditioner, is here. Without that they lose their main money earner. Without that, half the other families and groups on Karoda will attack them—they don't have a lot of friends. Word spreads. I wouldn't be surprised if there were some others beside the Soman allies heading for this area. They are worried about that, so we should be too. Or at least aware of them."

"How long do we have?" asked the captain. "And have you gotten in contact with the *Venture 7333*?"

"First ground forces should be here in less than an hour. There are quite a lot of fliers on their way from further afield, but they're arguing about how close they dare bring them. They know the area is under heavy surveillance by Iradalia. The actual location of their headquarters is something they want to keep from being obvious, which a bunch of fliers heading in would make it. It's why they don't have any here, and only use routes in the caves through the mountains. I've had Vezzarn asking for instructions. He's paid the port fees, so we can up and run when we get there."

"Tell old Vezzarn to get the tubes warmed up and have the nova guns ready for action. I'll be there shortly."

"How, Captain?" asked Goth.

"The Egger Route. There is nothing else for it, I think. It took about four hours to get here, and the Soman drivers knew the way. There are a lot of the Soman Consortium heading here as fast as they can. We need to get the Arerrerr out of here before they start shooting at us, while we try to load it up."

He sucked breath through his teeth, thoughtfully. "We transported the *Venture*. We could probably transport the tank."

"It didn't go well, remember?" said Goth. "Look, if you and I go we can be back here really fast. And I am, of all of us, the most experienced at using the Egger Route."

"Makes sense to me," said the Leewit.

"It means leaving the Leewit and the others here. Or are you suggesting we try to take them without the tank?"

"The Egger Route, huh, no thanks," said Leewit. "When we have to, but right now—no. We'll sit tight in the tank, with you on comms, and work on getting people out of the Soman caves. You and Goth go. There is nothing much you can use for padding, though."

"I guess we'll have to make do without it. Oh well. We're bruised and battered anyway," said Goth, taking the captain's hand. "Best to get it over with."

Pausert nodded. "My cabin, I think. Leewit, take care, and if I don't get back soon remember to wash behind your ears."

He got the *sudden death* stare from the Leewit, as he and Goth vibrated, blurred and disappeared.

Ta'zara turned to Me'a. "You get used to it, eventually. Or, like Vezzarn you just find reasons to be elsewhere when witchy stuff is going on."

"I can see the sense in that," said Me'a, wryly. "I suppose we'd better see if we can let the former slaves know it is safe to flee this place."

So they did. Some of them even collected the floater trucks from the parking bay, and started for the fringe of the forest.

The distance in Egger space bore little or no relationship to the distance in ordinary space. Pausert knew that. It was just remembering it that he'd failed at, he reflected, as they swam through the strange place that was somehow between everywhere and everything. His klatha senses relled that there were vatches in it, somehow. Of course, in Egger space there was no telling just how far off they were, either. But at least he was with Goth and she was with him... and vibrating and bouncing and shaking into his cabin on the *Venture*.

It helped a lot that they held each other tightly throughout. But they still needed a couple of minutes to recover. As every time they used the Egger Route, Pausert remained obstinately convinced they were doing the pattern slightly wrong, just not quite matching that place right. However, his suggestions for tweaking it had been met with firm resistance, so far. One day, perhaps. But right now, he had a spaceship to fly, and to land in a forest. They really weren't designed for planetary work.

It would take a fair amount of piloting skill, and not just lying here, holding Goth. "Up," he said. "We've a ship to fly. The Leewit to fetch. An alien pet to rescue."

"Clumping nuisances, all of them," said Goth, smiling up at him. "You know, the more this goes on, the more I feel like we're a piece in some game being played. And we're only seeing part of the picture. Not all of it."

"Me, too. And I got the sense of vatches being in Egger space. That's new to me. But there are all sorts of links. The trees here. The rochats. Even that paratha stuff."

They'd walked through to the bridge by then, where Vezzarn was worriedly working his way through preflight checks. "Am I glad to see you, Captain! Takeoff is a bit out of my league," he said, standing up from the command chair. "You want me strapped in on the aft guns? Missy Leewit going to take hers again?"

"She's not with us. We're going to pick her up. Goth will be working the lateral rocketry, so you'll have to take the forward guns. Jump to it, we're going for a short hard boost and a bit of atmospheric flying. You've got Me'a's position logged?"

"You've got me on comms, Captain," said Me'a from the speakers. "You've got a couple of minutes before the lead elements of Soman fliers get to the area. When they detect a spaceship coming in, they'll stop worrying about maintaining secrecy."

"We're on our way, Me'a. We just need to find you and find a place to set down near you."

"We've cleared the tunnels, Captain, or at least as well as possible. Farnal has taken charge. He's quite an organizer. He has six floaters and perhaps two hundred former prisoners and slaves, and some arms. They could endanger the ship, wanting to escape."

The captain, his hands and eyes busy with the controls, was not too sure how to deal with that. The *Venture* could never take all of them, let alone pick up the Arerrerr—and they could not let that fall into anyone else's hands. He wasn't sure what they could do with it. It would be a potential problem almost anywhere, even, possibly, on Karres.

Fortunately, Goth, who had already dealt with her lateral checks, answered Me'a. "Keep a couple of them, ideally someone who can operate the tank. Use the PA to tell them that Soman troops are arriving and you're going to be rearguard. And then use the guns to clear a few trees to make us a landing spot. We'll be ready to blast out of here in about two minutes. It shouldn't take us long, so move fast. And then pull back. We don't want to flame you with our tubes."

"Will do," said Me'a, tersely.

Two minutes later they made one of the captain's typical firecracker launches toward the stratosphere. Really, that was the only effective way to use the main tubes for atmospheric work. You could do a few miles on the laterals but that was practically the limit. Otherwise it was hopping up and then controlling her descent and using the laterals. Because they had to make a landing, the descent had to be relatively slow. That made them a prime target for revolt ships or surface fire or rocketry.

The captain knew this all too well from his training in the Nikkeldepain Space Navy, and did his best to counter it. That was not easy on himself, the ship or the other people aboard. It meant getting his bearings once they had gained height, and then dropping as fast and far as he dared, before using the main tubes for braking, as Goth handled the laterals to try and put them as close to the location that they had from Me'a. She would only have seconds, fast-falling seconds, to get them on an exact heading. Miss it, and they'd either land in the metallic trees, doing Patham alone knew what damage, or he could try to boost them upward. That might well leave the tank or anyone below in the blast from the tubes at maximum thrust, something the tube liners also would not cope with well.

They dropped through the clouds like a stone—more like a meteor, really—winds buffeting as Goth steered and the captain watched the figures on the altimetry screen plunge. His knuckles were white on the thrust lever as they dropped toward the tiny clearing in the forested valley. At the last second he pulled back the throttle. The *Venture* shook like a leaf in a gale and then in a huge pall of smoke, as the captain killed the roar of the *Venture*'s stern tubes, dropped again...about a hand's breadth.

"Phew!" said Goth, from next to him. "I sweated a bucket doing that, Captain. And then I thought you'd left it too late. They were shooting at us!"

"Didn't notice," admitted the captain. "Vezzarn, did you get any shots off?"

"Too busy hanging on and being sick," said the spacer. "I'm getting too old for this, Captain!"

"*Venture, Venture,* can we come aboard, quickly?" said Me'a. Her voice sounded a little shaken. "We should have been a bit further away."

"Good landing, Captain," chirped the Leewit in the background.

"We'll open the hatch for you."

"Just open the cargo hold and get Goth on the grav-tractor-beam projector and grab us," said the Leewit. "We'll hang onto Me'a's wheelchair. We gotta pick up the Arerrerr, and the bad guys are coming as fast as they can."

Goth had already unstrapped and was legging it down the corridor before the Leewit had finished talking. The captain turned to his detection equipment and external screens instead, and transferred the laterals to his board. No need to worry about Goth. She could do her job. And sure enough, he got an intercom call moments later, as he watched the Sirius 7 tank turn and trundle toward the deeper forest. "Got them all, Captain."

"Get them strapped in. No. Wait. Send the Leewit to the aft nova guns. Tell her to let me know once she's there and strapped in. This may be rough. I'm tracking incoming aircraft."

"She's on her way, Captain. What do you want of me?"

"If either Ta'zara or Me'a can handle the tractor, I want you back in the copilot seat as soon as I put her down. We're going to grab the Arerrerr and run."

"Strapped!" yelled the Leewit.

"Lifting!" snapped Pausert, suiting action to his words.

The captain pulled the incredibly tricky move of boosting just slightly and then kicking the *Venture* over sideways so she could ride on her laterals, over the bleak cliff-edged mountainside to the lava hole that was the Arerrerr's little island of greenery. It was slow, careful work, which just couldn't be done faster. He knew they were coming under fire, and was dimly aware that the nova guns had fired in return. But all his concentration was on managing to set the *Venture* down. The gimbals swung his chair and his controls, but the rest of the crew would be hanging in their straps. Gently, on what was far too steep a slope for comfort, he put her down. The *Venture* scraped and slid slightly, making the captain grit his teeth and reach for the controls, but she stopped. "Opening the hold," he said calmly. "I hope you can manage to load it. We've got no time for tie-downs. Hold the creature with the gravity tractor."

"Do our best, Captain," said Ta'zara. Pausert was aware of the nova guns firing again. Goth, panting, dropped herself into the second's command chair, pulling the straps on to clip in.

"Tell us when we can close and run," said Pausert. "Goth. Transfer laterals, and set up a transmission on the frequency that will blow those forcecuffs."

"Righto," she said calmly, hand flickering across the controls. "Also have done a light-shift on the *Venture*, Captain. They can't see us."

"Good thinking," he said, looking at the detector screens and indicators.

"The Arerrerr's in, Captain," said Ta'zara. "Activated the hold-door closing circuit."

Pausert eyed his instruments again. "Hold tight! Goth, full lift on the lower laterals! And transmit!"

The *Venture* began to rise—this was not what the laterals were intended for—and as soon as they had clearance the captain gave the *Venture*'s main tubes thrust. He was attempting something that was more than just difficult and fuel-expensive, juggling thrust from various tubes to put the *Venture* in an accelerating curve, upward.

"Got him!" yelled the Leewit.

And then the *Venture* was buffeted by the slap of the force from a vast explosion from the Soman tunnels. The captain struggled for control, watching the damage telltales for warnings, as the *Venture* raced away skyward, free and clear.

Two minutes later, as he was beginning to relax slightly, Goth said, "Captain! There's a whole armada heading toward us from space!"

Indeed, there was. Literally, fifty ships. "What the..." exclaimed the captain.

"Iradalia. That's an invasion fleet. Heading for the explosion," said Goth.

"And we're between it and where it is going." He reached for the drawer where the wires that helped them with visualizing the pattern for the Sheewash Drive were kept. "Time for some especially fast running before they start shooting."

Goth nodded. "We're still stratospheric, but there is no help for it, I reckon. We can't go down—we've got the Somans' survivors and allies hunting us there. And we can't outrun them, incoming like that. They must have been waiting on the asteroids and moonlets, ready to pounce ever since we landed on Karoda."

"Time to go Sheewash," said the captain.

"Uh-huh!" agreed Goth, and a few moments later the strange flame of energy danced in the twisted wires. The *Venture*, already racing skyward, accelerated furiously at a tangent to her course, to miss the incoming fleet.

"Good part of the world to be leaving," said Goth. "Looks like they're throwing everything they've got at it."

"It's going to be messy," agreed the captain.

Some of the invading fleet obviously thought a spacecraft hurtling up toward them—even though it was angling away—was a threat. Shooting at the Leewit was definitely enough reason for her to respond. At this range, given the speed of the *Venture*, a hit was unlikely. The captain did a few evasive maneuvers, anyway. This was nothing like the full power of the Sheewash and they were still in exosphere and not out of Karoda's gravity well. The *Venture* was just a really fast ship, pushing its human cargo to the practical limits.

"You nearly waggled us into that beam, Captain!" said the Leewit over the intercom. "Leave off. They can't hit a barn door from inside, and you just made me miss. I got a hit on one, though."

As an ex-space navy man himself, the captain hadn't been impressed by the invasion fleet's shooting or their piloting skills. He said as much. "Unless they're much better infantry than they're pilots, and better shots with blasters than space cannons, they're doomed. I think some of them are going to plow into each other, or hit each other on the breaking blast."

"This is something like their nineteenth try," said Me'a. "And as most of their people outside of the religious police never pick up a blaster until they get conscripted, the gambling money says this one won't go a lot better."

"Still, they can claim to have destroyed the Soman base," said Goth.

"They'll have to get back, first," said Me'a.

They were now well out of range, and the captain was glad to let the Sheewash wires collapse. The cluttered area between Karoda, Iradalia and open space was tricky enough to negotiate. Besides, there were a few things about the usage he'd put the *Venture* through that needed checking.

CHAPTER 22

Once the *Venture* was comfortably out of the Irad system, and there was no pursuit visible on the detectors, the crew of the *Venture* gathered in the mess. Most of them did, anyway. Old Vezzarn had volunteered to stay on the bridge, watching their instruments so no nasty surprises crept up on them.

"Captain, I'm just a crewman. You decide where we're going and what we do next. You've proved you always come back for me, look after me. Besides," he said, with a wary smile, when Pausert called the meeting, "it'll probably involve witchy stuff I'd rather not know about." Vezzarn remained rather superstitious about klatha. "This way I genuinely can say to anyone from the Daal's secret police that I really don't know. What I don't know can't be gotten out of me by the Daalmen, and not telling them anything is wiser from the Wisdoms of Karres' point of view. And that is for the best, I reckon."

It was quite crowded in the *Venture*'s small mess. Part of that was not just the number of people but because the Leewit and Tippi were playing a complicated game which involved the rochat jumping to catch pieces of the seaweed biscuit it had become so fond of.

"Aren't you going to need that stuff to feed the Arerrerr?" asked Goth.

"Fed the Arerrerr already," said the Leewit, tossing another fragment of biscuit for Tippi. "It won't need much more for weeks. It's got a kind of slow metabolism. But don't go into the hold without suiting up or cycling the airlock. I've changed the air mix a bit, for starters, to make it more comfortable, and pushed up the temperature. There's a bit more sulfur in the air, too. I have made sure it can't scent-spray you, or work on your neural patterns, but no sense in taking chances."

"Well," said the captain, "that's rather what I wanted to talk about. It fills most of the hold. Now... Goth and I have a task to attend to, but we also have this... pet. It's a problem. From what I can work out it can't really look after itself—and anyway, it's been used to make slaves once, so the idea that that is possible is out there now. We really don't want it happening again. It seems the only really safe place for it will be Karres itself."

"Karres is short on the minerals it needs to thrive. They'd have to look after it very carefully. I think it would be miserable," said the Leewit. "We should take it home."

"That's all very well, but we have no idea where 'home' is," said Me'a. "I had never heard of such a creature. It's not like its owners are out looking for it, and putting up notices on the walls. We don't even know where to start."

"I think I do," said Goth. "And maybe they have even been searching. Something odd has been going on. I've been putting clues together. I have been checking on some of the star charts, looking up what information we have on the systems we've been to. And there is a pattern. And that pattern relates to metal-leaf trees, and"—she pointed at Tippi, who wrinkled her nose at her—"rochats."

"Cinderby's World and Na'kalauf don't have metal-leaf trees, but do have rochats."

"Rochats don't breed on Na'kalauf. They're brought in, mostly from Serax, which does have metal-leaf trees, or the Armbour system, that did, before they got chopped down. Cinderby's World... well, it doesn't. It's too windy, I suspect. But it's also a world with a lot more heavy metals than average—the same as everything I can find on the others. When you look at where the systems with rochats and/or metal-leaf trees are—there are only twenty of them, and they're in an expanding cone down this edge of the galactic arm. They weren't introduced by humans—they were there when the first humans arrived. The cone doesn't have a point, but if it did it would be outside the border of the Empire. Off the southwestern border zone. And the leaves of the metals trees are the Arerrerr's food. From what I 'read,' that is what it has always eaten, including a variety that's rich in selenium."

"I see," said the captain. "If we find the point of that 'cone' and we have the planet the Arerrerr came from. Well, it gives us an area of space, but there are a lot of suns out there..."

"I've got the coordinates," said Goth. "I've been there. I saw a rochat, was wrapped in a blanket of rochat wool, and it's full of metal trees, and has a plant the Arerrerr remembers—the paratha spice, that doesn't grow anywhere else. The world is scarred by signs of an interstellar war and has alien structures on it big enough to see from space. That might account for why the Arerrerr was left here. They expected to come back for it."

"You mean..." He looked at Goth. "The planet you got poisoned on? The planet my mother is on? The planet where my father was killed?"

"Looks like it. And it's all too convenient. I haven't gotten all the pieces yet. It's got aliens, little hairy-tailed ones, but they don't look like what the Arerrerr thinks of as its caretakers Something has been manipulating us. I really don't like that. I don't think Karres will either."

"So what do we do?" asked Me'a. "My own strategic advice would be to back off, and force the enemy to play on a ground of our choosing. But," she smiled, "I have learned that you do things in your own way."

"We're going in," said the captain. "Only we're going in ready for trouble. They may find us more trouble than they thought. I don't think they're likely to know what they're dealing with. They may find they have a lelundel by the tail. Besides, I want a meeting with whomever shot Goth. And with this Pnaden and his bunch of creeps."

"That's not a group that needs to get their hands on the Arerrerr. They'd be as bad as, or even worse than, the Somans," pointed out Ta'zara.

"Sounds like it. We'll have to keep a sharp watch-out for their ship," said the captain. "You said it was quite well armed, and bigger than the *Venture*, didn't you, Goth?"

"Yeah. But it is not going anywhere, unless they found the parts I stashed in the processing plant. And I don't think anyone had moved that cover in a lot of years," said Goth. "They're stuck there unless they have another ship."

"Cornered rats make dangerous rats," said Me'a.

"True enough," said the captain. "Well, we'll deal with it when we get there. But first we've got to get there. Let's get those coordinates, Goth. Do some calculations, and plan our route."

"It's a fair way outside the border, Captain. Fuel..."

"Vezzarn took advantage of sitting around at the spaceport in Karoda to refuel. We're near as full as we can hold, barring a little wastage on the atmospheric work," said the captain. "So: What do you have to say, Leewit?"

"It's best for the Arerrerr," said the Leewit. "So long as she's safe and these aliens can stop anyone taking her away. Do you think so, Goth?"

"The little aliens I saw? The Gaks, or as Lina called them, Gyak? Nope. But...something that is able to push Karres witches around. Maybe. And they have been pushing us."

The Leewit nodded thoughtfully. "We'll find out first. But I don't think I like being pushed around."   ⸙

"Neither do I," said Goth.

The run toward Lumajo was not without a bit of excitement. However, compared to some of the trips they'd been on, there were plenty of skilled and able crew now to take watches. It was a luxury, the captain decided, he could even get used to. There was a good chance of pirates out here—and they had to rely on the Sheewash to put them out of range of an Imperial Space Navy patrol. That put Goth in mind of the fact that the *Bolivar* had known exactly when and where the supposedly secret patrol routes were. She told the captain about it. "Well, we can drop a few words in relevant ears in the Imperial Court," he said. "Knowing it is happening will make catching them easier. Or if all else fails, we can go hunting."

"Later." She smiled at him. "Got things to do on Karres, soon."

"What?"

She grinned, pure Goth mischief. "You'll find out, Captain." And she would say no more.

"Hmm." He smiled at her. "Everyone is playing games with

me. Including, I suspect, vatches. I've been relling them for the last few days. So far off that I almost can't be sure..."

"Big ones or little ones?" asked Goth. It was an important distinction, seeing as the captain could handle the big ones. Pull them inside out, if need be. It was the little ones that were a problem. But other than petty mischief the little ones hadn't given them as much trouble, and a fair amount of help, when they felt like it. They were very like the Leewit's Tippi—they'd do things if they wanted to, if it entertained them. Human stage plays had amused them, but one never knew how long that would last.

As they swung into orbit around the world, there was no doubt that Lumajo had been subjected to...something. There were deep scars across her landmasses, cutting into her seas, and plainly where the variegated greens of her forest struggled to get a toehold. There were still plenty of the alien structures—some even on the path of whatever weapon had been employed from space to make those scars. The scars stopped where they hit them.

"So, exactly where are we heading for?" asked the captain. A world was a vast place. Finding just where Goth had set down with the *Bolivar* had been troubling him for a few days.

"Well," said Me'a, who happened be on watch at that time, looking at the *Venture*'s instruments. "There's a signal beacon transmitting. I'd guess that might well be them."

"It seems pretty likely," said the captain. "But unless they're hoping for a rescue, a bit surprising."

"It's not a very strong transmission. Let me see if I can amplify it." She fiddled briefly. A voice issued from the speakers, but not in any language that the captain knew. He turned to the Leewit. "What are they saying?"

The Leewit listened and translated. "They say: 'SOS. This is Colony Ship *Ascension*, First Lieutenant Rao. We have had engine failure, have made forced planetfall, require assistance.' And the same again. And again."

"An automated signal. It may be set up to respond to ships. I suppose we'll have to see what we can do. It is surprising that it's not in Galactic Standard."

"It could be a trap. I wouldn't put that past Pnaden and his crowd," said Goth.

"Yes, but why not say it in Galactic Standard?" asked Me'a. "You're more likely to catch people that way. I'm searching the

Imperial Ship Registry at the moment but it doesn't look like they have a vessel of that name recorded."

"Can we pinpoint the transmission?"

"Got it," Me'a was an expert with her ability to use almost any form of gadgetry, especially computerized devices. "I am getting a visual and instrument scan on the area."

She did. The screens showed a zoom on an area of deep, dark green jungle.

"That isn't the smuggler's base," said Goth. "Unless the trees grow up really, really fast."

"I'm getting the deep-radar image and heat scan. But the trees mask most things. There is a definite pattern in the trees though. They're not as tall down that line. Ah. Maximum resolution on the end area... Great Patham! That's huge."

It was. Even the trees couldn't hide the metallic width of it, although they overhung the edges.

"That's bigger than most battle cruisers," said the captain, awed.

"Yes," said Me'a. "Look at the measurements on screen. There hasn't been a ship that size built for a long time. They're just too inefficient."

"Is it a human ship?" asked Goth. "I mean species doesn't make any difference to the Leewit. She'd translate talking plants. And this place plainly went through a war. Maybe it is—or was—a battleship?"

"Was. There are definitely trees growing through parts of it. I'd guess it has been there a while," said the captain.

"I suppose we could set down somewhere near it, and I could read it," said Goth. "But that's not the smugglers."

"I think I have located those for you too," said Me'a. "I was looking for a landing site, when we zoomed in. Quite near that, relatively speaking. Hang on. I'll just find it again."

She did. And this was far more recognizable to Goth. Unlike most of the land area, it was clearly not forested. Zooming in they could see the compound and the landing field. It did have a spacecraft parked on it. "Ah," said Goth. "They didn't get very far. I don't think we ought to land there, though."

"No. Although the problem is: If not there, where? In the forest would be risky. On one of the scars?"

"It depends. They could be radioactive...but if not, at least they're not too full of trees."

"It is difficult to assess radiation from this height," said Me'a. "The world has not gotten a nuclear glow, and the encampment of the smugglers is relatively close to one. I doubt if there'd be a problem with touching down. We could leave in a hurry if it was 'hot.'"

The captain pointed to the screen. "If we land next to that alien structure, where the burn scar stops, we'd be relatively close to the wrecked ship. I think it is an automatic beacon and has been there a long time, but there could be people needing rescue. We'll probably find some of the locals too. It sounds like that'll be a starting point for finding my mother. And we may have to pay these smugglers a visit, but dropping in on them gives them the fire advantage. Besides...I feel good about that spot."

"Then it should be that spot," said the Leewit firmly, before Goth chimed in to agree. They knew the captain's hunches well, and trusted them.

It was a relatively cautious landing, since the captain was sure the smugglers would have some detectors. They might even have surface-to-air missiles of a sort. And a ship was vulnerable coming in to land. He was keyed up and watchful doing so...

And nearly lost control at the last moment, because he spotted something that could only be a spaceship at the edge of the forest. It was too late to pull out, so he set the *Venture* down. The instruments gave no hint of abnormal radiation, and as soon as the smoke and steam cleared he saw the other ship would be no danger to him. It was a wreck.

It was also a one-man Imperial scout ship.

CHAPTER 23

His klatha instinct had put him down a few hundred paces from his father's scout ship.

"You know he lived through that," said Goth as they stared at it.

The captain looked at the wreckage and shook his head. "Yes... but how?"

"Good question. And a better one is exactly what made him crash?" asked Goth.

"Or who? On another more immediate front—I'm relling vatch again. They're staying out of range, but they're about. And the next question is, just what do we do first?" asked the captain.

"What," asked Me'a, "do you think those out there will expect you to do? Maybe the answer is not to do that."

"Spoken like a true Ta'taimi," rumbled Ta'zara, who had come in with the Leewit. "But first the Leewit wishes to torture all of you. She has done so to me, already."

"It was just a little transdermal needle prick," said the Leewit. "And at least I did it to you. I had to do it to my own arm."

"What's this?" asked Goth.

"You don't have to have it, since you can't be killed by it twice. Your body will react to neutralize the poison fast. For

267

the rest of you, you need it so if you get the poison that nearly killed Goth, you won't die."

The captain pushed up his sleeve. "Me first. I want to go looking for someone."

The injection did smart a bit, and when it was done they were all rubbing their arms.

Me'a pointed to the external monitor screen. "Looks like we're picking up some kind of vibration."

The captain nodded. "Sound. Not really effectively transmitted through the hull, but there is something making a regular racket out there."

"Seeing as the air is breathable, if a bit sulfurous, perhaps we could crack the airlock enough to listen," she suggested.

"I was going to say we might as well go out there and find out what is going on—I know, not your way, Me'a, but it is ours. But let's have a quick listen first."

It was drums. A pattern of beats, being passed, drum to drum, throbbing out across the jungle. There was a peculiar urgency to it.

"I'd say these...Gyak are telling everyone and their cousin that we're here. Or was it like this when you were here last, Goth?" asked the captain.

"Nope," said Goth, shaking her head. "I barely heard a sound in the forest. I might as well have been alone out there."

"I'm guessing we won't be alone soon," said Me'a.

Goth nodded. "Unless that's a 'keep away' signal. It might be. From what I could work out the little natives initially greeted the smugglers with gifts and friendship. Things turned sour later. Not surprising, when you consider Pnaden and his crew. They treat the ones in the compound like slaves."

"We're still going to have to get out there," said Pausert. "We've got the Arerrerr to give back to them, and my mother...and what happened to my father to deal with. At least their poison darts can't kill us."

"They could still kill you in any number of other ways. We're low enough for infrared scan to work under these trees, Captain," said Me'a, pointing. "There's already someone out there, watching. Quite a few someones."

"I'd better go and see what they want," said the captain, stepping toward the airlock. "Maybe they want to sell us souvenirs, or charge us landing fees."

"Let's just give them a chance to show us. I'll light-shift a split image," said Goth.

"There seem to be more of them arriving, Captain," said Me'a, pointing at the screen. "Just a question: I'm not too familiar with the *Venture*'s pre-takeoff requirements. How long would it take us to boost out of here? We could do a night landing elsewhere, with Goth's cloaking skills."

"A few minutes. She's got the old-style fusion system, and of course the tubes need to be warmed again. There are checks to be run. We could use the nova guns if they get too pushy. Not too close to the ship, of course. We'd end up damaging our own hull."

"I think perhaps being prepared would do no harm. Vezzarn and I could start the preparations," said Me'a.

The captain nodded. "Do. But let's see what they think of our images."

The answer was they were worthy of a shower of darts and flung spears and a lot of yelling. A mob of the small hairy natives poured out from the forest. The *Venture*'s tubes were still too hot for them to get close. Her airlock, though open and now cluttered with darts and spears, was too high to reach—but they were doing something about that. They were hauling a ladder out of the forest. And just inside the second door of the outer airlock, now open for planetary work, the Leewit stood stock still, listening.

"Shall we try a few shots over their heads before we warm the tubes? The tubes will cook them," said Ta'zara.

"No," said the Leewit. "I need to talk to them. They think we're trying to keep them from the sky ship that was promised. Like the other bad men. They're trying to rescue the ship."

"What?" ask the captain.

"They're speaking the same language as the voice on the SOS message," explained the Leewit. "These are the survivors. Or maybe the descendants of the survivors."

"I can send one of my probes out," said Me'a. "They have speakers and I can transmit as well as listen in."

"I'll give you a visual image," said Goth. "So we can see if they throw more spears and darts."

"I'll whistle at 'em first," said the Leewit, darkly.

She did, too. Loudly enough through Me'a's probe's speakers to shut them up, at least briefly. The captain couldn't understand what the Leewit was saying. But he knew her tone well, so that was probably just as well. He might have had to threaten to wash her mouth out with soap again. The hairy attackers plainly did understand, however, by the sudden stunned silence from the mob.

The Leewit continued to give them a piece of her mind. Listening to it, the captain knew it was a much bigger mind than you would have thought from her size. "Right. We can go out now," she announced.

When the Leewit said things in that tone, she usually got her way. The captain was ready to shield and cocoon, Goth ready to light-shift, and Ta'zara ready simply to defend. Me'a, when she came down, looked harmless in her chair. The captain was ready to bet she was not, as they moved over into the shade of the trees.

The Leewit was gabbling away at the various little people, armed with blowpipes and spears. No one was waving them around threateningly anymore, though. That had stopped, oddly and abruptly, when Tippi had emerged from her shirt. The captain noticed that made a lot of them point and jabber to each other in their language. But the tone of it was entirely different. Then a little white-haired hominid with a really long tail came forward, and the others backed off leaving her to talk to the Leewit, while they all craned to listen.

"They think the ship has come to take them to the good place," the Leewit translated. "Or to bring them the cargo of good things. Maybe both. It was promised."

The captain groaned. "I haven't even gotten any of the old tinklewood fishing rods and all-weather cloaks in the hold. Just one large alien pet. A pet that doesn't belong to them, which they couldn't defend and I really don't think we should give them."

The Leewit slipped her arm in his. "We'll look after the Arerrerr until we find the right place for her. And you can stop being ready to cocoon us at a second's notice, Captain. It makes you look like you've got a toothache, and they aren't going to hurt us. I've made it all the smugglers' fault. I've explained that we're just a tiny little ship, far too small to carry them all. They can see that. That we'd heard that the cargoes of good things sent hadn't been given to them. The old one is telling me how the evil ones have stopped our gifts. That's sort of how they understand it all. For them the stuff the smugglers brought was real treasure. I've been telling them we're going to be punishing the bad guys for not giving it to them. They thought the stuff the smugglers brought was for them. They brought them gifts to say thank you, but the smugglers... well, I don't think they quite understood."

"We didn't," said the captain.

"They've been waiting a long time," said the Leewit. "Many generations."

"Can you ask them about the captain's mother?" asked Goth.

"They said she was on her way. The drums say she won't be long. They're very impressed that the captain is the son of the lieutenant, and the pilot. The old man says you look like your father, Captain. He was one of those who carried him to the camp of the cargo thieves."

Goth couldn't help but notice that the captain was looking a little pale. Space was vast, and even at the best speeds, travel was relatively slow, and subradio communication expensive. He'd been a young boy when he last saw his father and she knew that with the passing of time had assumed him to be dead... without having dealt with the grieving.

Now, faced with the crashed Imperial Navy scout ship, he was having to. "My mother never believed he was dead, you know," he said to Goth abruptly. "I thought she just couldn't accept it, and that it was easier for her to fool herself. Maybe if..."

Goth squeezed his hand. "And maybe if you'd married Illiya. We can't do time over again, Captain. Look. I think she's coming."

Indeed, the crowd of Gyak were parting. Lina jumped down from a litter carried by a dozen of the little hominids. She was even paler than the captain. But she wasn't looking at Pausert. She was looking at Goth, and rushing forward.

Not even the Leewit could have quite translated what she said as she hugged her and then her son, and then both of them, fiercely.

Besides, all the Gyak started cheering and clapping.

It took a while before anything sensible could be said. But when Lina could, she said, "Pnaden and his thugs are on their way. They've emptied their base, loaded up every weapon onto every vehicle they have, and are heading straight for here as fast as they can come."

"Good," said Captain Pausert. "If they want to fight, so do I."

"On the other hand," said Me'a, calmly, "why fight when you can just win?"

"What?" They all looked at her in puzzlement.

"They're desperate," said Me'a. "They're bringing their entire strength—correct?"

"Correct," said Lina. "They appear to have abandoned their spaceship, their base. They're putting everything they have into this. My people are watching them, and when chance allows, killing a few of them. But they're little hunter-gatherers against blasters and armored groundcars. Pnaden's thugs have some heavy weaponry. They might be reluctant to use it against the spaceship. But..."

"They need either the ship, or at the very least, the main sequencer's multiplier unit. The sequencer from the scout ship would do, if it is intact. But how long will it take them to get here?"

"They're struggling through the jungle. I would guess at least another three or four hours. It takes too long to cut a trail, so it's a case of finding a route."

"I remember that all too well," said Goth, with a grin. "It'd be quicker to walk."

"If they try that, the Gyak will certainly shoot them," said Lina. "But we have time. We can certainly prepare."

"We could," said Me'a. "Or we could just leave."

Lina looked troubled. "I can't just abandon the Gyak."

"Oh, we won't go far," said Me'a. "Just to their base. Tell your drummers to get the Gyak to head there. We'll wait until the smugglers are fairly close and take off. Captain Pausert can put us down on their landing field. We can deal with any defenders they've left there. I think the time has finally arrived for the Gyak to claim their share of the cargo there."

"And I can get their ship going again," said Goth. "The parts are there. Only...I'm not so sure that I can manage a launch."

"That is something I am capable of," said Me'a. "I'm not a pilot of Captain Pausert's skill, but I could do it. I could certainly manage a landing from orbit, but not the sort of atmospheric tricks the captain showed us he could do. But we will have their own fortifications there. It may not even be necessary."

"Besides, the captain and I could cripple their groundcars, if we had a few Gyak to guide us," said Goth.

"Yes...but I cannot go," said Lina. "The Gyak will think I am deserting them."

"I'll stay with you," said the Leewit. "I like them. They're funny."

Lina's eyes twinkled. "They say a lot of rude things. As they say you do too. The drums are telling about it. And you have one of the pucca. They all keep them, combing them for their hair. It is how they make their fabric here."

"If the Leewit remains, I remain," said Ta'zara. "I am her sworn bodyguard. If she travels overland, I must go with her."

Me'a grimaced. "That will be somewhat awkward for me," she said.

Lina smiled. "Do you imagine that they would let you walk or wheel yourself? They insist on carrying me everywhere."

Me'a nodded. "Then why not? We can set off now, and the captain can take off a little later. Maybe even take a few of these Gyak with him. If they think at all like the clans on Na'kalauf, they'll see that as a safeguard. Ours with them, theirs with ours."

"Just make sure they're not too frail," said Goth. "I'd go on foot with you too, but I'm going to work the laterals, and then the guns, if they're needed."

"Besides," said Lina with a trace of sadness, "you should stay with Pausert. It was a choice I wish I'd had. But the fact that you're alive and appear well... it gives me some trace of hope for Kaen."

"I thought he was dead," said Goth.

Lina closed her eyes, briefly. "Yes. Effectively, anyway. He's in the open-stasis tomb. He took the toxin from the dart intended for me. The Gyak insisted on putting him in there, at the last. He told them to. I...don't know if he was alive or dead, then. But..." she shook her head. "I didn't think a cure was possible. I gave orders for them to do the same for me, once I had finished his work. I think they may consider that to be destroying Pnaden's camp and capturing his ship. To be honest, if I have done that and seen my son find you, Vala, I would not be unhappy with that."

"I reckon we got some sorting out to do," said the Leewit, gruffly. She didn't deal with emotions comfortably. "Come on. Let's get going. We can deal with all of that once we've sorted out their base and them."

A few minutes later they'd all disappeared into the forest, barring the three young warriors who were going with the *Venture*. They were part of Lina's guard and had learned some words of

Galactic, having worked for her, and, previously, on the smuggler base. The Leewit had given them a slew of instructions, and seen them safely strapped in. They had the hatch open so they could hear the drums and could tell the captain when Pnaden's thugs approached—that is, if they noticed. Goth wondered if introducing them to ice cubes in the drinks she made for all of them had been a good idea. They were certainly jabbering enough about them. But she'd had to do something to entertain them, because it was proving a very long wait.

Sitting next to the captain, Goth said, "We'll come back. I want to go to those wrecked ships and read the story from them. Especially the scout ship."

"Hard to believe anyone got out of that alive," said the captain. "I wish I had known him better. Seen a bit more of him. I don't remember him that well."

"I'll tell you at least part of his story," promised Goth.

There was no need for the captain's trademark takeoff, but he gave it to them anyway. The first-time passengers did compete with the roaring of the engines with their yelling, but they were the first Gyak for many thousands of years to see the forest from the sky on the viewscreens. The captain did land better than their colony ship had, though.

Goth scrambled away to the forward nova gun before the smoke and steam of landing even cleared. The captain used his external scanners to survey the compound, and, particularly, the other ship. Goth shifted the nova gun to lock on it, but the larger ship's turrets never moved. The captain scanned the rest of the base carefully. There was no sign of life. "They can't all have gone, surely?"

"Guess they could, Captain. This lot don't trust each other much. How about if I go out in no-shape...?"

"No. We'll go together. Vezzarn can stay on the guns. Our passengers can wait a little. Lucky I got the Leewit to teach me the word for 'wait.'"

So they went out into the smuggler base. It was quite eerie and empty. Even the camp of the Gyak who had remained as very little more than slaves was empty. That had a broken-down fence. So Goth and the captain came back to the *Venture* and let the three Gyak warriors out. One of the three had a small drum with him and started beating on it.

In the meantime, Goth and the captain went to the paratha processing shed, and collected the electronic pieces Goth had stashed there. In the process they did find some people in the cells. Terrified, abandoned people, including Vanessa. "Let us out, please," begged Vanessa.

"We'll get to you later," said the captain, staying Goth's hand. "Right now you could be safer inside."

They had barely gotten the parts reinstalled and the *Bolivar* capable of flying again, when the drumming announced that the first of the Gyak had arrived. Unsurprisingly, they were carrying the Leewit, wearing a broad hat of metal-tree leaves. The others were not far behind.

Several hours later, there wasn't much of a base for the smugglers to return to. It was all broken down in a surprisingly orderly fashion, with startling speed, with everything demolished and carried off to the jungle. From the wire to the buildings it came down and was pulled apart, with Lina proving exceptionally adept at dividing things up. "I spent years uniting the various little tribes. Only one tribe stayed with the smugglers, believing they'd be rewarded in the end. They're hunter-gatherers, so they live in small family tribes, and a bit of steel is a treasure. They're all happy so long as their own little tribe got something. Not that they don't have their own treasures, and tools and weapons, but this was a hard world for humans crash-landed with nothing to adapt to."

"They are humans then? I mean the hair? The tails?" asked Goth.

"The hair is just hair. And the tails are just plaited hair. They wear their hair over their faces to protect their skin in the sun." She cocked her head. "By the way, the drums say the smugglers are returning. They should get back a bit faster than they got there, as they now have a trail to follow. What are your plans then?"

"Well, the *Bolivar* is ready to fly. I think the despair of coming back to nothing, not even a base, will give them a decent lesson. We may add them to the other prisoners we've got locked in the empty hold on the *Bolivar*." Pausert sighed. "We still need to talk, to plan. I know this may seem strange, but we haven't actually discharged one of our main reasons for coming here. I think we may have been mistaken in that. We were looking for aliens...to return to them something they had lost."

"This was an alien world," said Lina. "It's still full of these huge alien structures. I know the smugglers landed originally to try and blast one open, but they failed. They should have tried the next one, the one you landed near to. It's open, or at least part of it is. It is a stasis tomb of some kind. Or I think that's what it is. Nothing rots or changes visibly inside. The Gyak use it as burial place for their lieutenants."

"Lieutenants?"

"Yes, the surviving officer of the colony ship was a lieutenant. And thus that's what their leaders have always been called. The tombs are very strange places. You can't go past a certain line, without the stasis field taking effect. They push their dead in with a long, flat paddle. I am their current lieutenant." She hesitated. "Forgive me. But I have been talking to the Leewit, and Me'a, and Ta'zara. I remember enough about the stories about my Great Uncle Threbus too...I don't dare to hope...but Kaen... Is it possible?"

"We'll find out, Mother," said the captain. "But even Karres can't do everything."

The drums could be heard beating like a pulse across the hot jungle during her silence. At length she sighed. "I already have more than I hoped for. The drums say that one of the lead vehicles broke down. A fight started between the smugglers from that one and the next two. Three of the vehicles are burning, and they are fighting each other. There are only two vehicles left. I don't think a lot of them will be coming back."

"And when they do," said Pausert, "it will be to nothing. I think that'll be a small payback for what they did to others, to the Gyak, to my father, to you, and what they would have done to Goth. We're going back to the wreck of my father's ship. I felt that was the right place to be. Let's let Me'a know she has a ship to fly. I think I'll give her Vezzarn to help with the process. He is experienced, even if he doesn't have the confidence. If any of the Gyak would like a flight—we will have some space on both ships."

Lina smiled. "Well, the three warriors who came with you are very occupied in telling everyone what great sky-travelers they are, so, yes, just to stop them becoming too vain—they're nice youngsters—I think we should take as many as you can. I can go with you, I think, this time. Let me go and arrange it all. It's best to keep busy, I find. It stopped me brooding. I will arrange for the surviving smugglers to continue being watched."

So they returned to the site of the scout ship's crash. "I think," said Pausert, when both ships were safely set down, "that we ought to go and have a look at this alien building. Maybe take the Leewit along too."

Lina nodded. "But, honestly, it is something that should be handled with some respect to the Gyak. It's their tomb of kings, so to speak. They have a feast planned to celebrate that the cargo has finally come and I owe them that much. They're still not sure about a ship to take them home. A lot are saying that this is home."

"That's true, I suppose. Look: The Leewit is feeding the Arerrerr. She says it is very happy with the leaves—they're all the right kind of leaves," said Goth.

Lina laughed. "About half the food here is leaves of some sort. It's a strange world. Quite surprising the little Gyak have adapted to it so well. Would you like to visit the original ship? It's very old, and is now something of a temple. The original crew must have been desperate for rescue. There's an old treadmill that the Gyak treat like a prayer wheel. They keep it turning night and day. They claim it calls to heaven for help to come and fetch them."

"It does," said Me'a. "It still sends out a weak signal."

They went down the trail to the old ship, while the feast was being prepared. It was... strange.

"Where did it come from? I've never seen any ship quite like it," said the captain.

Goth touched the wall of what must once—long before trees now taller than the *Venture* grew through the twisted I-beams— have been a control room. "It came from what we call old Yarthe. In the days before the first Empire," she said in a curiously singsong voice. "Take me away, please, Captain. I don't want to be here anymore. Too many thousands of people died here. Too many dreams died here."

So they left. "Your father made extensive notes on the old ship," said Lina. "Fully half of it is engines, but he recognized none of it. He wrote that it might be some kind of dimensional manipulation drive. I think he might have hoped to get a working ship built out of it—but that, it seems, was a dream. The Gyak don't even really work metal—they just use pieces of the metal-leaf trees. He wrote textbooks for them. They have some ancient texts—on metal sheets, from the ship, but the script was not anything he recognized. He was teaching them..." She sighed. "I went on with his work. Of course, his expertise was astrogation, engineering, and space combat. Mine was xenobotany. So we took different directions."

"But they're better off than they were?" asked Goth.

"Maybe," she said with a smile. "They're generally a happy people. They like to hunt, they keep their pucca, and they love their families. There are worse places to live and people to live amongst, now they have gotten rid of those smugglers, who were set on making them slaves and clearing their forests."

She cocked her head. "Speaking of which, the surviving smugglers are apparently killing each other again. The drums say they're out of lightning to throw, and are hitting each other. And both of their surviving vehicles are now burning."

"Lightning?"

"Blasters."

Goth laughed. "The boxes of spare charges are still in the lubricant store on the *Bolivar*. I found them there."

By the time they got back to the *Venture* the feast was prepared under the trees. There were hundreds of Gyak, with bright sashes of woven rochat hair, and various bright seed ornaments in their hair. Everyone, the *Venture*'s crew included, sat on the ground around the cook fires, as people brought platters of food to them. They were of course brought the first and choicest of platters.

"What do we eat with?" asked the Leewit, looking at the piled leaf platter.

"Your fingers. And they're waiting for us to begin." Lina took a small piece of the varied pile on her platter.

"Stop," said Goth, sniffing at the food. "It's full of paratha."

Lina began to laugh. "You'll struggle to find any food on Lumajo that isn't. And if I'd finished my work on Morteen on the supposed drug instead of getting myself on board the smuggler's ship, there probably wouldn't be any there, or in half the Empire either. It's entirely harmless, except for binding some toxic metals and making them safe to eat—without which the Gyak would starve. The problem with paratha is not that you eat it, it's not eating enough of it. If you only eat a flake, all you want is more.

If you just keep eating it, you get mightily sick of it. I worked it out fairly fast as a prisoner. I could have told Pnaden and his thugs too, and helped them succeed in growing it. Honestly. It's a shade-loving forest plant. Grows wild all over the forest. It likes a compost of metal-tree leaves, and lots of moisture. And they're trying to grow it as a field crop in the blazing sun, after they had their fallout with the Gyak tribes. It's stunted and most of it dies." She put her morsel in her mouth and chewed. "Eat it. You are quite safe."

So they did. And they found that it was true. At first all you could taste was the deliciousness of paratha. But, by the fifth bite, that had worn off.

CHAPTER 24

Lina had spoken at some length with the elders of the various Gyak tribes, and after the feast they set out for the place where the Lieutenants of the Gyak were laid to rest, the point being made that Pausert and his tribe—the easiest way of explaining the *Venture*'s crew—had had no chance to pay the final respects due to his father.

The alien structure was huge. The entrance, which was only one of the eight sides further round, took nearly an hour for them to walk to. It was a vast, cavernous opening, which would have accommodated several spacecraft. Goth reached out a hand and touched it . . . and pulled it away, hastily. "If you're looking for where the Arerrerr is heading—this is it. It's a pet shelter. They loved them a lot."

"I think I will avoid telling the Gyak that," said Lina. "They might not take well to finding out that this is a pucca house. From what I gather this is the only open one on the planet."

Tippi had slipped out of the front of the Leewit's shirt. And now stood up on its hind legs and faced them. "It is only open for the pet to come home," the rochat said.

The Leewit stared openmouthed and incredulously at Tippi.

They all did . . . but the Leewit's jaw was almost dislocated. Finally she said, "You don't have the brains to talk, Tippi! I'm a healer. I've examined you inside and out from head to toe. I had to work out what you needed, make sure I could fix you if you got sick. I love you but you don't have that much brain. No speech center."

"That is right," said the rochat. "But I am not Tippi. I only speak through her—she is a conduit. We made them, because we do not move easily or fast. When your species came to our old worlds we modified them so that you would like them."

"I don't like what you're doing with my rochat," said the Leewit flatly. "Leave her alone."

"She is the only way we can speak to your kind, unless you step into the time-dilation field. Then we could speak face to face. But it would be many years of your time before you emerged. We are very grateful. We have had our creatures search over and over for the little one we lost. We had found signs of her work but not her. We have watched how you have cared for her. But we long for her; we want her back. She will be happy to be back with us."

The Leewit's posture had eased slightly, but she was still suspicious. "Yeah? So why didn't you just talk to us through Tippi ages ago?"

"Because we do not have the ability, outside of this structure. Time dilation barriers are difficult to cross. We did hire intermediaries who are outside the normal framework of time. They have worked on our behalf."

"You hired intermediaries? Like who?" asked Goth.

"The creatures you call 'vatches.' They are not entirely of this dimension. We had considerable traffic with them, before the war. We used them to move across space."

"That explains why I was relling vatch," said the captain, relieved.

"They are extremely cautious around you. And, I am afraid they regard dealing with you as a game. A dangerous game, but one indulged in by the smaller ones. Apparently they discovered that you are able to manipulate force in a way that could even trap the small ones. They had been able to undo your earlier work. Now they cannot. So they have been pushing events, to achieve ends. They say they have learned a great deal from watching some human art form called a game . . . a 'stage play.' They have been making their own."

"The big ones transport spaceships. Why didn't you just get them to bring the Arerrerr to you?"

"Because she is made in such a way that the things you call vatches could not move her. We did this because they played certain tricks on our little ones. They could have moved in something. A spaceship, for example. Once she was in one, they could do so easily. But not yours. They won't go near you. And the vatches—several of the little ones—assured us that you would be the best and most reliable and kindest transporters for our little lost one. They are correct. We have observed you through Tippi's eyes."

"You could still have sent us a note or something," said the Leewit, grumpily.

"The concept of 'writing' is a new one to us. It was not how we recorded things. But we have tried to assist. We tried to cure your sister. We have modified the creatures you call 'rochats' to help with your species' illnesses, as the pet you call the Arerrerr does with ours."

"Just one question," said Lina. "What happens once you get your pet in here?"

"That is sort of relevant," said Goth. "We really don't want the Arerrerr falling into the wrong hands again."

"The unit will close," said whatever was speaking through Tippi. "They are impermeable, the space-time barrier allows nothing in and nothing out. Nothing will reach within for a million revolutions around the sun of our world. Our calculations indicate that our old enemy will be dead by then. We believe you have had the vatch deal with their last strike against us, the Nanite creatures, but they may still endure. They breed and live much faster than we do. We decided to simply wait them out. Few species live as long as we do, and with time dilation, it is a short wait."

"My man, my husband, is in here. I plan to join him," said Lina. "If...if he can't be cured."

There was a long pause. Then an answer: "There are various members of your species here. We will retain them if it is desired. It is no inconvenience. You can join them. Time passes exceptionally slowly in this field. We are using massive high-speed computing to communicate across it."

"Are any of them alive?" asked the Leewit.

"One," was the answer.

"I'm afraid before we bring in the Arerrerr we're going to have to look at him," said the captain, keeping his voice steady.

"It is possible. There is a large paddle that was used to push him into the field."

A few minutes later, Pausert got to look at his father's face. And to see the man's eyes open and take in both his son's face, Lina's.

"Lend me strength, Captain. Goth," said the Leewit, and knelt to work. Tippi looked on. So, presumably did something else.

After a few minutes, the Leewit stood up. "Push him back. Quick," she said.

So they did.

The silence hung for a long time. Finally Lina spoke, tears streaming down her face. "It's too late, isn't it?"

The Leewit stood there, obviously looking for the right words to say. Eventually she said, "Sort of." And sat down.

Pausert put his hand on her small shoulder. "You did your best."

"Yep. But he was much farther gone than Goth. The poison I have stopped. I started some repair work happening in his liver. But I can't keep him alive." She took a deep breath. "He needs... something to breathe for him. He needs his blood replaced. And then he needs several organs, either grown new ones, or replaced. I can't do that. We can't do that."

"But they used to," said Goth. "They used to. You know, that terrible reading I had in the old colony ship. That...room. That was the ship's hospital. I read...I read of them trying to do that. Trying to do what could be done back where they came from. They sent me into the past to meet you, Captain. Can we send him into the past? Down the Egger Route?"

The Leewit shook her head. "I can't. It's too far and too hard on his body in the state it is in. And I 'member Toll saying there are all sorts of difficulties going back before you are born. I know we did it by accident, but I don't know how. He hasn't got long to live. Take him out of that field, and he's going to live maybe half an hour. Even in the disminded state Olimy was in...it is not going to work. Take him down the Egger Route and he'll just die. It takes a lot of power to jump that far around time. Something like Old Windy could do it..."

The captain straightened up. He looked at the watching Tippi.

"You said you were grateful to us for bringing the Arerrerr home. That you would reward us."

"Indeed. We are aware of what your species considers treasure and we will heap it on you. Our plants were made by us to extract metals. We have many shiploads of your precious metals for you."

"We weren't looking for a reward, you know. But the best reward is that which the person you reward wants. We're giving you something you love. Can I ask that you give us help with something we love?"

There was a longer silence. Then the voice that was not Tippi spoke: "This seems right and fair. We would. But we cannot cure the human. We are genetic engineers, not xenoveterinarians. In some ways our species is ahead of yours, but in the medical and technological area you often surpass us. We have made some small changes. But they will only help his offspring."

"It isn't medicine I want help with. You have some deal with vatches. We need something from them. And they won't come near me."

There was an even longer silence. "You wish the human transported to where he can be helped. The great vatch says it can be done, if you will promise not to attack it. It also says..."

Pausert was suddenly aware of relling a vast vatch, close. And... Little-bit, the tiny vatchlet that had taken delight in playing with the Leewit, a thing almost seen, the sound of scent, the smell of a touch, an awareness for which he had no proper words: *Hello, big dream thing. We led you in a good play. We can take him. But we cannot bring him back. We can transport one way only, for dreamstuff. It would break you if we did. But you are not to use your vatch-hooks. They hurt the big ones. You are not to put me in the hard vatch-egg stuff.*

"Agreed," said the captain. "What do we need to do?"

He will need something for us to transport him in. He needs to breathe and be protected from the space between that we move through.

"What is going on?" asked Pausert's mother.

Captain Pausert realized she could hear his half of the conversation, but all of this would be unfamiliar territory for her. "You've heard of Karres, Mother?"

"The witches of Karres. Yes. It was a rumor, a story to be laughed at. I gather it isn't. I gather Vala and her sister are from

Karres, that they are what have been called witches, and are tremendously powerful in ways I had no idea were possible. It seems my wayward Uncle Threbus was one too, for all that he came from Nikkeldepain."

"So am I, for all I also came from Nikkeldepain. And I'm using that power to arrange for Father to go back in time, to old Yarthe itself, to a time before the first Empire, when they could treat the problems the dart caused. The Leewit has dealt with the poison, but she can't keep him alive long enough to heal him. They can. But it is a one-way trip."

She nodded. "Can I go with him?"

"We can't bring you back."

"I know," she said calmly. "But we'd be there together. And he will need me to get medical help to him in time."

"I'll ask," said Pausert. What else could he say?

Two is as easy as one. But what will you send them in? Which ship? We must take it straight to place of healing.

"I could send them in the *Venture*," said the captain.

Your ship has traveled in time before. Not good. And the other one is bigger. Make a ship for them that is the right size.

"Make a ship?"

An egg-stuff hard case. You could show me how to undo it, said the little vatch, doing her best to sound artless, and failing.

Pausert had to laugh, despite the circumstances. "Thereby stopping you having to worry about what I can do to you in the future. Right. I'll make one and take you through undoing it. If you can follow what I do with the klatha forces."

Of course.

So the captain did.

Simple really.

"When you know how."

Then it was time for practical preparation. Inevitably, it was Me'a who came up with questions like *What will you do to communicate?* and *What will you do for money?* She had the Leewit dictate a message onto a message cube she had with her, in the language of the old ship, giving all the symptoms and requirements. She also produced a pouch of gold coins. "They usually have value," she said, handing them to Lina.

Then...it was time for farewells, for Lina to bid a tearful farewell to her son, and give her blessing to Goth and Pausert's impending marriage. "I can't be there. But you'll be happy, both of you. I ... was. Will be."

Lieutenant-Commander Kaen was drawn from the slow time anomaly again, to have his wife lie down next to him. His eyes opened, seeing her, and then blinked at his son, standing there with Goth.

"Better go quick, Captain," said the Leewit, gruffly, touching Pausert's father. "He's counting down in minutes now. I've done what I can."

So the captain knelt and kissed them both, quickly. Goth, he saw, did the same.

And then he wove the cocoon...

Which, in the relling of the presence of the massive vatch, vanished, leaving them standing in vasty emptiness.

Pausert took a deep breath. "Right," he said. "We'd better bring the Arerrerr in. That's going to be a bit of a job"

"There will be no need," said the alien speaking through Tippi. "We will have our carrier fetch her, if you will go outside. If you call your ship and have the hold opened."

"If you give me Tippi back," said the Leewit, before the captain could get himself to call Vezzarn.

"Of course. We give her and their kind into your care. Once we have our lost one back we will no longer use the energy required to keep in contact across time." And the rochat, nonchalant as always, walked over and climbed into the Leewit's shirt, and snuggled into her.

There was nothing more to do but to instruct Vezzarn and to walk out into the harsh sunlight of an alien world.

There was a sudden sharp hiss and, turning around ... the huge door wasn't there anymore. Just, as with the other walls, a smooth oily-looking surface.

"Well," said the captain. "I guess we can go home now."

Back at the *Venture*, sometime later, the captain found himself sitting with Goth, looking at the octagon wall and the forest. The others were doing various tasks, and the two of them were alone. He sighed and turned to Goth and said, "It would seem that I just found my parents again ... to lose them both again."

Goth squeezed his hand. "It had to be done, Captain. She'd come so far and risked so much to find him. She wasn't ever going to let him go again. And, in a way, a piece of both of them is with us. Always. I don't think I'll ever let go of you either."

It had been a while developing, but the Leewit had finally reached her decision when she saw Goth and the captain kiss Lina and Kaen farewell. They were couples. She wasn't. It was time...and there was a galaxy full of Karres work, and healing to do. Now she just had to organize the practical details.

Even with the Arerrerr restored to her owners, there were still some matters to attend to. The *Bolivar*, the few surviving smuggler prisoners, and, of course, what to do next. "Home to Karres," said Goth firmly, when they met to decide.

"I've made up my mind," said the Leewit. "I'm not going back to Karres with the *Venture*. You go, Goth. I've got a perfectly good ship." She pointed at the *Bolivar*. "It just needs a bit of cleaning. I've got Me'a as a pilot, and Ta'zara for crew. I might even recruit a few of the Gyak. We'll be coming and going from here. Me'a has some ideas about some trade for them, and we're also going to be following up on the database of the Karoda slaves. Me'a downloaded it when she penetrated their systems, before you blew the place up."

"You can't cure them, Leewit," said Goth.

The Leewit smiled sweetly. "No. But I can give their 'owners' the same problem. I can duplicate what the slave feels for the master in them. They might not be nice people, but they will spend the rest of their lives loving and looking after their slaves. Being slaves...to their slaves. It's the best answer I can come up with."

The captain knew he'd been entrusted with the care of what had been the three witches of Karres, then the two...and then the one, because honestly, Goth did as much caring for him as he did for her, and now the Leewit was stepping up to that responsibility too. It was something he'd seen coming, and it was time. "Very well. The *Venture* will always be your home if you need it or want it, Leewit. But...well, you must take Vezzarn too. He's as near to an engineer as we've got, and you will need him more than I do. But I'm going to miss you."

She jumped up and hugged him. "I will miss you too, Captain. And I'll remember to wash behind my ears. Always."

EPILOGUE

Some ship-time later, back on Karres

"The Leewit will be returning to Karres soon with her new ship, and crew," said Pausert. "I think we can rely on Me'a to see that the ship's registration and origins are suitably adjusted. I suspect that she'll see to it that it remains a profitable ship, not that the Leewit hasn't got a firm grasp of the value of a mael. And while it is less fun than the circus, I think it will be good for her."

He and Goth sat on the porch of his Great Uncle Threbus' cottage on Karres, talking to Toll and Threbus. "Of course, we can't know what happened to my father and mother, but it seemed like the best choice to make."

Threbus nodded. "Indeed. We all have to make these decisions from time to time, and we make the best ones we can."

"Yes. Well, sending us into Karoda with a bomb could have been ugly. Especially one large enough to be seen from space," said Goth, with a slight edge to her voice.

"We made a mistake," said Toll. "We thought it was some kind of hyperelectronic tracker. The Soman base was apparently quite heavily shielded with multi-frequency jammers to deal with anything but short-range comms. They had a relay station on the Maciree Mountains which converted all their own short-range transmissions into long-range closed-beam messages—which is what Me'a tapped into. That's how they kept contact with their various other holdings."

"Should have checked," said Goth, gruffly.

"We thought we had," said Threbus. "The information we got was that it was a signaler... which it was, sort of. We knew that agents from Iradalia had spent a huge amount of money on buying the company that makes the forcecuffs that the Soman Consortium regularly ordered. The amounts were big enough that the Daal's bank on Uldune tipped us off. They were keeping an eye on transactions out of Iradalia, at our request. We arranged for the regular vessel to have a breakdown, so we could get the cargo onto the *Venture 7333*, as an apparent charter to deliver. Of course, the Iradalian authorities were waiting for the regular ship, and then got news that the cargo was coming on another vessel. But seeing as the vessel normally brought Soman cargoes, they let the Soman Consortium know. The Iradalians were in a terrible state, not knowing which vessel it was on, or exactly when to expect it."

"Which explains the performance with their customs," said Pausert.

"Yes. Nothing else went to their plan either. Their bomb had a radio-frequency response—which they tried but the jamming and shielding were too good," said Goth.

"Besides, we'd changed the trigger mechanism," said Pausert. "But why did it work when we did it?"

"You had destroyed the jammer with their command-and-control setup," said Threbus. "Or that is what we think."

"Well, at least with the Arerrerr out of the equation, I hope that there's no more danger to Karres and the future from that pair of planets," said Goth, her fingers still twined with the captain's as they sat together.

Threbus smiled. "They've vanished pretty much from the prognosticator's horizon. Without the money from slaving—the high-value Karoda slaves were fetching in excess of a million maels apiece—and taxation on that effectively supporting Iradalia..."

"I thought Iradalia taxed so high to make the slave trade unprofitable?"

"Maybe originally that was the idea. But it became their main source of revenue. So now both Iradalia and Karoda have suffered a big cut in income. The Iradalian invasion was possibly the worst disaster they've yet had. They threw everything at capturing the Arerrerr, and their troops and populace knew it. Of course they failed, and less than ten percent of their troops made it home. It caused enormous political unrest. So they have a new high priest of Irad."

"I hope he's somewhat better than the last one," said the captain.

"Oh, I think so," said Toll. "Oddly, it's none other than your friend Farnal. He came out of there, able to claim success, with a caring bunch of new converts. He and his group of 'siblings' are busy transforming a theocracy into a charitable organization, by all accounts."

"Well, that's another situation dealt with, although it was one the vatches almost certainly had a large hand in. I'm not sure I like being a plaything and manipulated," said the captain, seeing if he could rell vatch, and failing.

Toll smiled. "And now you will be getting married."

Pausert was still coming to grips with that. Something in his expression made Threbus laugh.

"None of us are ever quite ready for that moment, youngster." He nodded toward his daughter. "We do what we do without that readiness, just as we do everything else. And just as Karres changes the human galaxy, we change each other. It's not just you and Goth. Look at your parents, Pausert."

"Yes," said the captain, saddened a bit at the thought. "I wish...I wish I knew that had been successful. My mother and my father gave up so much for each other. They deserved some happiness at the end of it. I mean, yes, they had a few moments, but it would be nice to imagine more."

Threbus smiled slyly. "There is no need to imagine, Grand-nephew. We *know*. Your parents gave birth to a Karres witch, in you. A fortuitous combination of genes, with only a small linkage to Karres, and not a direct one of being born the child of a Karres witch, with the ability to manipulate klatha. It's a rare thing, and we watch out for it and recruit them. That's how I ended up on Karres. But where did it start, you may ask? As it happens, we do have very good records going all the way back to Karres' founders. They left from old Yarthe and settled on Karres—bringing with them the design of the engines from a ship of a type Yarthe had abandoned. Engines that could move a whole planet, with a little klatha help. And their genetic line was known to have produced a Karres witch before. That line produced children who could manipulate klatha."

Goth started laughing, before Pausert worked it out. "You mean..." he said incredulously.

"Yes," said Toll. "You're marrying into your own family, many thousands of generations removed. And yes, they lived long, happy and full lives. We have records. And I believe there's a message from them waiting for you, to be read at your wedding."

The captain didn't know whether to be elated or disgruntled. He settled on both. "Do you mean to tell me you—you and Toll both—have known all along that Goth and I were eventually going to get married? That's—that's..."

He frowned at Goth. "And you too?"

"Nope. First I heard of it. But I knew pretty much right away it was going to happen. Bound to."

She smiled. "I'm a witch of Karres, don't forget. Might even become a prognosticator, one of these days."

Pausert shook his head. "Please don't. I'm pretty sure having a wife who knows me as well as you do is going to be enough of a challenge, without you being able to foretell the future as well."

She grinned, then. "I said. I'm a witch of Karres."